Dan -

Thanks for the conversation.

Chemical Agent: A Thriller

Sean Sweeney

Chemical Agent: A Thriller—paperback edition

This book, an original publication, was registered with the United States Library of Congress Copyright Office in January 2016.

Cover designed by David Wood

ACKNOWLEDGMENTS

The author would like to thank the following for their input and insight into the writing of this novel:

Jeff Beesler, Kim Tomsett, Bruce A. Sarte, and Laura Jennings. Also to Stephen Campbell, Dean Pace-Frech, and Tanya Smith.

Of course, big thanks to the readers for continuing Jaclyn's story and for spreading the word, especially those who have been with Jaclyn since the beginning.

And as always, my wife Jen, who is my sunshine on cold, Jaclyn-less days.

Chemical Agent: A Thriller

Sean Sweeney

Chapter 1
The Warwick Hotel
Lenora Street
Seattle, Washington
Friday, June 13/Saturday, June 14
10:31 p.m. PT/1:31 a.m. ET

With tired eyes turning toward the south, Alexandra Dupuis stood on her suite's balcony, a grin creasing her otherwise placid face. She felt a slight breeze coming in off Puget Sound ahead of her, and without hesitation, the longtime Director of the CIA inhaled deeply. The sweet, salt-tinged air filled her lungs, the weariness of transcontinental travel slipping gracefully from her shoulders.

What a long day, she thought, *and tomorrow is going to be even longer*.

The delegation from Washington, D.C. had flown to the state of Washington earlier in the day, the blue and gray fuselage of the famous Boeing VC-25 sliding onto the air strip at McChord Air Force Base shortly after noon Pacific Time. There were numerous events planned for this rather large group; along with Alex, the president, Eric B. Forrister, and his wife, Veronica, their adopted daughter Maryah, the vice president, Lucia DiVito—Alex hoped the vice president was comfortable in her hotel, several streets over, separated in order to maintain the line of succession in case anything happened to the president—as well as Alex's protégé, Jaclyn Johnson, and her husband, Tom Messingham, had arrived to great fanfare. Not only them, but a cadre of Secret Service personnel and the White House press corps had come toddling along, too. They were all in Seattle—Jaclyn's hometown—to honor Jaclyn's father, the late General Edward R. Johnson, a hero of the first Gulf War, a victim of the September 11th attacks, with a statue in Volunteer Park.

In Alex's mind, it was an honor long overdue: General Johnson was an outstanding cadet at West Point, an outstanding soldier, and an even better commanding officer during his time in the United States Army. The late President

Sarah Kendall was one of his many charges, and Alex had grown familiar with the general when she herself served under former CIA head Nathaniel Dyer. There was an instant respect between Alex and the general, a respect she carried to this day.

The sweet memories searing her consciousness, Alex smiled.

I hope I've done right by you with your daughter, she thought, her thoughts headed skyward.

Alex leaned her forearms against the wrought iron railings, her gaze catching the floodlights of Safeco Field a few miles away. Jaclyn and Tom were there, their tickets for the Seattle Mariners and Tampa Bay Rays purchased before the season started. Alex hoped the broadcasters wouldn't show her there, even though the papers had said she would be in town for the unveiling; she wouldn't hold her breath, though. She also hoped Tom would enjoy himself, if but a little; she knew Jaclyn would have a grand time seeing her Mariners at Safeco for the first time in nearly a decade and a half.

"Jaclyn, Jaclyn, Jaclyn," Alex whispered into the night air. There were few cars in the area to distract her, even though she heard a bit of music coming over from the Pike Place Market, not too far away. "Oh Jaclyn, how you've grown since I took you away from here."

Alex's thoughts wandered back to September 2001, even as the warmth from the steel seeped into her flesh. The country, horrified by what had occurred that morning in New York, in Pennsylvania, and in Washington, had demanded answers. The sitting president had demanded retribution. And while everyone huddled around their televisions as the dark reality of their times flooded their consciousness, Alex had met with her staff in the bowels of Langley.

"The president," Alex had said as they walked out of the secure elevator, "is going to try to capitalize on our tragedy politically."

"Huge shocker there, ma'am. He's a politician. That's what they do."

They had entered the bunker. The room was all in gray: soundproof, bug-proof steel surrounded them, so much so that the only method of communication to the outside world was via a red landline phone which only dialed in one direction—to the Situation Room at the White House. There were televisions encircling the room, all tuned to CNN. They had showed the towers in Lower Manhattan belching black-gray smoke, the jet fuel burning. Alex had shuddered, then spoke again.

"He's going to do several things," she had continued. "Mark my words: He'll go after Bin Laden. It's only a matter of time before he admits he's behind it; the evidence is right there. " She had pointed at the television with a light gesture. "Four airplanes used against us, against one of his former targets. That's a tell. This was no accident."

"What's the next thing?"

Alex had tried to swallow the bile threatening to rise to her mouth. The taste of sour milk had lingered on her taste buds. The thought had been on her mind since she received the phone call an hour before.

"The next thing. He will take this opportunity to go after Hussein."

Her aides had immediately blinked, the surprise evident.

"Saddam?" they had chorused.

"Right in one."

"Why?"

"It's quite simple, Dave. Saddam is dancing in the streets of Baghdad right now, especially after what happened ten years ago. The president will rally Congress to his side, and I mean both sides of the aisle. This isn't unprecedented. It happened in '41. Everyone and their grandmothers are scared. Shit, all of Congress is scared." Alex had taken a seat, breathing a little heavy. She had poured herself a glass of water, if only to calm her nerves; she didn't drink alcohol while working, even in this stressful working environment. She had shot a gulp of water back into her throat, if only to rinse her mouth out. "He will be presidential, I am sure of it. He'll go to Afghanistan first, strike them hard. Then he'll go back to Iraq, inexplicably, much like his daddy did. This time, I doubt that Saddam can avoid the military might of the United States of America."

"And seeing that we haven't been able to locate General Johnson in the wreckage of the Pentagon," another aide had chirped, "that means the Army is going to be pissed."

She had swallowed hard; Alex had drinks with the general and his wife the night before the attacks. She had tried to keep her tears at bay, even now. She needed to remain strong, if not for her sake, for her son's sake.

"Correct. They'll get Hussein for making the president's father look foolish. He'll say it's to bring democracy to Iraq." She snorted. "It has nothing to do with that whatsoever. He'll go with a lie that says Iraq has weapons of mass destruction. He'll pin the blame on us when that particular plan goes awry."

"Of course. Pass the buck."

Alex had nodded.

"Right. And while he's doing that," she had said, "we need to be proactive in this new war on terror, as well."

No one blinked.

"Suggestions, Madame Director?"

The director had folded her hands on the table. She still hadn't grown used to people calling her by that title, even after seven long years at the head of the CIA. To her mind and to her heart, Nathaniel was still the Director, even though he had been in the grave since 1994. He would always be the Director, in her eyes. The letter he had left on her—his desk, she reminded herself—remained in her purse, even after seven years. And as much as she wanted to read his words, it wasn't time yet. Not even in the face of a horrific tragedy such as what had happened on this day would she pull that letter out.

"I have an idea that needs to stay within the confines of this room," Alex had said, "and it may seem a bit unorthodox to most people." She had taken a short breath as she kept her eyes on her aides; this, she had known even then, would make or break her career. "There is a young girl in the Seattle area who I feel would be the perfect candidate for this program."

"A young girl?"

Alex had nodded sharply.

"A girl of 14. She may not look like much now, but with a decade or so of training at The Farm, I'm sure she can turn into one of the best."

"We can't just go and snatch a child off the streets and train her to be a secret agent, if that's what you're thinking, Madame Director. Don't you think her parents would have a problem with the United States government stealing their child?"

Alex had felt her throat grow tight as her aide's accusation hit her ears. Her eyes grew limned with tears. She had closed her eyelids tight, stemming the flow.

"I don't think," she had replied once she had opened them, "that will be an issue any longer."

"An orphan?"

"You can call her that now, yes."

"Now?"

Alex had firmed her lips and nodded.

"I'm talking about General Johnson's daughter. Jaclyn."

Soft moans filled the room. A pen tinkled across the conference table.

"Fuck."

She nodded again. "Fuck is right. General Johnson and his wife are survived by a teenaged daughter, one who has some family."

"Wouldn't it be more prudent to send her to them?"

Alex nodded.

"Yes, I'm sure it would be the smart move to send her to the general's brother. They aren't too far away from them, and the girl has some cousins to help her adjust. But I reiterate: I think this is an opportunity that we as an agency cannot let slip through our fingers." She stood, her fingertips tenting on the table. "We have the opportunity to defeat terrorism and to attack terrorism with an individual born from the ashes of terrorism itself. Don't you see this opportunity in front of us? We can train this young woman—this orphan—to go after the ones who made her an orphan to begin with."

Then, as she looked over the heads of everyone in the room to see another replay of the towers tumbling, she lost her cool.

"Can we turn off the fucking TVs?" she had yelled. "How many fucking times do we have to fucking see the fucking towers falling? It's like the God damn fucking *Challenger* all over again. We already know what fucking happened."

Another aide had hustled around the room, turning the televisions off. Alex had felt a vein throb near her temple, her heart ramming the inside of her breastbone as she waited.

"Thank you," she had said, before taking another deep breath. She had bowed her head and counted to ten, pursing her lips and rubbing them together as she tried to regain control of her emotions. She had raised her head half a heartbeat after she had reached ten. "I'm sorry for that. I'm usually more in control."

"It's alright, Madame Director. We're all a bit fidgety right now."

Alex had smiled a half-smile.

"True. Anyway, I want to move ahead with this. I think this is the right thing to do."

"We can't get to Seattle right now. The president has ordered all flights grounded with SCATANA."

"He has grounded non-emergency civilian aircraft," Alex had corrected. "A government-issued Gulfstream on the business of the country's national security doesn't count. I'm headed there in an hour."

"What if the president wants you at a Cabinet meeting when he gets back from Florida?" an aide asked as she turned for the door.

"Don't worry about that. He's going directly to New York, then coming home. I'm hoping to get home before he gets back, heavy one passenger."

"Shouldn't we tell him what we're doing? We don't have the budget for this."

Alex had shaken her head.

"No. We're not telling this particular president anything. She's not even on board yet, and it won't be during this president's administration that she'll be unleashed anyway."

She exhaled. "I'll tell the next president about her. This one is a little too trigger happy for my tastes. He'll use her before she's ready."

"But Madame Director," the aide interrupted, "why her?"

"Why her?" Alex had echoed as she turned. "Why her. It's quite simple, really. Think about it. Say you're a soldier in the U.S. Army—hell, say you're a cadet at West Point, and you hear the stories of General Johnson as he rose up the ranks. And some time in the future, you're at your stationing and you get a call. It's General Johnson's daughter, all grown up, and she is in a bit of a sticky situation. You have a group of soldiers, all who idolized the man; the man gave them confidence like you wouldn't believe. They questioned his orders without flinching. She calls—wouldn't you answer that call and go to her side as if the order came directly from the general? You bet your scrawny ass you would."

"The rumor is she's blind," the aide had continued, his protest vociferous. "What good would a blind girl be in the fight against terrorism?"

At the door, Alex had smirked.

"You have no idea what the quartermasters are coming up with right now. If you did, you'd gladly pay a little more in taxes every year. Now if you'll excuse me, I have to go tell her that her parents are dead."

Alex had her driver take her to Andrews, the driver not sparing the pedal. And despite some warnings from air traffic control, the Gulfstream took off the evening of September 11, bound for the west coast.

The next morning, September 12, Alex had awoken early, called her then-husband to make sure he got their son off to school, before hopping in her rental car and driving to Renton. It was a rather easy drive headed out of Seattle, all while everyone else headed into the city, the morning rush apparent. She had easily found the home. It was on a side street with a well-manicured front lawn, the house painted baby blue. Another government car, this one from Fort Lewis, had met her there. She had called Lewis on the flight and spoke with the base commander, Colonel David

Meadows, informing him of what she had planned to do with General Johnson's daughter. He wasn't against it—he had served under the general—and had said he would facilitate it the next morning.

"Before school," Alex had noted. "I don't want to deal with pulling her out of class once she gets there."

"I can let the principal at Lakewood know that you're—"

"No, commander," Alex interrupted. "No one outside of official channels can know where she's going. You may tell her that she is being withdrawn—I'm sure the principal knows that the general is among the dead."

"I'm sure he knows." There was a pause. "I can't believe Eddie and Martha are gone."

Alex had bowed her head. She didn't say anything about Martha Johnson's premonition the night of September 10. Instead, she reached into her purse and felt a piece of tissue paper holding a gold band. She ran her fingers around it, the paper crinkling under her touch.

I'll give this to her, she had told Martha Johnson, *when the time is right*. She sighed. *That should have been a warning sign, right there. Always trust in a premonition, regardless of what the non-believers say.*

"I can't believe it, either." She had cleared her throat. "I will see you at the Johnson residence in the morning." She had hung up without another word.

A pair of soldiers had stood at parade rest at the entrance, all while a few curiosity seekers, knowing that it was the Johnson house, had waited to see what was going on. She had showed identification and had entered the house after they told her the commander was inside. Alex had hid her dismay as she walked in the door.

"We should have done this in the overnight, when I arrived," she had said to the commander. "That way we wouldn't have a circus. That's on me for not thinking."

"I wouldn't worry," the base commander had replied. He was a man of about 50, with short gray hair and a little bit of black mixed in for good measure. "Besides, Jaclyn told me that she was asleep, and the security alarms set. I called her this morning and let her know we were coming."

Alex had nodded.

"Where is she?"

"She's in her room."

"Packing?"

The commander had shaken his head.

"Thinking."

Alex had paused for a few moments, then nodded, her lips pressed together tight.

"Of course. Of course she is. Lead the way."

The commander had nodded and turned, leading Alex up the stairs. There were no creaks in these steps. Family photos in wooden frames emblazoned the wall to her left. The photos had shown the general smiling, raising a can of beer to the camera. It was a wooded area with a small lake in the background, pine trees in the foreground. The general was on a lawn chair, stretched out. Martha Johnson was in another photo, peeling off the Saran wrap from a bowl of potato salad. It might have been pasta salad, though. Alex couldn't wager a guess. And next to both parents was a scrawny blonde-haired girl; the girl had on a pair of sunglasses Alex knew helped give her eyes a rest from the painful rays of the sun—and from any fluorescent bulbs when the family was out and about.

Alex had grinned.

Hope you're ready for a new life, kiddo, she had thought as she ran her fingers along the frame.

She had hurried the rest of the way as she heard the commander speaking with the girl.

Alex had approached as soon as the commander stepped aside, and as she crossed the threshold, she saw, for the first time, the young woman who would someday put fear in the hearts of terrorists around the globe.

There, sitting on the bed, was a somewhat gawky teenage girl. Alex had noted that the girl's hair had the color of honey, her skin creamy. Her complexion was as close to flawless as a 14-year-old's complexion could get, her nose on the coquettish side; Alex had wondered just how it kept those sunglasses on and upright. And while the Director saw the girl had dressed in jeans and a t-shirt, as if she had gotten ready for school just like any other day, she appeared as if she had no interest in going. She held a small teddy bear in her hands; Alex thought it resembled Winnie the Pooh at one point.

Alex smiled.

"Hello, Jaclyn," she had said. "My name is Alexandra Dupuis. I'm an old friend of your mom and dad's."

Jaclyn had turned her head.

"Hi."

"I hope you know that we're very sorry for your loss."

The girl had taken a deep breath at that. Alex had looked for any signs of tightening eyes and quivering lips, but surprisingly, nothing appeared. It looked like the girl was in a daze. The girl's cheek, though, did twitch a couple of seconds later.

"Thank you."

"May I sit down?"

The girl had nodded, and Alex had parked herself on the edge. Whatever pains were in her feet evaporated just by sitting down.

"Have you been OK?"

Jaclyn had given her a soft shrug of her shoulders.

"I guess."

"Has anyone checked on you?"

This time, she shook her head. She still hadn't lifted her head to look at Alex.

"Doesn't your father's brother live around here?"

Jaclyn had offered a little nod.

"I don't think Uncle Bill knew that mom and dad were headed out. At least I don't think so."

Alex had made a note of that. *That would explain the head shake*, she thought. *Poor girl.*

"Have you been to school?"

"Yes. I don't skip school. Never have."

"So you went yesterday, even after everything that went down."

This time, the skin around Jaclyn's eyes had tightened a bit. The head had drooped a little more, as if she had tucked her chin as close to her chest as she could.

Alex had grimaced at her stupidity.

Damn you, Dupuis, she thought. *Not the exact time to use that terminology. What would Nathaniel tell you? Be a little more sensitive, you jackass.*

"I'm sorry I used that phrasing," she had said. "I want you to know that I'm not a truant officer or anything. I work for the CIA."

This got Jaclyn's attention. She had gasped and looked at Alex. The Director had noticed the tear streaks even through the girl's dark sunglasses.

"You're a spy?"

Alex couldn't help but let a grin spread.

"Kind of. You can say I'm the head spy in our country."

"Who are you spying on now? The people that took down the towers? The ones who plowed into the Pentagon?"

Alex had nodded. Her heart had fluttered at the mention of the Pentagon.

"Yes, and no. Our agency is looking into all possible leads, working with the authorities in New York and D.C. to try to find out who was behind it all."

Jaclyn's face had fallen a little, as if she had hoped the country's response would be rapid.

"Oh."

The pair had sat in adverse silence for a few seconds before Jaclyn spoke again.

"I had hoped they would have gotten out," she had said softly. Alex had heard every word. "I had hoped that they would have called last night. I figured that the cell service was overloaded. I thought, 'OK, they'll call this morning.' I stayed by the phone; shit, I practically slept on it. Oh, I'm sorry for swearing."

Alex had waved it off with a grin.

"Don't worry, sweetie. No one will know."

"I didn't even go to practice yesterday; I told coach that I had some women's issues, and she understood. I got home, I checked the answering machine." She shuddered. "Nothing. So I waited. Into last night, I waited. Made myself some cereal. Mom had left some chicken, ziti, and broccoli in the fridge, but I didn't want to touch that just yet. And then

Dave called me. I thought it was Mom or Dad at first; even answered it, 'Mom?! Dad?!'" Alex then saw the tears dripping out from underneath the girl's sunglasses. She had sniffed hard, her nose full. Her lips had turned into sharp edges, the corners turned down as the tears continued. Alex noticed her heart had begun to race; she had wondered why this girl, this 14-year-old girl, would open up to her like this. She didn't know Alex from Adam; Alex only knew of her from the tales Martha and the general had told her. Why did she trust her so much? She remained silent and let Jaclyn speak; she had somehow turned from the Director of the CIA into a guidance counselor as soon as she had perched herself on the edge of Jaclyn's bed. "Dave said that he needed to see me this morning, and that it was about Mom and Dad. I told him that I needed to know right that minute." A hard, long sniff—then a scream that Alex knew that she would never forget for as long as she lived. "He said they were dead! The fucking terrorists killed them!"

Alex had bit her lip as the girl's grief snapped apart. She had flung herself forward onto the bed, her face buried in the comforter as her tears flowed. As footsteps approached, Alex had brought her hand over and put it on the girl's back in a comforting manner. The base commander had appeared at the door, unbidden, with a few tissues in his hand; he had passed them over. Alex had nodded her thanks as she took them. He had ducked out into the hall once again.

She had waited until the girl had finished crying before she spoke again. Jaclyn had wept until she shook, her flesh trembling, the saline draining her. As soon as she lifted herself back up into a sitting position, Alex passed the tissues over. Jaclyn offered a mumbled "Thank you" before she blew her nose.

Alex had taken a deep breath as the girl filled the tissues. She had come to the reason of her visit, but she had to be careful: she was an adult in a position of power, and she didn't want to seem like she was misleading her. It was okay to sway her to her side, but no, she needed to lay everything out for the girl. She couldn't leave anything out.

"It is okay to grieve, Jaclyn," she had finally said, "and your parents deserve every ounce of your grief. But can I tell you something?"

With the relatively clean sides of the tissues, Jaclyn had dabbed at her eyes and nodded. She had pulled the sunglasses away by a few centimeters; Alex heard a slight wince as the daylight, which slipped through Jaclyn's drawn shades, hit the girl's eyes. She had noticed that the retinas were clouded.

Alex pursed her lips again.

"There are ways to channel your grief to get revenge."

"How?"

This is it, Alex thought. She swallowed her heart back down.

"Your father would want you to fight for us. I want you to fight for the CIA."

Jaclyn had shaken away her confusion.

"How? I'm only 14."

Alex wet her lips.

"I'm starting a program back in D.C. At the Farm, actually, in Virginia. It's a program that will see us train the new line of spy. A Super Spy, if you will. A spy born from the ashes of terrorism itself, one who'll stop at nothing to thwart the ones who wish to cause harm through fear."

Jaclyn had stared at her through the sunglasses, Alex knew, as if appraising her. The croak in her voice, though, left her.

"How long will the program last?"

Alex had exhaled through her nose and gave the girl a soft smile.

"The rest of your life."

An hour later, Jaclyn Johnson had finished packing up what she had for clothes, as well as a few keepsakes of hers and her mom's. Alex had offered to help her, but Jaclyn shrugged it off. Alex had nodded and backed away, then waited for the girl to come downstairs. The colonel had instructed the soldiers to help carry Jaclyn's bags to Alex's rental. Then, after Jaclyn had taken one last look around her parents' house, she had walked with Alex next to her, her sunglasses tight on her face. Alex had watched as Jaclyn tried to not look at anyone—but Alex did see a teenage boy with flaming red hair about Jaclyn's age break through the flood of people off to the side, screaming his head off.

"Where are you taking her?!" he had cried. "She's done nothing wrong!"

Alex had heard Jaclyn gasp in surprise, pulling her head up as the boy approached. The soldiers leading the women to the car had ordered him to stay back, but as Alex plainly saw, the boy's face was hard, but frightful.

"It's okay," Jaclyn had said. "You guys can let him pass."

"I don't think that's okay, Jaclyn," Alex had replied.

"Really, Alex," the girl had said, turning toward her. "It'll be okay. I just want to say good bye to him. He's always been so nice to me."

Naïve girl. That's because he wants something from you, Alex had thought.

"All right, but not a word about where you're going. The first thing I'll teach you about being a secret agent is that secrets matter."

Jaclyn had nodded, then walked over to the boy. Alex had observed the pair, the two teenagers standing only a few feet apart. The boy really didn't have too much to say; Alex had noted disbelief flooding his face as Jaclyn spoke, rocking him on his heels. She heard Jaclyn speaking to him, then reach down—she towered over him by a few good inches—and gave him a peck on the cheek. She had turned and walked back toward Alex, her pace a touch rapid. They all got into the rental, and as soon as the Hummer ahead of them pulled away, Alex had pulled behind them.

"Are you okay, Jaclyn?" she had asked, looking in the rear view mirror at the teenage boy, who stared at the rental's rear bumper as it departed.

Jaclyn had nodded.

"Yeah. Just sad about my parents."

"That is completely understandable."

"And sad that I have to say good bye to all my friends."

"You know that we're not stopping at the school, right? We're on a bit of a tight schedule."

Out of the corner of her eye, Alex had watched as Jaclyn's face fell.

"I know."

"You got to say good bye to your boyfriend, at least."

"He's not my boyfriend," Jaclyn had fired back, a little too rapidly. "He's just a boy who's a friend."

Alex had smiled and nodded.

"Right."

"I've never had a boyfriend."

Alex feigned shock.

"No way."

"Way!"

"It's okay. Boys are stupid anyway."

Jaclyn snickered a little.

"You can say that again, Chief."

Alex had grinned as she repeated herself. For the first time, Alex had heard Jaclyn's full laugh. It had lightened the Director's heart to hear her happy, despite everything she had endured in the last twenty-someodd hours.

They had driven on.

Over the course of the next few years, Alex recalled, Jaclyn had developed from the gawky 14-year-old into a younger version of the beautiful woman she knew today. Her complexion had cleared up, her skin flawless. She had worked out every other day, turning the baby fat into hard muscle. Kick boxing was one of her favorites. She went through daily weapons training, along with a rigorous education, mainly on laws and foreign languages. At night, she sparred hand-to-hand, doing her level best to knock her partner off their feet as the sweat poured down her face. Alex would drive to The Farm several times a week to inspect her training, and she always found the girl striving to be the best at what she did. Alex had watched as sweat sprang from her skin as the trainer gave the trainee a hard wallop against the back of Jaclyn's head, stunning her—but the teenager bounced back quicker than Alex had thought possible, turning defeat into a victory with a roundhouse kick the trainer apparently didn't see coming.

Good, Alex had thought. *That's something that will come in handy.*

As the girl grew older—she had turned 18 on May 19, 2005—they grew closer, even though Alex was her boss. They would make frequent trips to the mall in Alexandria, mainly for clothes, and sometimes a day of leisure, away from the world of intelligence briefs. Alex smiled as a memory of the two in the food court—and the modeling scout who had approached Jaclyn then, which gave the girl a rather incredible brainstorm and a way to fund her operations for the government—came to her mind.

Another warm breeze off the Puget snapped Alex back to the present. Sniffing, she checked her watch. It read 10:45 p.m. She looked toward street level and saw a black SUV pulling up to the sidewalk, the rubber grinding a touch as the driver applied the brakes: Jaclyn and Tom had returned a little early from the ballgame; before she stepped outside half an hour ago, she had checked the score. The Rays were ahead by a bunch in the sixth inning, and it was only a matter of time before the fans made a rush to the exits to beat the traffic.

She smiled as she saw the taillights turn off.

I'm so glad that she's found happiness in this life, she thought, *especially after all she went through to get to this point*. She sighed. *Edward and Martha would be so pleased and proud, I'm sure*. The doors to the SUV opened; Jaclyn climbing out of the driver's seat, of course. Tom followed from the passenger side. Jaclyn double-clicked the remote starter, setting the security system before they headed inside the hotel, holding hands.

"Time to go in. It's getting late. I'm going to need a good night's rest if I'm going to get up at 6 a.m. for the morning briefing. How many will that be now?" She sighed. "God knows I can't count that high."

Turning, she entered through the doors to her suite and closed them behind her with a slight *snick*.

She didn't see the shadow cross the moonlight.

She brushed her teeth vigorously before rinsing with a miniscule sip of mouthwash. She didn't bother flossing; the boys weren't around, and she figured that what they didn't know wouldn't hurt their teeth. Alex grinned at what their reaction would be if they found out, especially after all the times she had harassed them about their dental hygiene. She returned to her suite to get ready for bed just as the shadow grew larger, blocking out the starlight.

The breaking glass made Alex's head snap to the left, a sharp gasp slipped into her mouth. She watched as what looked like a parachute finished tumbling away, all while an intruder barged into her suite, feet first. The warm breezes pulsed in through the broken door. The intruder, she quickly discovered, was a man dressed all in black. It wasn't black Lycra like Jaclyn wore; it was more of a pullover shirt and cargo pants, with hard-soled leather boots to match. Weapons dotted his rather bulky frame; he had the appearance of a linebacker that didn't need pads to make a tackle. He wore a black harness, the straps making his deltoids look a tad larger. She suddenly felt naked without her gun, left behind in Washington. A breath caught in her throat. Her heart motored along, the muscle trying to outrun her adrenaline.

The intruder had landed on his feet as he crashed through the doors, which were now kicked open with spiderweb etchings remaining where the glass did not fall out of the frame. He had a gun out as soon as he landed, and he had it pointed straight at Alex's chest. Frozen in place, she looked straight down the barrel of the snub-nosed Baretta.

"Where's the Johnson bitch?" he demanded.

"Not here," Alex said after a beat. Yet, her thoughts rolled. *Keep him talking; Jaclyn will be here in a second. She has on her HUD; the warning tones and the schemata of the hotel will tell her where the trouble is. She'll come running. I know. She'll be here.* "What do you want?"

The intruder sneered.

"Her life. Yours will do, though."

Just as Alex's brain recognized the words, she heard the concussive blast half a heartbeat before an indescribable pain—one she had never before experienced—rippled out from between her breasts. The momentum took her off her feet, her backside colliding with the floor all before she cried out with a throaty moan.

The pain turned into a lengthy burn as she felt her life pouring out of the wound.

Her eyes closed, Alex realized she had been shot. She tried to get up a few seconds later, just as the intruder approached, the material of his boots crinkling as he walked toward her. She then saw a flash of light quickly cross her vision as her skull imploded.

For the last time, she grew still.

***

En route to The Warwick Hotel
Seattle, Washington
Friday, June 13/Saturday, June 14
10:43 p.m. PT/1:43 a.m. ET

"I've said it once, I'll say it a thousand bloody times," Tom Messingham said as they neared Olive Way on Sixth Avenue, "I will love you until the day one of us dies, but I promise you this: I will never, ever fall in love with baseball. So boring."

Jaclyn Johnson sniffed as she smirked.

"And I will repeat to you, my sexy British man: test cricket. So boring," she replied. "At least you caught a foul ball. Do you know how many fans go to so many games and they never catch a foul ball? Good on you to do it on your first try. And bare-handed, off the façade of the upper deck, too. I thought you were going to turn two there, for a second."

"That would have been six runs in cricket, not a strike." Tom palmed the scuffed baseball in his left hand; Jaclyn knew his right had the indentations of the ball's stitching against his palm. "You have to admit, though, Americans are little Nancies when it comes to fielding in baseball, with the gloves and all. Cricketers don't wear gloves."

"They wear enough padding to make a hockey goaltender blush."

"That's only when they're batting."

Underneath her HUD, Jaclyn rolled her eyes.

"I'll remember that for the next time you bring up American football and fifty pounds of Kevlar, dear."

They drove through the intersection, the black SUV a loaner from the Secret Service. Jaclyn eased off the gas as they approached the Stewart Street and Westlake Avenue intersections, the red lights halting traffic. To the left, Jaclyn saw a light in the Westin Hotel turn off. There were plenty still on.

Jaclyn took a deep breath as they pulled to a stop.

"I'll tell you, sweetie. It's good being back home," she said, turning to him and grabbing his hand.

Tom grinned.

"I'm sure. I get that feeling when I get back to London. And remember, you're supposed to meet with your dad's family tomorrow after the unveiling."

Again, Jaclyn rolled her eyes. The light turned green. Jaclyn hit the accelerator.

"Yes, how can I forget."

"You're really not happy to see them, are you?"

"I barely know them any longer," she said. "It's been how many years? I'm a different person now than I was in 2001."

"Yes, but you've changed in other ways, too." Jaclyn made the turn onto Lenora. The Warwick sat on the left, across from the Cinerama. "You've regained the sense of family that you lost."

"Yes," Jaclyn said, exasperated. "You and Tasha have given me a better reason to live these last few years than just killing terrorists every day." She hit her left directional and pulled up to the hotel's sidewalk. An attendant wouldn't touch the car, seeing as it would be needed for tomorrow's motorcade to Volunteer Park. Jaclyn peeked out the tinted windows. "Alex is out on her balcony, it looks."

"Catching another breath of fresh air, which is good for the lungs. I will say," Tom noted and he unbuckled his seat belt, "that there is something about the west coast air compared to that of the east coast that just screams healthy."

Jaclyn unbuckled her seat belt and opened the car door.

“We’re in a green city,” she answered. “A lot less pollution from these gas guzzlers, so the air is a little bit better to breathe.” She patted the steering wheel. “It means more outside time. Come on. We have a long day tomorrow, and we need our rest.”

“Yes, wife o’ mine.”

Jaclyn grinned and leaned toward her husband.

“Don’t you ever forget it.” They kissed tenderly before they broke apart. The couple exited the SUV, shutting the doors with a snap. Jaclyn walked a few feet toward the hotel while Tom walked around the front. Jaclyn turned and double-clicked the remote. A horn beeped just after the doors automatically locked. They grasped hands and headed inside.

A Secret Service agent smiled as he stood by the elevator.

“Evening, Steve,” Jaclyn said as they approached. “Everyone else in?”

Steve the Secret Service Agent shook his head in the negative.

“Not yet, Snapshot. The president, first lady, and the first daughter are across the street watching a late movie to get Maryah to sleep. Other than them, and now with you two in, everyone else is here.”

“We were going to stop in on the V.P. on our way in,” Tom said, “but me first lady here vetoed that idea.”

Steve chuckled and pressed the button behind him. The doors slid open.

“That’s not the first time a wife has vetoed a husband, and it certainly won’t be the last,” he replied. “Have a good night, you two.”

“We will,” they chorused before stepping inside the elevator. Tom pressed three. While the doors closed, Jaclyn watched the agent lift his left arm to his mouth. He said, “Mr. and Mrs. Messingham have entered and are in for the night.”

“I’m still not used to that,” Jaclyn said with a grin as soon as the doors slid shut. She felt her heart flutter against her ribs. “Mr. and Mrs. Messingham. Rolls right off the tongue, though.”

Tom showed two rows of perfect teeth.

"Aye, it does, love." He grabbed her waist and pulled her close to him. They kissed, their lips colliding hard. The kiss deepened as the elevator broke free of its mooring, the cables outside pulling it toward the sky.

"Mmmf," Jaclyn moaned as she broke away. "We didn't even kiss in the elevator in Las Vegas."

"Someone behind us would have honked had we not moved fast enough for them."

Jaclyn smirked at the memory: she and Tom at a stop light on the Famous Las Vegas Strip, their lips locked together. As the light turned green, someone immediately behind them honked their horn, breaking their smooch.

"Screw them."

The doors opened as soon as the elevator settled on the third floor. The hallway and its taupe-colored walls was empty, the Secret Service detail for the president presumably with him. Alex's room was at the far end of the hallway, while Jaclyn and Tom's sat to the right of the elevator. The president, first lady, and Maryah Forrister—Jaclyn always smiled when she caught sight of the former Syrian refugee the Forristers had adopted a year or so ago—had a room to the left of it. Melanie Ruoff's room was to the left of the president's, with a connecting door inside. The Secret Service agents took up the other rooms. Tasha, Jaclyn's ward, was not present for the unveiling; she had just graduated high school the weekend before, and chose to spend the last week with friends at Virginia Beach. After seeing the room assignments plotted out by the White House Advance, the Secret Service disagreed and had switched the rooms up as soon as they learned the set-up: as a just in-case, they wanted Jaclyn and Tom, both of whom were armed, across the hall from the president. The Director had agreed to the change.

"I can't wait to get this bra off," Jaclyn said as she rubbed between her breasts. She felt the front-facing snap as Tom slid their card key into the slot, rubbing the front to suppress an itch underneath it; a bread crumb from the hot dog bun had snuck into her shirt. He opened the door and held it open for his wife. "There are days that I wish men wore this damn thing and women got to go around without something hindering the girls. Ugh."

"I'm not revealing what I did at Eton, no matter how much sex you bribe me with."

She grinned as she pulled the snap apart before reaching into the sleeves of her Mariners t-shirt and pulled the strapless garment out. She tossed it aside like a slingshot.

"You are so kinky sometimes," Jaclyn said as she wrapped her arms around the back of her husband's neck. She leaned up, getting onto her tiptoes. "How about you get me down to my knickers and see how much noise we can ma—"

A mighty whine from her HUD snapped Jaclyn's head toward the door, breaking her head's momentum. Tom didn't move nor ask what was going on as the device flashed the word DANGER across the lenses, before she saw the red dot center in at the other end of the hall.

A breath immediately caught in her throat. Her heart rate instantly accelerated as the realization of current events dawned on her.

"Alex," she cried, prying the word out of her voice box. She leaped onto the bed and reached across to her bedside table. She slipped the drawer open and reached inside just as her HUD whined a second time; she easily heard the first gunshot. She choked off a cry, not even looking the way the shot came from as Tom moved to his table and did the same. Jaclyn grabbed her Walther P99 from within its depths and rolled off the bed. She raced for the door. Tom followed.

Together, their combined footsteps made it sound like a stampede.

The hall looked vacant, but the second shot sent Jaclyn's heart toward her throat. She and Tom moved forward, keeping her HUD on Alex's door. They made it halfway down the hall when Jaclyn saw the handle swing downward. She halted their progress and steeled her nerve as she brought her Walther to bear just as the door opened. Tom followed suit.

Out stepped a man wearing all black, who froze as he saw Jaclyn and Tom standing there, their guns up.

"Drop the gun, slimeball," Jaclyn yelled.

"Johnson," the intruder growled. "There you are." He tried to lift his gun—

Jaclyn immediately dropped the barrel of her Walther and pulled the trigger three times in succession. Three quick blasts poured from it, and within heartbeats, she heard the intruder scream mere seconds before he collided with the floor face-first. Jaclyn hurried in and kicked the gun out of his hands, sending it into the corner. Tom eased in with his gun up as the intruder writhed in serious pain.

"Oh, stop your whining, you little bitch," Jaclyn said, reaching down and hefting the man over and onto his back. Behind them, the elevator dinged; half a moment later, the doors slid open, and another stampede met her ears. Jaclyn caught Tom turning and bringing his gun up while she inspected the prisoner. She had shot him in the legs, incapacitating him; one of the shots had shattered his left kneecap. She drove the still-hot barrel into his left nostril. He kept moaning. She imagined the pain he currently experienced, and she felt her cheek twitch as she reveled in each pitiful-yet-glorious syllable. She ground her teeth together. "You even think about moving, I pull the trigger and send your brain screaming for your mommy."

"Jaclyn," Tom said, jarring her out of her focus. "Steve and I'll look after this bell end. Go check on Alex."

Jaclyn breathed and was now keenly aware of her racing heart. She nodded just before the prisoner started laughing. She felt her blood turn to ice as she looked down on him.

"You're not going to like what I've done," he said with a painful smile. "She's d—de—" He started coughing while his eyes tightened.

Jaclyn turned and saw that Alex's door was still open, the perp's foot resting against it.

That's good, she thought. *We won't have to wait for the guy at the desk to come up with a back-up card. Timing is everything. Please Alex, please be okay.*

Without another hesitation, she entered Alex's suite.

The room's lights had remained on as she walked in, keeping the door open a crack. She saw the destroyed double doors that led out onto the balcony, and on the floor, she saw a body on its back.

"Alex," she breathed as she launched herself away from the entryway. She took three steps before halting; she now saw what had happened in the moments prior to her taking the intruder down.

She gasped.

"No! Alex! NO!"

Jaclyn felt her insides roll as she found Alex's body where the intruder had left it. She wasn't moving, and Jaclyn saw why: a crimson stain marred her chest, and another bullet hole had ripped through her forehead. Her eyes were closed, as if asleep.

Underneath her HUD, Jaclyn's eyes were wide.

She tried to swallow, but it felt as if her windpipe had shrunk to half its normal size, making it feel as if she had swallowed sandpaper. She felt her body go numb, so numb that she was on her knees before she even knew it. She dropped the gun only a few inches to the floor, not even setting the safety before she let go. She felt the blood leaving her face in such a rush that she didn't know if she had the ability to hold onto the contents of her stomach. Her jaw had locked, her mouth open, wide enough that her breath came out choked. Every thought in her mind had evaporated in the time it took her to hit her knees.

Jaclyn knelt in disbelief, her gaze not leaving that of her mentor's—her surrogate mother's—body. Thoughts rolled through her mind as if on a theater-sized screen; their first meeting, seeing Alex through her HUD for the first time—and when she had come to London to give her aid when she had gone rogue. Tears filled her eyes. She did not know how long she stayed in that position, but after she felt her chest heaving and filling with air, she had no other alternative.

"TOMMMMMMMMM!" she screamed. "TOMMMMMMMMM!"

Half a moment later, she heard the rapid footsteps approaching the door, before it opened. Tom burst in.

"Are you o—oh my God," Tom said with a gasp as he walked in and paused where Jaclyn had. He then walked a little slower as Jaclyn's arms opened of their own accord. Jaclyn felt herself being scooped up as Tom wrapped his arms around her.

"Tom, she's, she's," Jaclyn cried.

She couldn't get the last word out.

"I know what she is, love," Tom replied. "Don't say it. Don't say it, please. Don't give it finality just yet."

"That—that son of a bitch—"

"We're going to get whoever ordered this," Tom said, his voice hard. "Come on, you shouldn't be here. We have to call the po—"

Jaclyn screamed as she broke Tom's embrace and grabbed her gun off the floor. Tom reached out and tried to pull her back, but she evaded his grasp. She rushed to the door, opened it, then leveled the Walther at the downed man. The Secret Service agent also had his gun trained on him; the bastard, Jaclyn heard, kept on inhaling sharply through his teeth, the pain certainly ripping a hole in his nerves. Melanie Ruoff, in a bathrobe, had already emerged from her bedroom, a cell phone in her hand.

"Who the fuck sent you?" Jaclyn yelled just as the Secret Service agent said, "Agent Johnson, stand down!"

The intruder simply laughed at the question. He didn't answer.

Jaclyn snarled as she rushed forward a step. She had reared her foot back and immediately sent it careening into the man's groin. This time, the intruder's moans bounced off the walls as he rolled into the fetal position.

Jaclyn quickly felt a pair of arms encircle her from behind, pinning her arms down.

"Tom, no, let me go!" she demanded.

"No love, you can't do this, you can't," Tom replied as he dragged her around the intruder, bringing her toward Ruoff. He grabbed her gun as the White House Chief of Staff wrapped her arms around her. "Melanie, stash her somewhere. But not in the bloody hallway."

Tom went back to the Secret Service agent.

“Melanie, God,” Jaclyn moaned. “Alex is—Alex is dead!”

She heard Ruoff gasp before her embrace tightened.

“Come on. Inside. You’re no good to us out here,” Ruoff said as Jaclyn heard the Secret Service agent speak into his wrist mike; “All agents, we have a national security emergency inside the president’s hotel. Director Dupuis is dead. I repeat—Director Dupuis has been murdered in her room. Alpha and Bravo, corral the president and escort him to his suite. Charlie, Delta, secure the vice president. Suspect in custody.”

Then, finally, without another word, Jaclyn broke.

Chapter 2
Seattle Cinerama
Lenora Street
Seattle, Washington
Friday, June 13/Saturday, June 14
10:57 p.m. PT/1:57 a.m. ET

Thanks to the generosity of the Cinerama's manager, President Eric B. Forrister and his wife Veronica had arranged for a late night showing of the latest kids movie. It was a way, hopefully, of getting their adopted daughter, Maryah, to fall sleep. The plan was to sit her down with the big screen in front of her, and treat it like any other day out at the movies: it had been a long day for Maryah, especially with the time change from Eastern to Pacific Time, and running here and there to the first lady's functions. She hadn't run out of energy, though, and she hadn't napped.

Still, the movie did it: she was asleep half an hour into it. Her container of popcorn sat between her tiny legs, hands inside it, even though her upper body had tilted toward the president.

Forrister, sitting to Maryah's left, grinned as he looked to Veronica, sitting on the other side.

"That didn't take long," he said. "It would be a shame to pull her out of here and bring her across the street. I don't think the manager would like that, either."

"No, I'm sure he wouldn't. But you know," Veronica said, "that she's going to know she missed the movie and will want to see it again."

The president nodded.

"It'll have to wait until we get to the plane. There'll be no time tomorrow until then."

"You try telling her puppy dog eyes that in the morning."

Forrister couldn't help but chuckle.

"Those puppy dog eyes are like Kryptonite."

They watched the movie together for five more minutes. They had the entire theater to themselves, the Secret Service standing outside the main door; Forrister had bought them a bag of Skittles each to tide them over until it was time to head back across the street. The door, Forrister saw, opened a touch, a sliver of light caressing the screen. It was then that Donald, their lead Secret Service agent, slipped into the aisle and took a seat next to Forrister. The president leaned toward him.

"Sir, we have a national security emergency back at the hotel," he said at a low timbre, as if not to alarm the first lady.

"What's wrong?"

Forrister heard an audible sigh coming from the agent.

"I'm sorry to say that Director Dupuis has been murdered."

Forrister's eyes widened as he turned to face him. He felt the blood leave his face. His breathing seemed choked, as if he needed a crow bar to pry the air out of his lungs.

"What?" he finally said. His heart thrummed at a pace he hadn't felt since Las Vegas and the monorail incident.

"Eric, what's wrong?" Veronica asked, but Forrister wasn't listening. He held a finger up to shush her.

"About five minutes ago, sir. It all happened very fast. I don't have all the details yet, but a suspect is in custody. Agent Johnson took him down."

Forrister closed his eyes and exhaled hard, before opening them again.

"Are you sure she's dead?"

The agent nodded.

"Agent Johnson confirmed it."

"Eric—?"

"I'll be right there," Forrister said before he turned to Veronica. "Sweetie, stay here. There's a big problem at the hotel."

"Did he say murder?"

Forrister tried to swallow as he stared into his wife's eyes, but doing so was a task. He knew he had to play this safe—she and Alex were friends, after all; Veronica had been the one to tell him what she saw in Alex's eyes during Jaclyn's Sydney adventure, something he knew he didn't have the wit to see—but there wasn't any way around it being anything but a hard shock. She couldn't hear it from anyone else. It had to be from him.

He nodded.

"I'm sorry, my love. Alex is dead."

If his eyes had done what his wife's had, he knew that there would be a few deep breaths coming soon. He watched, even in the darkness, as the tears started lining his wife's eyes. He held his hand out to her for her to hold. She grabbed and held tight, as if she didn't want to let go.

"I have to go across the street. I need you to stay here with Maryah. Keep her calm and out of sight," he said. He tried to remain calm even after delivering a mighty blow to his wife's heart. "I don't want her to see them roll Alex out of there."

"Eric, please," Veronica said as the tears ran down her cheeks, "take care of her, please."

He nodded.

"You know I will, love." He leaned over his precious daughter's sleeping form and kissed his wife tenderly. "I'll leave an agent here. We'll radio to him when it's safe for you to bring her over. Okay?"

Veronica tearfully nodded. Forrister brought his hand to his lips, then placed his fingers on Maryah's forehead. He slipped out of the aisle and powerwalked to the door.

"Papa Bear's moving," Donald spoke into his sleeve mike.

"How in the hell did this happen, Donald?" the president said as they marched hard through the lobby. "Pete, stay here and watch over them."

Peter the Secret Service Agent nodded and stayed put.

"You have to see it to believe it, sir. We've found a parachute lingering at the corner of the building."

"Lingering is better than loitering," Forrister grumbled before pausing. "A parachute? Has Seattle Police been called?'

"Yes, sir. Melanie called them."

"Good old Melanie," Forrister said with as much of a smile as he could muster. "Have her call the U.S. Marshals. This is their case. Seattle's to assist."

"Understood, sir."

They didn't say another word as they stepped outside and onto Lenora Street. The road was quiet, all save the sounds of approaching sirens coming from the north. Forrister looked to his right and found the parachute resting on the sidewalk, right up against the building.

Right under Alex's suite, he thought. As soon as the president and his Secret Service detail crossed the middle of the road, two Seattle Police cruisers—Ford Interceptors—whipped around the corner, their lights twisting in the darkness.

Forrister and Donald hurried to the other side just before the cruisers pulled up alongside the hotel.

"Mr. President," the first cop said as he got out of his cruiser, "we need to secure the hotel, sir."

"The hotel is secure, Sergeant. The parachute over there," Forrister said, pointing, "is evidence. Collect it. I'm going upstairs."

"Yes, sir."

"I want the chief roused and down here within an hour."

"Yes, sir. Will do."

Forrister and Donald entered the hotel. The night manager slipped out from behind the counter and approached.

"Mr. President, is there anything I can do?"

"Yes, make sure EMS have been called."

"They have been."

Forrister patted him on the shoulder.

"Good. I also need the card key to the Director's room."

"Certainly, sir."

The manager grabbed the key from the other attendant—who had already gone into motion seconds before Forrister spoke—and brought it back.

"I'm so sorry, sir."

"If any of the other guests," Forrister said, deflecting the man's condolences, "complain about what happened, please extend the White House's apologies." He walked to the elevator before the night manager had the chance to say another word.

"This isn't the way I wanted to end my night, Don."

“I’m sure you didn’t, sir. The suspect is in one of the side rooms, I understand.”

“I want to see Alex first, then I’ll see this scum-sucking piece of shit.”

“Understood, sir.”

They entered the elevator and were silent as it took them to the third floor.

The doors parted as soon as the elevator came to a rest. Forrister stormed through it as soon as the doors were wide enough for his frame to squeeze out. Even with the wailing coming from Melanie Ruoff’s room, he powered his way down the hall, ultimately sidestepping the bloodstain on the carpeting in front of Alex’s room. He slipped the card key into the slot. The light immediately turned green. He hit the lever down with his palm and walked in. Donald did not follow him inside.

The lights were still on as he entered, and he saw first-hand what had occurred. He saw the damaged doors, then looked to Alex’s body. A long grimace flowed.

“Shit,” he said. He walked in a little further and caught the full breadth of the body, his hands at his waist, his coat thrown over his wrists. “Damn it all.”

Sending a blast of air from his nose, the president crouched down next to her. He saw the bullet hole in the woman’s forehead and knew that was the shot that had killed her; he also knew that the shot to her chest was just to stun her. He felt his grief welling in his eyes and throat as he stared hard at his now-former Director of the CIA.

“I’m so sorry, Alex,” he whispered. “I’m so, so sorry.”

He kept looking at her still form, staring in disbelief. Memories suddenly rolled through his mind, though, knowing the end had come for his dear friend and confidante. He saw himself meeting her prior to the election which had won him the vice presidency and Sarah Kendall the White House, and how she had handed over the so-called nuclear football codes to Sarah on Inauguration Day. He remembered shaking her hand, noting the woman’s powerful grip that belied her stature. He recalled the day Alex had told him Sarah had committed the ultimate sacrifice to her country, and that *he* was now the President of the United States of America.

God, he thought, *now both of them are gone*. He shivered, a chill wrapping around him.

He recalled the daily meetings with her, dealing with the London episode, the incident in Vegas—*damn, how much I needed to hear your strong, comforting voice, even while I tried to keep it all together for the people in that station*, he thought—as well as when she disobeyed his orders regarding security in Atlanta. Tears filled his eyes as his thoughts moved to the Detroit fiasco.

He wiped his eyes with the back of his hand.

You were a good friend, Alexandra, his thoughts continued. *You were just one of many strong women in my life: you, Sarah, Veronica, Lucia, Jaclyn*. He swallowed hard.

"We're going to get the persons responsible for this, Alex," he said aloud, even though he knew she couldn't hear him; her sense of hearing had long departed. "The person that did this had to have been acting under orders from someone else, but don't worry. We'll get them. I'll make sure Jaclyn—"

Forrister stopped short. He had the feeling he couldn't send Jaclyn after this loon, he knew; she had already taken out the fucktard who had taken Alex out of the game, and she had found the body. He had heard the secret agent's crying even through the closed door. That was enough for him.

She's in no shape to go after these people, he thought with another hard swallow. He inhaled deeply. *At least not right now*.

"I'll see you when I see you, Alexandra," Forrister said, bringing his fingers to his lips before pressing them to her nose. "We'll take care of your boys for you. I promise you that."

The president rose to his full height and took a deep breath as he looked down on her one last time. He wiped his eyes, then headed out of the room, closing the door behind him.

"Where is the son of a bitch?" he growled.

Donald motioned to the door to the left.

"Pete's room," the agent said.

"Pete's going to have to double up tonight. Open it up."

Donald nodded, procuring the card key from his jacket. He brought his sleeve to his mouth. "Papa Bear incoming." He slipped the card into the slot, then drew his Sig-Sauer. Forrister opened the door and walked in, the agent trailing.

He found the intruder resting on the edge of the bed, which was now stained crimson thanks to Jaclyn's handiwork. The room, Forrister saw, was much like his and Veronica's. Pete's bag was open off in the corner, but the president soon put the accoutrements of the room out of his mind. Forrister leveled the intruder with a hard, dark stare, but the man simply sneered his defiance. The two Secret Service Agents in the room had their guns drawn, too; one had it leveled at the bastard, ready to plug him if he had the gumption to fight the pain away and make a move toward the Leader of the Free World.

"You picked the wrong government to fuck with, pally," the president said. "Who the fuck sent you to kill her?"

The intruder's sneer turned to a smile; he showed two rows of pink, blood-stained teeth as he chuckled his amusement.

"I'll never tell," he said.

Forrister growled as he pulled his right hand back, letting it fly half a second later. His fist violently collided with the man's jaw, bone meeting bone with a sickening thud. The killer moaned as he flopped to his right. Forrister immediately shook the pain out of his knuckles.

"You killed a highly-placed member of a sitting president's administration," Forrister said as the intruder raised his head. "You'll talk."

"You're going to pay for punching me."

Forrister sneered.

"Yeah, sure. You think anyone's going to believe that the President of the United States punched you? Maybe Fox News will believe you, but no one with a mind will."

"You should double-check the people close to you, Mr. President," the intruder said. "The person that helped us is free as a bird right now, and I'll never give him up."

Forrister ignored him.

"We'll go through your cell phone, your mail, everything. You will give up who ordered the hit on her."

The intruder snorted.

"No phone. No home address on record. Besides, your bitch there was collateral—"

Forrister's upper lip flared as he reared his fist back a second time. He groaned hard as his fist displaced air. The sound of cartilage snapping filled the room, half a heartbeat before the prisoner moaned and grabbed his nose. He sneezed hard; blood and mucus covered Forrister's shoes.

"Damage," the intruder finished. "She wasn't the target, old man."

Forrister breathed hard as he stared down on the bleeding man as he processed what he just heard. He added up everything, then felt his eyes widen slightly as he came to a conclusion he didn't think was possi—

Well, he thought, *that's not entirely true, and yes, it is possible. It is well within the realm of possibility that someone our top agent had either apprehended—someone with ties to Senator Farrell, perhaps?—or had killed wanted her dead. It wasn't much of a reality stretch. The fact that the bastard considered Alex collateral damage can only mean one thing—her death was a mistake.*

He nearly choked on air.

"Thanks for the information," Forrister said as soon as he cleared his throat. "Nice talking to you. Enjoy Terre Haute. I'll be at your execution; you can be assured of that."

"If I can escape these two goons," the intruder threatened, "you can be sure you'll see me before then. Maybe I'll have to give your wife the business, too." Lewdness tinged his grin as he shot a wink the president's way.

Stiffening at the man's verbal diarrhea, Forrister restrained himself from not just throwing his fist at the intruder, but his entire body at him. It would be an easy fight, he knew; the man bled from three bullet holes in his legs—*smart thinking by Jaclyn for going about it the way the authorities in Europe would handle it, taking out his lower extremities instead of plugging him in the chest and abdomen; that has to be Tom's influence, I'm sure*, he thought—as well as from a couple of punches. Hell, it had been way too long since he had gotten into a brawl, and right now, with this son of a bitch taunting him, daring him to make a move—

Forrister took a deep breath.

"You're lucky you did this now and not a couple of years ago," he explained. "Jaclyn would have killed you without thinking twice." He turned to the Secret Service agents. "If he tries to get up, kill him."

"With pleasure, Mr. President," the one on the left said.

Forrister left the room.

"Jaclyn's in Melanie's room, correct?"

"Yes sir," Donald replied, following half a step behind. Forrister didn't hear any more wailing as he approached. "The Director shouldn't be dead, if I understood everything that quack just said."

Forrister cleared his throat.

"No. She wasn't the target. But he wouldn't have had much of a chance had the true target been in that room like he thought. He would have been dead instead."

He walked two more steps before he knocked on the door to Melanie Ruoff's suite. He waited a few seconds before the door opened. At the same time, the elevator dinged. The doors opened to reveal a pair of EMT's pushing a gurney out of it. The Seattle Police sergeant followed.

"The bastard who killed her is in that room, right there," Forrister pointed. "Don't give him a safe drive. And the body is in that room there." He pointed to Alex's suite. "Don't touch it until the federal marshals get here."

The sergeant blinked.

"Excuse me, sir?"

"You heard me."

The sergeant walked toward the agent's room, muttering something about jurisdiction before the president turned to his friend. Melanie looked tearful as she stood in the doorway. His lips twisting, Forrister walked in and gave her a hug as she wept across his chest. He patted her shoulders and upper back a few more times.

"It's going to be all right, Melanie," he said comfortingly. "It's going to be all right."

She pulled away a little and wiped her tears away.

"We have a constitutional crisis, Eric," she said.

"Anything like that can wait," he replied. "I need you to call Lewis and get a few federal marshals up here to secure the scene. This is a federal crime, federal marshals will take the lead." He exhaled. "How's Jaclyn?"

"In shock. She's in the bathroom washing her face." She turned her head. "Tom's here, too."

"I wouldn't expect him anywhere else than by Jaclyn's side," Forrister said. He walked in and found Tom sitting on Melanie's disheveled bed. As Melanie made the phone call to Lewis, the MI5 man stood as the president entered. Forrister wrapped him in a hug that Tom was initially wary of, but the stress seemingly washed away. Jaclyn's husband melted half a moment later.

"Alex wasn't the target," Forrister said.

"Who was?" Tom asked.

"Your bride."

Tom swallowed.

"The bloke had said Jaclyn's maiden name and, 'There you are," before he brought his gun up. My honey bunny dropped him—and then she kicked him in the giblets. That explains quite a bit, and makes sense, too."

Forrister nodded as the bathroom door opened. Jaclyn spilled out. Forrister saw that she had stopped crying, but her grief remained on her face. Her lips crinkled as she approached. They embraced. Her upper body rose and fell with her breathing, but she didn't seem to want to cry again.

"Are you all right, Snapshot?" he asked.

She nodded.

"I will be," Jaclyn replied. "It's not every day that the woman that practically raised you through your teenage years dies at the hands of a sick fuck down the hall from you."

Forrister frowned.

"I know," he said, then waited a few seconds before he spoke again. "Do you feel up to having the unveiling tomorrow without—" he swallowed, cutting off the obvious.

Jaclyn grimaced and shook her head. She sat down on the bed, tucking her chin toward her collarbone.

The president nodded.

"I think that's the right decision, love," Tom said as he sat next to her, grabbing her hand, before he looked up at Forrister. "When should we reschedule?"

"When we have the bastard behind it all locked up," he replied. He crouched down in front of Jaclyn, his knees cracking a touch as the cartilage popped. "I know this will be hard for you to do, kiddo, but I need to hear everything that occurred tonight from your mouth."

He watched as Jaclyn took a long, deep breath, as if collecting her thoughts.

Then, without further hesitation, she relayed the details of what had happened.

***

A few minutes later, Jaclyn finished her story; Forrister trusted her to tell the truth, and she did. After another quick hug, the president said he would see them in the morning. Jaclyn and Tom left for their own room. He kept Melanie there; at the same time, the EMT's wheeled the intruder toward the elevator. Forrister saw that they had sedated him; he wasn't even awake.

"Are the marshals on the way?" he asked.

She nodded.

"They'll be here in an hour or so, and they'll take possession of the scene and the—the body—as instructed," Melanie said as she yawned. "Is there anything else?"

"You read me like a book. Pay another call, this time to McChord. Inform them that we'll be leaving for the east coast at 10 a.m. and to have Air Force One prepped. Then call Lewis again and tell them that we'll have to reschedule the unveiling. Then inform the Cabinet of an emergency meeting tomorrow evening. That can wait until tomorrow morning."

"Already on it; I told Lewis there wouldn't be a chance of the guest of honor being up for it."

"Remind me to book a different hotel for when we come back. I don't want Jaclyn to go through the trauma."

"Will do, Eric. Get some sleep."

"I will. Has anyone called Roger?"

Melanie blinked.

"Roger?"

"Alex's ex-husband."

"Oh." She shook her head.

"It can wait until the morning. I'll have Donald wake me in a few hours so I can call him before the news crews report it."

"Let's hope no one lets the cat out of the bag, so to speak. Get some rest, Eric."

"You, too."

The president left. Donald fell in behind him as they walked the few feet to the Forristers' suite.

"Contact Peter and let him know that the coast is clear and that the First Lady can bring Maryah over. Marshals will be here in about an hour. We're headed home in the morning."

"You got it, sir." Donald carried out his orders.

Forrister clapped the man on the shoulder before he entered his own room. He leaned against the door.

"Damn it," he muttered. "Damn it, damn it, damn it."

***

Jaclyn and Tom's hotel room
The Warwick Hotel
Lenora Street
Seattle, Washington
Saturday, June 14
12:05 a.m. PT/3:05 a.m. ET

Tom held Jaclyn tight after they finally undressed from their long day. They simply laid there without saying a word to each other, knowing there really wasn't anything to say. They both had seen what had happened. Words were beyond them.

Jaclyn's mind rolled along the breezes coming from the partially open window; twisting red and blue lights continued flashing outside the hotel. As she squeezed her husband—there was nothing to hold against him for what he had done earlier; he didn't want her to lose her mind when she needed it most, she reasoned, and she loved him even more for it—she thought about her life with Alex.

She shuddered.

How, she thought. *How is Alex dead? I was just with her seven hours ago. She was alive. She was breathing. Her eyes looked tired—shit, we all were tired—but she's been tired for two decades, maybe even more. She didn't look dead.*

But now...

Jaclyn trembled again, disguising it as she curled closer to Tom. In the darkness, she had removed her HUD and simply stared into her husband's chest. While she saw nothing but the utter blackness of Tom's t-shirt, her mind's eye saw, clear as day, every memory she had running haphazardly through her consciousness.

She looked like she was asleep, Jaclyn thought, *but how would one sleep with bullet holes in your chest and your forehead? How does one move on from something like that? Who will look after your boys?*

The secret agent tightened her eyes.

Alex, she thought. *I miss you so much. Why? Why did you have to die? If I could trade places with you, I would do it in a heartbe—*

Jaclyn gasped, everything rolling into her mind at once. Every box clicked, a virtual pencil expelling lead on the page.

That's it, she thought, bringing her fingers to her lips. She pulled at the bottom one, rolling the tiny flesh counterclockwise. *That's it, that's it, that's it.... But why? That may be what we need to discover.*

She quickly rolled out of Tom's embrace and made for her HUD, then turned the light on. Tom snapped awake. His eyes looked heavy.

"Love? What's wrong?"

"It was supposed to be me," Jaclyn said. "I was supposed to be in that room tonight. I was supposed to die. That was supposed to be our room. Remember? The Secret Service moved us out of there to protect the president. We have guns, and Alex wasn't armed. Instead, Alex was put in there."

"It could have been either of us who died tonight, then."

Jaclyn shot a heavy frown his way, crossing her arms underneath her breasts.

"Seriously? Are you the one who has made enemies in every corner of the globe since 2012?"

Tom nodded right away.

"Yep," he replied. "The day we got married, it was as if millions of men cried out in terror, and were suddenly silenced the moment you said, 'I do.' I became public enemy number one that day, and I made all the haters of the world me itty bitty bitch."

For the first time in what felt like hours, Jaclyn managed a smile.

"I love you," she whispered.

Tom grinned wider.

"I know."

"But you know what I mean. We were supposed to be in that room. It should have been one of us who died at that wanker's hand after he crashed through the doors."

"That would have been dreadful for either of us."

Jaclyn rolled her eyes under her HUD.

"Yes, I'm sure it would have been dreadful for you, my dearest love." She paused, nibbling on the inside of her cheek before she gasped, her thoughts thinking back to Sydney. She thought of her phone calls with Alex, and then of their conversation in the hotel the day Jaclyn and Tom had tied the knot. Jaclyn's face grew passive. "They took away the choice for you."

"Pardon?"

Jaclyn blinked as if startled out of her reverie. She found Tom staring at her, as if looking over a pair of eyeglasses her way. He looked confused, as if the man didn't understand that she wasn't speaking directly to him.

"Sorry, babe. I was just thinking back to what Alex had said on our wedding day; before we left the hotel, she had told me that she wasn't retiring."

"Right."

"Which means she would have had that choice sometime in the future had she not been—" Jaclyn felt her eyes close as the realization hit her. She slapped a hand over her mouth as she shook, falling back into Tom's embrace.

Tom swallowed as he held onto his weeping love.

"I know, love. I know."

"They took that choice away from her, Tom," Jaclyn cried, the tears streaming down her face once again. The corners of her mouth had turned down, the angles sharp. "They took it away from her."

Tom held her tight the rest of the night, and deep into the morning.

Chapter 3
Home of Darren Drake
Inglewood, North Seattle, Washington
Saturday, June 14
6:59 a.m. PT/9:59 a.m. ET

Fresh coffee in hand, the red-headed bachelor Darren Drake watched the early-morning news on KOMO at his kitchen table. He wanted to pay close attention to this particular newscast, and one story in particular. He had to figure that with the president's arrival yesterday, there would be plenty about the Commander in Chief's arrival—and especially after what had occurred at his hotel last night.

The man grinned as he loosened his robe. He wanted to enjoy this moment. He wanted to flaunt his superiority over the Leader of the Free World, as well as get his rocks bubbling in case he saw her: He also had a mild crush on one of the anchors, a hot blonde that reminded him, somewhat, of his childhood crush. Oh, how many masturbation sessions had the anchor fueled in the last few years? He sat there, mug in his left hand, his right covering his crotch. He stroked downward with the heel of his palm, bringing his muscle to life with a twitch.

Maybe they'll show both hotties in the same newscast, he thought with a lascivious grin inching toward his cheeks. *How lucky would my eyes be then?* A giggle slipped out, filling his kitchen with mirth.

The broadcast turned immediately to a shot of the hotel he had sent his associate—*yes*, he thought, *associate is the politically correct term to use here*—in order to kill Jaclyn Johnson, that runaway bitch, last night. The hottie anchor had turned it over to the reporter on scene. Police officers and yellow police tape surrounded the building, while he saw what looked like the Secret Service—they all wore suit coats and ties, even wearing sunglasses in the shade; he saw their tiny earpieces, even from distance—milling about the entrance. There was footage from the overnight of a police officer directing what limited traffic flowed along Lenora, as well as another officer hauling in what Drake knew was a parachute. Then, from a helicopter's angle, they showed the damaged doors, the glass cracked and shattered, the inner frames busted.

Drake's grin didn't fade in the slightest.

It went down exactly how I diagrammed it out, he thought. He wrapped his palm around his junk, through his boxers—

But as he listened in, he quickly discovered things had gone wrong: The Director of the CIA was dead—not the target.

So that's why I never heard from him last night, Drake thought as he set his mug down. He reached up and ran his palms across his unshaven jaw, his developing hard-on forgotten. The grin turned into a slight frown. *He's been captured, if the report is correct. I have no doubt that's true; he hasn't been in contact with my attorney, as far as I know. My attorney would have called me in the middle of the night. They said that they took him to a local hospital. I'll have to have my attorney call every single one, but making sure that my name stays out of it*. He nodded. *I have to be able to continue my work.*

Drake shrugged the thought away as his smile returned.

"Jaclyn Johnson still lives. But the person who took her away from me all those years ago is dead." He grasped the mug, the heat radiating through the kiln-fired clay to his fingers. "Such a pity."

His grin peered over the mug as he sipped deeply.

"Alas," Drake continued, "the runaway bitch will die sooner or later. I do hope it will happen sooner rather than later, and that the pain and torment she experiences in the afterlife far exceeds the heartache and heartbreak I went through from 2001 to now."

He continued listening to the field reporter, who then noted that the main reason for the president's trip—the unveiling of the statue—was now off due to the third-floor murder, and that the president and his entourage would return to the capital that morning.

Drake twisted his lips as he realized that part of his plan just evaporated on him.

"Damn," he muttered as he reached for his tablet computer, a brand of his own creation. He pressed the icon for his email account—an app of his own creation—and up sprang a blank message window. He scrolled through his address book for the addressee, then typed his message:

Dearest,

Our plan has gone slightly awry. The one who took our adversary away is dead in her stead, and now, the second chance has slipped away. There is no time, realistically, to change the plan and attack them via the AFB; too many military around. We must be cautious in how we play our next hand.

Looking forward to your ideas.

Darren

He clicked send and watched as the message spun away in a rush, the screen pixelating as if it represented a tornado racing across the expanse of glass.

Once he was sure it was away, Drake exhaled mightily as his memory took him back, the broadcast and the hottie anchor driven from his mind.

***

Teenaged Darren Drake grew up in Renton, a few houses down from the pretty blind girl, Jaclyn Johnson. He had spent hours staring at her and wishing he could buck up the courage to ask her out on an innocent date, whether it be to a movie or to the bowling alley. His staring had caused him to lose focus in school; there was something about the girl, the young woman he wanted to get to know far away from the curious eyes of their classmates, that he couldn't deny appealed to him. To his long memory, he had recalled she was rather gawky and wiry, and while her hair hung off opposite sides of her scalp, she did dress rather conservatively, which made his heart tremble at the sight; her jeans always clung to her thighs and waist—memory failed him here; were they at her waist, or did they come to rest just at the tops of her hips? Sometimes when he saw her in his memory, he wasn't truly looking at the girl's waist; his inner eye looked more toward the smile she flashed every time they approached their history class than anything else. He also recalled her button-down shirts she always wore, and the occasional whiff of lilac and cherry, which seemed to pour off her. She was, to his mind, perfect.

He had tried to ask her out, but as was typical for early teen girls—he would soon notice this rather peculiar and annoying trait had extended to young women in their early to mid-20's when he went out to a bar—he never had the opportunity to, for the lack of a better word, corral her in order to ask her out without having the Giggle Police show up and embarrass him to high heaven.

Fucking girls, he had thought at 13, *have this insane ability to synchronize their bladders at the same time, too. That may be the bane of my barely-teenaged existence.*

She had always been nice to him, he had recalled, noting that in the previous two years she had given him a valentine with a heart dotting the letter N in his first name. Seeing that made his heart flutter a few times, skipping beats with regularity every time she had looked at him. He even made sure to check with the other boys in the class, especially those with an N in their names.

None of them had the heart over it.

His eyes danced when he found that out. Plans to ask her out soon developed in his mind and heart.

Despite these wants and desires, he still didn't do it. Even as the school year closed and kids made plans to see each other over the summer—and even though he and Jaclyn lived a couple of houses apart—he heard the whispers of rejection tickling his inner ear.

She'll never go out with you, the whispers said. *She'll look at you through those sunglasses of hers and she'll smile as you're speaking, but then those corners of her mouth won't stop cutting into her cheeks. She'll start turning crimson, the blood staining her flesh as a bit of mirth touches her lips. It'll come out slowly, rumbling out of her belly, churning and bubbling and ending with a repetitious snort. And as everyone in the hallway learns what you've done, and judging by them viewing Jaclyn's laughter and soon they join in, your shoulders try to swallow your head. You turn and walk away, trying to run for the stairwell to get away from the amusement chasing you as you retreat with what remains of your dignity, your proverbial tail ducking between your legs.*

The whispers followed him, even now in his late 20's, and remembrance of them made his eyes leak with embarrassment.

Yet as the summer of 2001 began, and even though he had plenty of opportunities to ask her out without the swell of bodies growing around them, he chose a different path to attract her: he chose to work out and develop his arms, hoping Jaclyn would hang off them one day. He barely saw her that summer; she had taken to remaining in her house, or sunning herself in the backyard, or headed off with her gal pals to a remote beach at which he wasn't welcome—at least that's what he had thought. Instead of brooding on that, he had focused his mind on making himself as desirable to his female classmates as possible, so much so that Jaclyn wouldn't be able to stop herself from wrapping those arms around the back of his neck, pulling him close, and dropping her lips against his. Every time he thought of that, his heart skipped a beat.

School started in earnest that September. Drake had taken to wearing shirts nearly half a size too small for him, and as he strutted through the hallways, the reaction was, in his eyes, priceless. His arms bulged as he walked, and he noticed some of his freshman classmates—the females, of course—had turned their heads as he passed, as if their necks had snapped his way with the force of a stretched elastic band. Some had whipped their heads around and connected with his biceps as if their eyes were magnetized. Jaws dropped. Eyes widened. One girl that he didn't know, he noticed, had to wipe her mouth clean of the clear liquid that had instantly seeped out from between her lips.

But Jaclyn—Jaclyn didn't seem to notice any changes in him the first week of school. She went about her business as if nothing was amiss. He knew she had the ability to see—hell, she had to have known where the finish line was when she ran in the dash in middle school—even with the sunglasses protecting her eyes from the vicious rays pouring from the sun, or the painful glare from the fluorescent lights in school.

Why wasn't she noticing me? he had thought many times in those first days. *I did this all for her; yes, the attention from the other girls is nice, of course, but my older cousin said that a girl will always try to gain someone other girls want. He wouldn't lie to me, unless he said it to give himself a bit of extra entertainment at my expense. Surely that's not it. It's like Jaclyn seemingly doesn't care that I turned myself into a hottie for her.*

Then, as they sat in school on that Tuesday morning, they watched as the towers came down during their first period classes. There was such a silence hanging over the students that any movement, any movement at all, received a stern look from the teacher. It was when the news showed the Pentagon and the resulting hole from Flight 77 that a horrid cry rose up from Drake's right—Jaclyn Johnson had to stifle herself, her hand clamping over her mouth, before she ran out of the room; the teacher had run after her, and Drake recalled the man had returned, shaken. No one in that room saw her the rest of the day. Drake had filled himself with concern for her, and even tried to knock on the door to Jaclyn's house when he arrived home from school that afternoon. No one gave him an answer at school, and no one answered the door, either. It seemed as though Jaclyn had disappeared on the morning of September 11, 2001, never to be seen again by anyone that she had called friend.

The next day, though…

The next day came the changes that set about the rest of Drake's—and though he didn't know it at the time, Jaclyn's—life.

It was Wednesday morning, and he had just gotten out of the shower. Standing in his room wearing only a towel, he grabbed a set of 25-pound dumbbells out of the corner. He started to do his morning curls, hoping the exercises would make his arms pop in his sleeves, giving the girls, mainly Jaclyn, something to look at when in class. In the middle of a set, he watched as a Hummer in Army camouflage arrived at the Johnson house. Another car, this time with a woman getting out of the driver's side, pulled up about ten minutes later.

Strange, Drake had thought. He finished the set, then got dressed.

An hour passed, but Drake hadn't left for school yet. He wanted to make sure Jaclyn was okay. And with a pair of soldiers standing guard at the front of the house, Drake wasn't sure that everything was copacetic over there. It was when an older man and the woman who had arrived escorted Jaclyn out of the house, Drake seemingly lost it.

They're taking her away, he thought. *They're taking her away from me*.

Steeling his nerve, he shouldered his way through the crowd of people who had gathered on the sidewalk.

"Where are you taking her?!" he screamed. "She's done nothing wrong!"

He then watched as Jaclyn gasped, then pull her head up and her gaze toward him.

"Son, stay away," one of the soldiers said, his hand raised in Drake's direction. Drake's lip flared as he looked at the bastard in green; an accomplice to this kidnapping.

Then that angelic voice broke his stare. He looked from the soldier to Jaclyn, and for the first time, he saw her face red with tears.

"It's okay," Jaclyn had said. "You guys can let him pass."

"I don't think that's okay, Jaclyn," the woman on her left had said.

"Really, Alex. It'll be okay. I just want to say good bye to him. He's always been so nice to me."

The woman, Drake noted, tried to appraise him with a calculating gaze.

I wonder what that's about, Drake thought.

"All right, but not a word about where you're going."

Jaclyn had nodded, then walked over to Drake.

"Hi Darren," she had said.

"Hi," he replied.

They stood there, a few feet apart, hardly speaking. It wasn't until Jaclyn, shifting back and forth on what looked like rubbery ankles, finally spoke, and subsequently sent Drake's heart plunging for the abyss.

"I'm sure you know by now, but my parents are dead. I'm leaving here, headed east," she had said. Drake felt his jaw tumble away, the flesh over his skull slipping as disbelief settled in his throat. "You've been a great friend to me, and I want to thank you for that." She leaned down and put her lips on his cheek, then turned and headed back to the car, the peck on the cheek seemingly a good bye. Drake simply stood in place as the Hummer and the car both pulled away from the curb. He watched helplessly as the car shrunk in size until it turned away, out of view for good.

A hollow swallow filled his throat. She was gone.

The cry, he thought. *The cry makes sense now. Perfect sense. She's an orphan now, and she's trying to make sense of the world and where she's going.*

And even though he held out hope that he would see her again—he never mentioned anything about being there that morning to his friends at school, or in the days following—hope waned as the years passed along.

He graduated high school, his focus clearly returned with Jaclyn Johnson's forced absence from his life. He attended Washington State University and studied business, graduating close to the top of his class. With seed money he received at both his high school and college graduations, he began a small computer business which slowly turned into a massive rival for another computer-based business in the Seattle area. His wealth grew, but he remained a bachelor in name; he had a few dalliances, including one with a rather attractive woman that he had gone to school with since the third grade; it was funny to him, seeing as she hadn't acknowledged his existence until he hit it big. Her marriage had tumbled into the Sound, and before long she had ensnared him more than the blind girl ever had. He eventually gave her some seed money in order to start the business she had always wanted. He felt paying it forward in this way would help him reach his business goals—the total and utter defeat of Net Neutrality.

Drake had developed a keen business sense over the years, and he knew if the bribes he had paid to congressmen and senators worked, he had the opportunity to put the kibosh on free enterprise as the world currently knew it. He wanted those who bought his computers and tablets to use his, and only his, apps, ranging from his tornado email app to movie downloads and games, to web programs people used on an everyday basis. He wanted those other applications to take a back seat into the slow lane. They took from his bottom line; in his mind, they had stolen the opportunity for him to make more money than he had ever dreamed—much like the world had taken Jaclyn away from him a long time ago.

That is, until he had rediscovered her in 2012.

Eleven years had passed when he had heard she still lived, thanks to a high-ranking official blabbering about what she did for the country. A beating in his chest, long dormant, returned to life as soon as he heard her name. It couldn't have been anyone else. And when the news stations grabbed hold of a picture of her, he had no doubt in his mind. It was her. She was alive, and now, they said she worked for the government, with a side job as a fashion model.

Feelings he had thought suppressed returned to his consciousness, and even though he was involved with that other classmate, he did his best to conceal from her the blossoming strength rushing through his veins. He felt alive for the first time in a decade, as if hearing her name and knowing she still walked among the living, albeit on the other coast, was pure oxygen for his stale lungs. He didn't care that the high-ranking official—*what was his name*, Drake thought; *was it Bennett? Bennis? Benefits? Who cares, really*—had declared her an enemy of the United States. It didn't matter to him in the slightest.

She. Was. Alive!

Distracted, he tried to find everything possible. He discovered she had modeled for numerous magazines in the past five years, and had truly turned into a beautiful woman, her handicap not slowing her down one bit. She had filled out in all the right places—a stirring between his legs noted it—and it seemed as though she had grown wealthy, indeed. But as the weeks turned into months following her alleged traitorous behavior in London, the press soon learned what she truly was: a well-trained government agent with the ability to thwart terrorism.

Admiration filled his eyes, along with long-held tears. His heart raced along as he read about certain things she had done—things the government had rendered classified, but the press got a hold of it anyway. He started writing to her, care of Langley, to let her know how proud he was of her, and to let her know that he still loved her. He found it so much easier to say it in print than to her face. He had told her that he wished he could have said it the day she left, but he didn't have the nerve, even with all the work he had done that summer. The feelings he had held deep within his heart had unlocked, pouring forthwith onto the paper.

He sent them.

He waited.

She never wrote back.

Disheartened, he did more research: he discovered she had been in Las Vegas, and then Atlanta, defending the president against a member of the Ku Klux Klan. It was when he found out that she was engaged to be married, the world he had created fall apart. He had discovered the lucky man was a British secret agent. His heart had dropped, shattering on his pelvis as what he perceived as a betrayal of his feelings—he had even built something for her in another room!—reverberated in his mind. He had also discovered the identity of the woman that had taken her away in 2001: Alexandra Dupuis, the Director of the CIA. Knowing that she was still alive made his eyes darken.

And when he read about the unveiling of the general's statue in the Volunteer Park, he discovered who would be there: the president, the vice president—two people he didn't care for, if he had to be honest with himself—as well as three people he would never forget: Jaclyn Johnson—the name Messingham had replaced Johnson, noting that she was the late honoree's daughter, the marriage had seemingly already taken place—Tom Messingham, and Dupuis. And since he knew there would be great security around this event, a great deal of caution and planning would go into his attack.

There was another nugget in the paper which interested him: the person in charge of the event was another old classmate, one who had come too late to know Jaclyn, but had stayed until they had turned their tassels.

Smiling at this knowledge, the wheels in his mind started churning.

***

A rush of wind poured out of his tablet, the indicator that a new email had arrived, snapping him out of his daydream. Hearing the television in a commercial, he leaned toward the table and read the message.

It read:

Dearest,

The news that Johnson did not die disturbs me, but if you're happy that the other one is dead, then consider me happy. I do want that bitch dead, however.

The fact that they are pulling out of Seattle matters not. They will send her back. Mark my words, they will send her back to deal with this. It may be a week, it may be two, but they will send her back. And before you can ask how I know this, I have watched her more than you have.

We can meet tonight at the plant to discuss our next move. You get what you want, and I'll get what I want.

Love you, sexy.

KG

Drake nodded to himself as he read the email message. His eyes lingered over Dearest's words, "They will send her back," which sent his pulse into overdrive. His palms felt slightly damp; he wiped the sweat onto his robe.

"She will be back," he breathed. "That's all I want, to look at her again."

Without another thought, Drake's hand slithered back to his crotch.

Chapter 4
The Oval Office, White House
1600 Pennsylvania Avenue
Washington, D.C.
Thursday, June 19
12:34 p.m. PT/ 3:34 p.m. ET

Tasha had returned from her week-and-a-half-long post-graduation trip on Thursday morning. Jaclyn had noticed her ward had drawn a bit of attention from the sun, her skin now copper instead of rose. She had worn her bikini top home, the triangles keeping her girls covered and protected, as well as pair of cut-off jean shorts. She had her hair tied back into a ponytail, and her wide-lens sunglasses sat on her nose as if the sun penetrated their apartment in Foggy Bottom. She had greeted both Jaclyn and Tom with long hugs; there was a whiff of stale beer lingering around the back of her neck, but neither adults said anything. She was a high school graduate, and high school graduates, when at the beach for a week without their adults breathing down their necks, were going to drink. It was a fact of life they understood, even though they had never done so at her age.

Jaclyn hadn't texted Tasha that weekend, except when Tasha had texted them in the morning to let them know she was on her way home from Virginia Beach with the rest of her gal pals. She didn't reply with anything hinting her about her mood, for she wanted her ward to have a few more hours of happiness before she dropped a major bombshell in her lap.

"So the boys on the beach, let me tell you," Tasha said, slipping her sunglasses off and setting them on top of her bags. "Hunks. Absolute hunks. I mean, seriously gorgeous teenage boys that I would have given anything to drop my bikini for. But you'll be proud of me, I didn't succumb to temptation. Not even once."

Jaclyn tried to force a grin, but failed.

"That's good, Tash," she said, before she looked hard at her. She wore her special contact lenses instead of her HUD. "I have something to tell you. You should sit down."

Tasha did so, picking up on the seriousness of the situation.

"What's up? How was the unveiling? I'm sorry I missed it."

Jaclyn felt her heart skip a solitary beat.

"It didn't happen."

Tasha's eyebrows crinkled.

"Why not?"

Jaclyn took a deep breath as she steadied herself. She reached out and grasped Tasha's hand.

"Alex was murdered Friday night."

Tasha's eyes widened a sliver as a gasp overtook her. She slapped her free hand to her mouth just as her eyes grew heavy with tears. Those tears flowed easily as soon as the realization sank deeper into the girl's mind. She wept hard.

Jaclyn had to bite her lip as she watched Tasha's sudden grief overtake her. She tasted the sweet metallic flavor as she ran her tongue over the interior wound before she opened her arms, motherly, and watched as Tasha tumbled into her arms. The young woman cried for several more minutes until she stopped short.

"Are the boys all right?" she had asked.

Jaclyn took a soft breath and shook her head. She understood why she asked that; over the last few years, with the exception of the adventure in Sydney, Tasha had spent time at Alex's when Jaclyn went off to solve the country's problems. If Alex was a surrogate mother to Jaclyn, then she would have been a surrogate aunt to Tasha. Besides, it was Alex who had shown a great deal of trust in Tasha to help in the situation revolving around her friend from home, mainly regarding how she was involved in a major sex scandal involving many House Republicans. It was that incident which set her on the road to paying off the debt she felt she owed Jaclyn for her kindness, and to portraying a version of Jaclyn, right down to the Lycra jumpsuit, during a part of the Sydney adventure Jaclyn would have preferred to forget.

"No," she said softly. "Jake is inconsolable right now. He's only 13 and he's going to grow up without a mother." Jaclyn took a deep breath as soon as she felt Tom's hand on her shoulder. "And Tommy." She paused briefly. "Tommy's angry. He blames me for his mother's death."

"Why?"

"Because she was with me for an event," Jaclyn replied. "He argues that if she wasn't with me, she'd be still alive." She took a long, deep breath. "I know he's just lashing out at everyone. He's at that age—"

"He's my age, Snapshot."

Jaclyn conceded the point with a nod.

"He doesn't want me at the funeral."

"He can't stop you; shit, you've even said he and Jake were little brothers to you. What did his father say?"

"Nothing. He's never spoken to me. He blames me for the disintegration of his marriage."

"I'll straighten Tommy out right now," Tasha said, pulling her phone out and firing off a text to Alex's oldest son. "You of all people should be there. Well, along with the president, the vice president—you know."

Jaclyn smiled as she nodded.

"Thanks, Sex Kitten."

Tasha's eyes glittered. A smile instantly appeared.

"Hey, you remembered!"

"Of course. We're headed to the White House in a little bit to talk to Forrister about his plans for the agency moving forward. Do you want to come with us?"

"Let me have a quick shower, and then I'll get ready. I can't go over to the White House in a bikini now, can I?"

Jaclyn agreed, and Tasha hugged her again. "Don't worry about Tommy. I'll take care of him. He and I see eye to eye on a lot of things. I'll make him see sense."

She got up and headed to her room, which had been Jaclyn's old office until she had returned from her mission in Atlanta; with Tom in a right state after the Las Vegas incident, she had him sleep in her bed with her, while Tasha remained on the couch. After Atlanta, she had converted the spare room into a bedroom simple enough for a teenage girl. Jaclyn told her she could stay there while she attended Georgetown University, although Jaclyn had mentioned something over the last few months about moving the three of them to suburban Virginia; the old two-bedroom apartment at The Winston House had grown a tad too small for the trio. She had even spoken to the manager about the possibilities of upgrading to a three-bedroom apartment, one which would, at the very least, be big enough to have Tom's mother stay there instead of a hotel. In the end, Jaclyn and Tom had decided a small starter home would be good for the three of them to live in until Tasha decided she wanted her own place.

Besides, there was always the potential chance that the pitter-patter of little Messingham feet may appear at some time in the future. Jaclyn hadn't mentioned this to Tasha, at least not yet. She hadn't even mentioned it to Alex or the president. Jaclyn and Tom had discussed it in the previous few weeks, but nothing was for certain. Jaclyn truly didn't know if she wanted to have children, especially in the current climate of the world; after what happened this past weekend, she didn't know if she could do it, and then potentially die while on a mission for the president. There was also this thought they had to take into consideration: Having children might take her out of the game and relegate her to a desk position in Langley. That was something she wanted to avoid if she could help it. She really wasn't the type of person to simply sit at a desk and push paper and pencils. She was a doer. She put those thoughts aside; she wouldn't bring them up to Forrister now. Sometime in the future, probably.

Within half an hour, Tasha had showered and changed into something rather respectable for a meeting with the President of the United States. Tasha had put on a white button down shirt—Jaclyn made sure she had put on a white bra instead of something colored that would have shone through the thin material—as well as a pair of tan pants that flared out at the leg. She walked with a slight click, her low-rise heels striking the hardwood with great force. She had applied a little bit of make-up, even though Jaclyn felt she didn't need any for a meeting with Forrister.

The three of them headed to the White House once they had dressed appropriately.

The trip only took a few minutes as they wove through the traffic in Foggy Bottom to Pennsylvania Avenue, approaching The Cottage from the northwest. Jaclyn had refrained from picking up the phone to let anyone know they were en route. They had an appointment to meet with Forrister, and the president had blocked off the time to speak with them.

At the gate, the three of them showed identification; Jaclyn showed her CIA identification, while Tom showed a plastic card from MI5. Tasha produced her driver's license. At the sight of Jaclyn's card, the military police officer stiffened, then handed the IDs back to their owners.

Then, surprisingly to Jaclyn, the MP offered a stiff salute her way.

Jaclyn blinked and gave a meek one in return. She drove through the gates as soon as they swung open.

"That was weird," Tasha said from the backseat. "I don't think I've seen anyone salute you, like, ever."

Jaclyn sniffed as she smiled.

"You didn't know Dick Bennett. And that was a different salute, I'm sure."

She pulled the car up in front of the North Portico entrance and put it in park. It was a rather warm day in the capital, and Jaclyn felt the heat seeping into the back of her neck as they walked up the steps and entered the White House, a U.S. Marine holding the door open for the trio.

They weaved their way toward the West Wing.

***

Oval Office, The White House
1600 Pennsylvania Avenue, Washington, D.C.
Thursday, June 19
1:45 p.m. PT/ 4:45 p.m. ET

"You know," Forrister said, "I really have no idea why I watch this clown's show."

Veronica Forrister snickered.

"I think it's because you like to get a perverse view of the religious right's inner workings. It makes it easier for you to wade through the B.S. they spew on a daily basis."

The president thought about it and, with raised eyebrows, nodded after a few beats.

"That could be it."

The First Couple were in the Oval Office, watching the Reverend James McAllister's latest televangelist attack on the Liberal government. To Forrister, McAllister was high comedy, something he needed over the last few days. He had held up Air Force One until Alex's casket was loaded into the cargo hold, refusing to fly east without her. Add in the fact that Jaclyn wanted to avoid looking at the casket when they unloaded it at Andrews, it just wasn't a usual week in his life. Having McAllister's religious program on his television, the show laced with right wing dogma and political points, at least gave him a laugh and reminded him of the realities of his world.

"The funny thing about this is that this guy is getting away with every tax exemption known to man," Forrister said.

"And that, my dear husband, is sickening."

"Exactly. The taxes this son of a bitch is evading under the umbrella of religious exemption, even though they're all speaking on political matters, would feed a whole bunch of orphans," Forrister spat, the derision dripping away. "But no, today's right wing voter doesn't care about the orphans they can help with their taxes."

The president listened:

"I order the president, in the holy name of Christ Jesus, to revoke any and all abortion protections," the televangelist barked. "Also, I order the president to revoke protections for gays! Adam laid with Eve, not with Steve!"

"And that is why we base our laws on the Constitution," Forrister replied; it was more of a piercing shout aimed at the television screen, "not on the Bible." He had to laugh, though; the Adam and Steve bit always cracked him up. A knock on the door to the president's right pulled him out of the circus that played out to his left. "Come in."

The curved door swung open and a secretary stepped through.

"Sir, Jaclyn Johnson and associates to speak with you."

Forrister snorted.

"Making them sound like a law firm," he muttered. "Send them in."

The secretary stepped aside, and Jaclyn entered, her HUD nowhere to be seen. Her husband and ward followed her in. Forrister kept the television on as he stood and walked around the Resolute Desk. Veronica followed him across. The president wrapped Jaclyn in a hug for several seconds, before they let go. Forrister shook hands with Tom and gave him a light embrace as the first lady and Jaclyn hugged. Forrister then gave Tasha a peck on the cheek before they all sat down.

"We'll wait for Melanie to get here before we get started," Forrister said. "Are you doing okay, Snapshot?"

The secret agent paused, then nodded.

"It's been a weird few days, sir. Not having Alex here has been tough. Tom, though, has gotten me through it." She reached out and grasped her husband's hand just as the door behind and to their right opened, from the direction of a conference room, not the main reception area. Melanie Ruoff, Forrister's Chief of Staff, entered. With a wave toward Jaclyn—she returned it—she took a seat next to the first lady as Forrister grabbed the remote and switched off the show. "Interesting show, sir?"

The president grinned while he tossed the remote on the desk.

"Kind of. As my bride here says, I just take a peek into the world of the other side, and I have to admit that it thoroughly disgusts me how some of these preachers act; you'd think they'd have a little more compassion. The rumor on The Hill is that he wants to run for Congress, yet he's taking shots at me instead of the Democrat going against him in two Novembers time."

Jaclyn smirked as she huffed what seemed like impatience.

"I seem to remember another candidate going after a president instead of his opponent," she said. "The president went to Massachusetts, kicked a terrorist's ass, became a martyr, and the candidate died instead of winning his election. If my memory is correct, sir."

"I can assure you that won't happen in this case." The president came to the seat in front of them all. He sat down; the chair creaked under his weight. "Now that we're all here, I wanted to discuss how we're going to move forward. There's been some talk about how we should handle it. That guy," Forrister indicated McAllister with a jerk of his head toward the television, "wants us to dismantle intelligence and re-build it. I, for one, don't think intelligence is broken. Every agency will have blips; no one is perfect." He paused a few seconds. Every eye in the room had settled on him. "The far right of Congress is calling for someone from the outside—and I'm sure by that they mean someone from their party—to lead the CIA moving forward. I'm not so sure that's a good idea. In fact, I think it's a shitty idea. My hope is that as soon as we recover from the shock of what happened in Seattle, we can move on and show the country that our current set-up is what's best.

"I did want to talk with you about what happened Saturday. I want to know exactly who it was that was behind Alex's murder, and I want you to find that out."

He watched as Jaclyn nodded softly as she swallowed.

"So you want me to go back to Seattle and mete out justice." It wasn't a question.

Forrister's cheek twitched.

"Unofficially, yes. But that will come in time. Officially," he said, "I want you to lead the CIA until a replacement for Alex is found."

***

Jaclyn felt her throat tighten as she heard the president speak. She thought she had heard him say something about her leading the CIA, but it sounded tinny, as if someone held her underwater, the voices distorting and swirling a little in the swarming morass. She immediately sensed her heart thrumming rapidly, as if she had just undergone a mission in enemy territory, dodging bullets, chasing after shadows. Her throat went from tight to dry in a matter of seconds. Swallowing wouldn't help displace the arid desert which had suddenly taken up residence in her windpipe. She tried to get her jaw to move, but it felt locked, the muscles unresponsive, as if someone had wired the bone together with steel braces. But she found her voice, cracking, as she finally broke the hold.

"I'm sorry, sir. Did you say you wanted me to lead the CIA?"

Forrister nodded.

"Yes. Until we can find a replacement for Alex, from within, you are the boss for the time being. I have an idea of who it will be, but he's still out of the country."

"Why?"

Jaclyn watched as Forrister blinked. She had stunned him with her one-word reply, but he didn't stagger, punch drunk, like a boxer in the center of the ring. He swallowed his recovery and leaned toward her, his forearms resting on his knees.

"You would have been Alex's hand-picked successor, just like she was Dyer's in '94. She and I had a conversation about that after the wedding. She said, and I quote, that 'Jaclyn should be the next director, if she doesn't die in action first.' You know that she was an investigator, just like you, before she took the job."

Jaclyn couldn't help but nod. Her lips had trembled as they slipped into a Jack o' lantern's crooked line, and she did her level best to keep the tears from showing themselves again. Now wasn't the time to cry.

"That would be the only natural progression," Forrister continued. "Investigator, with the next stop being the director's chair."

"It's Alex's chair, sir." Her voice broke.

"She said the same thing after Nathaniel passed," the president countered. "Said it was Dyer's and it wouldn't be hers, ever. She eventually grew into it and made it her own."

"Congress will never confirm me, not after Bennett's tirade." Jaclyn knew this was, as the saying went, reaching. She looked for any excuse not to take Alex's job. She knew Congress would laugh in Forrister's face if he brought her name to Capitol Hill. She wanted to spare him the trouble.

"Congress doesn't get a say in temporary appointments," Forrister countered. "They'll know you're running the show, and I will come out in support of you. I've done it in the past, and if there's anyone who hasn't figured out that Bennett was an idiot for what he did back in 2012, then I'll deliver the message to them personally. You shouldn't have any problem getting your fellow agents to listen to your commands; you've been giving commands all your life."

Jaclyn smirked.

"I wouldn't say that."

"I would," Tom chirped in.

The smirk turned into a grin as she slugged him in the meaty part of his shoulder. A nervous giggle passed through the Oval Office.

"Jaclyn," Melanie Ruoff said, "the Cabinet has given you the go-ahead. We met last Saturday night after we got back. You're all set."

Jaclyn took a long, deep breath, then let it out through semi-pursed lips. "How long do I have to think about it?"

Forrister exhaled hard through his nose.

"I'll give you until Sunday night. And in case you forgot: I'm the president. I'll have you know that I don't like taking no for an answer."

The left side of Jaclyn's mouth crinkled into a half frown.

"How long would I be in charge?"

Forrister shrugged. "Hopefully for you, not too long. I know you don't want the job, and I just need someone in place until I can recall the person I want to take over. Let's just say that your term will be as long as necessary. And," he said, "the job does come with another title, one that Alex was, if I may say so, loathe to use. You probably never heard her use it. It's something I think you will treasure."

Jaclyn tilted her head a few millimeters to the right, intrigued by the president's tone.

"What's that?"

Forrister grinned.

"Lieutenant Colonel."

This time, Jaclyn blinked as her heart leapt. She straightened herself in the chair.

"Did you just say Lieutenant Colonel? As in a military commander?"

She swallowed her heart back down as the president nodded.

"Yes. I think it's about time that it gets used by someone in the clandestine services. You would enjoy the rights and privileges accorded to command personnel, even after your mission to find Alex's killer or killers is completed."

Jaclyn closed her eyes and tucked her chin toward her neck while her mind reeled.

A title, she thought. *A military title. Only the proud few get those. The ones who graduate from West Point, from Annapolis, from Colorado Springs*. She took a deep breath and felt the tears rise. This time, they fell. She felt Tom's hand encircle hers. *Daddy had one. Oh, Daddy, how does this make you feel? Your little girl, with a title, just like you! I won't command a unit like you did, but commanding the intelligence agency I've served since you died—*

She couldn't stop the sharp inhalation that came as she raised her head, her eyes full of tears; she felt one slip down her cheek.

"I think," Forrister said, "that she's saying yes."

Jaclyn wiped the tears away and nodded.

"Good. You start Monday. Take the rest of the weekend and rest after the funeral, then report to Langley Monday morning. Congratulations, Lieutenant Colonel. I want you to know, Jaclyn, that you have my full backing. We will not send anyone to Seattle in your stead. This case is yours.

"Now, I know that some people would frown on me sending you to Seattle in order to investigate Alex's death. You were close to her, and you might let your personal feelings get involved."

Jaclyn nodded.

"That's something that concerns me," she said. "I don't want to make the wrong decision."

The president immediately smirked his famous grin. "You won't. I *want* you to make this personal, Jaclyn. I want you to go after this son of a bitch and take him down for taking out a member of your family. I want you to go to Seattle, when we have all of our I's dotted and our T's crossed, and I want you to turn into the cold-blooded assassin that Alex herself trained you to be."

Jaclyn simply stared at Forrister while the goose pimples rose on her arms, the president's tone dark and foreboding.

"With pleasure, sir."

Chapter 5
CIA Headquarters
Langley, Virginia
Monday, June 23
5:57 a.m. PT/8:57 a.m. ET

Jaclyn and Tom had dropped Tasha off at The Farm shortly after 8:30 that morning before they headed to Langley. Jaclyn's chest ached as she drove, her heart somersaulting and bouncing against her inner sternum with every mile they passed. She felt the ache in her hands as she grasped the steering wheel hard, until a line of white crossed her knuckles. She blinked as she realized what she was doing, then took a deep breath as she eased off the accelerator, which she had nearly punched through the floorboards.

She caught Tom looking at her out the side of her HUD.

"Nervous, love?" he asked.

Jaclyn smirked. She kept her eyes on the road.

"A little bit. I'll be fine."

"Yes," Tom nodded. "You will be. The president supports you. Now don't crash the car into a bloody tree or else that investigation will be easy. I'll tell on you."

Jaclyn couldn't help but chuckle.

"For the record: Always taking the mickey out of your wife will lead to a lack of sex on your part."

"I have a hand," Tom immediately countered.

"I'll give you a hand if you behave yourself."

Tom hmphed.

"Consider me lip buttoned and me trousers unbuttoned."

Jaclyn feigned shock.

"It's 8:40 in the morning."

"Right, and it's 8:40 in the evening in China. When in Beijing, and all that."

This time, Jaclyn's laughter filled the car as it pulled to a stop. All of the worry and anxiety she had on her mind drifted away into the atmosphere.

They continued to Langley, pulling the car—Jaclyn now drove a 2010 Honda Insight, which even she admitted had the look of a spaceship slipping through the atmosphere rather than an automobile rolling on asphalt—up to what had been Alex's personal space nearly quarter of an hour later. Jaclyn really had no choice, as cars filled every other spot in front of the CIA Headquarters' glass main entrance. Twisting her lips as she pulled into the space, her heart resumed its frantic beating. As soon as the Insight's Auto Stop feature engaged, Jaclyn put the car in park, licked her lips, and then the two of them walked into Langley hand-in-hand.

"Welcome back, Agent Snapshot," the receptionist said. She nodded toward Tom. "Agent Scouser."

Tom offered a stiff wave across his body.

"Who is here right now?" Jaclyn asked.

"Pretty much everyone, ma'am."

"You don't have to call me, of all people, ma'am," Jaclyn corrected, breaking the hand-holding and placing her palms on the receptionist's raised desk. "Did Seattle send all the documents pertaining to Alex's murder investigation?"

The receptionist nodded.

"They are on her desk." She swallowed. "It's hard to think of it as her desk when she's gone."

Jaclyn put a reassuring hand on her shoulder.

"I know how you feel. I have to sit at it." She paused. "And all the morning briefings from the past week are there?"

"Yes," she replied with a nod. "It's like you already know how to do the job."

Jaclyn shot a crooked grin her way.

"I watched her for ten years leading up to my first assignment in Boston," Jaclyn replied, patting the receptionist's desk. "I made it my business to know her job." The pair of them headed up the stairs, Jaclyn's heels clicking away as they headed to Alex's—for the time being, her—office.

They entered Alex's office and flipped the lights on. At once, the room glowed white while the air conditioner hummed right along, filling the space with air some twenty degrees cooler than the air outside. Jaclyn walked over to the desk and found a stack of papers a few inches thick sitting to the right of her blotter, while a manila folder marked SEATTLE, all in uppercase and slanted across its cover, sat to the left. While every iota of her being wanted to grab the manila folder, she restrained herself and started reading the other files: dispatches from agents like herself currently in the field, relaying what they know about their current situations and surveillances. Some of them were dated the day after Alex had died, and it felt as if she read ancient history. There were memos—detailed memos—regarding ISIS and ISIL, Boko Haram and al-Qaeda. Memos regarding the Secret Service and their alleged indiscretions overseas—Jaclyn had heard something about that happening while Forrister was in Sydney with her and Tom, but she had paid it no mind; apparently, one tried to pull his weight with the Aussies, which got him knocked on his ass—made her raise an eyebrow at that, before she continued reading. When she read the daily reports, Tom flipped through the Seattle folder. Every so often, she peeked at him. His face was impassive, not letting on as to what he read in those reports.

It wasn't until 11 a.m., her eyes tired underneath her HUD, that she finally finished with the dailies.

"Hopefully it won't be as bad as that every day," Jaclyn said, slipping her fingers underneath the lenses to rub her eyes. She inhaled deeply. "I'm going to need some coffee to get through the rest of the day. Want some?"

"That would be perfect." Tom flipped the file folder closed. "A cuppa before lunch."

Jaclyn picked up the phone, pressing a couple of digits. She worked the phone much like she worked the runway years ago. It rang three times.

"Canteen."

"Can you bring two cups of strong coffee to the director's office, please?"

"Cream and sugar, ma'am?"

"Yes, put that on the side. Thanks." She hung up. "It'll be here in a couple of minutes." She stood and walked over to her husband. "Find anything interesting in that file yet?"

Tom shook his head.

"Nothing that sticks out at me yet. It's rather plain."

Jaclyn took the file and sat down next to him, playfully nudging him with her elbow.

"We'll see about that." She began reading.

Coffee came a few minutes later, and Jaclyn remained where she was; Tom had fetched it, thanking the girl from the canteen as his wife appeared in the zone.

Jaclyn noticed the report carried most of the details that she knew already: the fact that the intruder had busted through Alex's hotel balcony doors—the hotel room in which she and Tom should have stayed in, she reminded herself—shot and killed Alex, then had advanced through the hallway until Jaclyn herself had shot him three times. Her right index finger trembled as she read that line. Releasing a breath, she fingered the edge and flipped the page.

She swallowed as the file turned to the autopsy, which was not performed in Seattle. Instead, federal medical examiners had handled the case, and they had pulled the bullets out of Alex's cranial and chest cavities. The slugs, as Jaclyn surmised while her memory of that night returned, matched that of a nine millimeter Baretta, much like the one she had kicked out of the intruder's hand as he lay on the ground with her bullets in his leg. Seattle Police, in the report, had alleged after questioning the intruder, he had sailed over the city and had released the parachute as soon as he had enough momentum to crash through the double doors. Those were the facts as they knew them; they were unable to pry from him the name of the individual who had purchased his services as he had, to use their words in the report, "lawyered up."

"Of course he did," Jaclyn muttered as she pinched her dimpled chin between her thumb and forefinger, stroking it as she relieved the pressure. "The fucking cocksucker's a coward."

"What's that, love? Are you at the part about the muppet wanting a fecking barrister?"

She looked up at her husband, who took a deep sip of his coffee while passing a cup to her. She touched the side of her nose near the nostril, much in the way she had watched the Fourth Doctor do in old episodes of *Doctor Who*.

"It's basically what you said. Thin as a girl with anorexia."

Tom swung the chair around and sat down with his arms resting on the back of it. His thumbs ran around the brim of the paper cup.

"The bloke's mind is diseased, too. So what do you think we should do? We can't solve this shite with the file; there's no way of doing that."

"I'm thinking that we go with the old standby." Jaclyn stood and flung the report on her—Alex's, she corrected herself—desk before she finally took a sip of her coffee. She walked toward a whiteboard that looked as pristine as a blanket of fresh snow on The Mall. Alex had barely used it, it appeared.

"What, hypothesize? I thought you'd never ask."

Jaclyn's smirk filled her face. She grabbed a marker, making sure it wasn't a permanent one, uncapped it, and with the handwriting of a newbie physician, created a makeshift chart. She wrote "Switched rooms" and "Alex is dead," with a right arrow between the two. Then, below it, she wrote "Wanker in custody" and "Won't give up benefactor," again with a right arrow bisecting those facts.

"Okay," she said, re-capping the marker, "this is what we know."

"More bare than Everton's trophy cabinet," Tom replied. He sipped his coffee again. "But at least we can see the facts together without having to share the file."

"True."

"So the rooms, we think, were switched." Tom rubbed his face. Jaclyn heard the slight rubbing of skin against day-old stubble.

"They were. Remember, the Secret Service requested that we move rooms when Alex told the lead agent she wasn't armed. Moving us there accorded the president and the first lady a little more security if someone, somehow, managed to get by the Secret Service on the first floor."

Tom nodded slowly as understanding settled in.

"So who set it up originally? The room assignments, I mean. The hotel?"

Jaclyn frowned.

"Good question. You'd think the front desk would have issued the room assignments, but I'm not one hundred percent sure. That's how it usually works. It's how it worked in Sydney, I think." She jerked her lips to the side as she tossed the thought about, then nodded stiffly as she came to a decision. She power walked to her desk and, once again, made a phone call.

It rang twice.

"Yes, madame director?" the voice on the other end said. It wasn't one that Jaclyn recognized, but that wasn't the reason why she felt a cold shiver overtake her, the shiver spreading outward from her spine.

I'll never get used to that, she thought. *Please let this only be temporary.*

"I need you to call the west coast. Priority call."

"I can do that. Who am I calling?"

"The hotel that we stayed at last weekend. The Warwick, I believe."

"Calling them as soon as I pull up the number."

"Great. Patch them through to me when you get a hold of them. Thank you." She hung up. "I really want to know who made that decision."

"I'd love to know that, too. I mean, you said it that night: it could have been us who died if they didn't move us."

"So we're covering our bases and our asses by calling the hotel," Jaclyn said. She exhaled sharply through her nose. "It is, potentially likely, that it wasn't an inside job."

Tom blinked.

"Inside by whom?"

Jaclyn touched her nose again.

"Exactly." She slowly paced in front of her desk before the phone beeped a few seconds later. "Yes?"

"The Warwick Hotel on line two for you, madame director."

Jaclyn bit her lip as she reached for the phone.

“Thank you.” She hit the speakerphone and struck the button for the call. “Hello, who do I have on the line?”

“My name is Jared Simpson; I’m the manager of the hotel, ma’am.”

“Were you present the night of the assassination?” Jaclyn tried to keep the emotion out of her tone, trying to suppress any signs of her voice cracking.

“I was, ma’am.”

“Good. I’m hoping you can help out my associate and I with a question we have. It shouldn’t take up much of your time.”

Tom mouthed, “Associate?”

Jaclyn blew him a kiss.

“Of course.”

She took a deep breath.

“We were wondering who handled the room assignments for the president’s entourage, before the Secret Service switched things up.”

“If you could please wait a few minutes for me to find that information for you, I’d be more than happy to give it. Please hold ma’am.”

Tinny elevator music came on the line and filled the office with song. Jaclyn couldn’t place to band or the tune.

“What are you thinking, love?”

Jaclyn shrugged.

“Right now, not much. The answer may lie in what the manager tells me.”

“Tells us,” Tom corrected.

“That, too.”

The manager came back to the line.

“Normally we assign rooms as they empty and are cleaned, so they may be ready for the next guest,” he said. Jaclyn nodded at that. “However, it was asked of us to block off a certain amount of rooms to handle the president’s arrival. I’m going to go out on a rather long and sturdy limb and think you want to know who had requested it.”

Jaclyn nodded again.

“You bet.”

“It was the White House Advance.”

This time, Jaclyn blinked—but it wasn't in surprise.

"Great. Thanks a bunch."

"Is there anything else you need?"

"No, I think that will do it. Have a great day, sir." She hit the button for the speakerphone. Both lights for the speaker and the line winked out. She smacked her hands together. "I should have thought of that before."

"A White House Advance?" Tom asked.

"Yes. An Advance is mainly responsible for planning Forrister's itinerary and booking the hotels and such. There was an Advance who worked with Alex for Forrister's trip to Sydney. I had nothing to do with it."

Tom nearly had half of his coffee finished. He pulled the cup from his lips; Jaclyn caught a dribble of tan liquid hanging perilously from his bottom lip.

"Even though it was your wedding."

"Our wedding, you muppet," Jaclyn corrected. "The Advance. Who was it this go-around?"

"You're asking the wrong person."

Jaclyn stared a glance of death her husband's way. She picked up the phone and pressed the button to get her receptionist. "That was rhetorical."

Tom smiled and shrugged.

"Yes, Agent Snapshot?" the voice on the other end said.

Jaclyn blinked herself back to the present.

"Hi, can you ring the White House for me?"

"Do you need to speak with the president, ma'am?"

"No, I need to speak with the Department of Scheduling. The person I want is Barbara Branch."

"I'll give her a call."

"Thanks. Patch it to me when you get her." Jaclyn hung up.

"Do you know her?"

Jaclyn nodded and sat down at her desk.

"Yeah, we've run into each other at Forrister's state dinners. A little older, but on our side of fifty. Reddish-brown hair. Very approachable, so we should get somewhere with her. Is it almost lunch?"

"I could go for some fish and chips."

Jaclyn showed teeth.

"I bet you could. The chips sound fantastic, and yes, I know you mean French fries."

Tom's grin was devilish, but Jaclyn had to yank her HUD away from it as the phone beeped.

"Miss Branch on line one for you."

"That was quick, thank you," Jaclyn said before pressing the line. A woosh of what sounded like traffic buzzed over the speakerphone. "Barbara? It's Jaclyn Johnson."

"Hello there. What's up?"

"I was hoping you could tell me who the Advance was who worked on the president's trip to Seattle last weekend."

"Simple. Adam Hill. He's in the office right now. I'm on the road."

Jaclyn wrote the name down. She noticed Tom writing it down, too.

"What can you tell me about him?"

"About Adam? There's not too much to tell. He was super excited about setting this trip up for Forrister, since he's from Seattle originally."

Jaclyn blinked.

"Really? What part?"

"I believe he was from Tacoma."

This time, Jaclyn couldn't hold in her snicker.

"That's not Seattle. That's like someone from Pimmit Hills saying they're from D.C. because no one knows where Pimmit Hills is."

"You know what I mean," Branch snapped. "He made sure everything was perfect for the president; he thought he'd be able to move swiftly up the ladder if he impressed Forrister in his hometown. He planned the route to the hotel, to the park, the route to the schools, everything."

Jaclyn bit her lip.

"The hotel's sleeping arrangements?"

"Yes, of course. Why?"

"No reason," Jaclyn replied, eager to wrap this line of questioning up. "I was just interested. Do you have his number on you right now?"

"No," Branch replied, stretching it out half a beat. "Is there a problem with him? Something I should know, being his boss?"

Jaclyn felt her heart threatening to break through her sternum. Her brain shouted for her to throw the woman off. There was no time to make up a reason, especially with Branch throwing her weight around over the phone.

"Right now, I can't say anything, but please feel free to take it to Forrister if you don't think I'm answering your question. Thanks for the info. It's appreciated." She hung up without another word, much in the same manner as Alex had on countless occasions with her. "Shit."

"I guess you may have to watch your backside at the next state function," Tom said. "She may come after you with a blunt butter knife."

"I hope not." Jaclyn stood and walked to the whiteboard, scrawling Hill's name with the letters "WHA"—White House Advance—next to it. She directed it back toward the "Switched Rooms" heading with three question marks above the line.

"So she said that he handled the room assignments," Tom said as he walked to the board and stood next to her. He folded his arms across his chest.

"Right, and the Secret Service nixed that when they got there." She stared at the board for several seconds, then she remembered where he used to live. She wrote "Tacoma native" under his name in somewhat tiny print. "We know why they nixed that. That is known. What really isn't known is who Hill is."

"I don't even remember this guy being a part of Forrister's entourage."

Underneath her HUD, Jaclyn blinked.

"Was he? I don't know; most of that weekend is a blur now."

"That's totally understandable, love. But I think we need to figure out who Hill is, and I think you know of a guy who has access to that information at his fingertips."

Jaclyn caught her husband's smirk. She nodded somewhat enthusiastically.

"Why yes. Yes I do. Come on." She walked back to her desk and grabbed a notepad and a pen. She would write down what they found when they got downstairs. All the way downstairs. "Let's get some lunch and go check in on Salty Cakes."

***

Jaclyn had grabbed a B.L.T. sandwich—it was more along the lines of a grinder or a hoagie, the torpedo-like bread filled fat with crispy bacon and counter-ripened tomatoes—encased in white deli paper, a kosher pickle spear the size of a baseball bat taped alongside the wrappings, with a bag of chips and a bottled water for her lunch. Tom had asked for a rather bulky club sandwich with his type of chips on the side; Jaclyn smelled the vinegar wafting off her husband's tray. They also grabbed a chef's salad for Salt with light ranch dressing; it's what the tiny red-haired girl behind the counter said he liked to eat every day, all with a touch of strawberry springing onto her cheeks as she spoke. Jaclyn had smiled as she took her old friend's usual order from the girl, resting her sandwich on top of the plastic salad container. She peeped a gander at the girl's name—Margaret—and made a mental note before thanking her and turning away.

"You're going to tease him without any bloody mercy, aren't you?" Tom had whispered as they walked toward the check out.

"Uh huh," Jaclyn had replied, pulling the spear from her sandwich and munching away at the same time. "I will say this: I'm glad Salty is eating healthy. About time he got off the fast food kick that he's been on for the last ten years or so."

"That is good, yes, but I think the bird behind the counter wants to devour him much in the same way you're slurping on that pickle just now."

Jaclyn's teeth glittered in the fluorescent light. Tom matched it as he fished a twenty out of his wallet. Jaclyn made sure that it was an Andrew Jackson note instead of one bearing the royal bust of Queen Elizabeth II; he had grown more used to American funds over the last year or so. He left the change in the tip jar.

They headed to the elevators, and one had its doors already open, as if waiting for them. Jaclyn pressed the button for Salt's sub-basement. The doors immediately slid closed.

"How old do you think she is?" Tom asked as the elevator began its plunge into Langley's lower levels.

"Who, Margaret? I don't know, 20? 21?"

"And Salt is our age. Our little lad is robbing the proverbial cradle."

"If he has any clue who she is," Jaclyn said. "And if my memory serves me rightly, he already has a girlfriend."

"He may," Tom replied, "or he may not. She wasn't with him for the wedding."

Jaclyn clicked her tongue against her teeth. Her memory took her back to Sydney, and she saw in the corner of her mind's eye Salt standing next to Parkerhurst at the wedding. During the post-nuptial activities, she didn't recall seeing him with a woman.

"You're right about that."

"Well," Tom said as the elevator came to a halt, "you can ask him."

"You best believe I will." The doors slid open, revealing Jaclyn's favorite corridor in the entirety of the Langley complex: Salt's sub-basement. It was all painted the soft gray color of the Lincoln nickel, with a cinderblock construction which caused every step to bounce back at the person approaching; there were times Jaclyn felt as if she swam through the echoes while walking down this particular hallway. Jaclyn and Tom stepped out of the elevator, and Jaclyn immediately detected the sounds of music pouring from the closed door at the other end. She held her arm out and made Tom pause as she tried to discern the lyrics.

"Rage Against The Machine?" she asked.

"I wouldn't put it past the lad. He does like that type of music." He sniffed as he shrugged his shoulders. "Me, give me some Ferry Across The Mersey any day of the week."

Jaclyn smiled and kissed him softly on the lips.

"Oh, honey. Do be a love and make sure you send me a postcard from the 1960's when you get a chance."

Tom rolled his eyes as they walked toward the door. He opened it.

Salt sat with his back to the door, reams of data shimmying across his multiple computer screens; Jaclyn noticed there were dancing bobbleheads from various sci-fi and sports shows tucked here and there on his desk, and they all seemingly bopped along in time with Salt's music. With the music blaring, Jaclyn didn't have to tip-toe over. She walked right over and dropped his salad in front of him. Salt jumped as a few tiny leaves of arugula fell out and landed on his keyboard.

"Jaclyn!" he shouted over the music.

"Compliments of the hottie in the canteen," she replied, before gesturing toward the screen. Salt turned and clicked his mouse, opening the window. He scrolled over and clicked it again. The music ceased. "New girlfriend?"

This time, Salt gulped.

"No. Why?"

"Little Miss Margaret is seemingly sweet on you," Jaclyn said, teasing. "Cheeks turned the deepest shade of red I've seen in a long time when she mentioned that you liked a chef salad for lunch every day. It's like she's in tune with what the Salty Cakes wants." She smiled her infectious grin.

Another gulp preceded a similar shade of pink on Salt's face.

Jaclyn gasped and sat down next to Tom.

"Details, boy! What happened to the other girl?"

"She didn't like the fact I kept national security secrets out of our relationship," Salt coolly replied. "She didn't like the fact that I was at Alex's beck and call 24/7." Jaclyn felt her heart tremble at that. "And she didn't like the fact that I made more money than she did. She was kind of uppity about that."

Jaclyn listened, then shrugged her shoulders.

"Well," she said as she pulled the masking tape away and opened her sandwich, "there are other fish in the sea, and one of them, if I'm not mistaken, is three floors up."

"She looked sunburnt the way she blushed when she mentioned your salad, mate," Tom chimed in. "As you Yanks say, 'Go for yours.'"

Salt grew quiet as he opened the contained and poured the dressing over it.

"I understand you're the director now," he finally said as he tossed the tiny condiment container in the trash.

"It's a temporary position," Jaclyn assured him. She took a small bite of her sandwich. "I'm not going to be your boss for long."

"You hope," Tom said. Jaclyn glared through the HUD. He smirked as he took a bite of his club sandwich.

"And I heard you're trying to discern what happened in the hotel." He stuffed his face full of greens, ham, and turkey, and chewed away.

"Do you have some sort of Watergate recording set-up in Alex's office?" Jaclyn feigned insult.

"No, but I do have an email from the president," Salt countered. "What do you need?"

"I need you to eat your lunch first, then I need you to check into a White House Advance who set up the trip and the hotels."

Salt snorted hard.

"I thought you had something difficult for me to do. Give me a second. I can do both at the same time." He forked several cucumbers and shoved them into his mouth—a glob of dressing landed on the corners—before he let his fingers do their little dance across the keyboard. "What are we looking for?"

"His backstory. Pull up everything you can on this guy."

"Will do. What is his name?"

"Adam Hill," Jaclyn and Tom chorused.

"In stereo, too. That's good. And he's an Advance?"

Jaclyn nodded.

"That should be easy to find."

"That's why we come to you, Desmond."

The couple continued eating their lunch as Salt made the computer do his bidding.

"And boom goes the dynamite," he said as he punched the last key. "Found him."

Jaclyn set the sub aside and leaned in, her HUD taking in every detail of the screen.

"So what are we looking at?"

"His resume. A little skimpy in experience, but—"

"Zoom in on his address," Jaclyn said, cutting him off.

Salt moved the cursor to the top of the page and clicked the mouse. The screen shimmied and shifted until the words cleared up and came into better focus. Jaclyn scanned it and saw that he was indeed from Tacoma. She moved in and took command of the mouse—Salt grabbed his salad and leaned back as Jaclyn leaned over the desk—scrolling until she came to his education. She passed over his college—Washington State University—and came to where he graduated high school.

She quickly inhaled. The cold shivers returned, rooting her to the spot as if Salt's desk was an ice dam, and she had just turned into an ever-growing stalagmite of frozen water.

Out of the corner of her HUD, she caught Tom's look of concern spreading around a mouthful of roast beef, ham, and turkey.

"Are you all right, love?" he said as soon as he choked down the bite.

Jaclyn felt her tongue slide over her dry lips.

"No, not really. Here, look."

Tom's chair squealed as he stood and leaned over the other side. Salt rolled back a few extra feet, his salad in his hands. Jaclyn heard him munching away while she and Tom looked at the screen.

"What am I seeing?"

"This," Jaclyn pointed to the line which said Lakewood High School, Tacoma, Class of 2006. "He was a year behind me."

"You didn't graduate, though."

"No, I didn't," Jaclyn confirmed. "But Lakewood is where I was for the week-plus before Nine-Eleven. Who would have thought that two Lakewood people would work in the federal government?"

"I would call that a coincidence."

"And I don't believe in coincidences. Salt, do you have a picture of this guy on file?"

Tossing what remained of the lettuce in the trash, Salt wiped his mouth clean of excess dressing and wheeled himself back to the desk. A minimize and a mouse click later, the photo—his White House ID card, Jaclyn realized—popped up on the screen. He had a rather young face, one that didn't have loads of stress or student loan debt hanging over him; he looked fresh out of college. She checked the date of the photo—July 6, 2010—and figured he was, indeed, right off the collegiate assembly line. She didn't notice any gray hair in the photo, but since he worked for the government as part of two administrations, there was sure to be some semblance of discoloring now. Stress was a part of an Advance's job, getting the details just right. Missing details or details going against the plan, especially when you're working alongside the President of the United States, usually led to great amounts of stress.

His eyes, though—his eyes looked full of secrets. What those secrets were, she did not know. Not knowing gave her pause. She nibbled on her bottom lip.

She didn't like not knowing. She needed to know.

"Well, I don't know him. He didn't go to Woodbrook."

"Woodbrook?"

Jaclyn smiled at her husband and gave him a soft, reassuring pat on the shoulder.

"Woodbrook Middle. It's where I went to school when I lived in Renton before I went to Lakewood. It and another middle school fueled Lakewood's attendance, and this guy must have gone to the other one. It was a haul from the house," Jaclyn remembered, "but it was close to the base. Off Interstate 5, if I remember correctly. I had some good friends there, and of course, there were some cliques who thought I was a freak because I couldn't see properly like them."

"Those dirty cunts," Tom said, his tone dark and disgusted. "They should know you weren't a freak until you met me."

Jaclyn simply touched her nose again as she smirked at her husband's overtly sexual comment.

"Getting back on track," Salt interrupted, his ears turning crimson. "How is this guy involved in Alex's death?"

Jaclyn sighed.

"I don't know. He was the Advance last weekend, according to his boss. He had set up the hotel sleeping arrangements which originally had my hubby and I in the room Alex ended up in, and we switched out to Alex's room. The Secret Service asked for it, so we relented. It's the old adage: Do as the Secret Service asks."

"And Alex died in that room."

"Right. And he went to the same school you did." Salt tapped his fingers against his lips. It seemed as if the CIA's top computer cracker was deep in thought, mulling over what he knew, which Jaclyn didn't think was much.

"What are you thinking, Des?"

Salt didn't speak. He launched himself back at the computer and began a search, Jaclyn saw, for Lakewood High School Class of 2005 yearbook. His fingers moved like lightning, but with the skill of an impassioned lover caressing his one and only love—which, now that Jaclyn thought about it, wasn't too far off the mark for one of her oldest friends in the clandestine services.

"You have a brainstorm," Jaclyn said. It wasn't a question.

"Yes, I do. I have a brainstorm and a half."

"Well then, tell us about it, mate."

Salt pushed himself away from his desk.

"Let's review: You switch rooms in Seattle, after this White House Advance sets everything up. Alex dies thanks to this intruder. We're in Seattle, and it just so happens that this particular Advance and Jaclyn went to the same high school, albeit a year apart and they never saw each other. He was in eighth grade when Jaclyn was a freshman."

"Right, that's a coincidence."

"And I don't believe—"

"In coincidences, yes," Salt finished for her. "But I just happen to believe in my personal motto, my dear Snapshot: If it's incredibly hard to believe, then it's certainly believable." He breathed deeply, then turned to look at her. "I want to know who he hung out with. Maybe you knew some of them in your former life, before you were, shall we say, conscripted. Maybe," he added, "they were the ones who didn't like you because you were different."

Jaclyn didn't say anything, instead pursing her lips as Salt laid out his argument.

But Tom did.

"Are you trying to say that someone killed Alex because they had a rather superficial beef with me honey bunny back in fecking middle school?"

Salt nodded.

"I'm thinking Alex wasn't the target. The real target, I mean. I'm thinking they made a mistake and killed the wrong person." He looked up to Jaclyn.

Jaclyn instantly grew aware of her racing heart, the spot between her breasts aching as if someone had stabbed her and held the knife in place while she struggled against the hilt. Her lips parting with realization, she immediately sat down and grabbed her bottle of water, forgotten until now. Half of her sandwich remained; her appetite had long since departed. She twisted the cap off and drank deeply, the water helping to settle the twisting in her stomach. She took a deep breath as soon as she realized the two men—two of the most caring men in the entire world—looked at her with something resembling pity, and something resembling curiosity.

She looked to Tom.

"Remember what that guy said when he emerged from the room: 'There you are, Johnson.' He pointed his gun right at me, just before I shot him." She took a deep breath. "Salt's right, and I was right. You remember, that night in our hotel room. I answered the question before it was asked. It was supposed to be me."

“Right, and Forrister told me that in Melanie’s room, too. While you were in the loo.”

They stared at each other for several moments; Salt took the chance to look at the search engine. Jaclyn heard the clicking of a mouse as she felt a tear form.

“So,” she said with a slight breath, “someone wants me dead, and Alex was caught in the crosshairs. And Des, you think that the White House Advance who set up the situation last weekend has supposedly conspired with someone who has hated me for the last fifteen or so years to kill me. Is that right?”

Salt didn’t take his eyes off the screen.

“That’s exactly what I think,” he replied. “I don’t have any proof, of course, but I find it fun to play around with a hypothesis and see down what paths it leads us.” He clicked the mouse again. “The yearbook. This would have been your class. Let’s flip through it and see what we shall see, shall we?”

Jaclyn nodded and sat down. This was something she had never thought about before; the going back in time, somewhat, to what she should have been doing had the world not been turned on its ass that beautiful Tuesday morning. She should have been in this book, this keepsake: maybe she would have been on the track team at Lakewood, trying to become a record-breaking sprinter.

Maybe I would have had a boyfriend long before Tom came into my life, and maybe I wouldn’t have been, as Salt said, conscripted into service, she thought. *Maybe I would have had great friends.*

“Well,” Salt said, breaking her reverie, “this is interesting.”

Jaclyn looked up at the screen. A gasp quickly caught in her throat.

“I don’t believe it,” she whispered.

But with Salt’s motto from a few minutes ago lingering in the back of her mind, it truly was something she could believe: there, on the screen, was a group of students of that year’s senior class, and through her HUD, Jaclyn noted they were faces she would recognize anywhere. She blinked back tears as she saw that each and every one of them were so-called Army brats, just like her, who had attended Woodbrook with her.

And in this photo, taken from a bird's eye view, the shadow of the ladder clearly visible in the grass, each of them stood behind a homemade sign, the youngsters in the front row holding it at the top with both hands.

It read: *Wherever you are—we miss you, Jaclyn Ann Johnson.*

Jaclyn read it again, just to make sure she wasn't dreaming. She brought her hand to her mouth, and immediately she heard the rolling of wheels and felt an arm slink around her shoulders. Then she couldn't hold the tears back.

"They remembered me," she said through gulps of air. "God, I really can't believe that."

"And why not, love?"

"I left their lives so suddenly, so abruptly," she answered. "I was only there for—"

"A few years," Tom interrupted, before he nodded toward the screen, "but seeing that tells me you had an impact on them even after you left. That photo was taken what, three years or so after you headed east? They remembered you and loved you enough that they wanted to immortalize you as being a part of the class, even though you didn't get to graduate with them."

Jaclyn bit her lip and nodded. Her breath had grown choked.

"Do you recognize any of them?" Salt asked.

She nodded again.

"Every single one of them."

Tom's hand slipped into hers and squeezed.

"I'm going to put each of them through the facial recognition system and see what we come up with. It may be a waste of time, but maybe we'll grab a few connections to Mr. Hill here; besides, I love going through old photos, testing the limits and seeing if the system recognizes the past. And then, when I'm done taking a walk down your Memory Lane, we're going to search the rest of the year for him.” Salt turned to Jaclyn. “Do you want to keep looking over my shoulder, or should I bring these results to your office?”

Jaclyn smiled and nodded.

“I’m going to stay here.” she replied. She felt Tom’s hand squeeze hers again before she looked at the photo on the screen, the people she remembered as being part of her school family until the world as she knew it ended, and a new family—one now devoid a member, one rather important member—popped up in its place. “Wow.”

“Wow?” Tom asked. She caught his wink, then nodded again. Her smile, she knew, lit up Salt’s dingy little cubby.

“Wow. Just… wow.”

They looked on as Salt did his so-called dirty work.

Chapter 6
CIA Headquarters
Langley, Virginia
Monday, June 23
1:16 p.m. PT/4:16 p.m. ET

It wasn't until just before Jaclyn had to head to the White House for her first evening briefing—a briefing she knew wouldn't include anything overseas—when Salt finally found Hill's yearbook photo in the 2006 yearbook; he wasn't located in the 2005 yearbook, with Jaclyn's class. He had arrived at Lakewood in the fall of 2004, and for some strange reason, the yearbook committee that year hadn't deigned to include him in any group photos. Even though he was a junior, he wasn't seen mingling with the seniors; Jaclyn found that odd, as she noticed seniors with sophomores, juniors, and even freshmen. He didn't play sports, nor was he involved in a committee or in extracurricular activities. He was an enigma, it seemed, seeing as there was a photo of practically every student—even a photo of one who had departed the class prematurely—in the school in the 2005 book.

But in the 2006 book, he was everywhere. There were no photos of him with the sports teams, but he did hang out with several athletes in his senior class. He was even the class president.

"Well," Jaclyn said, standing behind him, "someone who went from total obscurity to the head of the class becomes a White House Advance. How curious."

"Orders, madame director?" Salt asked.

Jaclyn took note of his mocking smile and matched it with one of her own. He was Salt, her old buddy. She didn't care if he mocked her, or if Parkerhurst did: they were on her side and both knew she didn't really want to be in this position.

But, she thought, *I might as well act the part.*

"I want to know who hired him and when. Go back through his employment history with good ol' Uncle Sam. Then go back and check out this guy's cell phone records. I want to know each and every person he's spoken with since Branch gave him the assignment to set up the event. And then, Salty Cakes," she said, sitting next to him yet again and smiling, "you have to go ask that girl out. If anything, just for coffee."

Salt's cheek twitched as he smiled at her.

"I will."

"Good." Jaclyn leaned over and hugged him tight, planting a kiss on his cheek. "Let me know how that turns out, and let me know how this turns out. We're off to the White House."

Salt returned to his work, while Jaclyn and Tom took their leave of the sub-basement. They didn't speak again until they got to the elevator to take them back upstairs.

"Are you all right, love?" he asked, the elevator rising.

Jaclyn nodded.

"Yes. I'm just moved by what they did back then, and I didn't even know it until now."

"I don't think any of them had anything to do with it. They loved you."

Jaclyn pursed her lips and nodded.

"No, I know they didn't. It may be someone else." The doors opened. "Salt will find them. No one can hide from Salt's computer. No one."

They made their way toward Alex's old office. The warm setting sun blazed through the main entrance, the glass providing little cover as it sank toward the western horizon. No one had lowered the shades. Tom, Jaclyn saw, covered his eyes as he walked alongside his wife. Meanwhile, Jaclyn didn't break stride, not flinching.

The receptionist intercepted them just before they made the turn up the stairs.

"Jaclyn, the president has been trying to get a hold of you," she said.

"I wonder what that's about," Jaclyn replied, knowing it could be one of many things. She hoped it was about Hill. "I'll give him a call."

"There's no need to do that. He's waiting in your office."

Jaclyn froze, her heart pounding in her ears. She turned.

“For how long?” she asked.

The receptionist checked her watch.

“Ten minutes.”

Jaclyn let go of the breath she had held.

“Thanks for letting me know,” she said with all sincerity, but she was afraid it might have come out laced with sarcasm. There was no time for an apology right now. She hurried up the stairs, Tom on her heels. She opened the door and entered.

She found Forrister standing by an open window shade, staring east. Melanie Ruoff was with her. Barbara Branch wasn’t with them, for which Jaclyn offered silent thanks.

“Sorry to keep you waiting, sir,” she said. “I didn’t know you were here.”

Forrister turned.

“Already getting my people riled up on the first day,” he said with a smile. “Good. Keeps them on their toes.”

“I can explain my conversation with Branch.”

“I’d love to hear your explanation. I’ve been trying to hear about it for the past few hours, but your phone doesn’t seem to want to work today.” He said it with a little bit of his own presidential sarcasm, which she accepted with a grain of salt: Jaclyn already knew he had her back. Forrister walked to the front of the desk and sat down next to Ruoff. Tom leaned against the wall while Jaclyn took her seat. “She said you were asking about an Advance.”

Jaclyn nodded.

“Yes, sir. He was the one who took care of the planning for our trip, set the room assignments, et cetera.”

The president nodded this time.

“Go on.”

“We’ve discovered that the Advance in question went to the same high school I did, and we believe he may be attached to certain groups that want me dead. They may have found out, much to their utter despair and total chagrin, that yours truly did not exactly fall off the face of the earth in the last decade and a half since I left Washington State. Thanks to Dick Blabbermouth, of course.”

Forrister’s smirk lit up the room.

"Of course. And what have you found out about this?"
Jaclyn took a long deep breath.
"We're still working on it, and have been for the last five hours or so. Salt is currently cross-checking the Advance's phone records right now. I'm hoping we come up with something legitimate and concrete in the next few hours, and then I'd like to grill Hill in the Oval Office tomorrow morning."
"What is your thinking regarding his involvement?" Ruoff asked. "I know the way you work: you wouldn't come to this without a valid hypothesis to back you up."
"The Advance's job, of course, is to set the hotel sleeping arrangements and to make sure everything runs smoothly at the events," Jaclyn explained, then leaned forward. "Hill wasn't with us in the Seattle, which I find most curious. And there's the fact that I was supposed to be in that room with Tom when the Secret Service moved us to Alex's room, and vice versa. Do you remember that?"
Ruoff thought about it, then she nodded.
"So what's our next move?" she asked.
"We get the phone records, cross-reference them with their respective owners, and I do hope that somehow we find out exactly who was behind Alex's murder."
"And then?"
Jaclyn sniffed as she snorted.
"I thought you knew how I work, Melanie. Then I find the son of a bitch, wherever he is, and I kill him."

***

The Winston House
Foggy Bottom, Washington, D.C.
Monday, June 23
4:34 p.m. PT/7:34 p.m. ET

Jaclyn and Tom had picked up Tasha from The Farm before they grabbed some Chinese food at a place a block away from the Watergate Complex. Like the family they had grown into, they ate together and watched some television—

a re-run of *The Big Bang Theory*, Tasha's new favorite show—when the phone rang. Biting her lip as she noted the number came from Langley, Jaclyn automatically reached for the eavesdrop-cancelling cube Alex had given her years ago. She pressed the button in the center.

"This is Jaclyn," she said.

"Hey." It was Salt.

"What do you have for me?"

"So much information it will make your toes curl. Apparently, he was in touch with some of your old classmates, and they were all names on the list you gave me: the list of, shall we say, undesirables."

Jaclyn's blood ran cold as she listened, all while pressing down harder on the spot she nibbled. Soon, her mouth had grown full of metal, as if she had swallowed melted pennies.

"Do we have any idea what they talked about?"

"Unfortunately, no, we don't. And before you ask, no, there is no way to retroactively get a court order to listen to a past conversation."

Jaclyn snapped her fingers.

"Damn. Text me the names involved. I'll use them against Hill in the morning." She paused briefly. "Have you asked her out yet?"

A heavy sigh rippled through the line.

"No, not yet. She has to have gone home by now, and I've been a little busy working at the behest of the best secret agent this side of Moscow."

"That's no excuse, Salty Cakes."

"Send him my love!" Tasha said over her shoulder, her eyes not leaving the television.

"Tasha sends her love."

"Right back at her."

"He says right back at you."

Tasha replied with a single thumbs up. Again, no movement of her head. She had her eyes fixed on the season six episode where Sheldon and the gang were hauled in to Human Resources.

"I'll send that stuff to you right now, and I'll make sure I ask her out tomorrow, okay?" Salt said.

"I can deal with that. Talk to you tomorrow." She hung up, then pressed the cube's center button again. The eavesdrop-cancelling waves ceased. "Salt is sending me those names, and then he's going to practice asking Margaret out in a mirror when he gets home, if I know Salty like I know Salty."

"New girlfriend?" Tasha asked. No movement.

"New potential girlfriend," Jaclyn corrected. "They seem coy about it, but hey, everyone needs a little romance in their lives. How was your day?"

Tasha shrugged, then finally turned her head just as the show went to commercial.

"It was the usual. Hand-to-hand combat training, firearms. Then I had to read those all-important missives from the field to learn about what to do in certain situations instead of just plowing over them with the front of my car," she said. Jaclyn caught the reference. "Did you really blow up a soccer stadium?"

"Yes," Jaclyn said just as Tom said, "Football," in a correcting manner. "It was in order to thwart a major terrorist who had already killed upward of thirty thousand people threatening to kill more, including England's Royal Family. So, a football stadium was the most logical choice."

"Luckily no one was in it and the Olympic football competition didn't even look to Tottenham and their piece of shite stadium," Tom added, pronouncing it "Tott-numb" in two, quick syllabic bursts. "So I'd say that me wifey had a rabbit's foot or a four-leaf clover hidden somewhere in the Lycra that night."

Jaclyn's grin was tight as her husband spoke about that night. The memories churned, from the helicopter ride out of Arsenal's state of the art, then-six-year-old stadium to her making her entrance through the roof of the mosque, from Lavi Witz sliding the gun into her holster to Witz getting shot in the leg by the terrorist—to Jaclyn tearing the terrorist's gun out of his hands and popping him in the brain with each. She suddenly missed the Mossad man's presence. She faltered if only for a brief second, the frown she now wore masked only by the trembling of her cell phone's messaging service. She scooped it up and opened Salt's email.

As she read the message, a list full of the "undesirables" she and Salt had discussed, it felt as if she had just entered a time warp, back to the turn of the century, a place she originally thought she had left in the far reaches of her past.

But no, she thought, *the past can't stay buried when people with decade-plus long vendettas pop back in your life*. She shook her blonde head.

"A decade and a half is far too long to hold a grudge," she said aloud, mainly to herself as she let her finger slip up the screen. The image scrolled with it, the phone records of Hill's contacts from the time he began setting up the Seattle trip.

"What's that, love?" Tom asked.

Jaclyn blinked.

"Sorry, just thinking out loud to myself. Keeps me sane."

"Right. Anything in the email?"

Jaclyn's inhale was sharp. It felt as if needles plunged into her sides, the stitching tight and secure enough to leave marks on her flesh.

"Plenty. It was as I thought."

"We figured by the way you mentioned people holding a grudge," Tom replied. "How many stories are in there?"

"Again, plenty. One name that I expected to be on the list isn't there, which I find surprising." She took a deep breath. "And one name that I didn't really expect to see is in her place."

Tom leaned over, and Jaclyn put her fingertip on the screen, right under the name. He read it.

"Darren Drake?"

Jaclyn nodded.

"Darren Drake."

"Who's he? What did you do to him?"

Her lips crinkled. She stood quickly, her phone still in her hand, and walked to the window that overlooked 22nd Avenue Northwest. Leaning against the frame and looking through the open curtains to her left, she tried to look through the buildings to the Potomac River. The window was open, too, and she heard the partially muted cars going around Washington Circle a block away to the southwest; it certainly wasn't coming from DuPont Circle, several blocks to the north. A bus's air brake cracked through the din on K Street Northwest, just to the south of the building.

I didn't answer his letters, maybe, Jaclyn thought. *Any of them. One a month for two and a half years*. She dragged her bottom teeth against her upper lip for the briefest of moments. The faint taste of soy sauce, a hint of it, still lingered there. *How he fell in love—a teenage crush, I should say—with an awkward girl, and then to hold onto that absent love for over a decade and a half is mind-boggling.*

"I don't really know. The last time I saw him was the morning Alex took me away."

"It had to have been something major if he's on Hill's contact list," Tasha reasoned.

Jaclyn shook her head. She didn't want to hear this, at least not right now: to find his name, his particular name, on Hill's contact list, had to have been a coincidence—something, she reminded herself, she doesn't believe in—unless Drake had called Hill when he had heard about her father's statue unveiling and wanted to see if he could arrange a meeting between he and her.

If his letters are any indication, her thoughts continued, *that would be extremely plausible*.

"Okay, hold up. We're getting ahead of ourselves here," she turned and said, a touch of annoyance in her tone. "We don't know why Darren is on Hill's list, we don't know if Hill took orders from Darren, we don't know what they discussed. Maybe they were going to hook up for a beer in Seattle when he came home. Who knows?"

"But remember, love, Hill wasn't in Seattle with us."

Jaclyn breathed deeply through her nose and nodded.

"I know. That's something we can ask tomorrow morning, right?"

***

The Winston House
Foggy Bottom, Washington, D.C.
Monday, June 24/Tuesday, June 25
10:12 p.m./1:12 a.m. ET

Much like it had for the last week-plus, Jaclyn's sleep was restless that night.

In the darkness of her and Tom's bedroom, she stared at the ceiling in silence, her hands folded together over the comforter, all while her husband snored next to her. She begged for her mind to slow down so she could get some sleep. For the last few hours, even though exhaustion had threatened to sneak up on her as their small family of three watched an episode from that season of *Game of Thrones* they had missed due to Tasha's trip to Virginia Beach, Jaclyn seemingly caught an inadvertent second wind in the moments after the episode ran out. The timing, of course, was impeccable, she had thought at the time, and by the time Tom had flipped the lights off and they exchanged a good night kiss, she was wide awake again. Like usual, Tom was out the moment his head hit the pillow.

Jaclyn tried not to sigh her frustrations at her lack of slumber for fear of disturbing Tom, but she noticed he would have needed air raid sirens to rouse him. He was, for all intents and purposes, dead to the world and everything occurring around him, including his wife's poorly-timed bout with sleep deprivation. Every so often, she needed to touch his back to see if he was still breathing; she felt his heart beating slow, and that was good enough for her. Still, making sure Tom was alive only distracted her, if only for a few seconds, from what kept her awake.

It was like her past threatened to chase her down a long hallway, or a long tunnel with no side passages, no chance for escape; in her mind's eye, it was akin to the tunnel in *Back to the Future II* and *Who Framed Roger Rabbit?*, and all she tried to do was get to the end. She peered down the end of that tunnel, looking for the red curtain to rise, or for the multi-colored pennant to tumble into her vision and out from the DeLorean, before she felt gunshots ring out, and bullets breaking through the Lycra—*Why the fuck isn't it working?* she heard herself yell, the screams caroming off the concrete instead of it absorbing them—plunging into her flesh. She even heard her own heavy breathing in her mind, felt her legs tighten up as she tried to out-run her dreams: it was as if she had chased Clarence Butterfield-Smith again, but this time, it was four miles of continuous sprinting instead of two. It was phantom pains, yes, but those pains and thoughts kept her awake long past any time she considered prudent. She stuck the tip of her tongue out as her thoughts roamed about the wild, grassy prairie that was her mind.

Yes, she thought, *you've stayed up much later than this, and you haven't had difficulty the next morning. But this is different, Snapshot. You've never accused someone in your own government—with the exception of Jennifer Farrell, of course—of committing massive conspiracies involving a murder.*

She nodded to herself as she turned her body to the right, facing away from her husband.

It was a conspiracy, Jaclyn reasoned. A conspiracy to assassinate her, and a conspiracy to assassinate Alex.

If I can only completely connect the dots, this cocksucker Hill will crumble and give me everything I need.

She took a deep breath as her thoughts continued.

I'll put a gun right to his head, much like I've done to everyone else. I'll beat the answer out of him—right in front of Forrister, if I have to. I know he's not the big wig behind it all, but he knows who is, and he will tell me. I don't care how many laws I break, or have to break, as long as I get the ones responsible for killing Alex off the grid.

She nodded again.

Everything will become clearer tomorrow, she thought, *and if Darren Drake is behind it, then I have a good idea why. It's an absolutely fucked up reason, but yes, I'll have a good idea. And no, I won't take pleasure in killing my old friend.*

Jaclyn finally drifted to sleep, somewhat content but still troubled.

Morning would come quickly now. She knew it would.

She would deal with it, and all it brings, when the sun rose.

Chapter 7
The Oval Office, White House
1600 Pennsylvania Avenue
Washington, D.C.
Tuesday, June 25
5:49 a.m. PT/8:49 a.m. ET

Jaclyn and Tom did their best to keep their presence on the White House grounds as quiet as possible that morning, and they did so with good reason: after the somewhat hurried phone call with Branch about Hill the day before, Jaclyn knew there was the strong chance she had tipped Hill off about her inquiry before approaching the president about Jaclyn's behavior. And Jaclyn knew part of that had happened: Forrister had explicitly told Branch not to inform Hill of the investigation. Shrewd as she was, Jaclyn wasn't taking the chance Branch would obey her boss, though. No, she wanted to keep all of her bases covered, and knew she needed to resort to subterfuge in order to achieve her goals: it's what she did in the field, it's what she would do in the supposedly friendly confines of 1600 Pennsylvania Avenue.

There was also another reason why Jaclyn wanted the utmost secrecy about her comings and goings on this particular morning. It was expected of her as the head of the CIA to, at some point today, make an appearance in the West Wing with an intelligence and security briefing; she hadn't done it yesterday, seeing as she had one thought in mind when she arrived at Langley that morning. She had discovered, by accident when she returned from London, a few years ago that Alex usually parked at the North Portico entrance along Pennsylvania Avenue, across from Lafayette Square. Hill's office was, she had learned, in the northeastern corner of the Old Executive Office Building, which overlooked the North Lawn and looked straight up New York Avenue. Parking there, she decided, was a no-no, and parking street-side between the White House and the OEOB was out, too: she didn't want anyone in the Department of Scheduling who had possibly overheard Branch, if she had indeed disobeyed Forrister's order, to look out the window, add one and one together, and tip Hill off regarding her presence, sending him scrambling away—if he held any guilt, of course.

But thanks to a quickie 6 a.m. conference call between the president, Ruoff, the head of the Secret Service, the head of the National Park Service, and themselves, they managed to come up with a relatively concrete plan on how to keep the knowledge of Jaclyn's presence down to a fair few, and to draw Hill over to the White House for what Jaclyn considered "aggressive questioning."

First, Jaclyn and Tom would park at the Department of Commerce building on Jefferson Drive Southwest. They would then cross on foot to the Washington Monument, then meet up with a member of Forrister's Secret Service detail and a park ranger. From there, with the ranger opening a secure gate, they would delve underground to the tunnels Roosevelt had installed sometime after he had returned from Panama. The tunnel, as Jaclyn knew it, ran underneath The Ellipse and the South Lawn, taking them directly to the West Wing without any additional prying eyes on the lookout for her possible arrival. Jaclyn had said they would get to the White House, via their circuitous route, shortly before 9 a.m.

Secondly, and more to the point, Forrister would invite Branch, Hill, and the other members of that department over to the White House for a quick, first-thing-in-the-morning meeting to discuss Advance assignments for the next few months. The president assured them this would work and that Branch wouldn't suspect anything out of the ordinary, as they always had meetings such as these—except the president would have to keep Branch out of the loop as to the true meaning for the meeting; he had said he didn't want to truly play that game, but he had told Jaclyn that he wanted to see if Branch was loyal to him and not her people. Jaclyn had agreed at once, without trepidation.

The tunnels were rather warm this morning, Jaclyn noted, the bare bulbs providing illumination which didn't add to the heat building inside of them; a touch of sweat had already danced along the backside of her neck, dampening her collar, turning her lightly-bronzed skin clammy. She and Tom, along with a member of Forrister's detail who had traveled to Seattle with them—a hulking man of African-American persuasion who had played Jaclyn's version of football at Northwestern—walked north with quickened steps, the sounds bouncing back much like they did in Salt's sub-basement. It was a slightly uphill walk as soon as they crossed underneath Constitution Avenue, until they came to the long walk that led into the area near the Situation Room.

Jaclyn had never been inside the Sit Room, even though her voice had been inside of it on countless occasions. Even though she was the acting director, she didn't wish to step foot in it any time soon. That wasn't her domain, her squared circle; that was the domain of the president, the Joint Chiefs, and the one who would eventually take over Alex's job. Her arena, as everyone in the high reaches of the government knew, was the field. With a quickened heartbeat, she hoped today would be the day Forrister ordered her back into it.

We'll see, she thought.

"The president is meeting with Scheduling in the Oval right now," the agent said, pulling his finger down from the earpiece wedged into the thin canal.

Jaclyn nodded.

"Good. I didn't want to wait long."

They moved on.

The echoes turned harder once they entered the president's sub-basement, the hardwood floor replacing the concrete and stretching through the corridor. They followed the Secret Service agent to the stairs and they took them one at a time, bouncing off the front halves of their feet as they headed into the West Wing proper.

No one lingered in the hallway between the president's conference room to the right and the Oval Office to the left. They passed the president's private office before the Secret Service agent knocked on the curved door to the right. Jaclyn heard voices coming through.

"Come in," a voice called. It was of a masculine tone.

Jaclyn and Tom entered, the agent following behind them. Jaclyn made her walk slow and steady, unlike that of her model persona where she had to practically power walk down the runway, pause and genuflect with a hand on her hip, then turn and walk the other way, throwing her hips into it with every stride. At that instant, she wanted to make sure that every single eye in the Oval Office got a good look at her, making them know that she was out for blood. Behind her, she noticed Tom slip one hand into his pants pocket, the other holding onto a manila folder, as he and the Secret Service waited by the door.

"What is she doing here?" said Branch, sitting at the president's left hand and turning to see who had interrupted them.

Jaclyn grinned before she turned all Valley Girl.

"Oh, you know, making sure the president's security is up to snuff, and making sure that the Advances know that, too," she said, moving her head this way and that and checking out all the faces in the room. One appeared as if he had just lost all the color in his face, the skin turning translucent as he tried to make himself smaller. "We've had some issues with the security surrounding the president and his trips, and we have to cover all of our bases." She pointed to the faint-looking man, who had the look of the man she had spied on Salt's monitors yesterday. He had the same look, she noticed, albeit with a few extra lines under his eyes and a little more color near the temples. "Are you all right? You don't look so good. You want some help to the medical area? You know, the president has the best doctors here in the White House to check him for various maladies and ailments. Sometimes they just have nothing to do and are just sitting around, twiddling their thumbs and waiting for the off-chance that the president has a hangnail." She jerked her head. "Come on, I'll give you a hand—"

"You'll do no such thing, Johnson," Branch interrupted, her tone stern, before she turned to Forrister. "I told you that her behavior isn't right."

"I'll be the judge of her behavior," the president coolly replied. "Everyone else, please wait in the conference room down the hall. Barbara, you may stay if you so desire. He is your employee, after all."

The chairs shifted on the cream-colored rug as the other Advances, save Hill and Branch, stood and departed the Oval Office. Some, Jaclyn noted, took an awkward glance over their shoulders as they left. Tom took care to hold the door open for everyone before he closed it, leaving seven people alone. He then came over and casually sat next his wife. He tossed the folder onto the table between them.

Jaclyn had remained standing, though. She stared at Hill, the beginnings of a smirk outlining her lips. She watched as the man cringed under her long gaze. He didn't look to the folder.

"Mr. President, I have to object," Branch said. "This is a railroading!"

"Oh?" Ruoff said, answering in the president's stead. "A railroading? A railroading of what?"

"A man's character," she continued. "If Johnson is investigating him, you can be sure she'll be ready to slander his character."

"Why, whatever do you mean, Barbara?" Forrister asked. He flashed a sardonic smile her way, his teeth glittering. "I don't even know why Jaclyn is here this morning. Her presence is a complete surprise to me. Do you know something as to why she's here? God, I always hate being out of the loop."

Jaclyn watched as Branch's jaw started flapping twice, but she heard nothing emerge from between her lips—no meek gasps, not even a touch of spittle flying out. Her cheeks, from the corners of her mouth to her ear lobes, went from pale to strawberry in only a matter of mere heartbeats. She didn't utter another word. Jaclyn didn't think she wanted to incriminate herself.

At least not yet, she thought.

"Jaclyn, would you like to tell these fine folks why you're here?" Forrister said.

"With pleasure, sir." Jaclyn sat down. She clapped her hands together; Hill nearly hit the ceiling. "I hadn't spoken with Mr. Hill yet. I really wanted to go over old times, seeing as he and I have some mutual acquaintances back home."

The man in front of her swallowed hard.

"We—we do?" Hill croaked.

"Yeah," Jaclyn said with a smile. "But before we do that, I wanted to ask you about the set up you made for the Seattle trip."

"Adam, don't answer anything she asks."

Jaclyn jerked her head toward Branch.

"An answer you're afraid of hearing, perhaps? I don't see why two people with mutuals can't relive—"

"Oh, don't play coy with me, Johnson. We all know you're here to implicate Adam in the death of Alexandra Dupuis. I can answer unequivocally that he had nothing to do with it."

Jaclyn stared her down.

"And how do you know?"

Seconds passed, but Branch said nothing else. Jaclyn noticed a fire kindling behind the woman's eyes as she stared at her with an intense, brooding hatred. It was as if she looked into the eyes of Bennett, Farrell, and every terrorist she had brought down before now, and they all became this one entity, who just happened to handle the president's schedule.

She knows something, Jaclyn mused. *She knows something, and I don't know what it is. But maybe if I give her enough rope…*

She turned back to Hill.

"I understand you're from Tacoma," she said.

He nodded.

"And you went to Lakewood High."

Another nod, this one slower.

"Did you know that I went there for about a week and a half in 2001?"

Hill stared. His right cheek twitched briefly as he firmed his jaw, before he gave the nod Jaclyn figured would send him directly to Florence.

"Who told you that?"

Another twitch.

I've got him, she thought, not letting a look of triumph come anywhere close to the surface. She remained poker faced.

"People." His tone was calm, almost sobering. It was as if his fate was in front of him—which, Jaclyn knew, it was—and he didn't want to go through a long, drawn-out interrogation. Jaclyn's heart felt as if it dropped; her thoughts of roughing Hill up from the overnight weren't going to come true, it seemed. She had her heart set on trying to bloody Forrister's carpets.

"People," Jaclyn echoed. "Which people?"

He shrugged his shoulders, sending his head bobbing to the side.

"This one, that one."

"Being vague, I see. You handled the room assignments for our trip to Seattle last weekend."

Hill nodded.

"And you put my husband and I in a room at the far end of the hall from the president. Why?"

This time, Hill clammed up. Through her HUD, Jaclyn noticed that he was still among the living; his respiration was fine, but his heart rate had skyrocketed up near 150. She also saw the sweat beading on his forehead; a few strands of his hair had grown damp over the last few minutes. A bead of sweat plinked off the overhang in his ear, tumbling away into his ear canal.

"Nothing to say to that? It seems to me that you have something to hide. Protecting someone?" She looked to Branch, as if daring her to speak, before she returned her gaze to Hill. "Or are you protecting someone from Lakewood? I've seen the yearbooks, Mr. Hill, and I have your phone records from the time you took control of the Seattle trip and the unveiling of my father's statue. You were in contact with my classmates, the ones who were a year ahead of you when you got to Lakewood."

"You have no proof," he said, his breathing quite erratic, before he wiped his sodden brow.

Smirking, Jaclyn leaned forward and scooped up the manila folder. She opened it up—she had printed out Salt's email to her with all the names—and began to rattle off names. It took her about a minute to rip through the list, telling Hill how she knew them in case he didn't know. Some of them were girls with whom she had run track at Woodbrook, and then there were some that were, as she had told Tom and Salt, not exactly pen pals with her. Hill was stoic. However, Branch looked ready to burst. Her face looked as if cracks had developed in the flesh, and each one appeared ready to tumble away to reveal the monster beneath. Jaclyn made note of that.

And I have something that'll make you wish you were never born, she thought as she finished up.

"And then there's Darren Drake," Tom piped in. "What did you lot talk about?"

Jaclyn immediately stiffened.

"Oh, you mean this one's old boyfriend?" Hill said, jerking his head up to indicate Jaclyn. His face had instantly gone stone cold, the erratic breathing gone. Jaclyn felt Tom's eyes turn to her. "He wanted to get even with her for breaking his heart."

"I didn't break his heart," she corrected. She didn't notice that her voice had suddenly trembled, as if it lost its strength and had turned rubbery. "And he's not my old boyfriend."

"Yes, you did, and according to him, he was. You never answered his letters. He's pissed." By now, Hill smiled, as if he had the upper hand in this situation. He had turned the tables. His voice had turned stronger now, full of a confidence that wasn't there—or had evaporated, which was more likely—when Jaclyn had entered the Oval Office.

"I don't give a shit if he's pooped," Jaclyn countered. "Were you taking orders from him?"

"Don't answer that, Adam," Branch said.

"Shut up! Tom," Jaclyn said, looking to her husband, "if she speaks again, shoot her."

Tom drew his Walther and rested it on his thigh. Branch gasped before she turned to Forrister.

"Mr. President, are you going to let her talk to me that way?"

Tom flipped the safety off. Branch and Hill both stiffened.

"Barbara, I'm going to have to ask you to leave before you get blood on the carpets," Forrister said, pointing a finger her way. "Either that, or do as she says and shut up."

"I have something for you, too. Wait your turn." She turned back to Hill. "So, were you?"

"What do you want to know, Agent Johnson?" Hill said.

"I want to know exactly what went into your plan for the sleeping arrangements. I know there had to be a reason. Alex's death wasn't random. It was planned. My husband and I were supposed to be in that room, as you know. The Secret Service switched us. And Alex is dead as a result."

"Maybe the Secret Service set the rooms—"

But Jaclyn parried that thrust as she raised her voice.

"Don't go blaming the Secret Service for what you did, or I may have to ask our friend here to show you his Sig-Sauer," she said. "Or I can do it myself: it wouldn't be the first time I defended them. I have a witness who said you were the one who submitted the room assignments to the hotel, that it had your name on it. You signed off on it, Hill. So, I ask you again, true or false—did you take orders from Darren Drake or someone else from Lakewood High to put me in that room to potentially die as the intruder originally intended?"

Hill's lip curled.

"True."

Jaclyn kept her gasp to a bare minimum. The admittance had rocked her to her core, knocking her back into the seat. She had the first part of her answer.

Now to get the rest of it, she thought. Out of the corner of her HUD, she saw the dark-skinned Secret Service agent pry himself away from the wall. He moved to Forrister's side, pulling his jacket back to reveal his Sig-Sauer. No one else had noticed.

"Was it Drake? Or was it someone else?

Hill's nostrils flared.

"It was him. And he paid us good money—"

"Adam!"

"Quiet, bitch. I'm still waiting for the rest of it. Drake gave you plenty, so you shouldn't complain."

Jaclyn blinked just as Branch's jaw did that pseudo-flopping again. She caught the president staring at the woman, his eyebrows ramming together as his eyelids nearly closed in on themselves. Jaclyn then smiled; she had all the ducks in a row now, but she needed to know the reasoning. She needed to know why they did this, why they caused Alex's death.

"So you sold out the president. Both of you sold out the president, and Alex, and me." She kept her hands folded in her lap; if they expected her to ball her fists and let the muscles in her arms stand on edge, they were mistaken. She remained calm, keeping her emotions on a relatively low boil.

"Fuck you, Johnson," Branch blurted out, her fiery tone riddled with hatred. Her eyebrows were crooked, the interior corners sitting against the bridge of her nose. "No one cares about you."

"I beg to differ," Tom said. "And I think the president told you to shut your cakehole or else I get to shoot you."

Branch stared hard at Tom, but Jaclyn knew her husband had the ability to deflect and, as they say in England, take the mickey out of a person in any situation. She watched as Tom flashed a roguish grin and brought his Walther to bear, the barrel pointed directly at the woman's nose. Her blood thrumming to a drum line in her ears, she waited for the president to speak, to say something to disarm her husband, but he didn't. It seemed that Forrister wanted to see just how far Branch and Hill would push them before they replied in their subtle way.

For some reason, Jaclyn thought it the greatest show of support ever. He wasn't acting like a puppeteer, the players in front of him his marionettes dancing about for his entertainment. Far from it: he wanted to get to the bottom of this just as desperately as she. And if that meant Tom had to bury a bullet in the woman in order to get to that answer, then so be it.

Jaclyn returned her gaze to Hill.

“Getting back to the heart of the matter: you sold out the president over something that truly didn’t concern you,” she said.

“I didn’t like seeing Darren hurt by your scheming skirts,” Hill explained. “And he grew tired of your cock-teasing ways. He decided to put an end to his heartbreak, and he paid us a great deal of money to achieve his ends. He wanted you dead, Miss Johnson.”

She nodded.

“I understand that, and that’s Mrs. Johnson-Messingham, now. I’m trying to understand why he paid Branch.”

“So she wouldn’t take me off the trip and inform the president of what was happening.”

Jaclyn nodded again, then looked to Branch.

“Want to refute that before the federal marshals take you away, Barbara?”

Branch said nothing, even though the blush on her cheeks, now magenta, betrayed her rage. Instead, she stared at Jaclyn with an intent, controlled fury. Ruoff pulled a two-way radio from her pocket and pressed the transmit button. “You can send in the marshals now.”

A few seconds later, the main door to the Oval Office opened. A pair of men in plain clothes entered. Jaclyn didn’t take her gaze away from Branch as the men walked up behind her, grabbed Branch’s forearms, and lifted her from the couch. Jaclyn braced herself for a vicious, obscenity-laden tirade from the woman, but nothing save a few blasts from her nose and a bit of gritting teeth arrived. She turned and walked out without another word.

Two other marshals stepped behind Hill.

“Anything else you want to say, Hill, before I have the gentlemen here feed you your balls every morning in Leavenworth? Or will you enjoy the pleasant company of Tsarnaev at Florence?”

The man shook his head. The marshals took him away, too.

As soon as the door closed, Tom let a long-held sigh go. Jaclyn bit her lip as she watched him run his fingers through his hair. He stood and walked over to the windows that overlooked the South Lawn, while Forrister adjusted his tie. Jaclyn wondered what her husband thought about all this; the secrets of Drake's letters had to have hit him in the forehead with the force of a lorry. She watched as he shoved his hands into his pockets.

"So," he said, turning and looking at his wife, "I have a question: How many other lads are still holding onto first-year feelings for you?"

His wink, though, disarmed her. She couldn't help but smile back.

***

Oval Office, White House
1600 Pennsylvania Avenue
Washington, D.C.
Tuesday, June 25
6:32 a.m. PT/9:32 a.m. ET

"So you know this guy?" Forrister asked. The president stood and walked around the Resolute Desk. He sat down and set his own notepad down to the side.

Jaclyn had no choice but to nod. Hill had already let the proverbial cat out of the bag.

"Yes, sir. I went to school with him."

"And he's written love letters to my honey bunny," Tom added. He had moved over to where Jaclyn sat and held her hand lovingly, as always. Jaclyn felt her heart skip a beat as he did so, which only spread her intense love for him to every inch of her extremities, with so much warmth it made her fingertips numb; she knew he had every right to go off the handle like most men would do when they had discovered another man wanted to intrude on their marital bliss. But he hadn't, in truth. If he had any anger, he would never show it to her. "Which I think is as much of a crime as stealing a candy bar from the corner store when you're seven."

"You understand why I didn't tell you, right?" she asked, looking through her HUD right into his eyes. He shook his head.

"I don't feel I need to kn—"

"I'm going to tell you anyway. I have to make you understand." She sighed a little bit, then flattened a fold in her pants. "He started writing to me after I came back from London the first time, right after I had met you. He had said that he discovered I was still alive and out there thanks to Dick Bennett's scheming admission. He didn't even know I was a fashion model, which I find rather entertaining, to be honest. So he wrote and told me that he missed me, and that he finally had to tell me that he had loved me for quite a long time, starting from seventh grade to now."

Tom didn't speak, and neither did Forrister nor Ruoff. They all listened intently, sitting there without fidgeting.

"I didn't answer, of course. I knew I was in love with Tom, even then, someone who I knew would be there for me. I knew my future lay with this lug, not someone I hadn't seen in eleven years. But then, as I stayed at my apartment while I was *persona non grata* with the government thanks to Bennett's douchebaggery, Drake continued writing me, asking me where I am, what am I doing, how come I haven't answered yet—"

"If this wanker asked you for a pair of knickers, I swear—"

"No, he didn't," she said, reassuringly patting his hand. "He started writing every month, especially after I saved the day in Las Vegas, and then the cameras showed me with the first lady and the vice president on the tarmac in Atlanta. And let's recall that after Las Vegas, you were in the care of Tasha and I, and I had to send you back to mum before I went to Georgia. Between you with your jaw wired shut, me flying to Cali, getting Tasha enrolled in school, and getting comfy and cozy with you, I had pushed Drake out of my mind. It didn't even cross my mind to tell you, and you were in no condition to beat up anyone. I didn't hear from him again until after the election, and by then no other man mattered to me. Sorry, Mr. President."

Forrister smiled and waved it aside.

"No apology is necessary, Snapshot."

"Everything stopped, though, when we announced our engagement when I got back from Detroit, before Tasha and I went to see you and everyone in England," she continued. "And let us not forget that was when the White House announced daddy's statue would be commissioned. The letters abruptly stopped, and I had hoped that with my silence, he had taken the hint." She felt the tears building underneath her HUD, but she took a deep breath to reclaim her emotions. Tom's hand squeezed hers. "As we see now, I was wrong and misguided in my thinking. Ignore it, it will go away. That didn't happen."

"And now, he's found a way to get to you—through Alex," Tom said softly.

Jaclyn felt her lips roll in as she fought off weeping, right there in the Oval Office, but her emotions flooded the room. She fell into Tom's embrace.

A few minutes lingered as Tom comforted her. She had never felt his arms wrap that tightly around her body before, not even after they had made love the first time in Caesar's Palace. She clutched him just as tight, until she quickly ended the sobbing of her own volition, straightening herself and wiping the tears away.

"I'm sorry, baby," she whispered.

"It's okay, but don't get upset if some bird from sixth form throws herself on me the next time we're at the pub in London."

Jaclyn abruptly laughed.

"Yeah, like that's going to happen."

Tom tweaked her nose and kissed her tenderly.

"Now that we know exactly who he is," Forrister said, "and how he plays into your world, Snapshot, let's decide what we're going to do about him."

Jaclyn had turned and faced the president. Her heart raced at the prospect of—

"If I remember correctly, sir, you would have me seek out the killer and take he or she out of the game," she replied. "Is that option still on the table? I understand if it's not, seeing as I'm relatively close to the situation."

"You were close to the situation," Forrister corrected. "The suspect in question is a prior connection, yes, but I feel that you are well-separated from such a situation that you won't have a problem in making the correct decision. There is no conflict of interest, and I know where your loyalties lie. They lie with Alex's memory, with Tom, and with me, not with a twentysomething still struggling with his adolescence and his hormones.

"Agent Snapshot, you are hereby ordered to return to Seattle." Jaclyn's chest immediately swelled, her ears taking in every syllable Forrister issued. "Find this Darren Drake degenerate. Take him into custody, interrogate him, and if necessary, eliminate him. Use any and all methods necessary to find out what he's up to, and entrap him, if need be."

Jaclyn nodded.

"You can count on me, sir."

Forrister's smile was genuine.

"I know I can. And now if you'll excuse me, I have to go to another meeting before I fly to Chicago. I'm giving a speech at the Lincoln Library tonight." As he stood, the others stood after a beat. "I am sure you won't have a problem handling both jobs at once."

Jaclyn blinked, then remembered.

"Oh yeah. I'm still the director, aren't I?"

Forrister nodded.

"For now, Jaclyn. I think that we'll be able to relieve you of that post as soon as this bastard is in custody or in the ground, whichever comes first. Give me a call tomorrow and give me an update. I'll let you know what happens with those two cretins; I can assure you that they'll be looking for jobs in the interim, that's for sure. Take care, you two."

Jaclyn and Tom shook the president's and Melanie Ruoff's hands, before they turned and headed back the way they came.

"So what is the move?" Tom asked as they made their way down the stairs into the sub-basement.

"The move," she replied, "is to get a hold of Andrews and get the Gulfstream fired up and gassed up for another cross country trip. Then we get Tasha at the Farm, pack, then come up with a rock solid plan in order to get Drake to fall into our little trap."

"And I think it would be prudent to have your secretary make an appointment up for that thing we were supposed to attend when we were there last week."

Jaclyn's face fell. She froze mid-step, then caught her foot dangling a few inches from the top of the bottom step.

"Oh yeah, that thing." She swallowed, then shrugged her shoulders. "Yeah, why not? I'm sure we can squeeze it in. Heck, I'm confronting my past, pseudo love life in this whole trip. I might as well see old family members while I'm at it."

***

Darren Drake's office
Seattle, Washington
Tuesday, June 25
9:35 a.m. PT/12:35 p.m. ET

Darren Drake's fingers flew across his phone's keyboard, the clicking matching that of a stopwatch's second hand. He rocked violently in his chair, the leather crunching against the plastic with every nervy back-and-forth motion.

Where is she? he wrote. *She hasn't come back here yet. She should have been back by now.*

He pressed send, the text message sending with a sharp *veroop*. Drake bit his lip as he noticed the recipient had read it half a moment after he had hit send, and the display then showed the three dots blinking in tune as the other party began their reply.

Another *veroop* met his ears as it came across. Drake scooped his phone up and read:

She will come. We've read the dispatches from her past missions. When the shit hits the fan, she's the one the government sends. It is only a matter of time before she makes an appearance. And we must be ready for it. Be patient, lover.

As he read it and nodded, the person on the other side formulated another message, the telltale dots blinking side by side as the person typed on their phone.

When is your news conference about NN? Today? I look forward to watching it. I may have my pants off while you're on the screen, too.

Drake sniffed as he smiled, noticing the wink at the tail end of the message. He felt a stirring in his pants as they grew tight around his midsection. He typed away as he rubbed his dry lips together.

It makes me so hot knowing that you're going to be half-naked while I'm talking about our front. I may have to come over later and punish you.

He added a similar winking emoticon and sent the message. *Veroop.*

The person on the other end didn't reply.

Drake didn't mind that his most recent message received no response. His colleague had a business to run, as well, just as he did, and not answering a text didn't faze him; it had happened before, and Drake easily brushed it aside. He would see this person later in the day, and if luck held, well into the darkness of evening and into the next morning, too. They were partners in this scheme, the scheme to rid the world of the cock-teasing little bitch who had ruined his life in September 2001; this partner wanted to see her eliminated just as much as he did. And while he knew the person with whom he worked didn't exactly have the greatest reasons to see her killed—they were childish and flimsy, but he didn't care about that; he knew that one could raise the argument that his reasons were equally childish and flimsy—the side benefits were enough for him to join together in this endeavor.

Seeing as they've joined together in other ways, carnal ways, he didn't really care about their motivations.

He only wanted results.

After all, he had paid enough money for them.

Chapter 8
Jaclyn Johnson's apartment
The Winston House
Washington, D.C.
Tuesday, June 25
3:47 p.m. PT/6:47 p.m. ET

Jaclyn, Tom, and Tasha had rested a good portion of the day before they readied themselves for the trip to the west coast. Like usual, Jaclyn didn't worry about having the essentials or having more than a single weapon on her person for the trip there. She had already discussed it with Parkerhurst, who said he had something rather special for the trio. It would only take an extra day or so for him to finalize it before he assured delivery in Seattle. Jaclyn knew this was how he operated, and this was his art, as he liked to call it. For a moment, she had to stifle a grin as she sent her thoughts to her deceased father-in-law and how he had told a man at Thames House named Art—who had told Jaclyn that "you can't rush art"—to quiet down and do his job in the wee hours after Wembley came tumbling down.

Jaclyn had brought Tasha up to speed after they finished dinner that night. Tom had baked lemon pepper tilapia, rice medley, and steamed, fresh broccoli, and as Tasha rinsed the dishes off and put them in the dishwasher, Jaclyn stood at the sink, a mug of piping hot coffee in her hands. They had a long flight coming up, and Jaclyn wanted to be awake for it.

"So you have an admirer," Tasha teased, adding a teenaged "oooooooh" at the end. Both Tom and Jaclyn had to laugh. "What was he like, seeing as you haven't seen him in forever?"

"Back then, he was a quiet kid. I'd catch him staring at me, but I didn't say anything back. I was just as shy as he was."

"Jaclyn Johnson? Shy?" Tasha turned to Tom, feigning shock as she held a Pyrex dish in her wet hands. "Since when were we transported to Bizarro D.C.?"

Jaclyn simply tsked as her husband shrugged his shoulders, opened the fridge door, and pulled out a can of seltzer. He walked away as if nothing had occurred, leaving the women alone. Jaclyn pulled out a can for her and a can for Tasha. Neither opened them; Jaclyn wanted to finish her coffee first, and Tasha, wearing a spaghetti-strap tank top and comfy, thin pajama pants, had her hands busy in hot, soapy water.

"I can't believe those two idiots at the OEOB just blurted it out like that," Tasha continued. "Haven't they ever heard about self-incrimination?"

"They might have, once or twice, but these two were ready to burst when Tom and I walked into the Oval Office. It only took a few minutes, and they confirmed what we found out through Salt's computer. And hearing what I already knew from someone else just made me shiver. It wasn't a good shiver."

"Not like Tom makes you, at least."

Jaclyn felt her face burn with embarrassment.

"No," she said, "not like that."

"Do you think it will be difficult to kill someone you once knew?"

Jaclyn bowed her head slightly, taking her bottom lip between her teeth. She let her lungs fill with precious oxygen as she let her ward's question—a question which had lingered in her mind and had festered in her heart for at least the last twelve hours or so—fill her ears. An ache had developed in her chest, as if Hill had plunged a knife into her heart earlier in the morning by confirming her worst fears. The ache turned into a burning sensation which radiated out from the wound, but not in the way her eyes burned as a child: it felt like a slow charring had taken over, as if she had turned into a rotisserie chicken rotating on a spit.

"It may be. I don't really know."

"It looks as if you're struggling with that," Tasha said as she picked the silverware basket up and put it in the dishwasher. "Maybe you'll just shoot him in the leg like you did with his henchman?"

Jaclyn let a soft laugh escape.

"I almost forgot about that. I might have to do that."

"What do we know about him today?"

Jaclyn sighed. She moved slightly, resting her rear end against the cabinets.

"Other than that he's a psycho and that he owns a computer company? Not much more than that." After taking a long sip from her mug, she proceeded to explain his letters to her, how he had bragged about opening a company that rivaled Microsoft's operating systems—and made quite a bit of cash from it, to boot. "He tried to woo me."

Tasha blinked and shook her head rapidly.

"Woo?"

Jaclyn nodded.

"Woo."

"What's woo?"

"It's what teenagers do."

"I'm sorry, I was never wooed, nor did I woo. It was all, 'Hey girl' or 'Hey sexy, how 'bout you show me what's under that skirt.' There was no wooing."

Under her HUD, Jaclyn raised an eyebrow. It peeked over her Foster Grants.

"So you say."

"So I know."

"Anyway," Jaclyn said, a touch tired at the back and forth, "the guy from Scheduling said that there was some money exchanged, and that yes indeed, I was supposed to have died because I was a 'scheming skirt,' whatever the fuck that means. So that's an admittance."

"How are we going to do this?"

"Do you mean are we going to go in with all guns blazing? No. We're going to take this slow and steady. Build a more airtight case against him. Then we go in with all guns blazing."

"Sort of like how we did with Resnick?"

Jaclyn nodded.

"Sort of. Except I'm not getting tossed into Puget Sound. I don't think I've been thoroughly dry since then."

Tasha smiled.

"I'm in."

"Of course you are, Sex Kitten."

Tasha let loose a giggling torrent. She shook the suds from her hands and wiped them on a towel.

"Best. Code Name. Ever."

"Now," Jaclyn continued, "I think that seeing as I'm meeting my family for the first time in, what a decade and a half, I think I'm going to want to meet some of my school friends, too."

"Really? I don't think I would want to run into any of my old school friends. I don't even want to go to a Moreno Valley High reunion." Tasha opened the can of seltzer Jaclyn had offered and took two long sips.

"There's a good reason why I want to meet with them. I want to see if they have had any contact with Drake lately, and I want to see if they know where he lives. He doesn't have a home address listed on the city's tax records, and there's been no record of him living in Seattle proper for about five years. The letters all came from a P.O. Box in Renton. I had Salt check with the postal service, and he listed his business address."

"Which means he lives outside the city." Tasha tapped her fingers against the aluminum, then pointed at her. "You need a Facebook account."

Jaclyn blinked her confusion again.

"Facebook? Why Facebook?"

Tasha rolled her eyes.

"Everyone your age is on it? Perhaps?"

Jaclyn's lips turned down.

"I wouldn't know anything about that. The agency frowns on field agents using social media, especially those pesky location features."

"Well," Tasha said as she shifted her weight from right to left, "seeing as you're the head the agency right now, I think you can allow yourself a short-term use Facebook account for this mission."

Jaclyn pursed her lips and nodded while Tasha tossed a Cascade packet into the dishwasher. Jaclyn finished her coffee with a deep gulp before putting her mug in. Tasha closed the door and set it to run.

"There. Those will be clean and sparkly long before we return. If you don't know how to set up a Facebook account, I think I have the ability to help you. And besides, you know I'm a good judge of character. I can look at your posts and the ones of your old school pals, and we can see exactly who is fibbing and who is telling the truth. Or who's naughty or nice?" Tasha's eyes glittered mischievously.

Jaclyn chuckled.

"Santa Tasha."

The young girl showed two rows of perfect teeth.

"You know, I really should have a Sexy Santa suit in my repertoire," Tasha mused. "Low cut on the chest, high on the legs." She wiggled her hips. "Rawr."

"Oh, Sex Kitten, keep it in your panties."

Tasha immediately stiffened and gave her a sharp salute.

"Yes, Chief."

Jaclyn faltered for just a brief moment, but smiled and immediately embraced her ward. She felt Tasha's arms snake around and grab her shoulder blades.

"Thank you."

"No," Tasha said, her tone strong. "Thank you."

"Come on," Jaclyn said. "Let's go set up a Facebook page."

Smiling, the two women headed off to the living room, where Jaclyn's laptop sat on the coffee table. They sat down on the couch; Tom had a DVRed football match from the Euro tournament on the flat screen, England and Romania. From the pained look on his face, she knew England wasn't playing well. Jaclyn looked at the television and noted the score. It was 2-0 in favor of the Romanians. Only ten minutes had elapsed.

Jaclyn grimaced. She thought it was only a matter of time before Tom stopped the recording and violently deleted the match from the system.

Jaclyn and Tasha kept their conversation regarding the creation of Jaclyn's Facebook account to a dull roar while Tom kept his attention on Ian Darke's voice. The Englishman, in his usual manner, described the action, with former New England Revolution star Taylor Twellman adding insight as to why the Three Lions were, for the lack of a better phrasing, sucking it up in this Euro Round of 16 match.

"We need a picture of you, and an email address," Tasha said.

"A picture?"

"Yes, so they know it's you. And seeing as you're a top-notch fashion model, we can get you the blue check mark. That'll mean you're verified as being the celebrity in question who owns the account."

"I'm sure we can scan in a cover of Vogue if we have to," Jaclyn said.

Tasha did the hard work as Jaclyn looked on. They set up the account in minutes, with a picture of Jaclyn posing for the camera. She remembered it being the same one that Bobby Ray Rayburn's mother had her sign, only hours before that bastard shot and killed her. She shivered at that knowledge, wondering what possessed him to do that. She had never asked, but knew she would never get that opportunity: Rayburn was finally executed by the state of Georgia a week after Jaclyn had disarmed him, this time with guards flown in from other states, ones who weren't on the payroll of a racist organization.

Then Tasha asked for the names of the ones Jaclyn had said were friendly with her in middle school. Jaclyn gave them, and soon, Tasha had pulled them up through the search window. She sent them a friend request, then found others. By the time Tom's football match had reached the half hour mark, Jaclyn had received a few friend requests of her own from a few people that were outside of her circle, but not too far outside to be considered a part of the cliques that wanted nothing to do with her. There were a few of her track teammates—several of them posted "OMG!" to her wall, their surprise evident—and a couple of boys, now young men, on whom Jaclyn had hard crushes. That led to girlish giggles as she explained to Tasha who they were.

And then there were men who were close to Darren Drake. Jaclyn made sure they were accepted.

Tasha then set up an event for the Pike Place Market's Zig Zag Café.

Jaclyn typed:

I'm coming home, Woodbrook Middle School. Class of 2000, I want to see YOU at the Zig Zag Café. I'm looking forward to catching up and remembering old times, and learning about what you've been up to since I left.

"There," she said. "Now, I think we'll get some answers. Tom, make sure you pack a tie or two. Clean shirts, that kind of thing."

"Of course," he said, not tearing his eyes off the television. "I have to make sure I have a back-up in case I get blood on one."

"Or spill a drink all over yourself."

"That, too. Oh, come on, lads," Tom barked as he rose off the couch for a split second, then smacked his hands together, the resulting crack resembling a gunshot. "You need to pull the bloody trigger when you have an opening like that! Back line kept its shape at the worst possible time. The bastards."

Jaclyn shook her head as he sat back down. He shoved his hands under his ass and grumbled his frustrations.

"Men and their sports."

"So says the woman who has a rather extensive collection of Mariners, Sonics, Seahawks, and Sounders gear in her closet," Tom immediately countered.

Jaclyn blushed.

"Too bad there'll be no time for a game while we're there," she said, before she slapped her thighs. "Okay, it's time to head west. We need to get packed. Our flight leaves in two hours, and we have, believe it or not, reservations for The Warwick."

"And we have a dangerous terrorist to take out, too," Tasha added, spelling out the obvious.

Jaclyn paused, then nodded at her.

Yep, she thought. *He's a terrorist, as much as it pains me to admit it.*

***

Main Reception Hall
Drake Enterprises, Inc.
Seattle, Washington
Tuesday, June 25
4:30 p.m. PT/7:30 p.m. ET

Drake's executive assistant—it was a much more PC way of saying secretary in this day and age, something he really despised; he preferred the old ways—had sent out a news release to the media the day before, and the time had come for him to meet the members of Seattle's esteemed Fourth Estate. Drake had put on his best suit, a black number with a thin, matching tie which helped him cut an intriguing image. He was the young, handsome entrepreneur; his dark hair was slicked forward without a part, the front edges spiked upward. He thought, quite rightly in his opinion, he was the epitome of style and elegance.

He had mingled with the reporters before he took the dais. Some were unshaven louts, especially the one from the Seattle *Herald-Traveler*. There was an aroma of liquor around this one, but that could have been his cologne; a mix of Cool Water and Eau de Jack Daniels, Drake mused. The TV gal from Channel Four was a pretty blue-eyed blonde who looked a head-turner in a tight red number, the hem stopping short of her knees, but Drake had to wipe his palm full of sweat—hers—on his slacks as he walked away after their discussion. He shivered, thanking God he wasn't the one who shared her bed every night.

He had made sure that the tables off to the side had plenty of half-sandwich wedges filled with rare roast beef and turkey, crisp lettuce and mouth-watering tomatoes, bowls of pasta salad, and warm bread. It was an olive branch to the press, as Drake knew that they loved free food; on their meager wages, a free meal while working a story was a great way to generate positive publicity. He grabbed a small, four-ounce bottle of Nantucket Harbor water, cracked it open and chugged it. Over to the side, the gal from Channel Four nibbled on a chocolate chip cookie while she spoke with her counterpart from Channel Seven. The gal from Channel Seven was a red head, her back turned to him. He stared at her tight little caboose until he felt a tap on the shoulder. He turned his head a little.

"It's time, Mr. Drake," his executive assistant said with a wide smile. She was a young thing, a long-haired beauty fresh out of college, the smell of baby powder all about her. She was wide-eyed, seemingly unknowing of the pitfalls and predators of the world, even though Drake had done his homework on her; she had been the life of the sorority once upon a time, something she had tried to hide from him during the interview process. A quick search through a program of his own making allowed him to find out a little more about this girl, complete with pictures of her drunken debauchery; he had grinned at the scandalous photos he had found of her wrapped in the arms of another similarly-naked co-ed, along with the photos of her doing keg stands. Other than those attributes, he had liked her look from the moment he laid eyes on her, and it wasn't her education or business background which had clinched her employment. She wore clothing that gave her a look of class in her upbringing, one everyone expected an executive assistant to wear to work. Besides that, he didn't know if it was the girl's perky breasts or her blonde hair that made him remember Jaclyn Johnson when they first met in his office that day. Her eyes were what Drake thought Jaclyn's would look like had he ever seen them. He was taken with her from the start; he wondered if he had the potential to bed her, bed her in the way he wished to bed her lookalike once upon a time—and, if he admitted it, still wanted.

"Thank you, Carissa," he replied. Drake took another small bottle of water and walked over to the dais. Carissa the Executive Assistant followed, despite him wanting her in front. The pair stepped up onto the raised platform. Drake reached into his jacket and pulled out a set of notecards while Carissa, in her pumps, raised herself onto tiptoes to speak into the microphone. Drake admired her twentysomething runner's calves and the way they strained against her sheer hosiery. His eyebrow jerked toward his hairline, the beginnings of a smirk taking form.

"Ladies and gentlemen," Carissa said, "Mr. Drake is ready to begin. If you'd all like to gather 'round, we'll start the news conference."

There were no clapping hands as Carissa finished up. There was, though, the shuffling of feet as the reporters slowly made their way to the dais. Notebook paper slipped over and under, while pens clicked. Tiny red lights perked up and came alive, while the robotic tones of servos tried to rise above the print clamor, to no avail.

Drake took a long sip as he walked forward. He nodded to Carissa, who moved away with a smile. He kept his eyes on the throng of journalists instead of peering over and catching a glimpse of her ass in that tight little black skirt. The cameras, he knew, caught everything, including the surreptitious moving of eyes toward a lovely young woman's backside. He didn't need a scandal.

A scandal that everyone knew about, he thought as he grasped the lectern. *Ones that I create and keep on the down low are just fine.*

He grinned as he adjusted the microphone a touch.

"Thank you all for coming out here today, and I hope you've eaten your fill. Today, my company is proud to announce that with the help of our legislative delegation, we're filing an application that will, if approved by the Federal Communications Commission in the war against Net Neutrality, pave the way for Drake Enterprises customers to download our programs faster, as the devices intend, and to use those programs on a different speed of the Internet than those who are not Drake Enterprises customers."

He took a moment to watch the scribbling before he continued.

"We have enabled our devices to download apps more quickly, using faster speeds along the information superhighway, if you will. Only our products can do this. The only thing which needs to be done now to free our customers from the reins holding us back is approval from the FCC. There is no reason for this approval to not be forthcoming. There is no reason to restrain my customers from the bigger, better, stronger, faster equipment they have purchased and earned.

"I am Darren Drake, ladies and gentlemen, and I am the New Voice of Technology in America."

Drake heard the clicking of shutters as he stared out at the crowd of peasant journalists. This, he quickly realized, was his James Cameron moment.

His grin deepened as the questions poured from their mouths.

Chapter 9
The Warwick Hotel
Lenora Street
Seattle, Washington
Wednesday, June 26
8:05 a.m. PT/11:05 a.m. ET

Jaclyn, Tom, and Tasha had arrived in Seattle on the Gulfstream just before midnight Pacific Time. After procuring a rental car from Hertz, Jaclyn drove them into Seattle proper and The Warwick Hotel. Jaclyn had to steel her nerve as she made the left-hand turn onto Lenora Street, much like she had done a week and a half prior. Tom and Tasha hadn't noticed her distress; even though they were awake as Captain Kevin brought the bird in for a landing at Sea-Tac, they were still groggy, their heads lolling on their necks as they entered the city. By the time Jaclyn passed CenturyLink Field on Interstate 5 North, Tom had started snoring, his head against the passenger window, while Tasha had her legs tucked up under her butt.

She woke them as she pulled up to the curb, taking a deep breath to calm her racing heart. She shook their shoulders, and the pair soon snapped awake and spilled out of the car. Tasha was a bit cranky, but Jaclyn knew that she would be fine the next morning. They registered at the front desk—Jaclyn had wondered if she could leave a message for the day manager, letting him know she had returned and wanted to speak with him at his earliest convenience in the morning—and they took rooms on the second floor, one floor below where the unthinkable had occurred.

Jaclyn slept relatively well, and so, too, did Tom: both collapsed into bed after they got undressed. Tasha had the room right next to them, and Jaclyn felt sure she would also tumble into dreamland at the soonest possible moment. The interim head of the CIA awoke briefly at 5 a.m. and managed to go through the day's security briefings, even though all she wanted to do was sleep. After looking through them and seeing nothing out of the ordinary, she went back to bed for a couple of hours before waking up for the second time at 7:30 a.m. She and Tom showered, then got dressed in business attire. They let Tasha sleep in a little longer, even though she had stressed she wanted in on every aspect of this case.

It was a few minutes after 8 a.m. when they left the hotel room and headed downstairs. They found the lobby full of people searching for the breakfast buffet; some wore their PJs and a pair of slippers. The two counterterrorism agents strode from the elevator and found the day manager sipping his coffee. The manager set his mug down and smiled wide. He looked in his early 30's, with a full head of black hair. Jaclyn didn't see a wedding ring.

"Mrs. Messingham, Mr. Messingham," he said. "Welcome back to The Warwick."

"Thank you," Jaclyn nodded.

"You wanted to see me?"

"Yes, I wanted to let you know that we gained an admission out of the Advance. He confessed, and outed not only the source, but his boss, too."

The manager bowed his head.

"Thank God for that," he said, leaning forward with the weight of the world pounding on his back. "I can't tell you how much worry I've put myself through over the course of the last week and a half. When you called the other day and asked about the assignments, I felt my heart sink deeper than it had when I broke up with my last girlfriend. I knew I should have had a say in who sleeps where."

"Unfortunately," Jaclyn replied, "that wouldn't have made a difference. The Advance didn't know about the switch, and then everything went wacky. But I wanted to thank you for all your help the other day. There is a chance you'll be summonsed to federal court to testify against the Advance."

The manager blanched, but he soon swallowed whatever comeback he had wanted to issue her way. Jaclyn smiled and patted the counter, before she and Tom spun and headed toward the breakfast buffet.

The couple walked with easy steps toward the cafeteria. The aromas of eggs and pancakes and bacon hung in the air and filtered down the carpeted corridor. Jaclyn inhaled deeply. A grin plastered her face as she turned to her husband.

"Smells so good," she said.

"For an American breakfast, yes," Tom said. "It would smell marvelous if there were some bangers and mash in there."

She playfully smacked his shoulder.

"Just get us some coffee. I know how much you will eat, so I'll get our breakfast."

Tom brought over two Styrofoam cups of coffee, the tendrils of steam in a race for the ceiling. He also brought over several packets of sugar and a couple self-serve containers of half and half for her. Jaclyn delivered their breakfast, the paper plates weighed down with a mountain of scrambled eggs, two pancakes, three sausages, and a couple slivers of toast for each.

"No tomatoes and mushrooms, I take it," Tom asked.

Jaclyn simply stared at him as she shook her two sugar packets back and forth. He quieted down.

They ate in relative silence as the rumbles of conversation between the parties around them took over, with CNN over on the flat panel television mounted high on the wall off to the side. There was the rustle of newspaper nearby, as well as the beeping and booping of a child's video game. Jaclyn tried to keep her mind on her food, but even with Tom gulping down his coffee and doing his damnedest not to break his plastic cutlery while cutting his pancakes, her mind eased to today's endeavor.

"So," Tom asked as if prophetic, his mouth full of warmed pancake, "how much do we have to do before we meet your old classmates?"

"There's not much," she said. "We can sniff around the city for his building, if you want. I can easily look online."

"That's acceptable. And what else are we going to do today?"

"Rest as much as we can," Jaclyn answered. "I think that with the jet lag and the emotions of meeting with my classmates, people I've thought lost to me, that I won't be able to do much more than that."

"That may be the way to do it. I know I could sleep for another few hours. What time are we meeting them?"

Jaclyn checked her HUD.

"At about 5 o'clock. And then tomorrow," she said, feeling tension return to her shoulders, "while trying to find out more about Darren Drake's motives, we get to see my family." Jaclyn's face fell, her mood turning sullen.

Tom frowned. He had a sausage stabbed on the fork. A bit of maple syrup tumbled away from it slowly.

"You really haven't explained why this is weighing on you so much, my love."

Jaclyn set her plasticware down and swallowed.

"It's pretty simple, hon. I was never really close to dad's side. Mom didn't really have a side, either, since she was an only child. Dad had one brother, Uncle Bill. He married Anna, and they had a couple of sons. Anyway, since we moved around a lot, from post to post, we didn't get to see them often. Holidays were spent on base, and they had only just moved to Seattle only a few months before Nine-Eleven—I never saw them at Christmas, or birthdays. They were, and I'm sure I was to them, foreign.

"And when we did see them that summer, it was awkward. I sat in silence because of my handicap. The boys were boys, and they only wanted to play with other boys."

"I take it they are younger than you," Tom asked.

"One is. He was 12 when I was 14. The other was 16. He had girls hanging off his arms, but then his friends came over. He was a pretty popular kid. With the exception of him, they were the kind of kids that picked on me in middle school because I was different."

"And he didn't stop them," Tom surmised.

"No, they didn't say anything around me or to my face," Jaclyn answered, "but with the sunglasses on, I could still see them looking at me, wondering what was wrong with me."

"Teenagers have always been cunts," Tom said, reaching over and through their breakfasts to hold his wife's hand.

"Always have been, always will be. They can't see over the edge of their nose, and if they ever care to, they'll act appalled for no reason other than they don't understand."

Jaclyn firmed her lips and nodded.

"I know."

"Everything will be fine, and I will be there with you. It will be good to meet some of me lovely bride's family."

Jaclyn's sour disposition turned brighter as her husband threw a surreptitious wink her way.

They continued eating.

***

Seattle, Washington
Wednesday, June 26
10:23 a.m. PT/1:23 p.m. ET

As soon as Tasha had awoken, showered, and eaten her own breakfast, the three of them climbed into Jaclyn's rental. Jaclyn had done a little research online and had found the location of Drake Enterprises. He had several stores in the downtown area which sold his products, but she had the feeling he wouldn't be there. The main headquarters, though, was near the Space Needle and the Key Arena, a little toward the waterfront. It wasn't too far away, and they'd be able to return to The Warwick for a respite before heading to Pike Place for their first of two off-track meetings.

"So," Tasha said from the back seat, "why are we doing this again? Just to get me up to speed a little?"

"Surveillance 101, Sex Kitten," Jaclyn purred. "He doesn't know we're here, as far as we know, and it's possible that we may have to enter the building at some point in the future. So we take a seat outside, we scope it out, and hopefully not attract attention to ourselves."

"So it's basically what we did outside of what's his name's yacht," Tasha presumed.

At the wheel, Jaclyn nodded.

"Pretty much."

They found their way to the main building. Drake had taken a former abandoned building and had dumped a lot of money into its rehabilitation, turning it into a sparkling center of computerization and business. The building was set back about fifty feet from the road, leaving a long plain of green bisected by red and blue paving stones. There were no trees along the edges, the roots making the sidewalk buckle. Jaclyn didn't detect a weed growing anywhere, either; it was as if Drake had taken the old AstroTurf from the KingDome and had laid it on the lawn. Several blades of grass, though, danced in the breezes off the Sound.

Jaclyn had parked the rental around the corner in a public lot, and the three of them walked over to the other side of the street, where they had a good look at the comings and goings. Jaclyn took to wearing a Mariners cap over her blonde hair, a ponytail shooting out the back, while the other two simply wore sunglasses. It was a bright, warm sunny day in Seattle, with the temperatures ranging in the high 70's. There wasn't a cloud in the sky, and none were expected today, either.

"HUD," Jaclyn said as she took a seat next to Tasha on a wrought iron bench the city had positioned kitty corner to Drake's building; Tom had stopped at a small hot dog cart on the side of the road and had grabbed three 20-ounce bottles of Sprite for them, as well as a few hot dogs. Sweat had already started to streak down Jaclyn's spine, but she ignored it. "Let's take a peek at this building's security and layout."

The device beeped once as it accessed the schemata. As Tom handed Jaclyn her bottle and two hot dogs, the HUD spilled the data across the screen as if in three dimensions, showing means of egress and the amount of security around each. Jaclyn breathed easily as the data poured in front of her eyes, seeing that it was simple to access if one put their mind to it. She had disabled similar security systems with a press of an icon on her iPad, the device sending signals to the host that would tell it nothing was out of the ordinary.

"Now show me if there's an area marked conference room. Are there cameras we can tap in to right now?"

The device booped in the negative.

Jaclyn frowned briefly, but she nodded. The fact there were no security cameras didn't phase her. It meant there would be no record of her entering the building—whenever that happened to occur.

"Nothing?" Tom asked.

She shook her head.

"Not a bloody thing. HUD, pull up the security system's logs. I want to know their rotation schedule."

Another negative tone sounded, making Jaclyn frown.

"There's no rotation listed," she said, her tone hollow. "That's strange."

"Incredibly," Tom said as he sipped his soda. "You would think that someone who owns a company that makes computers and tablets would have some semblance of security to stop industrial espionage."

"They do," Jaclyn corrected. "I'm sorry, I didn't make that clear. The information isn't available."

"Which makes sense," Tasha chimed in. "Making that public knowledge would lead people like us or, like Tom said, his competitors to make plans to break in."

Grimacing slightly, Jaclyn stared as Tasha grinned at her.

"You're right, of course. But still, that makes me mad."

"Maybe Salt can access that?"

"I'm sure he could."

***

The Warwick Hotel
Lenora Street
Seattle, Washington
Wednesday, June 26
1:17 p.m. PT/4:17 p.m. ET

"You can't access it, either," Jaclyn groaned over the phone, flopping backward onto her and Tom's bed. She grabbed a hard hold on the phone before it slipped and bounced on her tummy. Out of the corner of her eye, she caught Tom and Tasha sharing a frown.

"It looks like it's several different layers of tight encryption," Salt said, his voice a touch tinny with a bit of echo attached as it came over Jaclyn's speakerphone. "We're talking about a computer mogul, correct?"

"Right," Tom said. "This lad isn't going to have simple security parameters set up, like mum or me sisters would have on the home network."

"Right, he'd have layers, and even if you defeat one, if you trip one, you may have to deal with several new layers slipped into the path." Even in Seattle, Daly's sigh was unmistakable. "This could take a while, Snapshot."

"Take as long as you need, Desmond," Jaclyn replied. "We may be here a while. Call me back when you've got something. Snapshot out." She ended the call with a touch of her thumb. "Damn." She tossed the phone next to her and crossed her wrists against her forehead. "Are we ever going to have a mission that's incredibly easy to close? I feel like we should have Drake under those hot, sweat-inducing lights by now."

"Sweat-inducing?" Tasha repeated. Jaclyn peered through her HUD and watched as her ward crossed her arms underneath her breasts. Even in the cool, air-conditioned room, her t-shirt was drenched. "Seriously? Have you been reading those steamy Donna Fasano romances again?"

Jaclyn slipped on her best McKayla Maroney smirk as her cheeks grew warm, tinged with pink. Tasha beamed knowingly.

"We've only been back here for about thirteen hours, Snapshot," she continued as soon as she got her cheeks relaxed. "How long had you been in Vegas before we met, and how much had happened afterward?"

"And what about when you came to London? You had been with me old man for barely a day before all the shite hit the fan and sent the poo spraying in so many directions."

"And don't forget about Boston, Moreno Valley—"

"Atlanta, Detroit—"

"Okay, okay, I get the picture," Jaclyn said, exasperated. She rose from the bed. "I'm anxious. I just want to get today and tomorrow over with so I can get a bead on Drake. All these extra things are just," she paused to shake her hands about, as if she flapped them like wings, "extra. Meaningless shit."

"No shite?" Tom winked.

Jaclyn exhaled and felt the left side of her mouth turn upward.

"I love you," she said.

Tom repeated himself, grinning like a fool.

Off the side, Jaclyn watched as Tasha rolled her eyes at them.

"We could, of course, race in there and question him," Tom said, "but I'm afraid guys like him will want a lawyer right away."

"Right," Jaclyn said, "and personally, I'd like to avoid the red tape, if I can help it."

The three of them grinned as Jaclyn's remark hit home.

Chapter 10
The Zig Zag Café
Pike Place Market
1501 Western Avenue
Seattle, Washington
Wednesday, June 26
4:53 p.m. PT/7:53 p.m. ET

Situated on the bottom floor of a drab, seven-story gray building, the Zig Zag Café itself was set back from Western Avenue, stuck between the surface road and the elevated Route 99, the Alaskan Way Viaduct. While Jaclyn heard several conversations as she, Tom, and Tasha approached the establishment, she couldn't avoid the sounds of cars streaming northbound; it felt as if she stood on the infield at the Daytona 500. Trees bordered the pedestrian walkway, while umbrella-topped tables sat close to the building. Several people, all of whom Jaclyn didn't recognize, sat with friends, discussing the day's events, or how their husbands had cheated on them with the maid.

"Amazing how the same story comes rattling off their tongues," Tom had said as he grasped the door handle and yanked it open. He stood aside as Jaclyn and Tasha entered a few minutes before 5 o'clock. "It's like it's all pre-rehearsed."

Jaclyn nodded and didn't say anything else, for she feared her heart would leap from her chest and show itself through her mouth. Her chest ached with every step she took, and now that she was inside the café, her nervousness had increased ten-fold. Even though she didn't truly care for this and even though she knew it was a rather instrumental part of her investigation, there was a fluttering in her stomach she had not foreseen: she was about to see people she hadn't seen in years, people who, despite her handicap, cared enough to give her a token of remembrance she never knew had existed before Monday.

She licked her lips as she spotted a couple of women over by the windows to her left. She watched as their faces exploded in instant recognition. Jaclyn had to remember that she wasn't wearing her sunglasses, and that she wore the special contacts that Parkerhurst had handed to her in Las Vegas instead of her HUD: Tom carried one of the tiny devices that Jaclyn had carried and set up in her shower in London to let her know of any activity that would cause mayhem to the café.

"Jaclyn Johnson," one of the women, a blonde, said as she stood and walked over to her with her arms spread. Another woman, a brunette, followed. "It's so good to see you again!"

"Carly Connors," Jaclyn breathed after a heartbeat. "It's so good to see you, too! And Maddy Parker. Wow, you girls haven't changed."

Except for the smell of chardonnay on your breath, Jaclyn thought, but kept it to herself.

"We've missed you. Tell us, please, what you've been doing other than modeling and saving the world!"

Jaclyn laughed.

"Oh, this and that and the other thing, you know. Pretty much those two things have ruled my life, except this big lug until recently," she replied, turning to look at Tom. He ambled forward and she slipped her left arm into his right.

"Hello," Tom said with a smile.

The two women starting giggling like a pair of schoolgirls.

"Ohh, he's British. We don't get that a lot up here," the brunette, Carly, had said. Her cheeks had turned a remarkable shade of rose in only a few seconds; Jaclyn debated quietly if it was embarrassment, attraction, or overindulgence with the wine that made the woman's flesh go hot. "How'd you land him?"

Jaclyn smirked.

"It's actually still classified, but I can tell you that he's the best thing to happen to me since I initially moved to Seattle way back when." Jaclyn beamed up at her husband, then noticed that Tasha had scurried off to a secluded spot, looking on with great interest. She sipped a mug of something or other. Jaclyn hoped it was coffee, straight, with nothing else added to it.

The small talk of husbands, wives, children, and jobs—she hadn't mentioned her new, albeit temporary, job in Washington, and they all expressed belated condolences about her parents and how they wished she had been able to stick around so they could comfort her then, immediately after the fact—continued for the next ninety minutes as other classmates funneled into the café and met with Jaclyn and Tom. Handshakes and hugs—a few longer than Jaclyn would have truly liked—and pleasantries were exchanged. There were some there who Jaclyn had invited, and she seemed genuinely happy to see them. Some Jaclyn hadn't invited directly, and one had blabbed they had noticed the event through someone else's Facebook page and had decided to crash. Jaclyn felt nauseating fear squirrel up her spine as she smelled the man's poor excuse for aftershave leaning against her neck and ears.

"Snapshot," she heard Tasha say over a tiny transmitter she had stuck in her ear, "we have two guys looking at you to your right. Both are in white button-downs with bad ties, both looking like they haven't missed many meals, either."

Jaclyn took a sharp glance that way. They were in the far corner, and they were as Tasha had described. The one of the left nodded her way and lifted a drink as if toasting her.

Her heart lurched just as her throat turned as arid as the Sahara.

She had recognized them. They both had put on a few pounds—everyone in the room had, but that was beside the point—but their hairstyles hadn't changed; one had a crew cut, much like he had in middle school, while the other had a comb-over that would have looked fine if his hair wasn't thin and receding. The coloring had changed, though, with one going slightly gray. She remembered them instantly, and recalled with whom they were best friends at Woodbrook: the one and only Darren Drake. Jaclyn firmed her lips.

"Jaclyn?" the person in front of her said, snapping her out of her distracted state. "You haven't heard from Peter Williams, have you? He said he may show up."

Peter Williams was an old boyfriend of Jaclyn's; boyfriend was a rather vague term, since they were 11 when they had “dated,” which meant they hung out on the monkey bars or shared a bag of Cheez-It. She recalled that Drake was a bit standoffish by this a long time ago, and just hearing Williams’ name brought a once-repressed memory to the forefront.

She shrugged her shoulders.

“I haven’t heard. Can you excuse Tom and I for a few moments?”

The woman in front of her had blinked at first. “Sure, do what you have to do.”

“Thanks, we’ll only be a little bit.”

Jaclyn left her standing there, somewhat dumbfounded. She grabbed Tom by the elbow and pulled him away from the bar.

“Drake’s friends are over there,” she said, mostly under her breath. “I’m growing rather bored of the small talk, if I’m being brutally honest. Tasha, keep an eye open on this.”

“I’ll keep two eyes open and my lips on my mug,” came the slightly sarcastic reply.

Jaclyn sniffed as she smiled. They walked a few more steps until the two men turned to face her.

“Hi there, Jaclyn,” the bulkier one with the crew cut had said. Jaclyn had forgotten his name, and truly didn’t care for it nor wanted to know it. He looked like he had gone on to play football—her kind, not Tom’s—in high school and college, but looked as if he had a desk job now; doing what, she didn’t give a shit. The other one looked like he had spent most of his time in front of a computer monitor while chugging Coors Lights: he wore rectangular wire-rimmed glasses and had slightly receding black hair, but his arms were wiry, as if he had an aversion to curling anything weighing more than twelve-ounce aluminum cans. A massive, angry paunch and a half was prominent around his belt buckle. A massive, angry whitehead was also prominent in the crease above his right nostril.

Jaclyn tried not to recoil.

“Hello yourselves. This is my husband, Tom Messingham.”

Tom nodded but didn't extend his hand to the men. Neither did Jaclyn.

"Can we sit?" the geek asked.

Jaclyn offered a curt nod, even though she wanted to shrug her shoulders in annoyance. They all took seats in rather comfy chairs. After standing for the last hour and a half, Jaclyn felt a little bit of relief strike her lower back with the force of a cannon ball slamming against a ship's hull. A slight groan came out like a purr.

"We wanted to tell you something that may be a little disturbing," the computer guy had said.

"Disturbing is what I do best," she replied. "Give it your best shot."

"Darren Drake. We've seen him periodically since high school," the bulky one said. "Jaclyn, we wouldn't have said anything, but we think this is pretty important: Darren is still pretty infatuated with you. He has a shrine devoted exclusively to you; I had stumbled on it during a pool party at his place. He doesn't know I saw it."

Jaclyn tried to keep her blinking to a minimum, even though she started to shiver. Her blood had turned to ice.

"I hadn't known that," she said softly. She tried to count the number of years between the time she had left Renton in Alex's care and now. The total frightened her; she did not feel touched by what, at first glance, seemed like long-held devotion.

Silence lingered as Jaclyn looked at her lap, the thoughts rolling.

If he was infatuated with me for so long, she thought, *why would he want me dead? Why would he have hired the aerial hit man to smash through the balcony doors and pop Alex in the chest and forehead? That doesn't make sense.*

"He has pictures of your magazine covers all over this room, along with newspaper articles over the last few years. There were other photos, too, and they were clearly, shall we say, faked."

"Where is Drake now?" Tom said, interrupting his wife's train of thought. She jerked her head upward. She had heard Bulky Boy talk about the shrine, but she couldn't respond.

She just couldn't, because she didn't trust the words to come out without sounding snarky or full of venom.

"Honestly, I couldn't tell you. I haven't spoken with him in weeks."

"That makes two of us," the geek added in. "He really hasn't been himself in about four or five weeks."

"Could be longer, though," the bulkier one said. "He definitely hasn't been himself. He hasn't returned our texts or calls. Every call goes right to voice mail."

"What has he been doing for work?" Jaclyn asked, feigning ignorance. They didn't know she knew about his company, and they didn't have to know that she knew. They told her exactly what she knew, then added a little extra.

"He had developed some web applications and cashed in right before the market crashed in '08," the bulky one said. "He lived off the proceeds for a couple of years."

"I always suspected he got some insider information," the geek added, "but he wouldn't confirm it for me. Meanwhile, people like me lost their shirts."

"And then, a few years back," the bulky one said, as if the rancor of his friend was lost in a buzzing maelstrom of thought, "he decided he wasn't happy just sitting around. He decided to build a company from the ground up."

That sounds so familiar, Jaclyn mused, trying to hide her feelings. She shivered a bit as she thought of what Grant Chillings had built before she destroyed it.

"And what company is that?"

"One of the largest computer companies the Pacific Northwest has ever seen."

"Microsoft?" Tom asked.

Bulky snorted.

"Bigger than Microsoft," he said.

***

En route to The Warwick Hotel
Seattle, Washington
Wednesday, June 26
8:45 p.m. PT/11:45 p.m. ET

Jaclyn, Tom, and Tasha had wrapped up their little shindig shortly after 8 p.m. There were still plenty more hugs between 6:30 p.m., when Jaclyn had confirmed what she already knew about Darren Drake, and when the party petered out half an hour later. Jaclyn was a touch distracted by what she had just learned, but she managed to put on a smiling face to all of her former classmates who had come out to see her. There were also plenty of requests to stay in touch. Many gave her their email addresses.

Jaclyn didn't offer hers in return.

They returned to the hotel with submarine sandwiches, a two-liter bottle of Sprite, and a copy of today's *Seattle Times*. Jaclyn didn't bother to check and see if there were any messages waiting for her at the front desk; no one in Justice would be stupid enough to leave a message for her with a complete stranger and a non-existent security clearance. She'd check her email for any missives from Langley or the White House—but those would have to wait a few extra minutes. She had a little more research to do on her old classmate.

Bulky and Geeky had, after telling them that Drake's company was bigger than Microsoft, subtly dropped the hint that he had tried to buy a bit of influence in Washington.

"And he just held a news conference yesterday regarding an application with the FCC about his business and his apps on his devices," Geeky said. "I'm sure there's something in the paper about it."

Jaclyn had blinked twice and firmed her jaw a touch before thanking them for the information. She had picked up a copy of the paper at a sidewalk newsstand and figured that she would read it over dinner.

Still, as they waited for their order to appear on the counter, Jaclyn sat down and whipped off the front section of the paper, while Tom took the sports pages; "I need to see if they have the football scores except for MLS," he had said. Tasha found the funnies easily enough, and before long started giggling over Garfield's antics.

And there, as Jaclyn eased her butt into place against the hard plastic seat, she saw him.

The story was the featured piece on the front page, a large photo that spread from above the fold to below, complete with a red isolation box surrounding it. The photo, of course, was a shot of Darren Drake, the photographer taking the picture from just below the podium, the lens making his nostrils look as if they were the size of a quarter. His mouth was open, the shot capturing him mid-speech.

She read the accompanying story, which indicated just what Bulky and Geeky had said: Drake had filed an application thanks to help from Washington's legislative delegation in order to do away with Net Neutrality.

"So my dear old classmate wants to be the new Apple, at a cheaper rate than the original Apple," she said when they got into the rental and headed back to the hotel; there were a few passersby walking along the sidewalk, and the pizza place was full of patrons. "And he wants to do away with the one thing that keeps the Internet at the same, level playing field for everyone." She started the car and pulled away from the curb. "Another snobby, rich megalomaniac that I am now ninety-nine percent sure votes Republican is trying to gain more power." She hit her directional to change lanes as she wound her way back to Lenora Street, grinding her teeth together as the thought sickened her; she had heard the whispers throughout Langley of those who had Facebook accounts and were liberals, politically, and they found out old classmates with whom they had enjoyed spending time together as children actually leaned to the far right-hand side of the aisle in adulthood. "Just what this country needs: another corporation buying control away from the ones who really should have it."

"Explain that one for me?" Tasha said from the back seat. She had her soda open.

"With pleasure," Jaclyn replied and pulled up to the stop light at the same time. She glanced into the rear view mirror and a reflection-full of Tasha came shooting back at her. "You're a businessman in today's world. What is the one thing you want, the one thing you covet, most of all?"

Her ward offered a shrug. "Money?"

"Yes, but even more than that. Let me re-phrase. When you were in Vegas—"

Tasha rolled her eyes and slumped back into the seat.

"Do we have to bring this up, Jaclyn?"

"Why, yes. It's my right as your matron to do this as I steer you along in the world. When you were in Vegas—" Tasha grumbled something under her breath that Jaclyn didn't pick up on, "—what was the one thing that the pimp wanted more than anything?"

This time, Tasha snorted.

"Other than forcing me to go down on his needle dick? Money from the Johns and Janes."

"Money leads to greed," Jaclyn said, as if ticking the line of thought off the flow chart, "and greed leads to power. Power is the one thing all businessmen want. The pimp wanted money, yes, but he wanted power over you, which he had until I kicked him in the balls." The light turned green, and Jaclyn shifted her feet, sliding the accelerator toward the floor. "Businessmen, once they have money, become greedy for more money, and once they have more money, they want the power and prestige that comes along with the ability to write one's own ticket, shall we say; it's like a drug, and that drug buys congressmen and senators to write laws in their favor and to use their influence with government agencies to look the other way."

"But how does this tie in to Alex's death and the attempts on our lives?" Tom asked.

Jaclyn bit her lip. Her thoughts rolled in a tornado-like maelstrom, trying to find the links of everything she had learned over the last few days.

"I have no idea—yet," she admitted. "It's just not making a lick of sense to me. They said that Drake is still infatuated with me, yet he hired someone to kill me, if we can believe the Advance."

"Not exactly something you'd find in a Hallmark card aisle," Tasha said dryly. "And from what you've said, the Advance as much as admitted it in front of the president."

"Right."

They drove on in silence, a silence that only lasted until they came to Lenora. Jaclyn turned left and slipped over to the left-hand side of the road at once.

"What is Parkerhurst bringing us this time?" Tasha asked as she undid her seat belt.

"No idea," Jaclyn replied. "But whatever it happens to be, you are not to use it to collide with the chest of Darren Drake's hitmen."

Tasha grimaced and snapped her fingers.

"Taking away my fun again."

"As the head of the CIA for the foreseeable future, it's my right to do that," Jaclyn said with a light smirk.

"If I remember correctly," Tom said as he opened the passenger door, "he comes at night, when the least amount of eyes are about, so probably tomorrow night. You'll get a call when we're at your aunt and uncles house."

Jaclyn grimaced and paused.

"It'll give us an excuse to leave, then," she said. Jaclyn got out of the car and tossed the keys to the valet.

"Love, remember: they are family, no matter the distance, no matter the last time you saw them," Tom said.

They entered the hotel.

***

The Warwick Hotel
Lenora Street
Seattle, Washington
Wednesday, June 26/Thursday, June 27
11:07 p.m. PT/2:07 a.m. ET

Too late in the day to call Forrister to give a sit-rep, the three of them ate their subs—Tom practically inhaled his—before Tasha went back to her own room, presumably to watch television. Jaclyn and Tom undressed down to their underwear—Jaclyn had unhooked her bra and pulled it out through her sleeve with a flourish, sending it flying toward the opposite wall—before they tumbled into bed. Tom, despite his exhaustive state, was raring to go, as Jaclyn noticed a rigid tent coming to life in his boxer briefs. She smirked.

"Think you're getting lucky tonight?" she said as she slipped her shirt off, leaving her standing at the foot of the bed in a skimpy pair of black, lacy bikini briefs. She hooked her thumbs into the sides as she awaited her husband's answer. A subtle rise in his eyebrows and a sure cockiness in his grin prompted her to drop them before she climbed into bed, slipping under the covers and letting her hands roam wherever they happened to land.

An hour later, the clock next to the bed reading 11:07 p.m. in bold red numerals, Jaclyn kicked her feet out from under the sheets as the cool air from the baseboard vents, purring through on low, nibbled at her sweat-stained flesh. She still had the sheet above her breasts, all while she leaned against her husband, who had his arms behind his head, as if victorious from an arduous battle. They had hopefully managed, they thought, to keep their exertions to a dull roar so they wouldn't disturb Tasha in the next room, or let her know through any deep, extraneous vocal inflections that they were, as she was wont to say, getting freaky-deaky over here.

Jaclyn listened to Tom's heart through his chest as she thought about today, just as he slipped into Slumberville. She lightly scratched at his chest with her nails.

She thought about the party, and how it was great—albeit uncomfortable for her—to see her once long-lost classmates. Many of them, she believed, seemed star struck in her presence, and Jaclyn, for some strange reason, understood the reasons why. She was a world-famous model and a terrorist killer, to boot, and she had elevated herself above the teenage drama she would have endured had she stayed in Renton after the death of her parents. She had changed greatly, and it felt, in some ways, that she was an outsider to everyone. Yes, they were all friendly and cordial and wanting to know how she was and what she had been up to—well, they had asked about the things she couldn't talk about, the things that were in the papers instead of the things that were under lock and key at Langley—but there were moments when she became ignored and somewhat pushed over to the side, and she seemingly stood there waiting for someone to speak to her.

But the real eye-opening part of the day came while she spoke about Darren Drake with Bulky and Geeky, his two pre-teen confidantes. They had given her so much insight in so few words that it made her head twist about and look back on the time when she thought she knew him. He was a kind boy in their prepubescent years, she recalled now, and quite attentive toward her. And there was a bashful quality about him, too, one that, as her memory took her back a decade and a half, and even longer, she finally recognized as one of puppy love. He had a crush, a hard one, and she didn't reciprocate those feelings. She did remember, though, kissing him on the cheek before she left for D.C. under Alex's charge.

How did he hold onto these strong feelings for me when I hadn't been around for him to look at me for this long? she thought.

Then the next thought, as she remembered her conversation with Bulky and Geeky, flung her eyelids back and brought her world full-circle.

My modeling pictures, the covers, she thought. *The shrine. They said he had built a shrine to me, and it was full of them. I've been modeling for years. There are plenty of pictures out there, plenty of shots of me in whatever article of clothing they threw me in, dancing about the Internet. There are so many that Drake could fill two walls, and maybe more*.

Jaclyn frowned, then pulled herself away from Tom's embrace. He didn't move or awaken. She shivered as the air bit at the newly-exposed skin.

Damn, she thought, sitting on the edge of the bed. *There are some people who need to move the fuck on with their lives instead of getting hung up on a perceived grade school romance. I know that high school sweethearts go on and get married, but this is ridiculous. I never gave him any indication that I was interested in him, and even so—I was fucking part-blind! Mommy and daddy were rather protective of me going outside, even if I had some gal pals over. Can you imagine daddy's ire if he knew a boy was interested in me?*

Jaclyn stood and walked to where she had stashed the pants she had worn today. She slipped her hand into the pockets and found the slip of paper she had stashed there. Pulling it out, she checked to make sure it was the right one and, once she discovered it was, she grabbed her iPad. She went straight to the Bing Maps URL and typed in the address into the search function. She took a deep breath and clicked the spyglass icon.

She didn't let the breath go until the address popped up on the screen.

Using the bird's eye view, Jaclyn got a good look at the property Darren Drake had bought, thanks to the address Bulky and Geeky had handed to her. It was a rather sprawling estate in Inglewood, and it lived up to all she had heard about that town while growing up in Renton. Inglewood was, according to her group of gal pals, a rather affluent city to the north of Seattle proper. It wasn't Beverly Hills, but she knew that it wasn't beautiful, downtown Compton, either. She had never been in Inglewood; even though she had lived in the Seattle area for a few years, there were some parts of the metropolitan region she had left unexplored by her person.

But there is always a first time for everything, she thought as she sat down in the chair, nude, the iPad in her lap.

Bulky had relayed the layout to her, and with her seeing the property for the first time, his memory was spot on. The main house was rather large, as it was two stories tall and sprawling away from the main entrance like a blocky, stone boomerang. The main entrance itself had a high arch with gargoyles clinging to the façade, with a wide lawn separated from itself by a rather wide, curving driveway. Jaclyn used her thumb and forefinger to rotate the image, giving her a view of the property from the backyard—which was just as immense as the front. There was an Olympic-sized, in-ground swimming pool—Jaclyn shook her head at the thought of how much Drake spent every year on chlorine, but figured he had the ability to afford it—along with a sizable back lawn that, if he wanted to and money somehow grew tight in the bank account, was rentable to the Sounders or Seahawks as a practice facility: the White House and the surrounding property, Jaclyn figured, had nothing on this place.

But it was the smaller two-story building just behind the pool house that drew her attention. The pool house was tiny, almost like a shed—but Jaclyn knew, from Bulky's description, that all the yard tools, including a massive John Deere riding mower, were almost a football field away to the northeast—and it fronted this building; in fact, Jaclyn discovered that they were built into each other, as if the pool house was an entrance to the larger structure behind it.

The shrine is in this building, Jaclyn mused, *if Bulky's words were correct, but also the security service that overlooked the property was in here, too.* She tapped the screen and took a look at it, looking for any way into it. Her heart raced at a furious pace as she looked for an outcropping, a balcony, anything—until she found what looked like a wrought-iron fence that resembled the fire escapes which had clawed at the brownstones in Boston, or the back entrance to the Football Association's old headquarters in London's Soho Square.

A tiny smile filled her face as she figured a way in for herself.

Then she remembered—*I'm not exactly alone in this, and Tom's not going to let me get inside by myself. And Tasha will be one pissed off little lady if I leave her out of this, too.*

Jaclyn let a bit of air blast off as she lowered the iPad, her face darkening, just as Tom stirred.

"Baby? Everything all right over there?" he said a few moments later. He sounded half awake.

"Yeah, I'm fine. Just doing a bit of extra surveillance on Drake's place."

"Put your glasses on and come back to bed, love. I'd like a look-see, too"

Smirking, Jaclyn stood and carried the iPad over to the bedside, where she had her HUD. Once they were on her face, Tom turned on the bedside lamp. She slipped back into bed and snuggled up close to him, feeling his furnace-like body up against hers. She suppressed a shiver as she passed the iPad over to him.

"It's like he said," he replied after a few moments. "That's the shrine building he talked about, right?"

Jaclyn kissed his forehead.

"Yep."

"And you've zoomed in on this bloody thing that reminds me of the F—"

Jaclyn interrupted him, lowering her lips to his and dragging the iPad out of his reach, off to the side. She forced the kiss to go deeper, until he reclined back, his head and shoulders hitting the pillow. Their tongues mingled together until she pulled the sheet down below his waist, exposing him to the world. She swung her right leg over his body and straddled him, slipping her hand down and grasping him; she grinned even as their lips remained together as she felt him swell in her palm. A few slow, methodical strokes later, she led him in just before she broke off the kiss, reaching over and slapping the light off, plunging their suite into utter darkness. Her HUD followed in the same general direction as the iPad, before she leaned toward his left ear.

"I don't want to talk about this any longer tonight," she purred as she sank onto him. Once she reached the hilt, she kissed his jaw line to his chin, then up to his lips. She felt his hands on her hips, his fingertips making tiny circles in her flesh; his thumbs traced a light line on the skin between her legs and waist. "It can wait until the morning when all three of us are looking at it. Besides, that FA thing is still classified."

The look in his eyes told her he understood her meaning. She thought she had him right where she wanted him—until he grabbed her around the waist in a bear hug and turned the tables on her, putting her on her back. This time, she had her arms snaked around the back of his neck as they touched foreheads. The iPad and HUD were a few inches away, but they had forgotten about them—for now.

Jaclyn couldn't help but give a low, throaty moan as Tom started rocking into her.

Chapter 11
Darren Drake's estate
Inglewood, North Seattle, Washington
Wednesday, June 26/Thursday, June 27
11:33 p.m. PT/2:33 a.m. ET

Drake's home office was in the main house, on the second floor in the rear, overlooking the pool and the vast swath of greenery he paid out the ass to keep manicured. His desk was positioned next to a window, the oaken furniture covered with sales data, as well as two flat-panel monitors for two desktop computers. An open laptop had its screensaver up—a picture of a relatively attractive blonde-haired woman wearing nothing but a terrycloth bathrobe—to his left. Outside in the moonlight, he heard the sloshing of water as that same woman—his current business partner—did her nightly laps, presumably in the nude as was her custom.

Drake smirked as he peered through the glass at the crystal clear water. There was a touch of froth about as the woman darted forward beneath the near-glassy surface; he saw the unmistakable line that parted her gluteus, even though it meandered and waved at him with wet hands. He turned his attention back to the multiple screens.

On one, he had Twitter up on several tabs, each with a different hashtag queued up. On the other, his real-time sales graphs on one tab, while his email queue took up another. He took a deep breath and looked at the time in the lower right-hand corner.

It read 11:36 p.m.

Okay, he thought, *here we go. Time to put part of my plan*—our plan, he corrected himself—*into action.*

He picked up his landline phone and dialed a number he knew all too well. It rang twice.

"Yes, Mr. Drake?" the voice on the other end answered. It belonged, Drake knew, to the pimply-faced computer operative he had hired fresh out of college a few months ago, a young man who reminded him so much of an old school chum, except without the encumbering weight problem in his trunk. He was a good kid, was always polite, but now it was time for Drake to corrupt him for the rest of his life.

"Are you ready to proceed with the task I have presented to you?"

There was a brief pause on the line before the voice replied, "Yes."

"Still have any misgivings with what you're to do?" Drake demanded.

He heard a bit of a shake come through the line.

"Not at all."

"Good," Drake said with a bit of a smile. He figured that was how Darth Vader reacted when Lando Calrissian acquiesced to his demands in *The Empire Strikes Back*. "You may proceed with the operation."

He rubbed his lips together furiously as the clicking of keys filtered through the connection, the kid typing at such a speed that Drake's mind spun on its axis. The operation was a relatively high-speed one; with it being late at night, most computer companies and websites had a skeleton crew on staff in order to maintain the system and to fix any bugs that cropped up.

But they have never, ever dealt with a coded bug like the one Drake was about to inflict on their systems—and more importantly, their sales systems.

The youngster had shown him, when Drake had asked, just how simple it would be for him to break into their mainframe without leaving a single digital fingerprint. It was only a few keystrokes as soon as he fiddled with the site's coding. One diversion in the code would muck it all up.

Drake wanted to go further than muck it all up.

He wanted to completely annihilate the code.

"Their security is like crepe paper," the young man said. "I feel like I'm intruding on a junior high dance, not a website of commerce."

Drake chuckled.

"They're not ready for high school, then. Once you're done preparing the codes for this one, move on to the next, then the third one. Then execute the files one at a time, right after the other. Then," he said, "we wait for the shit to hit the fan."

His operative clicked the keys several more times. Drake leaned back and waited patiently for everything to finish up, waited for the moment to arrive. By then, he had heard the sounds of water had lessened from outside, until he heard doors down the hall open and close. His body shifted, the chair rotating a quarter of a revolution to the left as he waited for his guest to emerge.

Shadows wrapped around the foyer to his office for a brief moment before a woman, clad in a white, terrycloth bathrobe, appeared in the doorway with a sultry smile. The robe was open only a little, but it was enough for him to see the inside curves of her pale breasts all the way to her stubble-flecked groin. She hadn't put on anything else after her swim, and her hair, just a bit darker now, was still damp and slicked back over her ears, down to just below her shoulders.

He covered the receiver.

"Have a good swim?"

She nodded.

"Yes, of course. Doing my laps every night keeps my heart racing during the day. Among other things," the vixen said, her grin shining. She perched herself on the edge of his desk, the robe hanging open. He tried to keep his eyes on hers instead of looking further south. "How is the operation going?"

He shrugged.

"It is proceeding as planned."

"Excellent. It will give the news stations something to chase while I start the next stage," she said. "And it will, eventually, mean the death of that jumped-up Army brat, which I've been waiting for for so long." She turned her head and looked at the screens.

Drake smiled half-heartedly.

"Mr. Drake," the voice on the other end said, "everything is officially ready. I'm in all three. The virus is ready."

"Are you sure the new code is layered?" Drake asked as he brought the receiver back to his lips.

This time, the young computer programmer's response had no delay.

"I'm absolutely positive that it is."

"Very well. Start the next step in the sabotage, and then lock it up nice and tidy."

"As ordered."

"Let me know when it is—no, never mind. I'll check in on Twitter. Everything will go there. Trust me on that."

He hung up without another word, then made sure that all of the screens were ready to show the aftermath of what he had just set in motion.

"Now, we will see just how panicked people are when they can't access their precious stores to buy their apps," he said to her.

"How long will it take?"

"Not long, I suppose." He brought the mouse over to the tab marked "Google" and clicked it. He found a gray bar with a number of unread tweets. He clicked that, and the tweets came into view. There was nothing regarding what he wanted to see yet, but he was a patient fellow. He did the same with the tab marked "iTunes" and then another marked "Apple."

Still, nothing.

Drake expelled a heavy shot of air from his nostrils as he waited for something to happen. He reached over and grabbed a can of soda, the fizz still tinkling against the aluminum as he brought it to his dry mouth. He felt a bead of sweat build on the back of his neck, his heart thumping a little wilder than before. Nothing was happening.

Yet as he took his bottom lip between his teeth, the panic began.

But the panic wasn't on his end.

It was on his prospective customers' end.

The tweets began with innocent questions of "Is the network down? I need to get that new game" or "How much longer until the site is back up? This is not good for eBusiness in this century." But after a few minutes, and with it nearing midnight, Drake knew several well-known computer businesses were in trouble, their sales tanking.

Showing two rows of perfect teeth, he opened a message window and put his fingers on the keyboard. The feel was perfect as he typed away.

"Reading," he mouthed aloud as he typed, "about the problems with my competition's stores. No problems with my store! Come over and see." He inserted a shortlink, plus a few important hashtags, then pressed Tweet. It appeared half a moment later.

"And now," he said to his business partner, "we monitor just exactly how our commercial sabotage is now worth to us."

The woman came over and slipped her body out of the robe, the heavy material dropping to the floor before she eased up behind him. Drake turned and slid the mouse about, making sure that the desktop didn't go to the screensaver while she brought her hands to his shoulders, easing her nimble fingers over his shirt, moving them to the base of his neck. He groaned lightly, settling back into his chair a little deeper. Together, they watched the real-time sales numbers slowly begin their climb, the graph turning into a steep, upward slide.

Drake grinned.

"It seems that it's working. Our sales are slowly going through the roof. By tomorrow morning, we should have a better idea of how many of my devices have been purchased tonight."

"And how much of that can be funneled my way?" she asked. "And how quickly?"

"Within hours, after the vendors are paid," Drake said. "I'm so lucky that I'm going to make more money on the apps that I'm willing to have you bend me over a barrel and send laundered funds to you."

"You send me the money because you've almost finished off the move to Oakland," the woman said. "And you love being bent over. Don't deny it."

Drake grunted as she reached over him and cupped his groin. She looked up with a look of pure lust in her eyes.

"Maybe when I get back from Portland Saturday morning," he said, his tone growing husky with each passing moment.

She squeezed him before she launched her lips at his. Her mouth mauled his, both taking in air through their nostrils until neither of them could breathe, just before their mouths opened. Tongues, feral and wet, sought out the other as the dance endured.

In the moment, Drake's mind whirled as she forced herself on him, and forced him to go along with her deviance. Soon, he found himself over the top of his desk, his pants and underwear at his ankles, and her behind him.

Just look at the sales numbers rise, he thought just as her tongue made contact.

Chapter 12
The Home of William and Anna Johnson
Forbes Creek Drive
Kirkland, Washington
Thursday, June 27
6:02 p.m. PT/9:02 p.m. ET

Jaclyn had spent most of Thursday catching up on CIA-related work while the three of them rested in their hotel. Fulfilling her role as the interim director, she spent several hours in a secure Skype conference with not only the president and the National Security Council, but she also privately briefed the president with what had happened so far in Seattle. There wasn't much to say, except the whole "Drake is still infatuated with me" thing they had learned while at Pike Place yesterday.

"Tread carefully, Jaclyn," Forrister had said. "We know what this scumbag is capable of, and we think he's responsible for taking out the app stores of several major computer companies last night. They've stopped selling, while his rankings rise, unaffected. And Jaclyn, you'll be receiving a call from Parkerhurst this evening. Be sure to clear your schedule after the dinner hour and await his arrival."

Jaclyn had shivered.

It is like I feared, she thought. *He is gaining more and more power. This sounds so much like—*

Her thoughts trailed off.

"I will wrap this up soon, sir, and I'll be sure to do the second thing." she had said, before she hung up and turned to Tom and Tasha. "Second thing's first: Parkerhurst is on the way." Tasha smiled and clapped her hands. "And in unrelated news, Drake's turned into Chillings." She explained her meaning, bringing up the Boston mission and how she had stopped a dangerous terrorist from poisoning that city's water supply, even after the deaths of nearly fifty people on City Hall Plaza, the poisoning of children at a Little League game, and the death of her then-partner, Mark Hanson. She wanted to refresh Tom's memory; she had told him all about it before she had departed London that first time. She wanted to bring Tasha up to speed, having never told her this adventure; she wasn't sure if Tasha had read the missive while under Alex's private tutelage.

She wanted to let them know what they were up against.

"It's basically as I thought yesterday. He's gaining power through economics and sabotage," she said, then relayed what the president had told her. "They want him in custody pretty quick, and they want me to rake him over the coals just as quickly."

"Think you can put the past behind you?" Tasha asked.

"It's already behind me." She checked her watch. "I suspect I should call my aunt and uncle and see if there's any way to postpone—"

"Don't even think about it, Snapshot," Tom warned. "It's already been postponed once. We can't postpone it again."

Jaclyn nodded, albeit reluctantly.

It was another warm day in Seattle, as summer took a hold of the Pacific Northwest even as June marched to its close, readying itself to welcome July with open arms. There was no rain in sight, either, until Saturday or Sunday, depending on which television station one watched. The three of them chose to dress in loose-fitting clothing, the girls in light sundresses and flip-flops—Jaclyn was wary of this; what if Drake or his henchmen interrupted their gathering, and Jaclyn had to make a mad dash after the culprit, leaping around the potato salad? The click-clock of her footwear would be an incredible burden—while Tom wore a white polo shirt, tan khaki shorts, and blue canvas shoes. None of them carried a weapon. Jaclyn wore the HUD, as her extended family had never seen her without it. She did, however, have on her contacts underneath it.

Jaclyn drove them out to her aunt and uncle's home in Kirkland, located on the eastern shore of Lake Washington. They crossed the lake on 520 East before venturing north on Interstate 405. They exited at 20A, took the left-hand turning when they got to the end of the off-ramp, turned onto Northeast 116th Street, and left again onto 120th Avenue. A right and a left later, and they were on the road that would take them to their final destination for the afternoon.

She gripped the wheel rather tightly as they approached. There were several developments off to the right-hand side, and nothing but trees to the left. Jaclyn felt her heart beat out a basso nova with every tenth of a mile that passed them by. She tried swallowing what remained of her spit, if only to dampen her throat, until, at last, she came to the driveway. She turned right into it, and put the car in park. Almost immediately, she spotted a woman, one about her age, looking out at them through the screen door at the side porch.

"Ready, love?" Tom asked from the passenger seat.

Jaclyn smiled.

"As ready as I'll ever be."

"Let's do it then."

They got out of the rental and headed toward the door. The woman who had stood there as they pulled into the driveway had disappeared, but as Jaclyn approached, another woman, this one older and recognizable, took her place. This woman opened the creaky screen door with, quite possibly, the widest smile Jaclyn had ever seen.

"Jaclyn," the woman said breathless. "I can't believe it's you. How much you've grown!"

For the first time during this trip, Jaclyn felt her heart soar as she watched her aunt come down the two wooden stairs with her arms stretched wide. Smiling, Jaclyn embraced her.

"Hi, Aunt Anna," she said.

Their embrace lasted a few seconds as a decade and a half melted away. Jaclyn didn't even feel a shiver overtake her as the closeness grew. Her aunt released her.

"And who is this young man?" she asked. "And this young lady?"

"Aunt Anna, let me introduce you to my husband, Tom Messingham, and the young lady is my ward and protégé, Tasha Verkler."

Anna Johnson, Jaclyn saw, tried not to weep. She flung her arms around Tom, who had smiled through it all. "Welcome to the family, Tom. And you, too, Tasha." She gave Tasha a hug that seemingly swallowed her. She turned to Jaclyn. "Your uncle and cousins are out on the patio. Come on."

They entered the house, and Jaclyn smelled barbecue sauce wafting through the rear screen door on the air right away. From the outside, it looked like any other on this street, complete with vinyl siding—their house was somewhere between pale baby blue and periwinkle—and a steep, gabled rooftop; the windows had faux black shutters with the letters W and A in a fine script on each. The lawn was perfectly manicured without a sign of dandelion or crab grass or clover, running right up to the mulched circles around the trees. There were spots of peonies around the edge of the house, along with a well-pruned rhododendron. What had remained of the pansies in the spring mulch clung to life.

Inside was everything Jaclyn had remembered of her aunt and uncle's house. The wall-to-wall hardwood floors, the polished wood paneling on the walls surrounding their in-wall oven from floor to ceiling. The fridge was stainless steel instead of the white thing most people owned, and the sink was stainless steel, too.

"Bill!" Anna Johnson called. "Jaclyn's here!"

"Great! Send her out!" called a booming voice from outside.

Anna chuckled.

"You heard him. Let me take this off your hands, Tom," she said, grabbing the trifle and setting it in the fridge. "Anything to drink, you three?"

Jaclyn and Tasha had asked for a soda, while Tom had a beer that Jaclyn knew he would nurse for the evening. Their drinks in hand, Jaclyn led the three of them to the backyard. She slid the screen door open and stepped on the covered patio.

The smiling faces of her cousins, Paul and Phillip, met her as she exited the house, and she smiled back. To her enhanced vision, they looked happy to see her. They wore nearly the same thing Tom did, although Phillip, she noticed, was barefoot, while Paul wore sandals. The women with them also wore sundresses, and were just as beautiful as Jaclyn. Her uncle had his back to her as he worked the grill, flames crackling as he turned meat over. In the yard, a quartet of children, two boys and two girls, played football together. The tallest one, Jaclyn saw, was the quarterback.

The older boys stood up and embraced their cousin.

"Hi skinny," Paul, the older one, said. He had a wide smile that didn't seem to end. "Is this your husband?"

"Yep, this is Tom. Tom, my cousin Paul, and his wife—"

"Sarah," the black-haired woman said. While Paul and Tom shook hands, Sarah held out a hand, which Jaclyn took, before Sarah kissed her on her cheek. "It's so good to finally meet you." Jaclyn felt her cheeks turn fiery.

Phillip was next, introducing his wife, Kathy, a blonde beauty. Jaclyn introduced Tasha to them, before she heard the grill cover closing shut. Her uncle turned around.

He was the spitting image of her father. He had the same build she recalled the general having, with a broad chest and strong arms. He had rosy cheeks, which she figured was due to the dark glass bottle of Avatar Jasmine India Pale Ale from Seattle's Elysian Brewery next to the grill. He wore a light teal Mariners t-shirt and blue and white plaid shorts that showed two feet of well-tanned leg. His hair, once brown like her father's, had turned white over the last fifteen-plus years.

"My niece," he said, "my beautiful, grown-up niece. Come here, girl."

Jaclyn grinned and came forward, her uncle's arms wrapping around her and enveloping her in a tremendous hug. There was the smell of beer, of course, as well as the smell of Right Guard and talc. And even though she smelled the aromas of barbecued chicken breasts clinging to his t-shirt, she felt the love pouring forth from her father's only sibling. It wasn't a hug like Tom gave her every day, or the way she felt his love when they held each other after making love in their own bed, but it was different and the same all at once.

It was a love she had not felt in over a decade.

Then she heard the sounds of tears and sobbing, and she thought it was her aunt appearing on the patio, overcome with emotion at seeing them together after their long separation.

She quickly realized, as they broke the hug and looked toward the entryway back into the house proper, that it wasn't her aunt that wept. She wasn't even on the patio.

It was her, and her own tears she heard.

The skin under her eyes had grown wet, and she tried to be sly about slipping her fingers up underneath her sunglasses to dry them. It didn't work. Tom came over and wrapped his arms around his wife, comforting her.

"Hello, sir. I'm Tom Messingham," Tom said, holding his hand out. Bill Johnson took it.

"Uncle Bill, this is my husband," Jaclyn finally said. "And this is my ward, Tasha."

"Good," he said with a smile. "Good. I'm so glad you're happy, honey. Ed and Martha would be so proud of how you've grown." There was an awkward pause, but it was brief. "The chicken should be done in a few minutes. Boys, let's get that table set."

"Eddie, Patrick! Patricia, Mary! Come on, help Grandpa set the table," Phillip had called to his children and nieces while he and his brother stayed seated, beers in hand. The wives, Jaclyn noticed, smacked their husbands off the shoulder as if in tune with each other. The children came running.

"Which one is Eddie?" she asked as Bill Johnson turned back to the grill. A gray cloud of smoke and steam rose up from within the depths. Paul pointed to the eldest one, who looked about seven years old. The others looked a couple of years younger and a head shorter.

"We named him in honor of Uncle Eddie," he said, holding Sarah's hand. He, like his brother and father, drank an Elysian IPA, while the wives drank tall glasses of pinot grigio. "It was really the only thing I've wanted to do since 9-11, and my beloved agreed that it was a pretty darn good idea other than asking her out."

Jaclyn grinned.

"Thank you so much," she said, fearful that she was about to turn on the water works again.

Uncle Bill brought a heavy platter of chicken breasts toward the table, the food resembling Mount Rainier. He set it right in the heart of the long red picnic table before going back for hot dogs and hamburgers for his grandchildren. Jaclyn's aunt brought out a vast bowl of potato salad, while the girls—Jaclyn had asked her aunt if she needed any help, which was quickly shot down—grabbed bowls of pasta and tossed salads. Jaclyn's little second cousins, who blushed and went silent when Kathy and Sarah introduced them to her, carried out a long plate of condiments, while Eddie brought out a crockpot. Jaclyn caught the smell once it was set on the table, and it triggered a memory she had thought lost to time and distance.

It was her mother's special recipe for barbecue baked beans. She smiled, and simply inhaled.

"There looks like enough food here to feed the Blues and Royals three times over," Tom said. "Thank God I didn't eat much at lunch."

"We like to make sure our guests are comfortable and have no reason for wants while they're here," Bill Johnson said as he sat down at the head of the table, next to Jaclyn. He lifted the lid to the crockpot; a veil of steam erupted, and he intentionally wafted it and its accompanying aromas toward his niece. "And seeing as this is a special occasion and the reuniting of my whole family for the first time in quite a while, we couldn't help but pull out all the stops."

The full Johnson clan all looked at Jaclyn with looks of love and admiration.

"I'm so glad you did," Jaclyn said, smiling. There was no sarcasm in her tone.

So this is what I've been missing all these years, she thought as her uncle served her some chicken. Whatever awkwardness she thought would happen at this gathering evaporated into the ether.

They all tucked in.

***

Once Aunt Anna, with the help of her daughters-in-law, had put away all the leftovers—and Jaclyn noticed there was so much food she had the feeling there would be three doggy bags headed back to Seattle—it gave Jaclyn the chance to talk with her aunt and uncle. Tasha played with the kids, while her cousins and their wives kept Tom occupied. Jaclyn heard some laughter coming from her husband, her cousins pulling him out of his British shell.

"We're so glad you got the opportunity to come back after everything that happened last weekend," Anna Johnson said. "The gentleman who had contacted us and told us about the unveiling of Eddie's statue had said you'd be unavailable to see us the next day. That had us rather confused."

Under her HUD, Jaclyn blinked. The unveiling was scheduled for the day after Alex's death, and she knew who had contacted them.

"He did? When did he say that?" she asked.

"The day you arrived," her uncle replied. "Why would he say that?"

Jaclyn settled back in her lawn chair a little deeper as she pondered this new piece of information. It only solidified what she already knew, and reinforced the idea that she was the true target: that Hill, the Advance, had betrayed not only her, but also the president and Alex. She wouldn't tell her aunt and uncle this. She brought her fingertips together and tapped them a few times.

"Jaclyn?" her uncle said. "Is everything all right?"

After a few moments, Jaclyn nodded.

"They will be. Let's just say that you'll never hear from him again, and he's not in charge of the re-schedule." Jaclyn reached over to her left and pulled a beer out of the cooler. A bottle opener hung on a thick strand of twine, taped to the cooler's roof. She uncapped it and drank deeply, if only to settle her anger.

"Jaclyn, I have to ask you this, and it's only because you're my late brother's only child—are you all right? Have you really been okay these last fifteen years or so?"

She nodded and smiled.

"I've been great. I've been shot at a few times, but I've been fine."

"We had no idea what had happened to you," Anna had said. "We were on that trip to Los Angeles, and of course, your parents had gone east. The boys were with my parents, God rest their souls. And then we couldn't get home. No buses or trains were running at a rapid rate. And forget about flying."

"And when we got home and found out that Ed and Martha were gone," Bill added, "my first instinct was to make sure you were okay. I made the drive to Renton faster than I think I've ever done it; got pulled over for going a few miles over the limit while I was at it. And when I got there—"

"I was already gone," Jaclyn finished for him. She grimaced just as she felt her heart skip a long beat. An emptiness she had felt once before took over. "I'm sorry."

Bill waved it aside.

"It wasn't your fault. There wasn't a memorial service for Ed and Martha, even though there should have been." Jaclyn noticed her uncle was venting now, as if he had bottled everything up over the last decade and a half. She knew he wasn't mad at her for what had happened, but it made her appreciate him all the more; it made her *love* him all the more. A couple of tears, Jaclyn saw, had formed in her uncle's eyes. "I miss my brother, now more than the years we were separated. For quite a while, our family was broken; there were missing pieces, so much so that we didn't know where to turn. We had to stay strong for your cousins. Over time, we recovered, and we added those beauties to the family; they made us whole again. And now, for the first time in quite a while, you're back to fill a piece we thought missing to us for years."

Jaclyn tried to keep the tears at bay, but she failed. Her aunt reached over and held her hand; she squeezed back. Words failed her.

They sat in silence for a few minutes until Jaclyn finally removed the HUD to wipe her eyes. She heard a gasp.

Looking up, with the twilight overtaking them slowly, she saw them staring at her.

"You found a cure?" Anna said, her hand on her chest.

"No," Jaclyn replied. "The government took care of me a few years ago. I still wear the sunglasses most of the time. I can wear the contacts, but really can't wear just the contacts for long periods."

Her uncle swallowed.

"I can't get over how much you look like Martha now," Bill said. He looked like he would weep any minute, but he took a deep breath and controlled it. Jaclyn felt tears rising, too; her face felt numb. "They would like Tom. Where'd you meet him?"

Jaclyn sniffed and set the HUD in her lap.

"We met in London, after his father died. The morning after, actually. During the Olympics."

"We had heard you were involved with that," Anna said.

"Everyone, unfortunately, did," Jaclyn replied, silently cursing the dead soul of Dick Bennett. "I was a prisoner in my own country in the aftermath."

"And Tasha?"

Jaclyn smiled at the memory of driving south on the Strip, seeing the then-16-year-old in the stereotypical Catholic schoolgirl kilt.

"Vegas."

"You've seen a lot in a short time, then."

Jaclyn nodded slowly.

"Yeah," she said. "I have."

***

Thursday, June 27/Friday, June 28
9:25 p.m. PT/12:25 a.m. ET

When the evening finally drew to a close, there were long hugs between Jaclyn and her long lost relatives. Her cousins, once learning she had a Facebook page, made sure to friend request her, along with their wives. Jaclyn had planned on getting rid of her account after the planned meet-up at the

Zig Zag, but now with family on it, she couldn't just delete it and disappear from their lives with a snap of her fingers—or a click of the mouse. They handed her their numbers, but unlike with her classmates, she did likewise.

And the boys—well, the boys apologized for how they and their friends treated her when they were kids.

Tom and Tasha made their way to the car while the boys, their wives, and the kids—Eddie had made sure he spent some time with Jaclyn, too—said their good byes, and went back in the house. Jaclyn hung back with her aunt and uncle.

"Are you sure you're okay, Jaclyn?" Bill Johnson asked.

Her arms crossed, Jaclyn nodded.

"I'm sure. My life was, for a time, in flux. I didn't know how I would get through life without mom and dad, but Alex helped me adjust, and she turned me into what I am today. I'm happy now. I have Tom, I have Tasha to look out for. I have great responsibilities to the country."

"We understand, sweetie," Anna said. "But remember that you still have family here who loves you."

"You can come home whenever you want," Bill added. "We'll always leave the light on for you three."

Jaclyn's face twisted as she rushed forward and hugged her uncle. Once again, his arms, corded and massive, swallowed her.

"I know."

"We love you, Peanut. We always have."

Jaclyn nodded against his chest.

"I love you, too."

She gave a kiss to her uncle before switching places with her aunt, hugging and kissing her, too. She waved good bye before she walked to her rental.

"We'll see you at the reschedule," Bill said.

"You've got it."

She waved one more time before getting in.

"That was a good visit, eh love?" Tom said as soon as she had her seatbelt buckled.

"It was." Jaclyn started the car and flicked the headlights on. "It was good to see them."

"And you're going to see them again soon."

Jaclyn nodded as she put it into reverse and backed out of the driveway.

"Of course. They said," she replied, getting a little choked up, "they said we can come home any time."

Tom smiled and patted her hand, slipping his fingers into hers. She pulled away, headed back to Seattle the way they came.

"Good. I didn't think it was right that you didn't get the chance to see family in the last few years when we've seen mine a few times. I'm glad you've gotten the chance to reconnect with them and re-establish your lives."

Jaclyn felt her heart skip a solitary beat.

"Yeah," she said with a smile. "Me, too."

Chapter 13
North Parking Lot
CenturyLink Field
800 Occidental Avenue South
Seattle, Washington
Friday, June 28
12:48 a.m. PT/3:48 a.m. ET

Jaclyn swallowed the vast well of emotions and remembered she had a job, a rather important job, to do. Yes, she was glad that she had re-connected with her father's family; the twelve terrorists who had taken over those four jets on September 11th hadn't robbed her of her family and life after all. It was something she now took pride deep within herself, something she knew she would use the next time she went up against a dangerous foreign-born terrorist with the testicles—not to mention the nerve and the pure stupidity—to attack the United States of America.

Of course, she knew she wasn't going up against an extremist Muslim hell-bent on trying to make her country kowtow to their perverse sense of right this time. No, she knew what she was up against: one of her own, one who had the sheer audacity to go after her for reasons she truly didn't know. And it was time to expose him for what he just happened to be—a duplicitous, deranged domestic terrorist.

But in order to do that, she needed a car.

The three of them changed into dark clothing when they returned to the hotel on Lenora Street, discarding the light summer clothes for something a little more suited for late-night surveillance. Jaclyn didn't have her essentials with her, much like she didn't when the three of them went on vacation to Sydney. She had received assurances she would have them tonight. For now, she wore dark pants and a black shirt. She would change in the cab of the tractor trailer.

When it was just about 12:30 a.m., Jaclyn, Tom, and Tasha got into the rental car and headed toward the Sound, but Jaclyn turned left onto Western Avenue and followed that road south. The roads were practically empty, despite to being late Thursday night and early Friday morning. The clubs were more than likely still going on, which meant the area should be well-protected from any stray voyeurs to the transfer of important secret agent materials.

She had received the text a few minutes beforehand, letting her know the site of the transfer was ready. She had made the trip already and knew how to get there, and thanks to the lack of traffic at this time of night, easily made it with time to spare.

There, in the North Parking Lot of CenturyLink Field, the home of her precious Sounders and Seahawks, she saw the long, black tractor trailer which had made several trips around this country—and even to international locales, too—framed by the famed north end and the north tower; behind the tower, she caught a glimpse, a shadowy glimpse, of the Safeco Field roof, retracted and yanked toward right field. Red warning lights blinked on and off atop the structures. She saw that the trailer had its rear compartment opened and the ramp already pulled out to the pavement, with floodlights rising off the truck's rear end to illuminate the area. She soon felt her heart thumping away, as if her subconscious pressed the accelerator to the floor. With a quick *snick*, Jaclyn hit the directional and turned into the near-empty parking lot. She revved the engine twice as she pulled up to the side of the trailer. The three of them got out the rental for the last time.

In the rear, she found two men, both familiar to her. One wore jeans and a plain white t-shirt, while the other looked as though he had just stepped out of a menswear catalog. The latter's tie was crisp and attached to his shirt with a tie clip, the bottom flap of the tie defying gravity when he bent over. He straightened as soon as Jaclyn and her crew approached the trailer's rear. There was nary a wrinkle in his khakis, she saw. The other—Charlie, the driver—raced up the ramp, thundering away without a word, as per usual.

And as usual, Parkerhurst had a smile applied that Jaclyn knew would slip downward when she went on the inevitable tangent of frivolity which marked their meetings. She tried to keep the giggle rippling through her mind from spilling out.

"Good evening, Snapshot. Scouser, Sex Kitten," Parkerhurst said, nodding to each as he addressed them. Both smiled his way, Tasha adding an inflection of curling fingers as she waved. "I'm sure that you are all ready to take on a dangerous terrorist causing havoc in the Pacific Northwest, so we'll get right to it—"

"Hold on," Jaclyn interrupted. She stepped forward and wrapped her arms around the back of his neck. Surprisingly, Parkerhurst reciprocated. A hint of musky aftershave caught Jaclyn's nostrils, along with the aroma of McDonald's French fries. "Are you doing okay, old friend?"

She heard Parkerhurst swallow hard. They had not spoken since before she had gone to Seattle initially, before their worlds had turned into this new, abrupt reality. He trembled in her arms a little, but she felt him take a deep breath.

"I'm doing okay. It's a little weird with Alex not around, ordering me here and there so you can blow things up."

"Do you need me to call and hang up on you without saying good bye?" Jaclyn said, smirking, just as the sound of an engine turning over, amplified and contained, erupted.

Parkerhurst's smile told her all she needed to know.

"You're a good friend." Rubber met steel as Charlie rolled the first car—candy apple red, Jaclyn noted—out of the trailer and down to the pavement. A deft turn of the wheel plus putting it in drive later, Jaclyn caught a full glimpse of what they had brought her and Tasha; Tom would ride with her, much like he did in Sydney. Parkerhurst cleared his throat twice before he began. "Your 2015 Chevy Cruze Sedan." Charlie got out of the car and tossed her the keys before heading back into the trailer to get Tasha's wheels, his footsteps carrying to the Sound. "You will find that, per usual, these cars come completely outfitted with everything that secret agents require in their day-to-day business for the president as well as Her Majesty's Government. Horses, oh yes, they have horses: 138 ponies under the hood, along with the following non-equine related items. Six speed automatic transmission, bucket seats, power everything, cruise control, AM/FM/Satellite radio on the off-chance you need it, GPS unit with Bluetooth wireless capabilities, concierge services—"

"Concierge?" Jaclyn blinked as she raised her voice over the roar coming from inside the trailer; Charlie had started the engine on car number two. "What is this, a rolling hotel? Is there breakfast in bed, too?"

Parkerhurst ignored her, even though she noticed the light flinch around his eyes. He did, however, take a quick, annoyed breath before he resumed his pre-rehearsed spiel.

"Four-wheel ABS, and airbags for everyone. As for the non-standard accoutrements, Snapshot, you'll find it is equipped with triple-plated armored glass, tinted of course, in the windshield. There are multiple license plates for use in Washington, Oregon, and Idaho. Turbo booster for a faster getaway, dual hood mounted machine guns, the usual full rack of STAs in the trunk, and your personal security setting via your iPad."

"Hover? Pontoons? Anything cool like that?" Tasha asked as Charlie finished rolling her version—this one in the color of champagne—off the trailer.

"It's vehicle of espionage, Sex Kitten," Parkerhurst said haughtily, "not a transformer. Your car is just as adequately equipped as Jaclyn's, and I'm sure that between the two of you, you can annihilate this fucking bastard."

Jaclyn had to pause briefly as she noticed Parkerhurst falter in both his mannerisms and his tone. She pursed her lips and grabbed his hand.

"We're going to get this guy. Don't you worry." She squeezed, and she felt his fingers rub along hers. "What else do you have for us?"

"I presume you want your essentials." Parkerhurst let go and walked over to the trailer's opening. He stepped up and in, then pulled two things off the interior wall. He didn't leap out of the truck, seeing as he was in dress shoes. He handed the garment bag to Jaclyn and the duffel bag to Tom before he eased his way down. He gave a soft groan as his feet hit; the grimace told Jaclyn that his shin splints just ripped pain up his legs. "You'll find your jumpsuit has had a touch of an upgrade since you last used it. Instead of pressing a button on your utility belt, the jumpsuit has a thin layer of Kevlar sewn into the lining. It has been tested repeatedly back in my lab, and we have shot at it with every type of bullet on the market. You'll be comforted to know that while the jumpsuit may tear if shot, the Kevlar lining won't even make as much as a mark. You have my guarantee."

Jaclyn nodded.

"I trust you, of course. What else did you bring us? New high heels, by any chance?"

"Oh, the usual, and no. I brought you things you could use. Extra magazines for your guns, plus a little plastic explosives and a detonator on the off-chance you need it."

Jaclyn's grin stretched across her face as she handed Parkerhurst the keys to her rental.

"Thank you, Parkerhurst." She blinked. "Plastic explosives? You've never brought that before. I could hide plastic explosives in high heels."

"For those times when you're away from the car and need to, shall we say, make a mess of things," he replied, seemingly ignoring her last sentence. "Happy hunting, Snapshot. Scouser. Sex Kitten." He nodded to each in turn before he helped Charlie lift and push the skids back into the underside.

"Parkerhurst, do you mind if I change in the trailer?" Jaclyn asked.

"I don't mind at all. Do you, Charlie?"

Charlie simply shook his head.

"Charlie's a man of few words, isn't he?" Jaclyn mused. "I've never heard him speak before."

"Oh, you should hear what he says during our road trips together," Parkerhurst claimed. "Swears like a sailor." He shot a wink Tasha's way. "We'll take your rental back for you. Just hop on up and close the doors."

Jaclyn did so, tossing the garment back on the floor and pulled herself up on the steel underframe. She grabbed the doors and swung them shut, before turning on an overhead light with a snap of her fingers.

"Now, let's see how the new suit looks," she said as she lowered the zipper, as if it glided on ice.

She removed the jumpsuit from the garment and stared at it. It was lighter than the original, the one she had worn several times in her missions. She slipped her fingers inside and felt the somewhat flexible lining. She nodded her approval—before she caught a glance at the shoulders.

It was the shoulders that made her gasp.

Seemingly stitched into the suit and a few inches from where the shoulder met the collarbone was a device she had seen many times in her life, and of course the memory of such brought the emotions back full force. She then remembered Forrister had made her one, since he pointed out her temporary assignment came with a promotion.

There, on the shoulders, were the silver oak clusters of a United States Army lieutenant colonel.

Jaclyn had to let a part of the jumpsuit drop as she reached up to wipe her eyes.

"This is for you, daddy," she said, her voice bouncing off the steel interior moments before she undressed and changed into the familiar confines of the jumpsuit.

***

Darren Drake's estate
Inglewood, North Seattle, Washington
Friday, June 28
1:57 a.m. PT/4:57 a.m. ET

The drive to Inglewood from the CenturyLink parking lot did not take long. Thanks to a little help from Lucy, Jaclyn's personal GPS voice, she managed to lead Tasha north with little difficulty.

Jaclyn and Tasha pulled their cars up along the side of the road, some distance from the address that Bulky and Geeky had told her the day before. The property looked quiet. There were a couple of lights on in what Jaclyn believed was the security residence, while the main house was as dark as the sky. She cross-referenced her location with the map on her iPad and found that they were an exact match. Confident, she fiddled with a couple of dials and came up with the supersonic parabolic microphone channel, the microphone resting in the grille of the car. She hoped she would pick up a stray piece of conversation from the security guards on duty, or of a dog chasing after dream squirrels.

"All we need," Tom said, "are a couple of blokes from Metropolitan Police to stumble upon the scene to make sure it's working."

Jaclyn smirked at the memory; it was just before Tom hopped into the passenger side of the Citroen, just before they leveled each other with their first kiss.

"Oh, you two," the voice of Tasha called through the speakers via the Bluetooth connection between the two cars. "Can you keep it in your pants for just a few minutes?"

"I'm trying," Jaclyn answered. "Time check, Lucy."

"It is 1:58 a.m. according to Seattle time, Jaclyn," the robotic voice toned.

"Which means it's just about 5 a.m. back home. Lucy, call Salt's phone, if you would."

Lucy didn't answer; instead, a light beeping of ten numbers followed by the telltale tones of ringing filled the car. Jaclyn tapped her fingertips on the steering wheel as she awaited—

The ringing cut out after three and a half rings.

"Morning," Salt answered, his voice garbled, presumably by his pillow.

"Desmond, it's Jaclyn. Wake up, I have something for you to do."

The unmistakable sounds of Salt groaning as he stretched filled the car.

"What do you need that couldn't wait until the sun was a little higher in the sky? And by higher, I mean at its highest point in the day."

Jaclyn rolled her eyes.

"Oh, Salty. Just get to your computer. I need some satellites moved into place." She gave him the address, and she heard the creaking of an office chair as Salt planted his ass in the one next to his bed. His tickling the keys were a faint yell through the speakers.

"Satellites are moving. There better be something in this for me, Jackie Baby," Salt said.

"I've already pointed you in the direction of a lovely young lady; what else would you want? Have you asked out Margaret yet?" she answered after a beat.

"Yes," Salt said, sighing. "We've been out a couple of times already."

Jaclyn's perkiness rippled through the line.

"Oh? You're going to have to email me the details, boy! Let me know when you have the satellites overhead."

"Okay, okay, give me a second."

Jaclyn laughed softly, singing, "Salty's got a girlfriend" like a teenager.

"So what are we looking for?" he interrupted.

"Pretty much anything that will fuck up our chances of getting in and out without being seen. Dogs, security systems, lunatics who kill people for no sane reason whatsoever. All of the above."

"Got it. Give me a few more seconds to see what they have."

Jaclyn waited, while Tom shifted nervously in his seat. She rested her hand on his thigh in an effort to calm him down. They shared a grin while they waited for Salt to finish up his surveillance from three thousand miles away.

"Okay, here we go." Jaclyn leaned a little closer as Daly spoke. "No dogs, but they do have a rather tight security system in place."

She nodded, mainly to herself.

"What can you do about that for me?"

"I could be a dear and disable it remotely. What I'm about to do is going to completely make you blind to everyone in that building."

"That," Jaclyn said, dryly, "would be a major switch."

"Right. I'm sending a signal that will interrupt the system. They will think that everything is hunky dory, but it will be the furthest thing from the truth. Think of it like someone opening up a porn site on their computers, thinking that since they have antivirus software, they are all set and nothing will happen. The company will have no idea you're there, unless you do something wrong, like knock over a filing cabinet or set the whole fucking place ablaze. Other than that, you three would slink in and slink out without anyone the wiser."

"Excellent work, Salty. Stay on the line." She turned to Tom. "Ready?"

"If by ready you mean am I ready to put a bullet in this guy's head for stalking my honey bunny? You bet I am."

Jaclyn's smile had tightened up.

"Sex Kitten? Are you ready to go?"

"That's a big ten-four, Snapshot."

"All right, let's stalk in quietly."

Jaclyn grabbed the Bluetooth device connecting her with Salt and promptly shoved it in her ear. The three of them eased their way out of the matching Cruzes, shutting the doors behind them without making the neighborhood come alive. All three wore black, and all three carried suppressed Walthers on their hips, just on the chance that someone unwisely got in the way.

They walked to their left as soon as they noticed a rather large front gate blocking their access to the driveway. Jaclyn hunched over as she led them to a small copse of trees.

"Salt, can you home in on me and get what I'm seeing here? I need to know what pitfalls are waiting for us. Are there any tripwires or other fences that ring this compound?"

"Not a thing to worry about," Salt replied. "The signal I sent will alert no one should you come across anything."

"I copy. We're going to enter the property now. Stand by."

Salt didn't acknowledge the order; Jaclyn knew he would follow it, and she heard the creaking of the chair to let her know that he was still on the line. She slipped into the small collection of trees that served as the western boundary of the property, trying to keep the rustling of bodies against leaves and crushing feet against twigs and sticks to a minimum. Jaclyn went first, her Walther P99 drawn, a suppressor screwed onto the barrel. Tom followed; Jaclyn felt his eyes right on her backside. He had his Walther out and at the ready.

Tasha picked up the rear.

They wound their way through a heavily wooded path, but Jaclyn managed to catch glimpses of the house, darkened and dormant, from between the trees.

"HUD," she whispered, "switch to heat signatures. Monitor the property and give tones if something comes up."

The device beeped its affirmative. The others maintained radio silence.

A minute later, they came to the end of the path, where it spilled out into the property's back yard. There were no heat signatures registering on Jaclyn's HUD. She breathed a little easier, but she felt her ribs tremble under the force of her rapid heartbeat. Tom was on her right, with Tasha to her left.

"Okay, give me the layout from this point to the smaller building," she added.

Her HUD obeyed with another beep. In heartbeats, she saw white lines pour across her field of vision. She saw the lines form bushes as well as stones, tiny stones that, Jaclyn figured, had the capabilities of knocking against each other if someone stepped on them; even the tiniest jostling was a noise that someone may hear. She saw the pool water, calm as the sea; the concrete surrounding it.

And there, on the building opposite, she saw the wrought iron balcony jutting out from the side.

Jaclyn nervously wet her lips as she stared at an incline. There was a light on the lower level, but not directly underneath the means of egress. She caught a glimpse of two heat signatures there, but none on the upper level.

"That's our entry point," she said, pointing toward the building. She saw that Tasha wore a small pair of night vision goggles. She nodded as she looked at what Jaclyn saw. "Salt, I'm counting two in the security house."

Tasha had turned to her left, to the far corner of the property. Jaclyn turned her head and gasped, seeing what her ward had in her field of vision: two men with flashlights, walking along the perimeter. They sent their beams into the trees.

Jaclyn had a quick brainstorm.

"We need to get back into the woods," she said. "Now. Make yourself as small as you can."

“Or climb a tree,” Tom said. “They won’t look up if we don’t give them a reason to.”

Without thinking, Jaclyn pressed her lips against his, kissing him hard.

“You’re not just another pretty face, babe.”

Tom grinned sheepishly.

“Help me up,” she whispered, stashing her Walther. Tom did as she asked, cupping his hands and, as she stepped up and into his palms, boosted her into the boughs of an elm. Catching her breath, she maneuvered her rear end to sit squarely on the branch, which felt as fat as a python’s girth. A few leaves rustled, but it was too far away from the oncoming guards to notice. Looking down, she saw her husband help Tasha into a tree with the same move, before he took two steps and launched himself up into the same elm with her. She watched with complete fascination as he swung his legs back and forth on another sturdy branch before flinging himself across to where she now sat.

He flashed a roguish wink at her. And while Jaclyn felt her heart race and flutter at his daring, all she did was tsk and roll her eyes under her HUD.

“So,” he said, his tone low, “we wait up here until they pass us by, then jump down and continue as planned, I take it?”

Jaclyn nodded.

“Sounds like as good a plan as any,” she said, before touching her ear. “Salt, we’re in a tree.”

“That is not the first time I’ve heard that in, like, ever,” he replied. “Operation on hold?”

“For the time being,” Jaclyn said after nodding. “I have two bogeys in my sights, both carrying flashlights.”

“I have a bead on them through the satellite uplink, Snapshot.”

“Can you jam their two-way radios?”

“From Washington? Not a chance in hell.”

Jaclyn’s lips twisted in a grimace.

“It was worth a shot,” Jaclyn replied as she peered through the leaves at her quarry. “Here they come.”

She pulled her Walther out of her right hip holster, flipping the safety off with her thumb. Her breath jarred her teeth as she inhaled hard, ready to hold her breath for as long as necessary.

The guards turned their lights this way and that, one sending the beam into the woods, at root level. The other, Jaclyn noted, had the beam out in front of him as they approached her location. They were thirty feet away, then twenty-five, then twenty.

Jaclyn's heart belted out Morse code as they came to within ten feet of their location, their lights slowly encompassing the search area.

Then they were underneath them. Directly underneath. Jaclyn heard their breathing, the air pockets within the cartilage of their necks popping as they turned their heads, their feet scuffing along the turf. If she concentrated hard enough, she surely thought the sounds of their hearts crashing against their breastbones would reach her ears, too. She bit her lip. They were a curious pair; the one on the left had the bulky frame of a defensive lineman, while the other had the slender-yet-muscular frame of a once-speedy-in-high-school cornerback.

Jaclyn figured she had the ability to take the cornerback down without an issue. The defensive lineman, though, may need Tom's assistance. Yet as she stared at the guy, she noticed him start to turn a bit; the back of that melon looked inviting. She didn't look at her husband for his non-verbal input on the matter. She kept her HUD focused on the targets instead.

The one on the left moved his flashlight over to his left hand and reached for his shoulder mic. The other was closer to Tasha's location.

"Walker One to Bravo Base. One and Two report the perimeter is secure. Repeat, perimeter is secure."

The reply came quick, with a burst of static added at the start.

"Roger that."

"Come on," One said to Two. One had a husky voice, as if his body style caused his tone to echo in the pit of his stomach. "It's almost time for a snack. My wife made me an extra large Ham and Swiss Piccolo today. A few slices of black forest ham, Swiss cheese, lettuce, roasted red peppers and red onions, a big leaf of lettuce, and a little Grey Poupon. Will go great with the strawberry shake I got at the McDonald's."

Jaclyn heard him extend the first syllable out to Mac. She shook her blonde head.

"Oh, I love those," Two replied.

Too bad you're not going to eat it right now, Jaclyn thought as she licked her lips and, without issuing an order, pushed herself out of the tree, Walther in hand. The drop happened fast, the air giving way to the Lycra clad angel.

Jaclyn landed right on the man's back, her feet colliding with the spot between his shoulder blades—and the back of his head, her aim partially true. He gave a cry of "oomph" as Jaclyn's feet made contact before she flung herself forward and twisted into a somersault. She rolled twice and righted herself, her Walther up and pointed straight at Two. Tom and Tasha then dropped from their branches, guns ready; Two had turned his head at the sound of their feet hitting the ground. One, she noticed, wasn't moving; he appeared unconscious and Jaclyn wondered if he dreamed of his wife's sandwich-making skills.

"Good evening," Jaclyn said. "If you would be so kind as to not reach for your weapon or your radio, I'd appreciate it."

The guard's hands shot into the air, the beam of the flashlight pointed over his head. Jaclyn made sure that it didn't flash toward the building behind her, as if alerting anyone that there was a situation outside that needed immediate assistance. The man's face had paled to near porcelain, his eyes wide.

Jaclyn stalked in and pulled a small roll of black electrical tape from within the confines of her utility belt. She passed it to her husband, all while keeping the barrel of her Walther trained on the guard's nose.

"Not a word. Hands down slowly and put them behind your back as far as you can," she ordered. "If you make for your gun, I will shoot to kill. Nod if you understand."

He nodded and did as he was told, getting them a hand's length away from the small of his back. Jaclyn reached up and disengaged his shoulder mic, then pulled his gun out of his holster. The ripping of tape and it pulling away from the roll was abrupt, but the sound didn't carry far. Jaclyn checked the safety and made sure it was in place before she handed it to Tasha.

"Put them a couple of feet into the woods," she said.

"Right." Tasha turned and walked a few feet before putting it down. Tom had wound the tape around the man's wrists and had done it so tight the guard had grimaced slightly. Then Tom wound the tape into a gag, shoving a few layers around and into his mouth. While he did that, Tasha tied the man's shoes together before Tom wrapped the top of his face, covering his eyes.

All the while, Jaclyn smirked his way.

Tom then picked him up, spun him around, then carried him into the copse of trees and set him down. He returned a few seconds later, albeit a little slower than when he walked in.

"Now let's take care of this wanker," he said.

"Just take his gun and radio," Tasha said. "Hopefully we'll be long gone before he wakes up."

"And if he's not?" Jaclyn asked. Tasha shrugged. "Tape him up."

Tom did as she asked.

"Remember that you have to take every precaution in the field, especially with a wanker like that," Jaclyn reminded her ward, her rebuke as soft as she could make it. It was her job now to let Tasha know this is how things had to be done in order to maintain anonymity. She could have buried the point home with harsh words, but this wasn't the time for harshness. "This guy can't identify us because we hit him from behind. And it's my hope the other one pissed his pants and he forgets he saw us, or what I look like. Now let's get busy."

They walked across the area between the main house and the pool, taking care to keep their footfalls as silent as possible. The darkness surrounded them. Jaclyn had hoped that if Drake had installed motion sensors in the rear of the house that Salt's signal would take care of it. She held her breath as they crossed.

No lights sprang awake as they approached the separate building.

They stopped just short of the building, a few feet from where the wrought iron balcony jutted away from the façade. The aroma of lilac swelled, but Jaclyn didn't let it bother her; her sunglasses prevented the pollen from reaching her eyes; the other two maintained a stoic posture next to her. She looked up at the balcony, then looked to where another wrought iron structure—a bridge—connected the main house with this building.

"What are you thinking, Snapshot?" Tom asked, his voice low.

"That door there," Jaclyn said, "is open if Salt came through for us."

"I can still hear you, Jaclyn," Salt said over the line.

She grinned.

"I know you can. Grapplers." Jaclyn pulled her favorite grappler from her utility belt and engaged it, while Tom and Tasha did the same. Parkerhurst had extras in the duffel bag, on the off-chance they needed them. Jaclyn pointed hers to the balcony. "When I'm up and over, you go next, Scouser. Then you, Sex Kitten."

"I love that name," Tasha replied. "Makes me want to claw someone's eyes out."

"Save it for when you get an assignment on your own. See you up there."

Jaclyn pulled the trigger, the grappling hook firing up and away with a *woosh*. She heard it connect and hook before she pressed the button on the side that pulled her up. It only took a few seconds to get up there, a much shorter amount of time than what had happened in London and the Football Association offices. The cord coiled up and stopped with her hands right at the railing. She let go and grabbed the cool iron, then pulled herself up until her feet gained purchase on the edge. She launched herself up and over, then disengaged the hook with the electrical charge.

"Come on," she whispered before she made herself one with the wall. Tom followed—Jaclyn had to make sure he made it over instead of falling to his death—before Tasha came up, too.

"I can really get used to this," Tasha said as she climbed over the fence.

"Let's get inside and find what we can find," Jaclyn said, sliding the glass door open, her breath held in her chest. No buzzing noises or sirens went off. She released the breath and headed in.

"So what are we looking for?" Tom asked. His voice, albeit soft, seemed to fill the room.

"First, we're looking for this shrine they told us about, then I want to find Drake's office."

"How about we do it the other way around," Tasha suggested. "Get to the office and gather the facts before we look into everything else."

Jaclyn thought it over, then pursed her lips and nodded.

"Good point."

"I'm not just another pretty face," her ward said, somewhat flippantly.

But Jaclyn grabbed Tasha's shoulder, making the girl freeze in place.

"Hold on, I have another idea: Salt, can you find where Drake's internet hub is located?" Jaclyn asked.

"Is Bin Laden dead?" Salt wisecracked. Jaclyn sniffed her amusement. "Give me a moment."

"Half of one would be better." She turned to Tasha. "Go search for this shrine that they talked about. We'll meet you there."

"You got it."

With a two-fingered salute from her brow and without an argument, Tasha turned and rushed off, her footsteps soft.

"Snapshot, I have the location. It's in the main house. For some reason, he left his computer on. All of his data is open to me."

Jaclyn's heart skipped a beat.

"Can you hack in for us and get all of his files? Financials, et cetera."

"Already on it. I'll upload and fire it over to your iPad for your perusal."

Jaclyn let go of a heavy breath that had lingered in her lungs for far too long.

"Thanks, Salt. I appreciate that. That means we don't have to linger in this place longer than we have to. Okay, moving to the shrine. Sex Kitten, we're incoming."

Tasha clicked her headset once. Jaclyn readied her gun as she felt her heart racing along as they entered the darkened hallway, the swift change in plans a distant memory. They went left, much in the same way as Tasha had only a minute before.

The duo took only a few steps before Jaclyn found the door in which Tasha had entered. It was off to the left, much in the same direction that Bulky had told them he had gone when he entered the building that day a few weeks ago, looking for the bathroom. They found Tasha staring at the corner so intently that she didn't even notice Jaclyn and Tom's presence joining her.

The room was slightly dark, save the ambiance of a black light illuminating the corner at which Tasha's gaze had settled. Jaclyn, too, stared, and with that, she felt icicles quickly encase her heart.

"Oh, fuck me in the arse and call me Albert Victor," Tom gasped.

Jaclyn paid her husband's outburst no mind as she kept her HUD on the display in front of her, and oh, was it ever a display. The scene covered the entirety of the corner, from window to window, from floor to ceiling. Photographs covered every inch of wall, from high gloss magazine covers to black and white newspaper shots. She recognized them all—they were all of her, just like Bulky had said. Her mind whirled as the memories of each of those shots came back to her, with each pose and shoot rushing through her mind as if she felt the hot lights, heard the clicking of a camera. But what truly frightened her wasn't the flecks of white-ish gold that stained the photos, no, not at first; it was what she saw dead center of the shrine—she quickly realized what it was: a one-foot high by seven-feet long slab of brown cardboard with the words "RUNAWAY BITCH" written in large, bold letters, written in pink marker.

Jaclyn felt her spine tingle just before she started shivering, but that did not suppress her growing rage. She soon realized she had held her breath, and her heart, because of this, was in the process of overcompensating; the spot between her breasts ached, as if a knife had punched through the jumpsuit and had plunged deep into her thorax.

She finally regained her breath and her voice. She shook her head, keeping the HUD poised right at the words in fluorescent pink. Now it all made sense, the details slipping together into a neat little row, and with the dawning of this numbing her mind, she came to grips with what Darren Drake truly was.

"This," she said, her vocal chords strangled by the grips of her tightened throat, "this is sick."

"That's what your old pals had said. This just confirms everything," Tom said. He swallowed. "This is more than just sick. This is—"

"Wrong," Jaclyn finished for him.

He nodded.

"This is disgusting. This makes me want to kill the son of a bitch."

"Not if I beat you to it," she answered, her tone cold.

Tom waved his hand toward the shrine, and Jaclyn, finally looking away from the insanity plastered into the corner, saw that his eyes had narrowed. On the other side of her, Tasha moved closer, seemingly inspecting it, also with narrowed eyes.

"This display is, is—"

"This display is full of the guy's cum," Tasha blurted as Tom fought over the words tripping against his tongue. Tasha pulled out her smartphone and ripped off a couple of shots for evidence.

Jaclyn suddenly choked on her saliva, her throat clenching, constricting. She struggled for a few seconds to breathe, her eyes watering.

"Babe, are you all right?" Tom asked, his tone full of love and concern. Jaclyn nodded.

As she tried to regain control, she heard the far off sounds of doors slamming shut, followed by the telltale sounds of rushing footsteps. She quickly inhaled, trying to quell her racing heart and her burning lungs.

"Snapshot, you need to get out of there right now," Salt said as she finally straightened, her hand on her heart. "Security is racing to your position."

"Well then, let's see exactly how difficult it is for them to shoot through a gray cloud," she said, her voice weakened by her choking. She walked toward the door and reached into her utility belt at the same time, pulling out two small, marble-sized spheres and tossing them toward the hallway. Jaclyn heard the smack of the balls against the wall, before she heard the fumes of the darkness bombs spill from inside their plastic casings, the hallway instantly turning into a tunnel of murky gray pitch. "Now," she said, her tone dark, the rage overtaking her as she turned and leveled the suppressed Walther toward the display, which sent Tasha backing up a few steps, "we send him a calling card to let him know how much we care about him."

She squeezed several rounds off, making sure that the wording received the brunt of the damage before letting her wrist turn this way and that, firing off a few more shots to poke holes in her pictorials until she had exhausted the magazine's supply. The Walther clicked. She knew she didn't have the time to re-load and fire off any additional bullets at Drake's shrine to her radiant beauty, to his despicable deviance. Jaclyn yanked the magazine out and replaced it with a new one as she moved to the window.

"Let's get out of here," she said as she kicked the balcony door open. They collided against the façade, sending shards of glass to tinkle against the stones below. "Grapplers."

The three of them grabbed their mini-crossbows and, starting with Tasha, shot, leaped, and repelled to the ground outside. Tom followed, before Jaclyn, who took a long last look at the display before she, too, fired her grappling hook to wrap around the bar. She felt her nostrils flare as she pulled herself away from that room just as the sounds of footsteps preceded mind-jarring confusion in the hallways.

Holstering her Walther, Jaclyn flung herself up and over, closing her eyes until she felt solid ground under her feet once again. A few seconds later, once the hook had retracted into her crossbar, the three of them stalked around the pool and across the backyard with dreadful purpose.

Tom and Tasha had skirted off to the left to head back to the Cruzes, but Jaclyn, her anger not sated in the least, kept walking toward the treeline. Behind her, her HUD informed her of a few lights flickering on in the guard house. Nothing flipped on in the main house. Jaclyn figured that Drake either wasn't there, or that the security guards let him sleep through the tumult.

"Snapshot? Are you coming, love?" Tom asked. He had paused near the corner. Tasha paused, too.

"In a second," she replied, looking straight at the prostrate heat signatures in the distance. "I have another message to deliver to Drake." She drew the Walther again and walked with hardened steps, her blood turning molten until her ear canals had their own heartbeat.

Tom and Tasha followed.

Jaclyn ducked back into the woods, trying to avoid low-hanging branches before she found Guard One face down among the ferns, still unconscious. Snarling, she didn't hesitate as she pumped the trigger twice, firing a pair of suppressed shots into his back. The body jerked twice. Then she turned, crunching leaves underfoot as she stepped twice, and found the second one all taped up and wriggling like a worm. With the barrel of her gun still tinged with tiny plumes of white-gray smoke, she pulled the trigger again.

The guard immediately shuddered and grew still.

Jaclyn let go of a long-held breath and inhaled the sharp aroma of cordite as she lowered her Walther, but she didn't re-holster it; she half-expected Drake's security forces to rush out of the house with guns blazing any second now, and she readied herself for the inevitable spin-and-shoot that was sure to follow. Her flesh tingled underneath the Lycra, her adrenaline rushing through her veins.

"Now that is what I call a calling card," Tasha said, impressed.

Her anger ebbing slightly, Jaclyn shrugged.

"It's better than leaving a small piece of cardboard that someone's just going to toss aside in five minutes," she answered.

Chapter 14
Darren Drake's estate
Inglewood, North Seattle, Washington
Friday, June 28
7:22 a.m. PT/10:22 a.m. ET

Drake's driver floored it.

As soon as his security back at home managed to get in touch with him, Drake roused his driver, then cancelled the rest of his meetings. Even going 80 miles per hour north on Interstate 5, Drake tried to will his driver's foot downward to send the accelerator crashing through the undercarriage to the pavement below. They ran into some early morning rush hour traffic headed into the city, but Drake remained patient despite the situation. Getting off the 5 and using side roads to go home wouldn't help matters much.

The pictures they had sent to his phone—Drake had told them to send the evidence to his email, too—were damning, but he told them not to contact the police. His eyes fed the signals to his brain, and his brain processed the information like he normally did. It was when he saw the bullet holes in his handiwork—all of his handiwork, he noticed—that he knew she had returned.

He also knew that, judging by the fact she had seemingly broken into his home without his security team knowing, someone he had trusted blabbed his secrets.

He didn't like it when someone blabbed his secrets.

Drake had stewed over this while his driver crossed from Oregon into Washington. *She has invaded my private sanctuary, the place where I go and remember what she has done to me*, he thought as he stared at the bullet-riddled pictures, the ones which bore his half-naked seal of approval many times over. *And in order for her to invade it, he must have told her. But how, and when?* It was information he didn't know, and it was information he now craved.

The fact the only damage was the shooting of his pseudo-pornographic collage and the damage to the balcony doors—they had also said they needed to air out the hallway of fumes, but that was painless—made Drake wonder exactly he was up against. He knew she was a covert agent, but the fact she is known for explosions and a bunch of destruction led him to believe she didn't want to thoroughly destroy the place.

He wet his lips just as his phone rang. He checked the number, and he grinned.

Drake hit the green button.

"You got my message then," he said, by-passing a greeting.

"I did," the voice of his business partner came over. "What happened?"

"Jaclyn Johnson happened. You were right. She came back." Drake explained everything that he knew so far, from her entrance to the building—"How she got inside, I haven't a damn clue; there's nothing in the security logs about an alarm going off," he said—to the vandalism. He didn't say what she had destroyed. It wouldn't help matters much, especially with her. His business partner hadn't been on that floor and didn't know how he still pined—oh, how he had pined!—for the once-toothpick-sized blonde.

"You should feel glad that she didn't set the whole place ablaze," his partner said. "It's time to make your claim have more weight, Darren. I'm going to have my operatives target what we've discussed in the past, and it should put the government at risk of tumbling. If they can't protect businesses, they have to capitulate to our demands. When they get rid of Net Neutrality—and, in turn, the money you funnel my way, will lead to our ultimate gambit."

Drake nodded.

"Yes. Yes, it will. I have something that I will have to take care of later today. Have you been in touch with Mr. Hill lately?"

"No? Why?"

"Call him up and tell him he needs to come to Seattle. Tell him that we're making a case against Jaclyn Johnson and that we're going to implicate her in the murder of her boss; a little misdirection. That will blind him to our true purpose."

"And what is our true purpose in this, Darren?"

He chuckled at her empty quip, his mouth closed.

"I thought you knew? Elimination, my dear. Sweet, total elimination."

She said she would call him in. Drake hung up. His driver drove on.

Drake clapped his hands together and rubbed his palms free of sweat. His heart still puttered along at a rather rapid pace, but it was slower than a few minutes before.

They eventually got through the traffic tie-up and slipped off 5 to the 522, motoring around the lake and into Inglewood.

He saw that his security team had heeded his warnings and had not called the police; the scene was empty of cruisers with flashing red and blue lights of their roofs, and with the exception of his car, there were no SUVs or television trucks lining his peaceful, suburban road. Drake let loose a deep breath that had threatened to strangle him as they approached his house. Suffice it to say, he didn't want the police involved, nor did he trust them to get an investigation correct, nor did he want to answer any questions about his pseudo-relationship with Jaclyn Johnson. That was drama he didn't need. He wanted to remain under the radar—even though it looked like, just from what the security chief had told him over the phone based on the woman's description, he had just made it square into the runaway bitch's crosshairs.

Drake bit his lip as his heart raced yet again. He didn't coil his fingers into a fist and strike at a defenseless seat in his growing frustration. He breathed as easily as possible just before his driver got out of the car and opened his door for him. He slid out just as his security head walked toward him. The large African-American gentleman looked glum, and for a former linebacker who had taken one too many shots off his bald coconut during his playing days, that was an improvement to his usual day-to-day demeanor of surly.

"Ed, what happened?"

Ed's shrug was one of blissful stupidity.

"We really don't know, sir. But we have two agents down in the woods over to the western side of the property."

Drake set his jaw and tried not to grumble anything unintelligible.

"Take me over there," he replied. Ed the Security Guy waved him forward. Drake followed.

They rounded the left side of the house at a light gait without urgency spurring them faster. There were a few others standing at the tree line, Drake noticed, some looking in and while other checked their smartphones.

"Both were dead when we found them after we had called you," Ed explained. "They were on a patrol in this vicinity when we last had contact with them."

Drake blinked. He wondered why they hadn't made an attempt to find them in the intervening hours between Jaclyn Johnson's sudden entrance and when they had called him—he had bought them big steel flashlights to go with their nice outfits and shiny guns, and in his mind he wanted to scream something about using them every once in a while—but he let it pass. They were truly of no matter to him, for there would be others, and they all were mere duplicates of each other. He wouldn't grieve; they weren't business assets with any tangible worth to him. As such, they were just another debit in the business of life.

They stopped at the tree line. The bodies, he saw, were covered in a blue tarp tented by the bushes and branches, presumably to keep anything larger than a squirrel from desecrating their remains. He knew that flies and other tiny insects had already started the nesting process in their open mouths and ears and nostrils, since they had been dead for hours and no one had moved them. Between rigor mortis, the flies, and the partially blood-soaked tarp, there was nothing for him to do. He wrote them off without further inspection.

"Take them into the basement for now," Drake ordered. "Tonight, though, I want them taken to the lake. Weigh the bodies down, sail into the middle, and drop them in. Make sure no one speaks of this."

"What about the woman and her friends that intruded on the property and killed them?" Ed asked as they turned and made for the guard house. He hadn't relayed the order, Drake noted.

Drake sneered as he focused all of his attention to the broken doors.

"Leave her and them to me. She will get what's coming to her." He issued a blast of air from his nose, shaking his head angrily as they skirted the pool. "How? How did she know?"

Ed didn't answer.

They entered through the bath house, weaving around the security desk and making their way to the second floor. Their footsteps echoed in the dimly-lit stairwell, Drake pounding away as he took the stairs two at a time. He found the door to the shrine open, and he chose to stand in the doorway instead of step through the threshold. From there, he saw, plain as day, what Jaclyn had done to his collage.

Pain rippled across his chest. The bullet holes looked larger than they were, as if the honoree gave him a massive middle finger with each shot. He grimaced in disillusionment.

How could she destroy this? he wondered. *It's all in homage to her. I painstakingly made sure that I found every shot of her and put it on display for my private viewing, and then she... she...*

He sighed hard, bowing his head.

"How?" he repeated himself, flinging his hands up toward his shoulders, dropping them just as fast as they rose. "How did she ever fucking find out about this?"

"I don't really—"

"Ed," Drake interrupted without a second's hesitation, his impatience overflowing. "Your gun. Hand it over, please. Now."

Swallowing, Ed drew his sidearm and passed it over, handle-first. Drake took it and flicked the safety off with his thumb. He pointed it at his security chief, the barrel practically shoved against the bridge of his nose. The man's eyes widened just as Drake pulled the trigger without any further hesitation. The concussive blast filled the hallway as if bouncing off the walls, along with blood and gray matter emerging from the back of Ed's skull. He dropped to the floor backward while the scent of cordite floated to the ceiling.

"That was a rhetorical question. I didn't want an answer from you." He turned to another man. "Take this corpse to the basement and make sure that the two outside find their way there, too." He repeated his other order before turning and making his way to the main house via the steel walkway between the two buildings.

Drake slipped into his office and found his computer still on like he had left it, finding nothing amiss. He sat down and logged onto his Facebook page, wetting his lips as he searched for his friend's page, his eyes going right to it. He clicked the hyperlink and started scrolling.

He didn't have to scroll far; his friend wasn't that big of a Facebooker, which meant finding the reasoning—or what Drake believed was the reasoning—wasn't hard to do. Drake stared at the event's title, his gaze unflinching from the screen. He felt naked and cold, as if the winds off the Sound reached him here and shredded his business suit to mere fibers and threads. A deep breath didn't sate his desire for warmth, nor did it control the panic welling in the pit of his stomach.

What was his friend's intent? he wondered as he reclined in his captain's chair, pinching his bottom lip between his thumb and forefinger. *Was it because I lavished him with gifts? No, that would be a shitty way to repay someone now, wouldn't it? I introduced him to his wife, that pretty girl who works in software. He has nothing for wants. Everything has been fine between the two of us. Except—*

Drake swore loudly, launching himself from his chair and immediately paced the length of his office. His steps came so easily that his heart raced to catch up, but neither caught up with the speed at which his mind spun.

He gasped.

"That cunt," he breathed, clenching his hands together until he felt his fingernails digging into his flesh. "That dirty, sneaking, half-witted cunt. He has a lot of nerve to tell my secrets to that runaway bitch." His lip curled.

Yet the next thought hit him straight between the eyes, much in the way the bullet bisected Ed's brain only a few minutes ago.

"Time to take advantage of the situation," he said, walking over and picking up the phone. He took a few calming breaths before he dialed a number he knew all too well. The line rang twice, until a familiar voice, one deep and sonorous, came through.

"Hello?"

"Chuck, it's Darren."

"Hey." Chuck's reply had come through as if there was a touch of wariness behind it.

Let's use that wariness to our advantage, Drake thought with a grin.

"What's going on? What are you and Madeline doing tonight?"

"Not a whole heckuva lot. Maybe dinner and dancing. Why do you ask?"

"I was hoping that you guys can meet up with Kim and I, have a few drinks. We haven't been out these last few weeks, and I'm sorry for that. Lots of stuff going on with the build-up to the Net Neutrality application and everything."

"Sure," Chuck replied after a few seconds, and it sounded to Drake that he was stalling for time before he finally answered. "We'll be at the Pike Place Market at 5."

"Great," Drake answered, smiling. "We'll be there with bells on."

"Awesome. I'll let Maddy know."

They hung up.

Drake rubbed his hands together.

"I do hope you have your funeral arrangements already made, because I know that women can be absolute blubbery when they have to do it," Drake whispered to the phone as their conversation ended.

***

The Warwick Hotel
Lenora Street

Seattle, Washington
Saturday, June 29
9:13 a.m. PT/12:13 p.m. ET

Bulky's death and the horrendous nature of it made headline news the next morning.

Jaclyn watched KOMO in silence, with Tom and Tasha next to her. She had leaned in to the point she rested her hand in her palm, her elbow digging into her thigh. Her heartbeat slowly drowned out the anchor's voice, the tension thick in her mind. An ache slowly built in her ribs, but she chose not to rub the pain away.

The reporter on scene—Jaclyn instantly recognized the background as Pike's Place Market—had said the deceased party died via a gunshot wound to the head, all in front of the man's obviously panic-stricken wife. An ambulance took the man, or what was left of him, to a nearby hospital, where he was pronounced dead. The wife, Jaclyn understood, was taken to a different hospital for a psychiatric observation. The reporter said that Seattle Police were still looking for the shooter, noting that witnesses had looked around and didn't see anyone at ground level who might have possibly pulled the trigger. Some looked to the roofs of the nearby parking lots and buildings. They saw nothing.

Exhaling a breath she had held for the longest time, Jaclyn knew she should get involved and tell Seattle Police her hypothesis, but she didn't want to jeopardize her mission or her investigation. She had the feeling that Drake was behind Bulky's death, but she truly had no proof of that; all she had was speculation and conjecture, and it wasn't enough to gain punishment for Drake. The fact she had just destroyed his shrine to her on Bulky's information, and now that Bulky was dead, wasn't at issue here.

Bulky was, unfortunately, expendable. She wouldn't shed tears for him, for she had no reason to do so. She had only seen him once in the last fifteen-plus years, and there wasn't a feeling of camaraderie between the two. He had given her information, she had subsequently acted on it, and he coincidentally ended up dead less than twenty-four hours later as a result.

Yet she did feel an obligation to tell Forrister, seeing as she hadn't briefed him on the situation here in quite a while.

Jaclyn dug out the eavesdrop-proof cube and pressed the center button before she called Forrister's cell phone. It rang once.

"Jaclyn! What's going on in Seattle?"

"Right now, sir, the fecal matter has hit the oscillator," she replied, explaining what happened last night and everything up until now. She left nothing out, choosing to run everything down for him all at once instead of in pieces; she made sure to inform him about the meeting at the Zig Zag Café, as well as the meeting with her father's family, which solidified her thinking about Hill. The president, to his credit, did not interrupt, instead letting Jaclyn exhaust him with facts. Jaclyn heard a bit of a breeze in the background, and quietly wondered if Forrister was in the midst of a round of golf, or out on a boat somewhere. That distracting thought evaporated. "I'm on the right path, though. I have clear proof that Drake was stalking me, and that he called me a runaway bitch. There is the testimony of Hill, the Advance—"

"Who no one has seen in two or three days," Forrister said.

Jaclyn bit the inside part of her cheek until she tasted copper flood her mouth.

"Shit. I didn't expect that."

"We never do. It's not like we could have incarcerated him for his protection."

Jaclyn nodded as she kept on gnawing at the tender flesh.

"We could have; let's not rule that out."

"Right. So what's next?"

"We have his company's financial records; Salt hacked them for us before I shot up his shrine to me, so I'll look at them today."

"Good. Keep me updated." The president paused to cough. "Sorry. I also want to keep you up to date on what's going on here. The new Director of the CIA is home."

Jaclyn blinked. She straightened.

"Oh? He moved fast."

"We extracted him Wednesday, and we got him home last night. He reports to the Oval Office on Monday."

Jaclyn breathed a heavy sigh of relief.

"So does that mean I'm back to being just a regular old secret agent-slash-model?"

"On Monday, you will be."

Jaclyn stared at the wall as Forrister's announcement rooted her to the floor. Her thoughts immediately meshed into one gigantic glob of tumult, one that made her eyes spin. She knew she hadn't truly given one hundred percent into the temporary job as director, especially in the time since she returned to Seattle: it wasn't her top priority, and she hoped the president didn't lack for knowledge of what had occurred around the world as soon as she left the capital to go on her vendetta.

"Good," she said, adding a sharp nod at the end. "Good."

"I appreciate everything you did during this time, which I know was hard for you."

Jaclyn didn't even notice that her lips had pursed. She released her hold on her teeth before a soft exhalation slipped out.

"I'm sorry I didn't put that job first when I should have, sir."

"Jaclyn, do you think I'm mad at you?" Forrister asked.

This time she blinked, wondering how he had come to such a conclusion so fast.

"No, sir. I just know I didn't really do the job that you hired me for."

"I didn't expect you to do everything Alex did. In fact, I knew that once you got a sniff of something in this matter, you'd turn into a bloodhound. Remember that I told you to go after this guy. You did nothing wrong, and I don't blame you one bit. You were following orders. As you've always done."

Jaclyn felt her heart swell as the president dismissed her fears. He could have done one of a hundred different things—she didn't think he still had the incident in Las Vegas at the convention center in the back of his mind to use against her, but it seemed that he had gotten over that slight breach and moved on—but instead, he chose to support her and build her up instead of tear her down.

"Thank you, sir."

"No problem. Just get this guy and get home."

And then, much in the way Alex had done in the past, Forrister hung up without a closing salutation. Jaclyn lowered the phone and clicked the lock. She tossed it on the coffee table.

"Forrister has seemingly forgiven you, huh?" Tom asked.

"Yeah," she said, nodding. "And I have a new boss."

"Someone to fear?" Tasha asked.

"No. In fact, it's someone I know only in training missives, but if he's any sort of an administrator like he is an operative, then the terrorists better hold on to their skivvies for the foreseeable future."

Chapter 15
The Warwick Hotel
Lenora Street
Seattle, Washington
Saturday, June 29
12:17 p.m. PT/3:17 p.m. ET

Jaclyn spent the next three hours or so pouring over Drake's financial records, her iPad propped up as she sat on the suite's couch, her legs tucked underneath her rear end. Tom sat nearby. Tasha was in her suite, doing something productive. At least that's what she hoped; Tasha was long past texting boys constantly, but she was, as Jaclyn recalled, still fresh out of high school. Anything like that could happen.

For the first few hours or so of her search, nothing popped up that gave Jaclyn pause, even though her eyes had started to sting from staring at the tablet for so long. There were regular debits and credits, all with simple explanations attached to them. It was as if Drake ran a rather reputable business.

It was when she got to the political contributions section that things got interesting.

"All right, here we go. Political contributions," she said, untucking her legs and sitting up. She scrolled through and found several contributions to Republican candidates—"See, what did I tell you!" Jaclyn had said, which prompted Tasha to enter the room to see what was up—only to find they were all within federal campaign guidelines. Jaclyn had grimaced at that, knowing that federal campaign finance laws, to some, was more important than murder and stalking.

Then she spotted a repeat contribution, but it wasn't to a politician—instead, Jaclyn discovered, thanks to a search, was a political action committee.

It was a PAC called TealSeattle.

"TealSeattle? Didn't we see a billboard for them when we first came to Seattle just before all the shit hit the fan a couple of weeks ago?" Tasha asked, hanging over the back of the couch. Her crop top rode up on her back.

Jaclyn nibbled on her bottom lip for only a few moments as she pondered it. She did recall it, the billboard near CenturyLink and Safeco as they came up 5 from SeaTac. She nodded, if only to let her ward know she was paying attention—but her mind slowly drifted. Having been away from Seattle for so long, she wasn't exactly sure what TealSeattle was or what their aims were. She felt her lips twist and turn, her mind weighing things.

She minimized the screen with a click of the home button before she opened Safari. A quickie type of "TealSeattle" into the search queue popped the company's website up. The touched the link, and it immediately sprang to life. The site, of course, was a backdrop in all teal, as if in homage to the Seattle sports teams she loved. Yet as she read on, she soon learned the company was devoted to continuing Seattle's "green" community aspects in the minds of all people, both residents and visitors alike.

In addition, there was a subsidiary of TealSeattle that provided energy to both Safeco and CenturyLink Fields, by way of solar power. Jaclyn read that TealSeattle was one hundred percent solar.

"Which has to suck on rainy days," she mused.

Jaclyn kept scrolling through the page, which she saw included a note from the company's CEO, a woman by the name of Kim Perkins.

She felt her lips wriggle of their own accord.

"Kim Perkins. That name should mean something to me, I think," she said aloud, more to herself than her husband and ward. She tapped her fingers against the tablet, searching her memory for seemingly lost information, until she finally shrugged her shoulders as she felt the weight of urgency press down. "Well, I can't think of it right now, and it's not necessary to what we have in front of us. I'm sure it will come to me in due time, but gee whiz, look at all the donations Drake gave her company." She minimized the company website and tilted the iPad their way to show them the obscene amounts of money Drake Industries handed over. "Just an absolute shitload of money."

"And look at these similar amounts going to non-PACs," Tasha pointed out. She ran her finger down the spreadsheet, scrolling it. "Yeah, it's great that Drake is so free with his money and his profits." Jaclyn turned her head and watched as Tasha rubbed her finger against her lips. "But I'm wondering who these others are."

Jaclyn narrowed her eyes toward her young friend.

"Are you thinking Drake's shadier than we realize?"

"It's possible." Tasha turned the rubbing into a tapping. "I'm not sure, but it's possible."

Jaclyn looked to Tom, who immediately nodded toward the phone. She picked it up and immediately dialed Salt's line. It rang three times.

"Yello."

"Salt, it's Jackie."

"'Sup, kid."

"I need you to look into a few records for me. You still have the files you hacked from Drake's home computer?"

"That's a big 10-4."

Jaclyn smiled.

"Good. In the financial records, there are several companies listed that have received funds similar to the ones donated to TealSeattle from Drake Industries. I need those companies checked out, from top to bottom."

"Got it. I'll call you back as soon as I get to it."

"Priority A1, Salty. We've delayed far too much on this."

"Fine," Salt sighed. "I'm typing away as we speak. I'll have it to you within an hour." He hung up without another word.

"He's on it. Meanwhile, I'm on a break. Let's go to lunch. I'm starving."

"That makes two of us."

"Three," Tasha chimed in.

The trio headed out and walked along Lenora to Taco Del Mar, a little place some three blocks away from the hotel on First Avenue; the place that Jaclyn wanted to go to—located barely half a block away from the Warwick on Fourth Avenue—wasn't open on the weekends, but she, Tom, and Tasha thought the second option was the better option.

There, Jaclyn ordered the Baja Tacos, while Tom had to have the Baja Burrito, a dish her husband noticed was as fat as his fist and filled with beef, beans, rice, and a little concoction they called *pico de gallo*: a mix of chopped tomatoes, onions, cilantro, serrano peppers, and salt. In fact, Jaclyn saw the *pico de gallo* on hers, too; the aromas filled her nostrils to overflowing. Tasha had the chicken quesadillas. They all tucked in.

And just as Jaclyn finishing licking her fingers clean of *pico de gallo*, her iPhone vibrated.

"Just in the nick of time," Jaclyn said as she answered Salt's call. "What do you have for me, Salty?"

"A whole lot of oh shit wrapped in a blanket of this guy's fucking nuts," Salt replied. "We need to talk privately."

Jaclyn's blood ran cold to the point that she automatically shivered.

"All right, give us a few minutes and we'll get back to the hotel. We're at lunch."

Salt chuckled.

"Was there any salt?"

Jaclyn wished he saw the wry smile she flashed his way.

"Plenty. We'll be back at the hotel in fifteen."

"Make it twenty. I have to use the loo," Tom said, grabbing his stomach.

"We'll be there in twenty," Jaclyn corrected. "See you there." She hung up. Tom slid out of the booth and headed for the restroom.

"What does Desmond have to say?" Tasha asked as they waited.

"Right now," Jaclyn replied, "a lot of worrisome stuff, but using as few words as possible. But we already know our target is fucking nuts, so that's not exactly breaking news. Hopefully he'll be able to give us something else before we approach him."

Tom finished up a few minutes later, and without anything else said the three of them made their way back to their hotel room, their steps buoyed by the knowledge—the potential knowledge—they were about to receive. As soon as they got back to the room, the sky outside had started turning dark, a sure sign of a Seattle rain. Jaclyn had the cube out of her purse and the button pressed as soon as they sat down. Tasha had grabbed drinks and they all sat down to pay Salt another call.

He answered after half a ring.

Must be really urgent, Jaclyn thought.

"That wasn't twenty minutes, Snapshot," Salt said as an admonishment.

Jaclyn checked the clock.

"It was nineteen."

She heard his audible swallow come across the line.

"Oh."

"What do you have for us, Desmond?" Tom asked.

"Quite a bit, actually. The funds that Drake gave to these companies was just fancy bookkeeping," Salt said.

Jaclyn blinked.

"Do you mean to tell me—"

"That he was cooking his books?" Salt interrupted. "You got it."

"Dummy corporations?" Tom blurted.

"You got it."

"Damn it," Jaclyn said, gripping the back of the couch, her arms up, over, and behind her head. "How many of those are dummies, Desmond?"

"All of them. They all have an operating address matching the one he uses for Drake Industries."

Jaclyn immediately bit off a curse that hung precariously off her teeth. She shot off the couch and side-stepped the coffee table and her husband's legs, bringing her hands together and wringing them.

"So either Drake thinks he's a smart cookie," she began, "or else someone at the IRS isn't smart enough to figure all this out."

Tom touched his nose.

"Bingo."

"You were right on the dot, Sex Kitten," Jaclyn praised. Outside, the plink of rain against the windows cracked, then deadened, then came in a torrent. "He's definitely duplicitous."

Tasha beamed her thanks, just as a touch of scarlet stung her cheeks.

"There's more, Snapshot."

Jaclyn froze mid-stride. Her breath caught in her throat; she didn't want to choke again. She swallowed hard.

"What do you mean?"

"The money he diverted, shall we say, also went to TealSeattle."

Her breath caught in her throat as Jaclyn felt her eyes widen.

"Does that mean that Drake Industries is a front?" she said when the breath returned.

"Yes, and no. Drake Industries is a reputable business, with real customers and a real product. They have assets, stockholders, they have people to pay—and he pays them pretty well—and he's making a killing, an absolute killing, on the apps people buy."

"So he's not exactly taking a bath in money, if he's giving multiple thousand-dollar donations to TealSeattle," Jaclyn mused. "Does he have an underground drug lab that the DEA doesn't know about?"

"I don't think he's into the drug trade, Snapshot," Salt cautioned. "Besides, we have enough on him for murder, conspiracy, stalking laws, money laundering—drug violations would get us laughed out of court."

"So he's like one of these millionaire playboy sport owners like in football," Tom said. "Some of them give money to players like it's nothing, they buy teams in other sports and ship money between the businesses—there are people in Liverpool who think that because John Henry gives X amount of money for an ace pitcher in Boston, that means we can't buy a striker, and I'm sure there are people in Boston who think the other way around—except this guy's breaking the law by doing what he's doing."

Jaclyn nodded. She heard the sounds of sirens growing louder and closer with every passing second.

"Pretty much what he's doing," she answered. "So he's giving money to this Perkins woman for who knows why. That's really what we have to find out. Who she is, and why she really needs all this money from one person. Isn't TealSeattle getting funds from others? They're a big PAC; surely they're getting more money elsewhere."

"I can check that out in a second. Who's this Perkins woman?"

"Give me a sec. I have it on the iPad." Tasha handed it to her and touched the Safari icon again, sending the app hurtling to life. She scrolled until she found the woman's name. "Kim Perkins. I swear I know who this woman is."

"I'll do a search. Quite frankly, Snapshot, I don't know why you didn't think of doing that first. Google is your friend."

Jaclyn sniffed as she heard Salt typing away, even though her face slipped into a grimace.

"I had lunch on my mind."

"Tell it to someone who cares. Okay, here we go, Kim Perkins." Salt hmmmed. "Not bad. She's a looker."

"I'm telling the girl in the commissary that," Jaclyn snapped. "Send me the image?"

"On its way."

Jaclyn opened her email account just as the pounding of keys on the other end finished. The message came through, and Jaclyn opened it with a simple pressing of her fingertip.

Her eyes sprang apart as the image came into clearer focus. She felt her heart skip a beat as she recognized the woman—calling her a woman reminded Jaclyn of just how old she herself happened to be—and recalled every little thing she had said or done in her miserable little life. The smirk, full of evil intentions without a bit of mystery, was unchanged in over a decade and a half.

"It's her," Jaclyn gasped. "That… that… bitch!"

"What babe?" Tom asked, coming up from behind. Tasha joined them, peeking over her other shoulder.

"She's one of the fucking undesirables I mentioned," Jaclyn said. "Except I don't know her as Kim Perkins. I know her as Kim Gibson. She went to Woodbrook with Drake and I, and all the people we met at the Zig Zag that night." She suppressed the growing urge to fling her iPad across the room like a discus. “She’s the CEO of TealSeattle.”

“Does she have anything to do with Alex’s—”

“I don’t know,” Jaclyn interrupted her ward, her tone a little more strained that before, “but I seriously wouldn’t put it past her.” She paused for a second and lowered her head, tucking her chin toward her collarbone. “She really didn’t like me much.”

She heard Tom’s swallow.

“Because you were different.”

Jaclyn nodded. She felt tears approaching the corners of her eyes at maximum velocity, and felt the stares of Tom and Tasha burn her face. If Salt were in the room, she would feel his stare, too. She was certain of it.

“There’s a little more, Snapshot,” Salt said.

Jaclyn blinked.

“More?”

“Yes, more. Drake is donations heavy into the religious world, too.”

Jaclyn gave a wry smile, considering the circumstances.

“Why does that not shock me?” she replied.

“I know it doesn’t, but to whom may shock you: he’s sent thousands of dollars to one James McAllister.”

Jaclyn felt her jaw drop. She looked to both Tom and Tasha and saw that they, too, wore expressions of disbelief on their faces.

“I know that name. That’s the guy who runs that—”

“Right-wing televangelist program that the president watches, bingo,” Salt finished for her. “There are regular donations to his program.”

“I wonder what that’s all about,” she said, the thought trailing away as the rapid knocking against her suite door made her jump. She quickly wiped her eyes while Tasha, at Tom’s nod, went to check who was there. She felt her flesh tremble; from what, she couldn’t guess.

“We’ll find out how she’s involved, love,” he said, comforting her. “We can’t jump to a conclusion about her. We’ll find out, and then we’ll act.”

Jaclyn nodded as Tasha turned toward her. She loved Tom even more for being her rock.

"There are two cops outside," her ward said.

"Show them in," Jaclyn replied, taking a deep breath. She hoped they weren't there to take her in for questioning, much like the police in Sydney had during their family vacation.

Tasha opened the door. The two Seattle cops were both in uniform, and both were roughly the same size in build.

"Agent Johnson, I'm Patrolman Beesler, this is Patrolman McGrath. We have a situation, ma'am. We need your assistance."

Jaclyn blinked.

"What's the situation, officers?"

"We have a jumper, ma'am. He says he knows you. He's asked for you."

Jaclyn grew aware of her heart racing until it hurt her ears.

"Who is it?"

"His name is Adam Hill."

Jaclyn's eyes widened for the second time in a few minutes. She turned to Tom.

"That's the Advance. Why the hell is he here?" As her husband shook his head and shrugged, thought quickly caught up with her. She blinked briefly, and as she remembered who she had on the other line, turned her head back to the cops. "Officers, may I see some identification, please? This is a highly sensitive situation that I'm dealing with here. I have to be sure of who you are."

They blinked this time, then pointed at their badges. She leaned in.

"Salt, I need to know if Seattle Police have these badge numbers on file." She spoke the numbers into the air. Salt gave a clicking of the keys in response. The officers, she saw, looked slightly concerned, but there was no sign of sweat nor an increased heart rate—save hers. "National security and all."

They nodded.

The wait for verification wasn't that long.

"Snapshot, they are on the up and up. Both active, and with records of good standing," Salt called.

Jaclyn grinned.

"Great work, Salty. I'll call you back later."

"You've got it." He hung up.

"Where is he, officer?" Jaclyn asked as she grabbed her gun. She checked the magazine and found it full, sliding it in with a soft snick. Tom and Tasha went to get light rain jackets, including a teal one bearing the Mariners logo for her.

"The only place one wants to go in order to make a rather dramatic statement," Beesler said, holding onto his utility belt.

Jaclyn paused and felt as if she had been plunged into the coldest depths of the Puget; the chill seeped into her bloodstream. She knew exactly what Beesler meant.

"You're kidding," she said.

In tandem, the cops shook their heads in the negative.

Twisting her lips, she grabbed her HUD on a whim, thinking she would need it even with the deluge which had intensified in strength over the last few minutes.

"Okay," she said, "take us away to Broad Street, guys."

They filed out of the hotel room. Neither Tom nor Tasha asked where they were headed; to Jaclyn's mind, they both knew exactly where this party would end up.

And somehow, she thought as she entered the stairwell to head to the lobby, *I had a feeling I'd be there at some point, too.*

The five of them exited the hotel and into the rainstorm, hopping into a waiting Seattle Police Range Rover, its engine still running, a plume of light gray smoke emerging from the tailpipe at a regular stream. Beesler slipped into the driver's side, with McGrath pulling his lanky form up and into the passenger side. The seats in the back were cushioned, unlike the ones in a regular cruiser. Everyone put on their seat belts, and McGrath flipped a switch in the center console. The sirens erupted and blistered the day as Beesler slipped into traffic, his wipers trying to catch up with the clouds' discharge. They turned right onto Fourth and zipped toward the north.

Off to the right, Jaclyn kept her gaze firmly on their destination—she caught sight the roof with her HUD, along with the various helicopters circling and hovering nearby—wetting her lips as they passed through every intersection.

Chapter 16
The Space Needle
400 Broad Street
Seattle, Washington
Saturday, June 29
1:47 p.m. PT/4:47 p.m. ET

The Range Rover pulled to a stop across the street from the 520-foot-high Space Needle, and through the tinted windows, Jaclyn noticed a small crowd of people had already gathered along the southern side of Broad, even in the semi-monsoon which had swept across Seattle. They all gazed upward, some pointing, at the day's spectacle. The roads, she saw, were also blocked off with sawhorses. Two fire trucks, an ambulance, as well as several other Seattle Police and King County cruisers were also there. Officers kept the people on the sidewalk, while some stood there with their hands in their pockets, trying to stay as dry as possible.

Beesler and McGrath led Jaclyn, Tom, and Tasha over to the command post, which was a cruiser, its doors open, practically underneath the structure. Jaclyn felt the rain plaster her hair to her scalp. Several men turned to face them. Jaclyn held out her hand, and the man wearing the bars of a chief took it. Calluses rippled across Jaclyn's palm. She shivered.

"Jaclyn Johnson, Justice. Where's Mr. Hill?"

"Hanging off the outside of the restaurant," he replied, then pointed up to the curved siding. He leaned to another officer. "Get a light up there."

White light immediately sprang to life and sliced through the mottled gray sky from nearby, and Jaclyn saw, through the pelting raindrops, a person standing outside on a ledge. He was, from this vantagepoint, tight against the glass, his arms outstretched and low, his palms flat on the surface. It looked as though he did that to keep his balance. His hair and clothes looked sodden, and from that height, Jaclyn had a hunch there was a breeze which would send several follicles, no matter how wet, tumbling about.

“How do you know our Mr. Hill, Agent Johnson?” the chief demanded.

Jaclyn didn’t see a reason to lie to the man. She explained his position—his former position—at the White House.

“We believe that he’s involved in the incident at The Warwick a few weeks ago. I thought he was still in Washington. We don’t have enough to charge him yet.”

She didn’t miss the chief’s lopsided grin.

“We can charge him with trespassing if we can get him down the hard way.”

“As opposed to the easy way,” Jaclyn countered, knowing exactly what the easy way was to police.

“Less paperwork with the hard way,” a lieutenant said.

“I got it,” Jaclyn replied. “Is the restaurant empty? It’s not rotating, I see.”

The chief nodded.

“We evacuated the place about half an hour ago and sent a man up to talk to him. Our guy tried to get out to him, but Hill just inched away from his grasps. He said his name and that he wanted to see you.”

“Did he give your man a reason?”

“Nope. Just said that it was time to go. Witnesses said he walked in, just past the maitre’d as cool as you please. Walked around tables, then slid the door open and stepped out onto the ledge there.”

“Damn it,” Jaclyn said, biting her cheek. “I’m going up there.”

The police officers said nothing.

“Tom, get Forrister on the phone and tell him what’s up. Tasha, take visual notes for me.”

Both nodded and Tom had his phone out right away. Jaclyn reached up and kissed him just before he started dialing.

“I love you,” she said.

Tom winked.

“You better, because I love you, too.”

Jaclyn smiled just as Tasha rolled her eyes. She went over and kissed her ward on the forehead.

"I'll keep in touch through the Bluetooth," she added before she turned toward the entrance. She walked underneath the steel lattice base, all while checking out the Needle from below. It was, to Jaclyn's HUD, one enormous disk that would, at midday, block out the sun; today, it did little to stop the sky's weeping. Once she stepped inside the pod-like elevator, she felt her heart racing, which drowned out the sounds of rain lashing against the glass. She tried to shake out her wet hair as the pod gave a lurch and began to rise; the quickly made a pony tail. She slipped her Bluetooth earpiece into her ear canal, just as her heart hammered out the beats. She figured it would take about half a minute for her to get to the restaurant; it would be another eleven seconds or so to get to the observation deck.

She didn't want to go that high. Wetting her lips, she donned her HUD.

Jaclyn drew her gun as her internal count reached fifteen. A few seconds later, the pod slowed. She took a deep breath and let it out, until the elevator chimed. The Walther snapped upward, and she was out and into the restaurant before the doors even finished opening.

"In the restaurant," she whispered, checking left and right, finding nothing. Thought crept quickly, and she noted that she wasn't wearing the Lycra jumpsuit. Her skin crawled, as if naked and exposed to the world—and every bullet imaginable.

She swallowed her fear and kept moving. She felt cold, but that wasn't due to her feigned nudity. Jaclyn had the feeling she knew why she was close to shivering again.

The aromas of abandoned meals clung to the walls and hung heavily in the air; if Jaclyn concentrated hard enough, she would hear the fizzing of soda languishing in its glasses, while smelling beer starting to skunk in theirs. Condensation rippled toward the napkin below. Jaclyn took a deep breath as she sidestepped several tables, the chairs flung out to somewhat impede her progress. She cautiously stepped around them until she came to a point that made her halt.

With the breezes, stiff and howling, coming through the window-like door, one for the window washers to use as a means of egress, there stood Hill; beyond him, a Seattle Police helicopter hovered, putting a light on the subject. He hadn't moved, growing increasingly wet as he stood there in the elements, clinging for his life some five hundred feet above the ground. His hands remained attached to the glass, so much so that Jaclyn feared those same window cleaners would need forever to pull his DNA away. One misstep, though, and he'd hurtle to the earth's face in half the time it took her to get up there.

She walked forward slowly, holstering her weapon as she approached. She made her way to the opening. Her head started hurting, the blood pounding rapid-fire in her ears.

"Approaching," she whispered. She kept her HUD on Hill; if he heard her, he made no sudden movements to let her know he knew of her presence. Taking a deep breath, she moved her head and shoulders into the opening. The wind made her pony tail bounce back inside. She looked at him and noticed that below his feet was a platform about a foot wide encircling the structure. There were outcroppings spaced a foot apart and each was all of two inches wide.

In order to get him out of here, she thought, *we're going to have to get him to come one step at a time, and carefully. There's very little margin for error, and he can't die: he's a witness—the star witness.*

"Hill," she said.

The man gasped as he turned his head sharply to the right. Jaclyn looked and, thanks to the light from the chopper, saw his growing disbelief plastered across his face. His flesh trembled, his upper body seemingly glued to the sides of the Space Needle. There was fright, yes, but there was something else at play in his eyes, something she instantly realized.

He doesn't want to die, she thought. *Someone has forced him out here. And I have a good idea who did that.*

"He's going to kill us," he said. His voice tried to defeat the wind.

Jaclyn shook her head.

"He's going to do no such thing, Hill. Come in and let's talk."

Hill violently shook his head back and forth, with bits of water swinging off and landing on the glass—or falling even further, well beyond her gaze. Other than his head, his body didn't move—except a bit of a shuffle in his feet, a couple of inches to the left, away from the door.

"No," he said, his voice quavering under the stress of the situation. "I can't. I—I have to stay out here and jump. He'll kill me if I don't, he'll kill me if I talk." The tears followed mere heartbeats later, his eyes tightening as he whacked the back of his skull against the glass. "He'll kill me if I don't do either." The man's weeping turned furious, stretching the final syllable out a few moments.

"Agent Johnson, we have sight of you." She recognized the voice of the chief in her ear—but it wasn't the Chief she truly wanted to hear right now. "Do whatever you can to end this peacefully."

"That's what I'm trying to do," she muttered, hoping that it didn't distract Hill. He seemingly didn't notice that she had spoken, his mind agitated by what Drake had ordered him to do. For half a moment, Jaclyn's heart went out to him.

"I can help you, Hill. I can protect you from Drake. You just need to come to the door and come back inside," Jaclyn said over the gale. She held out her hand.

Hill stayed where he was, as if standing defiant in the face of the deluge. A gust of wind picked up from the west; Jaclyn's left hand clung to the inside.

"Being alive and being in jail and in protective custody is better than being a red blob on the side of the world," she yelled. "Help me stop him, Hill. You've told me why he had you kill her—"

"That was a mistake," he cried in interruption. "It was supposed to be you!"

Jaclyn didn't flinch; he had already admitted as much to her in the Oval Office, but an admittance in the sky, one with such fervor and strength behind it, was something to take seriously.

"I know it was, and I need to stop him."

Then, the weeping stopped; if it was an act, Jaclyn considered herself all well and fooled. He had turned his head to stare into the wall beyond her. A tear still rolled, but he looked emotionless, almost like a corpse.

"You can't," he said.

"Yes, I c—"

Jaclyn's HUD came alive just as a concussive blast combined with flash of light from inside, then coincided half a heartbeat later with a slight crack of glass and Hill's body jerking away from the building. He didn't make another sound, and Jaclyn watched as the man flailed away stiffly, tumbling toward the park near Broad Street. His ankles clipped the outcropping, which send his body into a rapid, pinwheeling arc as he fell out of her sight. It wasn't until she heard the echoes of screams coming up at her from below that the public realized the man had died—whether or not they knew he had been shot, she didn't know, nor did she really care at the moment.

Jaclyn jerked her head back into the restaurant, her gun still in her holster. She saw a figure hovering near a doorway, a figure that was easily identifiable. The man held a gun, a wreath of gray smoke growing away from the barrel. His grin was wide, as if pleased with himself.

But it was the eyes—a pair of eyes that looked half-mad and half-full of desire—which really got her attention. He looked much older than the last time she had seen him, and he wore a suit which belied what he did for work. She wondered if he had a pinstriped suit at home, because with what she knew about his dealings, he likened him to a gangster of the 1920's to 1940's.

"Drake," she breathed.

Not hesitating any further, Jaclyn drew her Walther and pointed it, then squeezed off two rounds.

Neither hit the target, instead embedding themselves into the wall. Drake had moved away barely in time.

Without thinking, Jaclyn quickly gave chase.

Instead of skirting the tables and chairs the patrons had left askew in their haste to evacuate, Jaclyn vaulted them and even sprang up on them as she made her way toward the elevator—but Drake, she noticed, had moved toward a stairwell. Even as she hopped up and rushed across the tables two steps at a time and launching herself forward, the voices in her ears.

"Jaclyn, what was that?" Tom cried. In the background, helicopter blades thrummed.

"Hill's dead, I'd think that's pretty obvious," she said dryly as she hopped across a table marked 52. "Drake shot him, I'm in pursuit. No time to talk."

In her ear, she heard her husband relay that back to the chief.

She reached the other side of the room and dropped to the floor from the tabletop, trotting toward the stair door—the lone door—in this direction. She offered it a hearty kick, swinging it open; she could have simply opened it, but kicking it would have sent it slamming into Drake's head if he hadn't run any further and tried to catch her unawares. She brought her Walther up and at the ready as she slipped inside.

Drake's footsteps only went one way, though, and that way was up. She pointed her weapon that way and she slid to the wall, just as the echoes of his steps fell silent and died.

As sweat trickled down the back of her neck, her adrenaline kicked in. Jaclyn tried to keep her breathing as quiet as possible as she moved closer to the actual stairs, waiting for her quarry to make a move. Without looking down, she crossed her left foot and stepped up, then pulled her right foot up behind it, moving up another step. She did this three more times before reaching the next landing.

Then, Drake swung his upper body up and over the railing from two flights above, swinging his gun around, too. Two blasts came forth, both hitting above Jaclyn's head.

Tiny jagged pieces of concrete tinkled against her head just as Jaclyn fired. The shots clanged off the steel, the casings falling at her feet. But without hearing any wincing, she knew she hadn't hit Drake with either of them.

Jaclyn bit off a curse.

"Darren, come on, give yourself up," she yelled. Her voice immediately caromed back at her. "This is my only offer."

"Piss on your fucking offer," he called back, his voice echoing his vitriol a little, too.

Jaclyn gnawed on harsh-smelling, cordite-tasting air.

"So be it," she muttered, then pushed off and ran.

Drake ran, too. She heard his footsteps intermingling with hers as they both pounded away on the steel, but his were a little faster this time.

Jaclyn followed up several flights of stairs until she came to the final one, one that led to the roof of the observation deck. Drake, she saw, wasn't out in the open, which only meant one thing.

"Tom, he's on the roof," she said. "The very roof of the Space Needle. I'm going out there, too."

She hefted her Walther and opened the door, once again with a kick.

Jaclyn gasped as she stepped back into the storm. While rain, wind, and the sounds of the helicopter blades created a vicious cacophony of noise, she saw Drake inching himself toward the edge of the roof. She watched, mesmerized, as he lowered himself a little as he attempted to keep his center of gravity as close to the sloping roof as humanly possible, frog-walking until he could go no further. Much like Hill with the restaurant, one bad step or a slip on the soaked surface would send Drake plummeting to his death.

If he's going over there to jump, Jaclyn thought as she felt a touch of weightlessness approach her heart, *there's nothing I can do to stop him right now; I'm not going to risk my neck for Alex's murderer*. Closing her eyes for the briefest of moments, she inhaled sharply as she tried to steady herself. She didn't want Mother Nature to deposit her over the edge. With where her head was positioned, she now stood well over 520 feet above the city of Seattle. Jaclyn couldn't help but swallow the bile that rose, all while she tried to suppress her increasing vertigo. She kept as close to the door as possible.

"Darren!" she yelled. Drake jerked his head up and glanced toward her; she saw his face, pasty white, a mix of angst and fear colliding with each other. "Don't do it! Don't you dare fucking do it!"

Drake snarled. Off to the side, Jaclyn caught a glimpse of a black object approaching; she noticed that it was a helicopter, but she hadn't received word that Seattle Police had called for back-up.

"Who's going to stop me, Jaclyn? You?"

Without thought, Jaclyn slowly brought her Walther to bear on her old friend. His suit and hair were soaked.

"Jaclyn, what's he doing?" Tom barked in her ear.

"He's gone as far as he can," she said, before raising her voice. "You're done, Darren."

The snarl turned into a grin.

"You don't have the balls to shoot me," he said. "Especially since you don't really know everything."

The Walther's barrel fell a quarter of an inch. The thrumming of chopper blades drowned the sound of her blood pumping.

"You have nowhere to go," Jaclyn repeated over the din, trying to keep the conversation on track; she couldn't afford a distraction like the one he proposed. "If you value your life, you're going to get your ass back here as quick as you can."

"Why? So you can break my heart again?"

Jaclyn felt her nostrils flare.

"To answer for her death," she corrected, her tone strong and stern. "You know that."

Drake snorted.

"Sure. Sure. She took you from me, and she got what she deserved." He turned his head for a brief moment, then turned back to her. "Listen, I don't have time to chat; my ride's here," he said.

Jaclyn blinked in utter confusion, but then she caught the meaning of both sentences. Even though she heard Tom speak in her ear—"Where in the bloody hell did that one come from?" he had said—the first one disappeared from her mind, though she knew she had enough now; she had his confession. But the second sentence grew much clearer as her eyes bulged under her HUD. She now saw what Tom had seen, what everyone on the ground had seen: the approaching helicopter, as dark as the night and teeming with missiles, slide its cargo door open as it hovered closer, all before it started to execute a treacherous bank directly in front of her. Soon, the blades sent rainwater spraying into her face, distracting her from her purpose. She instinctively brought her gun arm up to ward everything off instead of to use it.

Then thought caught up with her. A gasp slipped from between her lips.

If those blades hit the spire, she thought, *there's going to be a shit-ton of explaining to do. The whole Space Needle may go up in flames, and here I am; on second thought, maybe I won't be the one who does the explaining, after all.*

Her panic grew stronger as her chest thrummed with what felt like a knife-inflicted ache. She glanced up and saw just how close the blades came to striking it. It was mere feet, maybe as many as ten, but at this distance, it was all too close for Jaclyn's comfort.

Jaclyn gulped as she watched Drake take his chance and leap toward the maw of the chopper, only to see his hands to slip a bit on the wet edge. Drake careened while he struggled to gain purchase, and Jaclyn felt her heart make a dash for her throat as she saw his feet dangle freely, the roof of the Needle too far away for a solid strike, and far too sloped for practical safety. Her weapon forgotten as her shock lingered, she stood helplessly as another man, all in black, instinctively reached out and clutched his arm. Another grabbed the back of his jacket and yanked him in to safety.

Without another second, the pilot went into action, pulling the chopper away from the roof. It turned around and headed back the way it presumably came.

Jaclyn stared as the copter, with Drake aboard, retreated. She ignored the feeling of her sodden pony tail clinging to the back of her neck, but she remembered her duty.

"We need that chopper followed, babe," she said as she eased herself to the other side of the door as slow as possible. A wave of nausea shuffled through her. Her eyes closed. “Oh, damn.”

“Seattle PD is swinging a chopper around,” Tom replied. “Are you okay, love?”

“Not really.” She tried turned the handle, but it wouldn’t budge. She sword and bit her lip, but the thrumming of helicopter blades gave her pause as they increased in timbre. Jaclyn turned just as the police chopper charged around the observation deck, the whirling blades sending another spray toward her. She spat out a bit of rainy mist. “I’m slightly nauseated, it’s raining, I’m on the roof of the Space Needle, and to wrap this all up in a neat little bow—” she paused, “—I’m pretty much locked out of the building.”

“Oh, bloody hell,” Tom said. “I’m coming up to get you. Stand tight.”

She inhaled as she closed her eyes.

“Okay, babe. I love you.”

“I love you, too. Scouser out.”

Jaclyn crept as close to the wall as possible and slammed her back against it as she watched the aerial pursuit. She swallowed hard again as the Seattle PD chopper grew smaller, Drake’s chopper just ahead.

Then, her HUD went golden as an explosion of light filled her field of vision in that direction. Startled, she tried to back her way through the retaining wall, but she went no further. She fought the urge to lean forward, fearful that she would lose her balance, in order to get a closer look at what had happened.

But she knew that just from the fireball and the tumbling shrapnel some distance in front of her, the Seattle Police helicopter had exploded; thankfully, she saw the fuselage’s remnants dropping straight into the Puget instead of over a populated area or a business, which would keep the death toll from this whole day down to those in the copter, and Drake murdering Hill, dead before he even hit the ground. Even through the slate gray curtain of rain and her current height, Jaclyn saw over the surrounding buildings and watched as a heavy cloud of raven, fuel-driven smoke rose and billowed about even after it hit the water, the copter buoyant and still partially aflame. She lightly gnashed her teeth together as she noted her memory and how the explosion had happened; now she wished she had risked everything, if only to throttle Drake and send him off the roof's edge, and to prevent his rescue.

Jaclyn bit her lip until she tasted metal. She sucked on it for about a minute, her chest still a dull ache, until the door finally swung open. She turned her head and sighed, her heart swelling. Tom stood there, a look of relief on his face. He, too, looked haggard, with water dripping off his head, but she knew that he didn't look half as haggard as she did right that second.

"Would it be so cliché of me," Jaclyn said, her body still up against the side of the spire mount, "if I said, 'My hero' right now?"

Tom nodded and smirked as she eased her way into the stairwell, her breathing coming easier as the feelings of vertigo ebbed away to nothingness. She wrapped her arms around the back of his neck as they kissed.

"The chopper exploded," she said as they broke apart.

"I know, I saw it on me way up. Missile from the bogey. It took Drake away?"

Jaclyn nodded. She felt a drop of water plink onto her nose.

"He confessed before he hopped aboard," she said. She didn't believe that she restrained her emotions, especially after everything that had occurred so far. "He said she took me away from him, and that's why—"

She felt his finger on her lips, quieting her. Her heart skipped another beat.

"Don't say it now. Let's get downstairs and let's get you dry."

Sighing, Jaclyn nodded. They headed down the stairs—Jaclyn a touch gingerly as she regained her footing—to the waiting pod elevator.

***

Darren Drake's secret hideout

Bainbridge Island
West of Seattle, Washington
Saturday, June 29
2:33 p.m. PT/5:33 p.m. ET

It didn't take long for Drake's getaway to come to fruition. He had planned every detail, right down to standing on top of the Space Needle.

In the seconds before he brought his gun up and shot Adam Hill from behind, he had pressed a button on a beacon, which let his people know he was ready for extraction. That meant he had a certain amount of time to pull off the killing and get to the rooftop to catch his lift; anything that went against that course of action was an unnecessary tangent. He had the feeling Jaclyn Johnson would chase him to the very edge of the world after what he had done—and he was right. She had fallen right into his game, and he left her there.

As they approached Bainbridge Island and his facility there, he thought about everything that went down in pulling it all off: he had lodged himself in a bathroom stall, his feet up against the moorings, while Hill, silently and reluctantly, walked through the restaurant and took his position on the ledge; the evacuation order came a few minutes later, and once it was quiet enough, he slipped out and waited for Johnson to come—as he had ordered Hill to do.

Drake toweled his head, breathing a heavy sigh of relief all while he slicked his hair back. He had ordered the missile launch to destroy the pursuing helicopter. He desperately wanted to keep his operations secret for the time being, and he knew that soon, the federal government would come in and shut his operations down. It was only a matter of time, seeing as he had exposed himself—but not in the real way he wanted to do it—to Johnson.

"Estimated time of arrival?" Drake asked. He tried to pull his sodden clothes away from his body, but they just re-attached themselves with a bit of a squelch.

"Three minutes, Mr. Drake. Miss Gibson awaits."

He cracked a smile.

"Good. Good."

The chopper flew on.

The time passed easily, and Drake spent it trying to regain all of his faculties: his heart rate slowed to normal, the danger gone. He breathed easier knowing that she wasn't on his tail again—at least not yet. Hearing her voice for the first time in a long time, though; he tried to keep it lodged in his mind, to hear it whenever he wished.

The chopper approached the facility, and from up here, the complex sprawled across the windscreen, partially camouflaged by the trees, their greenery shouting at anyone to look away. The walls were high and made of concrete, the thickness ranging close to two feet according to his specifications; he had wanted something which resembled the old G.I. Joe cartoon's headquarters. There was a concrete roof, too, save the two sunken panels dead center which, he saw, were in the process of sliding apart. His pilot made directly for that port, and Drake heard only the pilot's side of the conversation. Soon, though, the helicopter hovered over that spot before it dropped slowly inside, the blades not hitting the sides as they kicked up dust and pine needles during the descent. It was as if they had done it before.

Drake hopped out of the helicopter a few seconds after it landed, taking a few moments to steady himself on solid ground, all while the blades' wash enveloped him as they slowed above. Another deep breath later, Drake made the slow walk to his private office. He needed a change of clothes and a hot shower.

Yet the former Kim Gibson—now known as Kim Perkins, his business partner and the middle school nemesis of Jaclyn Johnson—intercepted him in between the chopper and the office.

"How did it go?" she said as she fell in next to him.

"As expected," he answered. "It went perfectly. Hill is no longer our concern. They'll be scraping him off the latticework from now until Christmas."

"And Johnson?"

Drake issued a shot of hot air from his nostrils.

"As far as I know, still alive. She chased me to the roof. I left her there."

"That wasn't how we planned it," Gibson said, her tone stern. "We planned that she would die there. We're now, as the baseball world says, 0-for-2 in this endeavor."

"Baseball is a game based on failure. We'll get her," Drake reminded her, even though he tried to keep his personal feelings down. Personal feelings had no place in a business relationship, even though the extreme nudity between the two had long disposed of feelings. "But what I need right now," he said as they slipped into his office, "is a long, hot shower, and a clean suit. And maybe even a glass of wine."

Gibson's smirk told him everything. He matched it as he closed the heavy door.

"You're lucky I foresaw your needing of wine," she cooed. "I took the liberty of pouring you a glass as you approached. That way I can get you nice and soused as I take advantage of your inebriated state while we discuss just what exactly we'll do with Johnson."

"We do have to make a move quickly," he cautioned, "but the shower first." Drake removed his jacket and tie, then unbuttoned his shirt and kicked off his shoes. Less than a minute later, with rainwater coating his fingertips, he managed to get naked as Gibson rested her ass on the edge of his desk, her ankles crossed over each other while she sipped a different glass of wine. Drake felt her eyes canvassing the slopes of his rear end—much like he had at his home—as he walked toward the shower.

She followed him into the private bathroom just as he stepped into the shower. She sat on the toilet.

"What is the move?" she asked, impatient.

"I have to keep moving," Drake said through the spray. "Since she saw me, you know the feds will be on my company rather quickly. You should be in the clear to do everything we've talked about."

"Killing Johnson is the main goal. You know that."

For the first time in a while, Drake was glad for the flimsy, partially-scalloped curtain separating them. He closed his eyes and bowed his head, all while the cloud of steam kept him as camouflaged from her sight as the trees outside did to his redoubt.

"Afterward," he said, as if he spoke to the temperature controls. "We have to make sure that those computer companies don't get back online any time soon, and I have to make sure all of my money is laundered out of my known accounts and sent to you."

"Don't send it to me," Gibson said. "Send it to TealSeattle."

"You are TealSeattle, my dear." He grabbed the bottle of Pert Plus from the shelf.

"Yes, but no one in the government truly knows that it's me."

Drake considered this, then nodded to the ceramic tiles. He hoped, however, that since Jaclyn had seen him, that they wouldn't find his financial records. They were on his home computer, he knew, one with heavy encryption.

"Of course. When do you want to go ahead with your plan?"

"Everything is in place." Her voice was a bit closer than before; a little stronger. "The people are in Vancouver and they have no fear of the U.S. Government. Their planes are ready at my command. The trucks will be loaded as soon as they get here from California, and they'll ship the chemicals up to the planes. We'll do it a few at a time so we don't arouse suspicion from the state police."

"There are tractor trailers on the highway at all hours of the night, in all directions," he countered as he slathered his hair with shampoo. "I doubt it will be an issue under these circumstances."

The curtain opened as Gibson flung it aside. Drake turned and found her equally naked, but dry. She stepped in as he had his hands to his scalp, shampoo falling to the porcelain floor. Drake saw that she had a come hither look on her face. She reached out and grabbed the curtain in her left hand, pulling it closed. She grabbed him with her right and pulled him closer to her. He twitched as her hand made contact.

Breathing deeply, he tilted his head under the light rain and rinsed.

They said nothing else as they shared the water.

Chapter 17
The Warwick Hotel
Lenora Street
Seattle, Washington
Saturday, June 29
6:15 p.m. PT/9:15 p.m. ET

Jaclyn tried to avoid looking at Hill's dead body, his form broken by the steel, as she and Tom exited the Space Needle. She and the chief had conversed, and she said that the debriefing should occur at the hotel. She figured that as the acting head of the CIA, she had the ability to postpone the debriefing until a time more convenient for her. The chief, knowing of the harrowing adventure she had just gone through, didn't put up a fight. They agreed on meeting at 6 o'clock. That gave Jaclyn, Tom, and Tasha plenty of time to shower, to get dry, to decompress, and to consult with the president.

She had showered with Tom, and both put on a pair of sweatpants: Jaclyn a pair of gray and teal Seahawks sweats, while Tom had a pair of Liverpool sweats, all in red. Each wore a different colored hooded sweatshirt with Seattle emblazoned across the chest in big, bold letters. Tasha came into their suite in sweats, too, but in the colors of the Georgetown Hoyas. They called for Chinese takeout.

For Jaclyn, the time in the shower had given her plenty of time to think, even with the strong hands of her husband scrubbing her skin.

The fact she had almost died on the roof of the Space Needle, without any protection on her body, rattled her. Drake had, of course, tried to kill her on the stairs leading up, but she remembered his hands were empty on the roof. All he was trying to do was keep his balance, trying to keep from falling like a stone while the helicopter made its approach to snatch him from her clutches.

There was also the fact he had admitted to killing Alex. But it was the way he had made his admittance, that and the tone he had used, that made her shiver.

"She took you from me."

Jaclyn had to fight off the urge to vomit, even there in the shower. Drake had thought about this, had used it to fuel his revenge and to bring death to Seattle, for more than fifteen years; the mere thought was more than she would ever fathom. Couple in the fact that he had built a shrine to her and had—

Even as soap raced down her back in a fight to cling from the top of her bottom, Jaclyn launched herself out of the shower to kneel in front of the toilet. She heaved twice.

Once done, and with Tom standing beside her, her hair in his hand, Jaclyn needed a moment to collect herself. She wiped a sheen of cold, clammy sweat from her brow before her husband helped her back to her feet and back into the shower.

"Thinking about what you and Drake had to talk about, I take it," Tom said as he slid the curtain shut again. Jaclyn had her face in the water, her hands rubbing her flesh slowly.

"We didn't have much to discuss, but yes, you can say that. That and the fact I thought about him with his pants around his ankles, and the result is now headed to the Seattle wastewater treatment facility."

Tom grabbed his belly as he faux stumbled backward.

"I'm hurt," he gasped. "I'm so jealous, you thinking of another bloke with his hand on his willy." He playfully huffed. "Mum was so right about you." He winked.

Jaclyn smirked, just before a wave of nausea hit her again. She inhaled deeply as she retreated a few inches into the corner; water peppered her bare shoulder from above.

"Four words: Kate Middleton's bare bum. Don't tell me you haven't Google'd it."

Tom shrugged.

"Maybe I have," he answered. "Maybe I haven't. You all right?"

"Yeah. Just residual crap from what Drake said. And no," she cautioned, "I'm not pregnant."

Jaclyn felt her heart fall just as Tom's face did the same.

"Oh."

She reached out and grabbed his arm, tugging it and pulling him toward her. She felt his pain even through his hand. The spray of the shower coated his hair and splashed her face.

"Not now, babe. Soon, though," she whispered before kissing him lovingly.

"How soon?"

Jaclyn lifted an eyebrow.

"Mum's giving you the business again?"

Tom nodded softly.

"She sent me an email while you were up fighting with Drake. I deleted it."

Jaclyn kissed his forehead.

"Maybe she should start with Chloe, then." Jaclyn tried to be as soft as possible, especially in a situation such as this where delicacy was needed; and while she wanted to become a mother, she knew—and he knew, and his family knew—right now really wasn't the perfect time for either of them. She knew this wouldn't be the last time this subject would come up, and truthfully, they both knew it was a discussion for another time; they were currently in the midst of an investigation, and it was the only thing that mattered right now. If children were thrown into the mix—Jaclyn really didn't want to think about it. It was postponing the inevitable, yes, but they really didn't have a choice. Did she want to grow old with Tom and raise a small family? Yes, but she knew her duty: she had priorities, and saving the country was her priority. Right now, raising children wasn't one of them. "She is the oldest child, and we are what we are. Maybe she should find herself a man and get it on."

"I think mum understands your feelings on that," he replied. "I think." He nibbled on his bottom lip. Jaclyn stroked his cheek with the fingers on her left hand. A dull ache shot out of her shoulder for reasons she couldn't fathom. She offered a slight groan, but bit it away.

"I wouldn't try explaining it. She knows we're in the service to our governments; she's been through it."

"I think she believes that since dad did it, we can do it, too."

"I think it's a different situation. What did mum do for work?"

Tom shook his head.

"She took care of us, and now Her Majesty's Government is taking care of her like she's a minor Royal since dad's been gone."

Jaclyn felt her lips slide into a pumpkin-like grimace.

"We'll have kids, and they'll be handsome like their father," she said, a light smile touching her lips. "But in a few years. Not right away. One of these days, we'll both be free of our governments, and we'll be able to take care of the baby-making. You don't think I could rock the jumpsuit with a baby bump now, could I?"

"Maybe," Tom said. "I don't know why I want to be a father so quickly. And they'll be as beautiful as their mother."

"No, mum wants to be a gran so quickly," Jaclyn corrected as Tom stared her down, his eyes warm and sensual, all while she felt her face burn and grow numb under her husband's flirtatious praise. "We're—we're going through the motions of dealing with our security-heavy jobs and societal pressures on both sides of the Atlantic. If it got out that I had a child, do you know how many foreign governments would try to kidnap him or her and use against both of our governments? I don't think I can do that now, or ever. I want to be the mother of your children, yes—but right now isn't the right time."

Tom nodded solemnly. Jaclyn knew he wouldn't protest.

They finished up their shower a few minutes later.

Tasha had placed the order, and they waited for it to arrive. In the interim, Jaclyn called Forrister. The phone rang once before the switchboard operator answered with a stiff "White House." Jaclyn soon discovered that the president wasn't at 1600 Pennsylvania at that moment; instead, he was around the corner at Nationals Park, taking in the Nationals and Tigers baseball game. The switchboard, though, patched the call to his cell phone.

The call rang three times before Forrister picked up. She heard the soft tones of the crowd and organ music chanting "Let's go Nats!" in the background, and she figured that the president was in a bullet proof suite somewhere near the press box. She quickly imagined Forrister sipping on a near-ten dollar beer and munching on a Shackburger.

"Hello," the president said.

"Sir, it's Jaclyn."

"Hi Jaclyn. I'm at the ballpark. What's up?"

"I know you are. I encountered Drake this evening, sir. He unfortunately escaped me."

"Damn. What happened?"

"He took off from the roof of the Space Needle in a helicopter, then shot a missile at a Seattle Police chopper that I ordered to follow it."

"And you were—"

"On the roof the Space Needle, yes."

"Damn. That has to be five hundred feet up."

Jaclyn closed her eyes. She hadn't put the HUD back on, and she swayed a little as the president's little reminder of the building's height sent her stomach to churning once again. She eased herself into a chair.

"Five twenty would be a little closer to the mark, but with five-ten of me, it's closer to 526."

"Damn."

"I'm meeting with the chief of police in about an hour or so to debrief, so I can call you back and see what we're doing about finding Drake," Jaclyn said, pausing briefly. "Sir, he pretty much confessed to me. About killing Alex. That was after he killed Hill, the Advance, from behind, as Hill stood on the outside of the restaurant. They're still peeling him off the base after his fall."

Forrister's groan was heavy and audible through the line.

"Why does all of the freakiest shit ever conceived," he said, recovering slowly, "happen when you're on duty?"

Jaclyn sniffed her amusement.

"I don't know, sir. I think someone has it in for me, or something. I'll let you know how this comes out."

"All right, you've got it. Forrister out."

Jaclyn disconnected the call without a closing greeting nor asking him the score of the game, just before their Chinese food arrived. She fished a pair of twenties out and handed them to her ward. While they ate, they checked out the local news to see recorded footage of just what happened at the Space Needle through the piercing lens of the Fourth Estate. Jaclyn gulped a few times as the camera focused on her leaning out of the window in an attempt to get Hill inside, followed by the flash and bullet that made him drop. She was quite happy they didn't show him fall. Then they showed a bit of her stare-down with Drake on the roof of the Space Needle. They didn't mention who it was.

Jaclyn fumed.

Looks like we need to set the record straight, she thought.

Once sated from the afternoon's excursions and the aroma of chicken fingers filled the room, they waited for the chief and his lieutenants.

They didn't have to wait long.

The chief arrived with a small entourage; Jaclyn didn't see Beesler or McGrath alongside the Seattle PD's brass. Jaclyn offered to make some coffee if they wanted, but a few of them had rather large cups of Starbucks in their hands.

"Did they get Hill's body off the base?" Jaclyn asked as they all took their seats.

"We did, yes," the chief replied. "Who was he again?"

Jaclyn didn't argue; she knew she had already told him, but with the stress of losing a few members of the brotherhood weighing on him these last few hours, she thought it prudent to re-hash the tale.

"He was responsible for planning the president's trip here a few weeks ago," she said as she launched into her story. She mentioned the room set-up and how it cost Alex her life; Jaclyn kept her composure as she relayed the details. She also brought up the sting they had set up in the Oval Office; even the chief grinned as Jaclyn spoke of it.

"What did he tell you up there?" he asked.

"Mostly, it was ramblings about how he would die if he didn't stand on the outside, and that he'd die if he talked to the authorities. He mentioned, in one moment of lucidity, that Drake can't be stopped."

"Drake?" the chief blinked. "You mean—?"

"Darren Drake, yes. The head of Drake Industries. It was Drake who shot and killed Hill, it was Drake's chopper that shot and destroyed yours. The son of a bitch is behind everything." She told them how she had attended school with him at Woodbrook, how she had used her federal authority to break into his home—the chief visibly bristled at that, adjusting his positioning in the chair—and found his so-called shrine to her, and how it all came together. "We're looking into his financials and we're finding many dummy corporations, as well as multiple donations to a company called TealSeattle."

Jaclyn watched as the chief and a lieutenant shared a look. She saw their heads practically move as one, their chins pulling toward the other as if magnetized. Her heart sprang into action, pumping away with punishing force against her inner sternum.

"TealSeattle does some good things in our city, but we've heard rumblings."

Jaclyn felt her eyebrows rise. She looked to Tom and Tasha, and she wasn't shocked to find that they both had similar expressions etched in their faces. She had to suppress a shudder—a good shudder, one which made her ovaries dance—as she caught Tom's eyes.

"And what rumblings are these?" she asked, returning her gaze to the chief.

The chief looked constipated, as if he had eaten a burrito that didn't agree with him.

"Can your associates be trusted?" he said, jerking his head toward Tom and Tasha.

"Seriously?" Jaclyn replied, her tone one of derisive amusement. "My husband has a higher security clearance than the Queen of England. My ward has a higher security clearance than *you* do." She snorted. "Yeah, I'd say they are rather trustworthy."

The chief nodded.

"Good. What I'm about to say cannot leave this room. It's part of an ongoing operation." The chief cleared his throat. "We have reason to believe that there are some shady doings at TealSeattle, but we haven't been able to get anyone into the building. We have no probable cause to get a warrant, and no one is talking—much."

"Much? But someone told you something," Tom said.

"No one told us anything. We discovered—well, stumbled on it would be a better description."

"How?" Tasha asked. "That would be a pretty big stumble."

The chief cleared his throat again, this time with a heavy load accompanying it. He leaned in; Jaclyn did so, too.

"We used drones. We had our crews do a fly-by of the city to see just exactly what there was to see. And when we crossed the channel to TealSeattle, we found a bit of toxic waste coming out of a pipe in the building, as well as a bit of venting steam. It made us ask the question amongst ourselves privately—"

"Why is a company dedicated to green energy and keeping Seattle green involving itself in anything steam-based or anything involving toxins or toxic chemicals?" Jaclyn finished for him, her chest aching as the words pierced her heart like a shiv.

The chief of police leaned backward.

"Bingo. Brilliant thinking."

"And according to Drake's financials, he's diverting truckloads of cash to TealSeattle, either directly or through his dummy corporations."

"The IRS," Tom said, "is going to have a fecking field day when they find out about this shite."

"Who's to say they don't already know and are just waiting for the right time to strike?" Tasha added.

"That wouldn't shock me," the lieutenant said.

"Well, I can tell you it won't be us who tells them," Jaclyn said, shooting out of the chair and walking over to the window. She stared southward, looking toward CenturyLink and Safeco, the rain still slicing across her field of vision, landing against the glass and rolling to the balcony below. As she crossed her arms across her chest, she tried to keep her gaze from moving up to the balcony above, all while she felt every eye in the suite turn toward her. She breathed heavily, the cold glass growing thick with gray, warm fog. Her mind rolled: between the actions of today and all she had learned today, the fact they continued to peel layers away meant they were getting closer to the truth of the matter. All they needed, she believed, was one, final push, and everything would come undone. She knew that deep in her heart.

Then, she took in a sharp breath. The realization hit her.

He's still in custody, she thought.

"We're going to get the drop on them."

"And just how are we going to do that, Agent Johnson?" the chief asked.

Jaclyn spun on her heel.

"Drones," she said. "Chief, get your drones in the air. How many do you have at your disposal?"

The chief blinked, as if trying to snap the dumbfoundedness out of his face.

"Three. What do you have in mind?"

Jaclyn powered her way back across the room, slipping into the small dinette and grabbing a bottle of Sprite from inside the fridge. Even in her stocking feet, she made the floor quake. She twisted the cap off and drank deeply. Her mouth had grown rather dry, and the soda managed to dampen it before she returned to her seat.

"Drake and his entourage fled west toward the Sound and practically beyond; by the time I looked up from the downed wreckage, their chopper had disappeared into the storm. I lost sight of them, begging forgiveness for the word usage. We had sent that chopper after them to see just exactly where they were headed; if Drake hadn't blown it up, we would already be converging on their location, and we'd have that scum-sucking son of a bitch under arrest for murdering Hill, at the very least, and his accomplices as accessories. So we've lost track of them."

"And you want the drones to snoop them out," the chief added, this time with a grin. "Agent Snapshot, if there is any way to steal you away from the feds, you have a job waiting for you here at Seattle Police. The way you think is uncanny."

Jaclyn felt her heart bounce into her throat like a basketball, forcing her to swallow hard. She recalled what her uncle had said the other day, about always having a home here in the Pacific Northwest—with the possibilities of a job and a home, she could give her mother-in-law what she wanted, and what she wanted, too.

"Thanks, chief. I'll let you know if that ever comes up. But until then, we have to focus on bringing down Drake and his cronies. Can you get those drones up?"

He nodded.

"Of course. You want them to head west?"

"Yeah. That was the way they were headed. Bainbridge Island, maybe even further to the west."

"We'll get them. But when we find them, what is our plan of attack?"

Jaclyn took another long sip. A small drop tumbled away from her lip as she pulled the bottle away.

"It depends on what our prisoner has to say," she said.

The chief had to blink again. Tom and Tasha, though, smiled. Jaclyn saw the recognition spring into their eyes.

"Prisoner? What prisoner? I wasn't made aware of a prisoner."

Jaclyn smirked.

"Actually, I'm sure you were. It's the one I shot that started this whole thing," she said, standing. "He's going to give me everything I want to know, and he's going to know first-hand what it's really like to turn into a target."

Chapter 18
Seattle Police Headquarters
610 Fifth Avenue
Seattle, Washington
Saturday, June 29/Sunday, June 30
10:03 p.m. PT/1:03 a.m. ET

It took a few hours to arrange, but Jaclyn managed to get the prisoner transferred up Interstate 5 to Seattle Police Headquarters for further questioning. The federal marshals had held him at Fort Lewis, her father's old base, and Jaclyn had a feeling the U.S. Attorney for Seattle had no idea there was a dangerous terrorist under lock and key; she hadn't heard from one, and she had expected a call from them shortly after hers, Tom's, and Tasha's return to the Pacific Northwest. It was either that, or she figured the president had leaned on the attorney and told him not to speak to the prisoner until well after she had completed her investigation into the matter.

As she thought about this while she, Tom, and Tasha walked into the station, she let a grin slither across her lips.

Well, she thought, *there may be no need for a trial after I'm done with this cocksucker. There may be nothing of him left to put on trial.*

She had dressed in her jumpsuit, complete with two suppressed Walther P99s and full magazines, along with her favorite black trenchcoat. She felt a few stares from several officers as she entered the building, the drops of rain running down the rear side of the coat. She had her blonde hair tied back, the sides of her Foster Grants tucked into the thick strands.

"Tasha," she said as she strode model-like down the corridor, "go keep an eye on the drone situation while Tom and I work this fucker over."

"You got it."

They met the chief and the lieutenant in the chief's office. They both looked rather tired. Jaclyn and her crew had downed a pot of coffee, now that they were in for a rather long night. The chief led Tasha to what he jokingly called the "Drone Room," while the lieutenant brought Jaclyn and Tom to an interview room.

"Is it soundproof?" Jaclyn asked.

The lieutenant nodded.

"About as soundproof as you'll get here."

"All right. Don't come running if you hear anything out of the ordinary."

He paused mid-stride and gulped hard.

"I'm actually on my way home—"

"Tell your replacement that, then," Tom said. "Who's bringing him up?"

"My replacement, as well as two servicemen. They'll be up in two minutes."

Jaclyn nodded.

"Two minutes. Good. We'll be in there. Tell him not to worry if the lights are out. Just shove the bastard inside, and we'll take over from there."

The lieutenant nodded, then rushed away, the blood leaving his face as he retreated. Jaclyn figured he didn't want to be a witness to whatever she had planned; she was sure he had heard of her prior one-on-ones with terror suspects, and her walking in there with suppressors screwed onto the barrels more than likely told him the janitors would be working overtime in the morning.

Jaclyn and Tom walked into the room, her heels clicking off the linoleum. As soon as they closed the door, she dove into her utility belt and pulled out a pair of darkness bombs, the tiny globes of thin cellophane she had created back at a Langley lab. She brought her hand up and tossed them down hard, the small crack filling the space just before spilling their contents out and up toward the ceiling. A pitch black nothingness encased the pair, but Jaclyn didn't feel out of her element; her senses, already heightened long ago with the partial loss of her sight, felt at home and comfortable.

"HUD," she said, "give me heat registry."

With a pair of beeps, the device complied. She turned her head and found Tom's heat signature bursting across her field of vision.

"You look sexy in reds and oranges, did you know that?" she asked.

She didn't catch her husband's facial mannerisms, but she heard his snicker. They maintained silence as they waited. Jaclyn's blood thrummed along in her ears as the anticipation built, only drowning out the deep breathing from her husband.

The wait was short. The door opened, and Jaclyn found herself staring at several heat signatures at once, but they appeared melded together as if a congealed mass of sunshine. Yet as the seconds passed, the signatures on the side made their way out of the room, leaving one fidgety signature standing only a few feet away. She heard the door shut right before the steel links of the handcuffs jingled once. A choked, nervous breath escaped his lips.

Jaclyn felt the left side of her lip twitch before she stepped hard and flung her left foot, stiletto and all, right into the bastard's gut. She heard him wince as his air left his lungs, right before he tumbled to the floor.

"Ah, your groans are a Top 40 hit to my ears, you bastard," Jaclyn cooed.

The prisoner wheezed as he tried to regain his breathing. Jaclyn's foot connected with the side of his skull just as the darkness bomb dissipated. He flopped backward, the chains on his ankles and wrists jangling off his body.

Jaclyn leaned over and grabbed him by the orange prison jumpsuit he wore, heaving him to his feet and throwing him into the steel table. He crumpled like an accordion, hitting his knees hard; the sounds of bone against steel preceded bone against linoleum.

"You know what I want," Jaclyn said from behind him. She looked down and saw that the sweat came in cascading rivulets, just near the point of being absolutely drenched.

"I don't know what you me—"

With gritted teeth, Jaclyn grabbed a heavy handful of the man's wet hair and yanked his head back. He screeched, but those pleas turned to blubbering as Jaclyn drew and placed the suppressed barrel of her Walther against his Adam's apple.

"You're not so tough without your precious gun now, are you? You can't shoot defenseless ladies and kill them, but now you're in chains, and I'm the one with the gun. How does that make you feel?"

Jaclyn received her answer not a second later as the sound of water plinked off the linoleum, followed by the strong, pungent aroma of fresh urine.

"You just pissed yourself, you piece of shit," Jaclyn taunted. "Only little boys with death wishes piss their pants."

"What do you—"

"What do I want? What do I want?" Jaclyn dug the barrel into his flesh a little deeper while bringing her lips closer to his ear. She ground her teeth together as she spoke. "I want my friend back, you cunt, but since that's not fucking happening any time soon, I'm going to take your life in payment. First, though, you're going to give me every little fucking detail you can about Drake and Gibson, and why TealSeattle isn't as green as they say they are. Then, and only then, I'm going to kill you."

"Why should I talk?" he said, even though the words came out through strained vocal cords.

"You're dying tonight," Jaclyn stressed. "Whether it's five minutes from now, ten minutes, twenty, it makes no difference to me. Your life is worthless; it's been worthless since you crashed through those balcony doors. The information you have within your itty, bitty brain is going to crack this investigation and take down the bastards who hired you."

The prisoner snorted.

"Then there's nothing in it for me."

"What's in it for you," she said, pulling tighter against the man's scalp, "is that you get to hear your pithy little voice tell me everything you know before your blood runs cold, your flesh grows hard, and your heart stops beating. If you don't start talking now, I start shooting fingers and toes away. And once I run out of fingers and toes, I'm going to make your face bleed." She pulled the Walther from his Adam's apple and tapped the point of his nose for greater effect.

The rattled gasp in response instantly fueled Jaclyn's desires. But when he didn't start talking—his eyes darted to Tom, and Jaclyn saw the orbs pleading with her husband to call her off; Tom simply stared daggers in return—she shrugged and tilted her gun toward his right hand, let go of his hair, and grabbed his shackled wrist instead. The barrel met his thumb, right at the joint where it met the palm.

"Three, two, one!" Jaclyn counted down without taking a breath, pulling the trigger the instant the final syllable poured from her teeth. The gun barely made a noise—but the prisoner howled as the sharp, instantaneous pain seared his nerves. His eyes flew open as two inches of bone, flesh, fingernail, and blood dropped to the floor. He tried to pull his hand away, but Jaclyn's grip had his arm stationary. She wasted no time, moving to the next knuckle. "Next finger! Three, two, one!"

She fired. The prisoner's index finger joined the thumb in a pool of crimson on the floor.

The prisoner's tears multiplied as he roared and whimpered, bawled and shat himself. Jaclyn paused briefly as he smartened up and balled what remained of his fingers together into his palm. She waited for the man to stop being a pussy and take his torture properly, adjusting her grip toward the forearm.

"Anything to say?" she sneered.

He shook his head violently.

Jaclyn snorted and shrugged.

"It's your funeral," she said, pointing the steaming Walther at his wrist.

That got his attention.

"Please, no," he breathed, stunned.

She didn't listen. She pulled the trigger again, punching a dime-sized hole into the man's flesh. Blood poured from the wound, coating his wrist in his own juice.

"Oh God," he moaned, "oh God, make her stop. Oh God." He clenched his eyelids tight. "Fuck, God, stop her."

Jaclyn made a noise that resembled a buzzer going off.

"Sorry, God doesn't recognize your plea for mercy. Try again next time." She leveled the gun at a point next to the wound and fired again. Another howl, one that seemed to come from his hips. He flexed his fingers, giving Jaclyn another opportunity to take off another digit.

And she did.

The prisoner's middle finger vanished with a well-placed bullet, and blood shot out of the wound with the force of a geyser, making a mess of what remained of the prisoner's right hand. Jaclyn let go, and immediately he grabbed it and pulled it close to him, all while bowing his head until his brow touched the cool steel. She saw sweat dripping off his hair, as if he had turned on a faucet and had turned it off just as quickly. He didn't bang his head off the table, which Jaclyn thought would happen, if only to distract the pain that burned its way up his arm and seared every inch of nerve within his flesh. If he felt the pain all the way in his toes, she wouldn't have been surprised by that.

"You have anything to say, bitch?" she said.

Head still against the steel, the prisoner shook his head.

Jaclyn frowned.

"Well, I think that this proves that American men are tougher than Muslim terrorists," she said, kneeling to the side. "What's your name?"

The prisoner raised his head. Jaclyn saw his eyes, red and full of terror, grow vacant. He squeezed that hand underneath his left armpit, but with the shackles, his arms looked like he had twisted himself into a position in which he couldn't escape, his makeshift tourniquet rather comical. He had lost a lot of blood in a short amount of time; Jaclyn figured that he wasn't going to make it much longer.

"Joe," he said. "Joe Fitch."

"Joe, you don't have much time left. You're probably feeling a bit woozy right now." He nodded. "You're going to die. You died pretty much for nothing, because I'm going to get Drake. I'm going to kill him, I'm going to kill Gibson, and every little thing you did for them is going to be for nothing." She grinned. "What is Gibson doing with all the money Drake has funneled to her company? Why is there toxic waste in her seemingly green plant?"

Fitch shook his head.

"I don't really know," he said. "I just tried to call your bluff. I know nothing of their plans; they hired me the week before, and the check cleared." He gulped. "Can you, you know, call the ambulance?"

Jaclyn simply stared, making no facial reaction. The look in his eyes, even with the pain, told her one thing.

He's telling the truth, she thought.

"No, I'm not going to call the ambulance," she said. He whimpered as her words hit, then brought his head back to the table. "I'm just going to sit here and wait for you to bleed to death, much in the way you killed my friend."

"It wasn't supposed to be her," Fitch moaned.

"I know. I should put a bullet in your brain and in your heart, much like you did to her, much like you wanted to do to me. But you realize that if you had tried to do that to me, you would have had no luck whatsoever."

He nodded, albeit slowly.

"I would have killed you the moment you entered our room."

To her surprise, Fitch didn't move. It was almost as if he didn't hear her.

"Your colleague in the whole thing fucked up. He didn't count on the Secret Service thinking about the president's protection."

Fitch still didn't move.

Grimacing, Jaclyn rose from her crouch and shoved her Walther up against Fitch's temple. Without another thought, she pulled the trigger. Fitch's head didn't even register a bullet had penetrated the skull. A mushroom cloud of brain, bone, and blood exited the other side. The corpse slid out of the chair and toppled to the floor, dead long before he hit it.

Jaclyn let a breath out as she stashed her Walther.

"I'm confused," Tom said, drawing her gaze. "I'm wondering about the whole Tom and I roughing him up part."

Jaclyn's teeth glittered.

"Figure of speech," she replied. "It's a euphemism for you to make sure he bleeds enough while I pump him full of lead."

Tom blinked, then nodded.
"Oh good, as long as we have that figured out."
"Come on," Jaclyn said. "Let's go see how Tasha's doing with supervising the drones. I want to nail this scumbag's balls to the wall."
Tom gave a British-style salute as they left the room and powered their way down the hall to the command center.
The room was dark and poorly lit, as if a darkness bomb had lingered for far too long and clung to every surface. The only light came from the computer monitors and a set of dim LED bulbs that were ensconced in the ceiling. They found Tasha standing behind a rather large captain's chair, her forearms resting on the back. She had her gaze fixed on the monitor in front of her. Jaclyn and Tom sidled up next to her. Jaclyn saw darkness mixed with reflected moonlight on the screen.
"What have we got?" Jaclyn asked.
"Drones are in the air," Tasha confirmed. "Rain has stopped. What you're seeing here is the drone's undercarriage camera. It's flying over the Sound right now."
"And what about seeing where it's going?" Tom asked. "I'm pretty sure we need to see where it's going."
"That's simple enough," the man in the captain's chair said. He reached over and flipped a switch. An infrared picture of the approaching shoreline popped onto the screen; to Jaclyn's HUD, it felt as if she wore a pair of night vision goggles.
"Did you get anything out of him?" Tasha asked, distracting Jaclyn from the view.
Snapshot shook her head.
"No," she said. "He had nothing to give except fingers."
Tasha smirked.
"And?"
Jaclyn's sigh rippled through the room.
"He's dead. Bled to death. Then I shot him in the skull to make sure."
"Feel better?"
Jaclyn swallowed; her throat felt raw.

"Not really. Alex can't come back. I just eased his pain a little more. Mine is still there."

"Drones are a few minutes from sweeping over the shoreline," the controlling technician said, interrupting them. Tom ran his hand around her shoulder, and she immediately felt the warmth and love from the two closest to her. While she appreciated it, now wasn't the time for a double cuddle.

"Where are they? Bainbridge?"

"Affirmative, ma'am."

"Can you pull it up on the map through GPS to show my husband and protégé where they are, please." It wasn't a question, and Jaclyn saw the controller didn't take it like one, either. He acquiesced and simply flipped a switch to bring the detailed 3D map, one with topography and satellite mixed together, up on the screen.

"Bainbridge Island," Jaclyn declared. "Located twelve miles from Seattle proper via the ferry at its farthest distance, and only a few miles from Fort Lawton north of the city. At its widest points, Bainbridge is four to five miles across, while as little as one—and maybe even less than that. A hodgepodge of homes, roads, businesses, small hills and forestry areas encompass the island, and somewhere within the twenty-eight square miles and its watery boundaries, Darren Drake is in hiding."

"So what are we looking for, Agent Johnson?"

Jaclyn cleared her throat quickly.

"Anything that looks like it can hold a fairly large helicopter," she said.

The controller nodded.

"Roger that. The drones will take a few swipes of the island." The controller grabbed a cup of Starbucks; Jaclyn kind of wished for a latte, too. After taking a deep sip, he set it down again and returned his gaze to the screens.

When she brought her eyes back to the screen, she watched as the drones soared over Bainbridge's South Beach, the southernmost point on the island. The drones swept over the tops of the trees, occasionally skirting over a pre-fabricated, barged-over home. To the northeast, Port Blakely was equally devoid of large structures. The trees bowed and waved with green hands, the bowing coming rather stiff and unnatural.

It was near Wing Point that a larger concentration of civilization popped up, but like at South Beach and Port Blakely, there was nothing there that screamed redoubt, nothing that screamed massive complex full of gun-toting underlings willing to go to the absolute edge to achieve their diabolical plans and nefarious schemes. There were large buildings, sure, but Jaclyn saw nothing that resembled a helipad, nothing that pointed to an evil genius at work. Jaclyn's jaw shifted several millimeters as she pondered if this was simply a wild goose chase. A deep breath scoured her nostrils.

The drones motored over the eastern coast of Bainbridge, cruising over a golf course.

It took nearly twenty minutes for the drones to finish the eastern reconnoiter before they turned toward the west. Jaclyn's heart made a direct line for her throat as she saw Hidden Cove, in virtual darkness, appear on the flat panel monitor directly in front of the controller.

"Check the Cove," she ordered. "There could be an escape vessel tied to a dock, or the redoubt hidden in the trees."

"True," the controller said, turning the joystick to the left. "We'll never know until we search. Bringing them low."

"Don't bring them too low. We want to make sure they can get back up."

Tasha snorted.

Jaclyn didn't even turn her head.

"That's not what I mean, Sex Kitten."

"I know."

"Cute double entendre, though."

The snicker that came from the recent high school graduate made Jaclyn grin.

The drones skimmed the surface of the Sound as they turned to the southwest and toward the inland portion of the island. A tiny island, not more than twenty yards across, fell away from the drone on the right-hand side as its camera panned the northern shoreline of the Cove. Each of the three counterterrorism agents paid close attention to a screen apiece. From what Jaclyn saw, there was nothing resembling a colossal hideout among the tall, statuesque pines.

"Continue surveillance," Jaclyn said. "Nothing there but pines and docks."

The controller didn't acknowledge the order vocally; instead, the moved the droves back toward the eastern shore, but cut that short and sent them southbound, away from the area they had already scouted.

By 11 p.m., the drones had scoured more than half of the island and had finally made it to the western coast. They swept around near Lynwood Center—nothing there, which earned a swift sigh from Jaclyn—and came about at Crystal Springs. The other half of Kitsap County lay on the other side of the water. The city of Bremerton appeared briefly to the southwest as the drones turned the corner.

"How much longer can those things stay in the air?"

The controller shrugged.

"Don't know, to be honest with you. We've been going for about forty-five, fifty minutes on this trip so far. They had full battery when they left, and the range is good for fifty miles, so if they peter out and slam into the ground, we should have a good idea of the battery life."

Jaclyn smirked.

The trees were incredibly thick here, and the darkness crept over every square inch of Bainbridge Island's surface, making it darn near impossible for anyone, or anything, to catch a glimpse of anything remotely tangible, anything remotely solid. The drones, scaling the sky higher and higher as if reaching out with metal hands to claw at the nothingness above, caught glimpses of a tiny body of water—Gazzam Lake—as they swept over Westwood, which barely consisted of enough beach houses to represent a quorum at a city council meeting. They kept floating along to Fletcher Bay.

It was just as the drones passed over the water again that Jaclyn raised her head to peer at what had just appeared; a light rustle to her left told her that Tom noticed it, too. Light filled the screen, the viewports of the drones catching it and transmitting it back to Seattle Police.

There, in full view, was a wide building that took up hundreds of feet from west to east across the screen, the western edge only some seven hundred feet from where the still waters of Puget Sound lapped upon the shore. Tree stumps remained near the base of the thick walls, while other tall pines seemed to act as spindly camouflage. But what really caught her HUD and smacked her right on the bridge of the nose were the tiny lights on the roof; they sent white, stationary beams of light into the sky, as if resembling beacons. Jaclyn thought not even a bit of fog would make the lights shimmer had Mother Nature deemed it necessary to disturb their peaceful vigil. The lights outlined a squared-off section of roof, which looked sunken from this distance.

A light lick of her lips later, Jaclyn felt sure this was where Drake had run to when he left her on the roof of the Space Needle.

"Get closer to that building right there," Jaclyn ordered, her tone a little louder than she had anticipated. She pointed at the screen before noticing that both Tom and Tasha held their breath as the drones moved into position.

A few heavy heartbeats later, the center drone slowed as it pulled overhead and went into hover, the screen now showing its undercarriage camera once again. Yellow pebbled paint covered the roof in a circular fashion, along with target hashes shooting off to the side to make it resemble a hockey face-off circle more than a landing area. The cut in the middle running across the breadth of the roof, though, told Jaclyn all she needed to know.

Her grin spread easily.

"Jackpot," she breathed. "We've found Drake's hiding place."

"Looks good enough to me," the tech said. "Getting the coordinates now."

"Good. Give me a fixed point on the map."

"With pleasure."

With the exception of fingertips on keys, the command center was silent. Jaclyn waited patiently to see the exact location of Drake's hideout, her fingernails at her teeth. It was un-model like, but she didn't care about that right now. Bitten-off fingernails could be grown back. She was one step closer to getting the man behind Alex's demise, and that's all that truly mattered.

Not a minute had passed before the tech had the location pulled up, a blue dot pulsing away.

"Is that an exact GPS fix?" Tom asked.

"Yes, sir." The tech zoomed in with a few mouse clicks, and showed the redoubt on the satellite map.

"Zoom out again."

He did as ordered. Jaclyn stared at it and rubbed her chin, a plan percolating as she weighed her options. Drake's hideout sat next on a plot of land called Battle Point, a triangular section of land sticking out from the western edges of Bainbridge Island. Getting to it wasn't difficult, but going via car wasn't exactly advisable, either, since one had to travel south through Tacoma and venture down and around the Puget to get to Suquamish. Once there, a bridge connected the two land masses. With timing being everything, that type of a trip was out.

Jaclyn had been there once prior to her world turning upside down, but she had taken the ferry, which was the direct route from Seattle proper. The ferry, however, didn't go directly to Battle Point; instead, it stopped at Wing Point to let cars off and to take cars again. Another ferry went to Bremerton, swinging around the south coast of Bainbridge. She could do that and swing northward when they got to Crystal Springs. There was also the possibility of going around the north side of the island and squeeze through the narrow waterway between Suquamish and Agate Point, but she noticed that way was directly in the line of sight of the redoubt. She didn't want to tip Drake's men off—or Drake, for that matter—that they were on their way.

Would Drake's men muster themselves if it was just them coming about in a smaller boat? Jaclyn thought. *Maybe not, but I wouldn't want to take the chance of them freaking out for a slow-moving rowboat.*

There were really only three options from which to choose, then: the first was to sail over to Fletcher Bay, lay anchor, and then walk half a mile northbound. The second would be to, yes, sail over to the Hidden Cove, lay anchor, and walk about a mile or so to the southwest.

The third, however, was perhaps the safest course, but also the one with the most physical exertion of the three: sail over from the city to the eastern side, lay anchor, then hike two miles across the island. The narrowest walk would be from the inlet between Manitou Beach and Ferncliff. The first quarter mile, she figured, would be the most dangerous: three people walking down a lonely street at an ungodly hour with black clothing and heavy armament before entering the forests which lay between the drop-off and the final destination. People looking out their windows may be alarmed at the sight, but that wasn't her concern; she'd have the chief of Seattle Police make a call to Bainbridge Island Police to let them know about the situation and the mission.

It was enough for her.

"Call the chief and request that he come down," she said. To the side, Tom and Tasha blinked in tandem. Their questions, Jaclyn thought, would have to wait for now.

"He's not going to like that," the tech replied. "He probably just got in bed."

"I don't care," she snapped. "Get him down here; I know he'll want to talk to the president. Then ready the SWAT and call the Bainbridge Island department and tell them to get ready for a show. We need to get mobilized and ready to move."

Jaclyn had her phone out as the three of them stormed out of the command center. She scrolled through her recent call list and found the number for the White House. She touched it and waited for the switchboard operator to snap out of their rest and answer the phone.

"So what's the move?" Tasha asked.

"The move," Jaclyn replied, the phone pressed to her ear, "involves a bit of hiking, and a bit of shooting."

"Excellent," Tom said. "It's a good night for both."

Chapter 19
Seattle Police Headquarters
610 Fifth Avenue
Seattle, Washington
Saturday, June 29/Sunday, June 30
11:51 p.m. PT/2:51 a.m. ET

Jaclyn had the communications set up and ready to go within half an hour, and all they waited on was the chief and the head of the SWAT. Forrister was on hold.

The chief and the SWAT commander walked in shortly before midnight, each wearing a robe. Jaclyn explained what they had found, and that it was time to act. Once everyone was assembled and seated, she started her spiel.

"Over the last several weeks, a rather corrupt businessman with ties to Seattle has perpetrated a ruse against the city and its residents, and has openly attacked and killed a high-ranking member of the Forrister Administration. Over the past few hours, he has killed a link in the chain, and in his escape, blew up a Seattle Police helicopter. We have tracked him to Bainbridge Island, to a fortress on Battle Point." She clicked the map to show the position of Battle Point in relation to Downtown Seattle. Then, she clicked the PowerPoint and showed the redoubt from the drone flying north. "Right now, our plan is rather simple: my two colleagues and I will take a boat over to the eastern side of the island, hike across it, and when we get into position, we will wait until you arrive for us to engage the enemy.

"We expect to find the businessman, Darren Drake, waiting for our arrival." She flipped a switch, and Drake's photo appeared on the large screen. She had taken the photo from the Drake Industries website; a chill wriggled around her spinal column. "It is also entirely possible that an associate of Drake's, Kim Gibson, also known as Kim Perkins, the head of TealSeattle, will be there, as well." She flipped the image to show Gibson's face to the men and women assembled. Jaclyn averted her HUD; she didn't want to look into the eyes of the woman who had tormented her in middle school until she no longer had the option. "There is a rather lengthy financial trail between the two, and we believe the money going from Drake to Gibson will be utilized in a plot that goes against TealSeattle's core beliefs." She took a light breath before continuing. "We believe that if we do not stop this duo, the plot they have concocted will come to fruition, to the detriment of Seattle society."

A hand shot in the air.

"Yes?" Jaclyn said, pointing to the man in the dark blue jumpsuit.

"Ma'am, can you tell us exactly how many men we're dealing with here?"

"Not for a certainty. What we do know is that the fortress in question has thick walls surrounding it, with plenty of trees on its outside edges acting as camouflage, as you saw in the photo. We've only seen it with drones, nor do we know the amount of entrances, nor do we know how many men are on this base. It is my hope that with the men and women in this room, we'll be able to storm the building and subdue any and all acts of sabotage, and any and all acts of aggression against our party."

"Shouldn't this be a job for the military?" the officer asked. "If the walls are pretty thick, you're going to need a rocket launcher or something to get us in. We don't have can openers on us."

Jaclyn grinned as the others chimed in with a bit of laughter.

"I'm sure that," she began, before a thought sprang into her head, making her pause mid-sentence. Her breath suddenly came out strangled and thin. She never got the end of the sentence out.

"Love, are you all right?" Tom asked. She turned and saw the concern scrawled across his retinas.

"Yeah, I am," she breathed. "The military. The military. That gives me a great idea; why didn't I think of that first? Mr. President, are you still on the line, sir?"

"Yes, I am."

Jaclyn heard the stiffening of backs as the president's voice filtered into the conference room. Several of them looked at their fellows, wondering if the voice on the other end was truly Eric B. Forrister. Yet as the noise died down, Jaclyn returned her attention to the speakerphone.

"Sir, correct me if I'm wrong: I still have *that* privilege, correct?"

Forrister's chuckle was tight-lipped.

"If your meaning of 'that privilege' is what we discussed two weeks ago, the answer is yes."

Jaclyn found it difficult to swallow, her throat tight. She felt the tingle of excitement crawling across her chest, but a blink and a deep breath calmed her just as quickly as the idea entered her mind.

"We'll use the military as a last resort," she said. "We're going to reconnoiter with our eyes, if you'll pardon the expression. We didn't have the drones do a full scan; I just wanted to pinpoint the location of this fortress before we set a full plan."

"And if this is not the right place?" another cop asked.

Through her HUD, Jaclyn issued a stare that simply said, "How dumb are you?"

"It's the only place on Bainbridge Island with concrete walls that are several feet thick, and a helipad sunken into the roof," she said. "Besides, the tech in the control room, while we planned this, did a search. The bastard we're looking for has the property in his name, according to the assessor's office. He's either there, or we're back at stage one."

"Let's hope he's there," Tasha said.

"Chief, you'll co-ordinate with your opposite from Bainbridge to let him know what's going on?" Jaclyn asked.

"Of course. He and I are old golfing buddies. I'll give him a courtesy call. He'll probably send a few officers to those roads nearby and turn anyone coming that way around." He cleared his throat. "Confidentially, he's confided to me that they wouldn't be able to do much more than direct traffic."

The SWAT guys laughed hard. Jaclyn sniffed a smile.

"Good. You may want to let him know that we'll be going on foot through the woods, and that we'll be as heavily-armed as we can manage it." She paused for a brief moment before turning toward the assembly. "Any questions, you guys?" None came. She felt every eye on her while several butts shifted nervously in their seats. Firming her lips, she gave a sharp nod. "All right then. We're going to head out in a little bit. We'll send a signal when we're ready for you. Dismissed."

The SWAT soldiers filed out of the room as if this whole thing was just another situational meeting, but Jaclyn tuned it all out as she leaned over the speakerphone again. The Seattle chief and the SWAT head remained with them. The noise soon died away once the last SWAT member out closed the door behind them.

"Most of these men were all military before they joined the force, ma'am," the SWAT head said. "I apologize for that man passing the buck, so to speak."

Jaclyn waved it off.

"Thank you for your concern, commander. It's no matter. He actually gave me the idea to call in the military. Mr. President, should I make the call or should I let you do it?"

Forrister's laugh filtered through and filled the small auditorium.

"I'll do it, of course. The guys at Lewis always love a call from the C-I-C."

"Good. Saves me a nickel."

"I'll call them now, and I'll call you back on your cell." The president sighed softly. "3 a.m. Veronica is going to kill me, you know. She doesn't like it when I'm not in bed with her every night. I can't even begin to tell you what happens when I go overseas."

Jaclyn had a good idea what he meant; if SnapChat had existed before she and Tom got married, she probably would have set up a private account to send him racy photos, but it didn't matter now since they practically worked together and weren't separated by the Atlantic Ocean any longer. There was the little phone sex tease from before Tom dropped contact while she was in Las Vegas, but that turned into a passionate love-making session when he arrived.

"My apologies to the First Lady, and give Maryah a smooch for me when she wakes up."

“Will do, Snapshot.” The president hung up.

Jaclyn let a deep breath go before turning to the chief.

“Any way we can get an unmarked motorboat to ease our way across the Sound?”

He nodded.

“You got it. The waters should be clear right now, no one to impede your progress. And I’ll have dispatch send landline calls to our officers on the Sound to clear your way in case anyone gets out of line.”

“Give us two hours,” Jaclyn noted. “We need to get changed and make sure we have enough firepower ready, just in case it turns into a firefight.”

The chief nodded again.

“I’ll have it ready for you. Pier 69. 2 a.m.”

Tasha slapped her hand over her mouth as she became overcome with girlish giggles.

Underneath her HUD, Jaclyn rolled her eyes at her ward. The chief grumbled something unintelligible as he pulled at his robe. The SWAT commander followed him out.

“All right, let’s go. We have some weapons to check and some dark, skin-tight clothes to put on,” she said. They left Seattle Police Headquarters and headed back to The Warwick.

“They seemed a bit apprehensive,” Tom said a few minutes later.

“Yes, and there’s a reason for that,” Jaclyn said, her tone even and calm.

“Which is?” Tasha asked.

“It’s quite simple. They want the U.S. government to take the fall instead of the Seattle Police Department. We all know that the police are getting a bad rap in departments throughout the country. They wanted the military to do it so that in the event of a massive fuck-up, blame wouldn’t be placed on the department. The military, however, has been able to evade criticism from the so-called patriots, as no one would utter a peep for fear of being labeled anti-military. The so-called patriots would instead say that it’s a failure of a Liberal president, as they’ve said time and again. So they were only looking out for their best interests, and I have no problem with that."

"True. True."

"But will there be a fuck-up?" she said to the air, just before striking the switch for her directional. "No. No, there won't."

***

Darren Drake's pleasure boat
Leaving Bainbridge Island, Washington
Sunday, June 30
12:15 a.m. PT/3:15 a.m. ET

Their shower and change into dry clothes complete, Drake and Gibson left the island via a small sloop Drake had docked in Hidden Cove for just this type of emergency. They departed the fortress in a small Ford, a driver behind the wheel in order to take them to the small harbor. Drake had him avoid the main roads when at all possible; he didn't need police interference just now, and he was sure that the proper authorities were on to them now that Jaclyn—*oh, my sweet, sweet Jaclyn,* he thought as his heart swelled—had laid eyes on him.

The pair didn't speak a word to each other as Drake maneuvered the boat backward and forward, making their way out of the island and into the open water of the Puget. Drake kept his eyes focused forward, even with her arms around his waist from back to front, her head resting between his shoulder blades. Yet even as he piloted the sloop, even with the comforting presence of his lover, all he thought about was trying to avoid Jaclyn killing him before Gibson had the chance to do the same to her.

His quandary, however, was larger than a cat-fighting tiff.

At the moment, he didn't know exactly where he would find refuge: Drake knew he couldn't go to the main residence in North Inglewood, seeing as Jaclyn had been there, had the address, and was sure to give it to the police. He couldn't go to his place of business or any of the corresponding stores, for he figured there would be dawn raids at those places. Files would be secured, the locks to those establishments' doors changed.

In a word, he knew he was fucked.

There were, of course, other hiding places dotted around Seattle and the metropolitan area that Drake owned through subsidiaries. Those, he knew, did not have his name on any financial documents the government might get their grimy little hands on, and he also knew that he wasn't on the listings of board of directors or anything searchable on the Internet.

Or, he thought, *the best place to hide is in the open.*

Nodding mainly to himself, Drake bared to starboard as they hit the open water, beginning a slow roll toward the south.

"Where are we headed, love?" Gibson asked.

"Your plant," Drake replied with a slight grin; he didn't turn his head to look at her to gauge her reaction, only feeling her grip tighten on his waist. "I need a place to hole up until this blows over. You can be sure that first thing in the morning, Johnson will have the police and the federal authorities barging into my businesses, examining records, securing computers, et cetera. They'll freeze all of my assets. They will blockade my manse. They will do everything to keep me in the country."

"So why don't we sail to Vancouver and hitch a flight to somewhere without an extradition policy?" she replied. "You and me, living off the proceeds of our scams, illegally in a country where their exchange rate makes the dollar look puny. That would make me happy."

Drake smiled.

"Yes," he said. "That would be wonderful."

"Then let's do it."

This time, Drake's lips twisted into a frown. Even though it made complete sense, he didn't see the need to do it just yet. All he needed to do was hide. He was sure of it.

"I can't. Not yet."

"You need to get out of the country. *We* need to get out of the country. Our scams are set up. We have nothing left to do."

"Are the planes readied?"

Gibson said nothing, the silence caustic against the sounds of water splashing against the hull. The outboard engine purred along, its hum low.

"I thought not."

"They will be readied tonight. I will make sure of it."

Drake spun partway and finally looked Gibson in the eye. For the first time, she quailed under his gaze.

"That is why we need to stay in-country; I will not fully trust this task to underlings. Once the planes are readied, once they have sprayed Seattle with the chemicals, and once we have assurances that the city is alight, then we can make our way out and aboard. We'll cancel the phone lines and we'll declare bankruptcy once and for all. We'll be far from the reach of the tax authorities, and well far away from the reach of Jaclyn Johnson."

Gibson paused and swallowed, then finally nodded her approval.

"You're right," she said. "You're always right."

Without another word on the matter, they sailed toward Gibson's private pier in Seattle proper.

Chapter 20
Bainbridge Island, Washington
Sunday, June 30
2:30 a.m. PT/5:30 a.m. ET

The boat Jaclyn, Tom, and Tasha climbed into was an older Seattle Police boat, the chief assured her, one retrofitted for a nighttime assault. Its hull was in matte black without SPD insignia or serial numbers on either the port or starboard side, which Jaclyn thought necessary for this mission. The black would meld well with the stillness of the water and, with a new moon hanging over the Pacific Northwest, there was barely any light to let anyone over on Bainbridge Island know that they were on the way. They would appear wraith-like to anyone who cared to look eastward, and with it being closer to 3 a.m. when they planned to come ashore, Jaclyn counted on no one witnessing their arrival.

Like the hull, the three of them were all in black, too, with Jaclyn and Tasha wearing their jumpsuits. Each had several firearms and a couple of spare magazines just in case. Jaclyn didn't want to do a lot of shooting—that was what the SWAT was for—but if she needed to draw a weapon and fire off a couple of rounds in order to take Drake's men down, then so be it. She mainly wanted to do the in-person reconnoiter, report in, then, when the SWAT had finished doing their thing, drag any survivors out of the fortress and beat the answers she desired out of their mouths. At least that's how she felt the plan should go.

They didn't speak as the motorboat raced across the Puget, the outboard motor at a low roar as they made their way to the west. Jaclyn had brought Lucy along, seeing as there was no need to bring the Cruze along for the ride. She did, however, wish the car had pontoons like the one in the Detroit mission, but the whole headlights on thing would more than likely put a damper on secrecy. She hoped that she wouldn't need the car again, but that was more than likely a fool's hope. Lucy made sure to chide Tom, who served as the pilot, whenever he strayed a smidge off-course.

The trip across did not take as long as the normal ferry ride: Jaclyn remembered the usual thirty-five-minute trip taking longer, as she was only a pre-teen when she had made the voyage to Bainbridge last. But with the smaller vessel and with a bit of speed behind it, the trip took about twenty-five minutes to complete.

"We should be at Battle Point by 3:30 a.m." Jaclyn announced as Tom tied the boat to the dock at the harbor between Manitou Beach and Ferncliff, "as long as none of us twist an ankle while we're walking through the woods. Flashlights will only get us so far. We have to hope that there are no pitfalls the closer we get to Drake's redoubt, since we'll need to go light-free in about an hour."

They set off from the docks, Jaclyn in point position, with Tasha in the middle. It took only a few minutes to escape the clutches of civilization; for Jaclyn, she felt like Aragorn leading the hobbits away from Bree as they stepped into the wooded area. No dogs barked at their sudden appearance—another thing for which Jaclyn had prayed would go their way.

Route 305, Bainbridge Island's main highway, was deserted. They crossed it at a trot. At this stage, there was no need to hunker low to the ground. Jaclyn noticed that the air was still a tad moist from all the rain which had drenched not only Seattle, but the island, too. As she stepped off the far side of 305, she felt the wet ground give way a little underfoot. She kept her balance, taking a deep breath and letting it out as she managed to stay upright.

"Be careful," she warned. "It's slippery."

They elected to walk along the roadways which wound away from the Puget until they had no choice but to enter the forest. They turned right and then left again until they came to a horse farm, the barn as large as an aircraft carrier. They avoided the sure-to-be electrified fencing before they finally plunged into the wooded area adjacent to the property. The chirping of crickets and crunching of leaves underfoot surrounded them, the noise of a light breeze seemingly absorbed by the pines. The sweet scent of sap filled Jaclyn's nostrils and reminded her of climbing trees when she was in her single digits.

"We just need to bear directly toward the west," Jaclyn said, pointing that way. "If we stray from that to the south, we'll have a little more walking to do. And we don't know what Drake has for people on patrols. We need to be as quiet as a church mouse in these woods."

"Right," Tasha countered, "because snakes eat church mice."

Jaclyn grinned and kept walking. A road interrupted their path, but like before, there were no cars on them in either direction.

They finally arrived in the area known as Battle Point, the woods spitting them out and depositing them in the southernmost section of a rather large park. From Jaclyn's map study earlier, there was a small riding ring and a trio of softball fields dead ahead, and beyond that, the redoubt lay nestled in the trees. Farther north was a small street hockey rink, a pair of tennis courts, a playground area, and two soccer pitches that she knew she had to keep her husband from seeing, or else he'd want to channel his inner Steven Gerrard for a few hours.

From the park, Jaclyn saw the topmost level of the fortress, as well as the beams of lights she had seen from the drones a few hours ago. A yellow light blinked on and off slowly, once every three heartbeats, cutting into the night. A small rise was also in the distance, and that is where Jaclyn believed was the best place to get a good look at the layout.

"Lights out," Jaclyn said, and the three of them extinguished their flashlights. With the exception of the redoubt's lights and the stars, there was nothing to see. "Let's go."

They trotted away from the woods' edge and entered another copse of trees to the rise, a blemish on the surface.

A few minutes later, they found themselves overlooking the redoubt, an immense structure now that the three of them had the chance to see it up close. Through her HUD, Jaclyn saw several men with submachine guns walking along the top, looking here and there for an intruder.

Or us, Jaclyn quickly thought.

The walls were thick, yes, but she also noticed there were several spots near the forest floor on the southern side with several openings which, ironically, had garage-door type enclosures. And they were, to the best of Jaclyn's knowledge, wooden garage doors. There were several stumps like she had seen before, but those were off to the side. The ground in front of the openings was clear of the forest remnants, with freshly-turned earth smoothed out. Several puddles dotted this area, but they weren't exactly expansive or deep.

"Some fortress," Tasha snorted.

Jaclyn beamed before turning to her companions.

"Who in their right mind creates a fortress with thick concrete walls, but the means of egress on the ground is through a pair of flimsy, wooden garage doors?" she asked aloud, her tone soft.

"Someone without a lot of brains," Tom answered. "This is going to be easier than we thought. The SWAT team can flash-bang the shite out of that, flush the bastards out with baton rounds and water cannon," he continued, before Jaclyn saw his face fall, "and now I sound like David Cameron. I need a bath." He trembled with a full-body shiver.

Jaclyn pulled out her iPhone and immediately dialed Seattle Police. The line rang twice.

"Seattle Police, Dispatcher West, this line is being recorded." It all came out in one long, pre-rehearsed spiel that Jaclyn figured the dispatcher said it so many times in a day and could drop it into regular conversation.

"This is Jaclyn Johnson," she said, trying to keep her voice from carrying into the dell. Even from here, she heard the light lapping of the westernmost part of the Puget against the shore. "Get me the chief. I have a sit-rep for him. Priority one."

"Right away, ma'am. Please hold."

The line went from the softness of the communications center to the dulcet, acoustic-like tones of Nirvana. She only had to wait a few minutes for the chief to take her off hold, cutting off Kurt Cobain's raspy, grunge crooning on *Heart Shaped Box*.

"Agent Johnson, what's happening?"

Jaclyn's cheek twitched.

"Chief, the fortress, if we can call it that, is just a flimsy excuse for a concrete shell. The walls are thick, like we thought, but the means of egress on the ground is via the old garage doors you'd find attached to a house in the 1970's."

The chief snorted.

"Sounds like the ones on my house. Wooden, with a metal handle at the bottom?"

"We haven't gotten close enough to check," Jaclyn replied dryly, "but that's what I'm betting. What do you guys have that can bust those doors down and get the SWAT and us inside?"

"A little of this, a little of that. Is there any place for us to put people down?"

"There's the park to the east, and I'm sure you can put choppers down on the roof. There are people there on guard duty, so there has to be a means of egress there. It's just a matter of finding it. There is a tower there, hidden amongst the trees, so there has to be a door there."

"I hope it's just as wooden and not password-protected."

"Hopefully. ETA?"

"Dawn is about two hours away, sunrise at 5:15 a.m. We're going to launch in about an hour and half. Choppers should be incoming just before then, and we're going to put boats in the water half an hour before that. We figure that it'll take an hour to sail over and around, even going full speed."

Jaclyn nodded.

"All right. We'll sit tight and try not to disturb the locals. Shoot me a text when you're incoming."

"You've got it. I'll be with them, on the last chopper in."

"I'll see you then. Sending you our coordinates via text." Jaclyn hung up without another word, then found the longitude and latitude of their current location on her HUD before typing it into a text message. She fired it off, her iPhone *veroop*ing as it sent. "They'll be here in about two hours, so we just sit here and wait."

"You know that waiting isn't me strong suit, love," Tom said. "I'm going to get antsy."

She reached over and patted his hand lovingly.

"Just calm down, dear, and think of Liverpool winning the League Cup."

Tom's grin spread, filling the points between his ears. Jaclyn saw his teeth glittering in what remained of the starlight.

They remained quiet as the minutes ticked away.

***

Battle Point, Bainbridge Island, Washington
Sunday, June 30
5:17 a.m. PT/8:17 a.m. ET

Jaclyn heard the whine of engines just as the eastern sky grew a touch lighter. She picked her head up—Tasha had closed her eyes and had dozed off, while Tom had his back up against a pine, his eyes closed but still alert—and looked that way.

"HUD, magnify," she ordered. Tom turned and looked that way, too, the two of them trying to peer between the thick, tightly-packed trunks. It took a few seconds for the golden red sky to frame them, but Jaclyn's heart swelled as she saw the tiny pinpricks of darkness grow larger as they zipped toward Bainbridge Island and the landing zone nearby. "SPD incoming."

Tasha grunted as she popped awake.

"Great, it's about time. I'm starving to shoot someone."

"It'll take them a few minutes to land, disembark, and get through the woods," Jaclyn cautioned. Tasha nodded, albeit swallowing a response to that. "We have to hand it to Drake; he picked a secluded spot to build this thing so that it would take a few minutes for any attackers to get to the front door. It is, for the lack of a better word, ingenious."

"Yet he gave us a flimsy entranceway," Tom countered. "He may be a genius in some respects, but he's a fucktard in others."

Jaclyn didn't disagree.

"We should hear the boats soon, too. They may get there quicker than the ones in the choppers. The north side of the jetty is close by."

"And we're on the south side," Tasha said. "So do we move or what?"

Jaclyn bit her lip as she gave it some thought.

"Too bad I don't have a sniper's rifle," she said. "This would be the perfect opportunity to pick a few of Drake's guards off."

"Remember Snapshot, we need some of them alive," Tom said, his tone rather stern. "We can't kill all of them willy nilly."

Jaclyn slapped her forehead sarcastically.

"Right, how silly of me."

The boats came in from around the northward side, and the three of them heard their engines blistering the dawn even over the din of the choppers growing closer, hovering, and landing in the park to the east of their position. Jaclyn felt her phone's light purr, even through the leather of her trenchcoat. She checked and found a text from the chief: *We're here*, it read. *Commence the attack.*

Jaclyn's grin lit up the day.

"All right, it's go time. SWAT on the ground, racing this way, ready to distract the guards."

"Some distraction," Tasha said. "I just hope they don't distract me."

The trio crept low to the ground as they abandoned their brief campsite, slipping through the forest as they grew closer to the redoubt. Jaclyn had her Walthers out, one in each hand, safeties flicked off with her thumbs. Tom had his out, too, and she heard the slight grinding of his thumb sliding the safety back and forth a few times, her amplified hearing making it sound as if the weapon screamed. Her chest ached as they picked up speed, just before the sounds of gunfire sprang up off in the distance.

“We’re late to the party,” Tasha complained. “I need to shoot someone!”

“Calm down, you’re going to get your chance,” Jaclyn said as she hustled away, Tom and Tasha following.

They drew to within twenty yards of the fortress, coming up on the southeast corner. Jaclyn noticed the dark forms of the SWAT team members racing through the trees, their weapons up, as they approached from the eastern side. She also noticed another one of those garage doors on that side, and her heart skipped a beat as it slowly opened, the sounds of tiny wheels drowned out by that of gunfire.

And from those doors, yells of “Attack!” poured out as Drake’s foot soldiers—twenty of them, Jaclyn counted—poured forth. She relayed the number to her fellow agents.

“That’s it?!” Tom said. “Only a score of the bastards. This is going to be easier than we thought. We thought they would flow out like ants in a nest.”

Several of the foot soldiers dropped before Jaclyn even got to them, their bodies riddled with a couple of bullets their cheap body armor failed to stop. She aimed and fired, taking two out while in motion, her bullets shattering their helmets, the bullets burying themselves in their brains. They dropped easily and just turned into loose obstructions for the SWAT team and the trio of counterterrrorism agents to vault over. Jaclyn leaped, spun, and drove the heel of her boot into a foot soldier that didn’t get his weapon up in time. She wiped the sweat away from her brow as she noticed several of the soldiers backing away.

Inside, Jaclyn spied the chopper, its engines off. It still had missiles, but not the same amount that it had when Drake made the daring leap for safety. Even in the midst of the fighting, Jaclyn noticed Drake’s men had kept the garage door open, and bullets flew haphazardly on both sides.

If one of those bullets strikes, she thought, leaving the rest of her thought dangling as she tried to keep her breath in her lungs. Her chest quaked under that knowledge. She turned and, using every bit of speed as possible, headed toward the southern side proper.

"What are we doing?" Tom asked. "Aren't we attacking?"

"Not here," she said. "This side could blow up at any minute, and I don't know about you, dear, but I'd rather not turn into a fireball."

She glanced as Tom and Tasha both blanched as they caught sight of the weaponry anchored to the helicopter. They turned and hurried away, catching up to her just as she turned and headed for the other entrances.

"Certainly one of these other entrances open as easily as that one," Tasha said.

"That's my hope."

They continued racing along the edge of the building, a few feet from the sides.

Jaclyn's HUD suddenly whined, the high pitch sending both Tom and Tasha into rolls along with her, the bullets missing the three of them by inches; behind her, Jaclyn felt the plumes of dirt kicked up by the bullets as the particles slammed into the jumpsuit. She finished her somersault and came up firing, the twin bullets catching their would-be assailant in the neck and chest. She watched as the bastard staggered twice and fell, dropping his submachine gun out of his weak grasp. The weapon fired into the concrete repeatedly, until it had exhausted the magazine.

Jaclyn ignored the sweat that rushed down her forehead and threatened to slip under the brim of her HUD and sting her eyes. She tapped the Fosters Grants as if to say, "good job."

They kept moving toward the gate—just as it started opening. The three of them paused just feet from the door and watched as another foot soldier ducked under, his helmet low. He was the only one that they saw. He shouted a hearty, "Let's go!" toward the back. Jaclyn's HUD recorded his adrenaline levels as running a little too hot.

Jaclyn pounced and jammed the barrel of her hot Walther into the eager soldier's craw. The man stiffened as if someone plunged a knife into his lungs, stopping in place.

"Where's Darren Drake?" she asked, her tone demanding, just as two more soldiers rolled underneath. Out of the corner of Jaclyn's eyes, Tasha sprang and dropped one with a swift kick to the chin. Tom simply held the third at gunpoint, freezing the soldier in place; he cheekily grinned and inched his barrel upward. Tasha kindly removed his weapons as soon as he had his hands up. Jaclyn smirked at the one she held.

"I don't know," the soldier replied. "He's not here."

Under her HUD, Jaclyn blinked.

I was afraid of that, she thought, just before she tasted a tiny bit of copper flooding her mouth. The inside of her cheek tasted raw.

"Where did he go? When did he leave?"

The soldier blanched and swallowed hard.

"A-A couple of hours ago. Shortly after midnight," he replied, his tone meek.

"Who's in charge now? Was Gibson with him?"

The man nodded. The sounds of gunfire continued spraying around.

"The commander is back h—"

Everyone fell as the tremendous explosion rippled away from behind. Jaclyn felt a jarring pain in her left shoulder as she hit the ground, yet she managed to leap up to her knees and keep her prisoner under her Walther's barrel. She saw his eyes widen, his cheeks slacking, as if he knew his chance to escape was now long gone. Then, through her HUD, she caught the results of the explosion: the fire had eaten most of the concrete, with some of it tumbling around them, the larger chunks hitting the ground with heavy, deadened thuds. The heat from the explosion set several pines alight, the smoke and fire stretching for the sky, giving a wholly different meaning to an early dawn meeting a late dusk.

The other soldier, with Tom on the ground, got up and sprinted away toward the west. Tom had dropped his gun, and so had Tasha, and by the time the two of them had recovered their weapons, the other soldier was already too far away for an accurate shot to drop him.

"Don't worry about him; someone else will round him up. We have a prisoner right here," Jaclyn said.

More SWAT members came around to the southern side from the western side just as the two garage doors opened. Several of Drake's foot soldiers spilled out, but Jaclyn noticed none of them had weapons. She got to her feet and made sure she had Walther No. 2 out and up. Tasha took care of the prisoner Jaclyn had collared; the one Tasha had kicked was still out cold, unmoving.

"Who's the commander of this base?" she called out. The sounds of gunfire had stopped for the most part, but the cracking of flame and the smell of burning fuel filled the valley. Several of the soldiers had stopped walking and looked to their fellows, but one, Jaclyn noticed, kept walking toward her wearing an expression that resembled vinegar.

Tom moved into action and leveled his own Walther at the man. That made the soldier pause.

"I am the commander," he declared. His face, as plain and unappealing as it was, showed every bit of revulsion at the mere thought of surrendering to a woman.

"Where's Darren Drake?" Jaclyn repeated.

"He left." The commander's expression turned smug. "He said you would show up, and he needed to give you the slip." Jaclyn grimaced, wondering just how much wider this man's slimy grin could go. "And he has."

"Where did he go?" She slipped her left Walther into its hip holster.

The commander shrugged.

"I really could not tell you. He sent me a Facebook message to tell me that he arrived safely at his destination, but he didn't tell me where." He shrugged, but Jaclyn noticed his grin was as patronizing as he could make it. "Sorry."

Jaclyn cleared her throat for a second.

"Facebook for Mobile or do you have a computer set up here?"

The man fished his hand in his pocket and pulled out a small square. He tossed it over, softball-style. Jaclyn snatched it in her left hand.

"I'd say you throw like a girl, but that would be insulting to girls everywhere." She turned it over and gawped.

“BlackBerry? That’s so 1998.” Stashing the other gun, she manipulated the touchpad in the center and moved to his messages. “Is he blocking everyone else save the people on his feed?”

“I’m not sure. Why do you ask?”

Jaclyn shrugged this time. A look of concern passed over the commander’s face, but that concern rapidly morphed into something resembling fright. He took a step forward—“You can’t,” he said, just as a bunch of submachine guns behind Jaclyn swept up and trained themselves on the commander’s skull, Jaclyn ignoring the whine of the HUD at the same time—but she already had her fingers typing.

“I am coming for you, Darren,” she spoke as her fingers danced on the keypad. “Give yourself up. The chopper you used to throw off Seattle Police is shishkabob, the commander of your foot soldiers is pretty much a dead man.” Jaclyn grinned as she looked up to gauge the commander’s reaction; his eyes had narrowed as if to tell her that he wanted to rip her apart limb from limb, but the splotchiness of his complexion made her wonder if he was about to wet himself. “Seattle Police are freezing every bit of your assets. This is over. Find me on Facebook, send me a message there, and we’ll arrange your surrender.” She signed it with her name, then clicked send. “There.” She turned to the SWAT team. “Take these men into custody.”

As they all moved in, Jaclyn felt herself swoon a bit. Tom caught her.

“Time for some sleep, methinks,” he said.

Jaclyn couldn’t hold in the yawn.

“Yes, that sounds like a great idea,” she said. “It has most definitely been a rather long day. Tomorrow night, though, will be longer.”

Chapter 21
TealSeattle Headquarters
East Marginal Way South
Seattle, Washington
Sunday, June 30
9:07 a.m. PT/12:07 p.m. ET

Drake stared at the Facebook message with a mix of dread, of longing, and of genuine, cold fear gripping his racing heart. He wondered how she had grabbed a hold of his underling's Facebook account, but he dismissed the thought just as quickly as it came to him; how she had done it was of no concern. She had done it, and that was that. His eyes, widened for nearly two minutes, threatened to shoot out of their sockets while his heart threatened to burst. A breath strangled him until he finally commanded his throat to relax.

He kicked the covers off and sat up, naked, swinging his legs over the side. Cool air from the baseboard air conditioning vents gently hummed and nibbled along the tender flesh of his inner thighs up to his groin, to the point where he shivered. Cell phone still in hand, Drake stood and walked to the window.

He coughed his gasp as it choked him.

His attention drawn to the northwest and beyond Harbor Island, he saw the column of black still crawling for the sky. His jaw dropped by two centimeters as the distant inferno kept his gaze rapt and rigid. Judging from the distance on the other side of Bainbridge, it had to be—

There can't be anything else on the island that could contribute to a blaze that size, he thought. *There just can't. And now—*

Drake swallowed hard as he looked down at the phone in his hand.

And now Jaclyn has me by the balls, and not the way I want her to have me by the balls, either.

He grimaced as he brought the phone up and tossed it on the bed. Gibson, who slept equally nude next to him, didn't stir as the device bounced half an inch.

Good, he thought, letting a breath filter away. *Stay asleep. My thoughts are rolling, and I don't need you and your constant antagonism confusing me right now.*

He walked to the small washroom and turned on the cold water, cupping his hands underneath the stream as he thought about this new wrinkle, this new predicament he had hoped to avoid which had now become unavoidable. With enough water in his hands, he lowered his head and splashed his face with it, rubbing the sleep counterclockwise from his eyes. He turned the faucet off and grabbed a hand towel to dry his face.

Jaclyn, he thought, *I can't simply surrender to you in that way*. He tossed the towel aside. *I just can't. There is too much at stake, too much going on that the mere thought of going against that turns my stomach. But the thought of seeing you—damn.*

The images of last night, of trying to evade her when all he wanted to do was to reach out and hold her tight, even in the driving rain and on the roof of the Space Needle, made his head ache and groin twitch. The fact she was there—*within twenty yards of me, and then she chased me! It was like the playground in elementary school all over again, albeit with another girl, the cock tease*—had sent life scurrying to every inch of him. And while he had gone on living after the day she had departed, the day that woman stole her from him, he had never felt more alive than when he looked around the corner and saw her pleading with Hill to get him to come inside, just before he raised his gun and pulled the trigger. He had to suppress the longing in his heart as he saw her, knowing he had a job to do. There was a confliction in his heart, the confliction of wanting her for himself while casting Gibson aside, and the confliction of wanting her dead while Gibson rode him in absolute victory. That confliction—that desire—nearly cost the operation everything. He had to eliminate Hill; who knows what he had told her back in Washington? Eliminating him set the chase in motion, and after that, the near-fatal extraction.

And Kim wanted her dead, Drake thought. *She had hated her back in middle and high school because she was different, and she ensnared me later in life with that luscious ex-cheerleader body of hers. She takes from me financially, and only gives sex in return. What kind of life is that?* He felt his lip curl, the hatred boiling from his gut. *But if I break it off with her, she'll tell everything. It's her word against mine, and we all know the world believes the word of the scorned woman over that of the so-called philandering male.*

Drake swallowed.

I'm in over my head, he thought, *and there's no way to get out of it. Unless—*

He looked toward the sleeping form of Gibson. She had the covers up past her breasts, her head against the pillow, her legs a triangle underneath the sheets.

If Jaclyn can take Kim out of the picture, he thought, *that would free me of that burden. We can keep our combined crimes hidden, and Seattle would still go up in flames.*

The thought gnawed at him while Gibson stirred. He let the thoughts of betrayal evaporate before she finally came awake.

"What's wrong, hon? What time is it?"

"A little after 9," he replied. "I received a message a few hours ago. From Jaclyn."

Gibson's eyes sprang open as she sat up, the covers tumbling to her waist.

"What did she want?"

"She wants me to give up."

Gibson blew a raspberry.

"She doesn't want much, does she?" she added, a snort careening from her lips.

"I think she wants everything and then some. Look," he said, pointing toward the window of her high-rise building, "she's destroyed the redoubt."

Gibson's eyes flashed to the window.

"Fuck!" she screamed. "She is ruining everything. She needs to be stopped. What does she say?"

"She wanted me to message her on her Facebook account and arrange for my surrender." He swallowed. "This is the end of the line, Kim."

“No, it’s not,” she said, before she muttered something about spineless men. She got out of bed and walked over to him. “Let me see this.” She snatched the phone from the bed and went to the messenger service. He watched as her eyes darted back and forth as they took in Jaclyn’s words, all while he tried not to stare at her nipples, which stood pronounced in the cold room. She blew another raspberry as she tossed it back on the bed. “The commander was an idiot anyway.” She turned and walked toward the bathroom door; on a hook hung her robe. Drake loved watching her walk away from him—but for how much longer? “We need to set this bitch up, and set her up good. I need a number of your foot soldiers. Not more than ten.” She grabbed the robe.

“There are no more,” Drake said. “They were all at the fortress. And judging by the fire out our window, they are either dead or in police custody.”

“What about the ones guarding your home, your office?” she said, donning the robe, covering her gluteus from view.

“Jaclyn said they were all raided,” Drake said, as if resigned to his fate. “It’s over, Kim.”

“It’s not fucking over until I say it’s over, Darren.” She turned and tied the robe, her breasts covered by the thick terrycloth. She flung her tresses out from the top and back. “And it’s not over. Not by a fucking longshot. You message that blind bitch back and you tell her to come here, alone. No cops. Just her. She wants you to surrender?” She blew another raspberry. “Fuck that. She can come here by her little lonesome and arrest you. Meanwhile,” she said, her rant flowing from her lips, “I’ll be there to get the drop on her—and finally kill that unpopular piece of Army trash, like I’ve wanted to do for a decade and a half.”

Drake grew aware of only his racing heart as he stared at his business partner-cum-lover as her face morphed into one of deranged desire. He kept his own true feelings hidden, not wanting to upset the woman in the room—even though he wanted the exact opposite of her goals. He wanted to stop her, but his penis gave a little quiver, and that was enough for his heart.

He nodded, then sent Jaclyn the message.

***

The Warwick Hotel
Lenora Street
Seattle, Washington
Sunday, June 30
1:37 p.m. PT/4:37 p.m. ET

Six hours after returning to the mainland and falling asleep in the hotel, Jaclyn finally awoke, somewhat refreshed from the much-needed slumber. Her head still felt a little heavy and she knew she needed a few more hours' rest, but right now was not the time. She knew she had the time to sleep when this was all over, and her racing heart told her it would be sometime today.

Wearing a Mariners t-shirt and pink bikini panties, the blonde counterterrorism agent hopped out of bed, but not before placing her fingers to her lips and dropping a fingertip-laden kiss on her husband's forehead. Slipping her HUD on, she walked over to the windows and flung the curtains open, then crossed her arms underneath her breasts as she leaned against the warm glass, looking toward the south.

Even though her gaze took her HUD toward CenturyLink and Safeco, she looked beyond those buildings to where the Duwamish Waterway bisected the southern half of Seattle proper. There, beyond the two athletic palaces, lay what she figured would be the target for this evening's events—if Drake returned her message, which she thought he would do, his blatant infatuation his undoing.

She hadn't checked her Facebook account, but she figured the message would be there. Tasha had told her to check her "Message Requests" channel, messages sent by people that weren't on the friends list. Jaclyn had grinned in her half-sleepy state on the way back to Seattle.

"I don't know what I'd do without you," she said.

I do hope, she thought as she stared out the window, *that you have replied. I do hope that so very much. That way, I can end this farce and make sure you rot in hell.*

Jaclyn turned and headed back to the bed. Her iPad sat on the bedside table. She scooped it up and did the usual motions to wake it up before touching the Facebook icon. And there, as it finished opening, Jaclyn spied the message box all lit up in red. She touched it and noticed the number one in parenthesis next to the message requests.

It was, of course, from Drake. Her arms trembling, she touched it and it sprang open faster than she ever recalled a message opening. The message, she saw, was rather brief. She sighed with great thanks as she noted it wasn't a remit of teenage longing.

She wet her lips as she read:

My dearest Jaclyn,

You are welcome to come to the TealSeattle plant this evening and negotiate my surrender. However, I only want you to come. No TV cameras, no one else but you, and especially no police.

I await your reply. 10 p.m., after the city falls asleep? It is Sunday, after all.

Sincerely, and with love,

Darren

Jaclyn forced the bile back into her stomach, leaving her with a foul taste on her tongue, clinging to her tonsils. The words love and Darren did not belong together, and her name and dearest certainly did not belong together, either.

Yet as she read the message again, she realized, quite suddenly in fact, that he wanted her to walk into a trap. Going in alone, into a building owned by her middle school rival, and without the police to back her up—*yeah*, she thought, *that may be considered suicidal of me*.

The smirk came gently, and the smirk turned into a light lilt.

But they really have no idea what I'm capable of, her thoughts continued. *They don't realize that I am a walking army capable of destroying a contingent of foot soldiers all by my little lonesome.* She typed in her reply—*"All right, I'll be there. 10 o'clock."*—and sent it.

Jaclyn set the iPad down and slipped out of bed again, padding over to where she stored her ammunition. She dragged her Walthers out of the holsters and, with the safeties on, removed the magazines and checked them, pulling herself down into a crouch. She had only used a few bullets in the most recent escapade, plus sending a few shots Drake's way inside the Space Needle's staircase. Biting her lip, she counted the remaining bullets in each, and quickly nodded her satisfaction. She slipped them back into the weapons with a snick, then put them back in their holsters. The spare magazines, she saw, were full.

She took in a great deal of air through her nostrils, filling her lungs and holding it before letting the breath out slowly.

I'm ready for this, she thought, *but I have to tell Tom and Tasha that they can't come in with me. That may be the most hurtful thing of all. Tom will understand, even though he will fear for me. Tasha will protest vehemently; she just wants to be on the front lines. And that is why I love them both. However, thinking about what that SWAT officer said, there may be a way to avoid the instructions—*

Behind her, she heard Tom stirring, the comforter shifting as he moved his legs into the vacancy next to him. She gave him a light smile as he opened his eyes, then slipped back into bed with him.

"Is there something wrong, love?" he said.

One deep breath later, she told him what was on her mind.

***

2:30 p.m. PT/5:30 p.m. ET

Jaclyn set up the FaceTime call with the president. The three of them sat next to each other, huddled around the iPad. When the call connected, Jaclyn wasn't surprised to see Forrister sitting alongside Melanie Ruoff and Lucia DiVito, the vice president. From the looks of the background, Jaclyn believed they sat in the Situation Room, several flights of stairs below the Oval Office. The wood paneling was a dead giveaway.

Without another thought, she pressed the center button on the cube Alex gave her long ago. She felt a closeness to her mentor now, even though she was gone.

Time to put the person truly responsible for her death away, she thought.

"So I've brought Melanie and Lucia up to speed," Forrister began, "especially with what happened this morning. You said you were going to contact the target. Has he responded?"

Jaclyn nodded.

"He has, sir. He wants to meet with me, tonight, with the following conditions held: me alone, no TV, and no cops."

"In other words, he's setting you up for something," the vice president mused aloud.

Jaclyn nodded again.

"That is my thought, ma'am."

"Are you really going to go in alone, Jaclyn?"

Jaclyn felt her cheek twitch.

"Truthfully and officially, I don't really have a choice, Melanie. It looks like this is the only way he will surrender, with me, alone, in the same room with him. That being said, he is not as stupid as we think. He is sure to know that I have shared everything with someone else on the chain of command, and that someone will come for him if I am to die or fail to report in. Whether or not his partner in crime knows this remains to be seen, but I wouldn't be shocked if she didn't know." She took a deep breath. "I've already sent him a message confirming that I would be there, and that I agree to his demands."

She watched as the two women on the other end of the call frowned. Next to her, Tom and Tasha barely responded.

"I'm thinking, though," Forrister said, "that you have something else in mind. Unofficially, of course."

Jaclyn grinned wide.

"You know me too well, sir. I'll go in alone, as intended, but if you'll recall, the gentleman from the SWAT team mentioned—"

"I remember, yes," Forrister replied coolly as he interrupted.

"I think it's time to call them in. I'm not sure how many I'll need, but a few might suffice. They don't even have many of their own soldiers left, I don't think."

"I haven't heard the latest update, but I'm pretty sure that all of his holdings have been raided, and everyone with a gun taken into custody rather swiftly; none of them should be a bother, as you said. I'm not sure you're going to need them, but I'll make the call and we'll try to keep it quiet… Lieutenant Colonel," he said, a grin touching his lips. "We can't truly send you in there without some semblance of backup, Snapshot."

"Thank you, sir. But only a few. The three of us can overwhelm them as it is. We just want to make sure they don't escape us."

"Are they going to escape?" DiVito asked.

Jaclyn didn't swallow, for she knew the vice president was always cool, calm, and collected. DiVito wasn't someone to issue threats or threatening words.

"They better not, ma'am. I'll be rather pissed if they do."

A few nods filtered between the two locations.

"Jaclyn, as always, you have my full backing and support. I hope that when we speak again, this bastard will be in custody," the president said, his hand moving toward the screen on the other side. "Happy hunting, you three."

The connection winked out without another word.

Chapter 22
TealSeattle Headquarters
East Marginal Way South
Seattle, Washington
Sunday, June 30/Monday, July 1
9:58 p.m. PT/12:58 a.m. ET

"Are we all connected?" Jaclyn asked, her finger touching the Bluetooth earpiece.

She sat in her Parkerhurst-issued Chevy Cruze, alone, only a few blocks away from the target. She had just pulled out of the CenturyLink Field parking lot after giving her husband a long kiss, the men nearby not paying any attention; some of them, she noticed after pulling away, looked up at the North Tower, seemingly minding their own business. The similarly clad teenager didn't look, either. Jaclyn was glad for that, since the girl would have made immature kissy noises had she looked on. Instead, she scoped out a few of the younger camouflage-wearing men, who, in turn, checked her out.

"You've got it, Snapshot," Tom said, his voice coming over the car's speakers.

"Right on," Tasha added. They were, Jaclyn knew, both in Tasha's Cruze. Even with the two of them right next to each other, there wasn't any feedback whining through the system.

"Good, you're both on. Sex Kitten, you keep an eye on Scouser now. Don't let anything bad happen to him."

"I will be sure to throw myself on top of him like you would should a bullet come his way," Tasha said jokingly. Tom, too, laughed.

Turning the wheel and her Cruze onto East Marginal, Jaclyn rolled her eyes to the air.

"Uh huh, that'll be enough out of you. What if I did that to your boyfriend, kiddo?"

Tasha giggled for several long seconds.

"I would give you a big hug and thank you, since it would make him extremely randy for little ol' me. Oh, the fun I would have that day." She sighed a heavy, dramatic breath that sounded as if a long burst of wind scoured the inside of Jaclyn's Cruze. "Alas, that will never happen, for my mentor doesn't like teenaged boys."

That time, Jaclyn sniffed as she smiled.

"All right, you can quit the faux guilt trip. I'll check in when I get there. It shouldn't be long. Maintain silence until ready. Scouser, my darling, I love you."

"You better," Tom replied, "because I love you, too."

Smiling, Jaclyn blew him a kiss over the Bluetooth.

"Snapshot out."

A few minutes passed as she sped along, just before she turned right into the TealSeattle parking lot. She killed the engine as soon as she brought it to a stop, the service entrance right in front of her. Firming her jaw, Jaclyn stared at the building through the windshield. Directly in front of her lay a steel garage door, presently closed, as well as a combination of steel and concrete making up the façade of the tall, ten-story building. There were windows, too, dotting the second through fifth floors before a logjam of concrete filled the rest of the way to the top floor. The top of the building, which was also encased in glass with steel bordering the windows, was dark at this late hour.

And here we are, she thought, clicking her tongue against her teeth. *Time to show this muppet who's boss around these here parts*.

"HUD," she said, "calculate the thickness of those walls for me, please."

The device beeped once just before it spat telemetry diddling across her lenses. She felt an ache slowly stream across her chest as she waited for it to finish, only realizing she had held her breath for far too long. It beeped again as the numbers stopped.

Approximately nine inches thick, it read. *Care to blast it?*

Jaclyn swallowed hard just as her lungs tingled with what felt like fiery fingers, the question circling her consciousness.

I can end this, she thought. *The computer has the right of it. I can end this right here, right now. I have six S-T-A's, and all six should be enough to obliterate the building—and everyone in it.* No one would inquire why it had happened—at least she didn't think so. She felt her cheek twitch just before she touched two fingers to her chin. *Drake and Perkins would certainly get crushed to death; maybe the shrapnel would tear into important arteries and make them bleed to death as the chaotic scenes develop all around them. It would free me up of ever seeing those two pretentious jackasses ever again; it would take days to sift through the rubble for their corpses.* A sneer quickly touched her lips. Jaclyn moved her hand toward the switch that would turn the servos and gears behind her, raising the rack into place—but she stopped herself just short of it. She held back, cautiously flexing her fingers as she brought her hand back to the steering wheel.

Her throat had turned dry as she contemplated her options, counting them off on invisible fingers. Ending it right now was certainly high on her list, but the negative downside to that would be not asking Drake and Perkins the true reasons why they had acted the way they had. Drake had already admitted his role, and had admitted his long-requited love for her, but Perkins's role—Gibson's, she corrected, remembering the past and all the shit memories it brought to the forefront—in all of this still truly confused her. Did this woman still hate her after all of these years? It didn't seem plausible; wouldn't the years apart and the distance and maturity quell those thoughts? Was Tom right in thinking that Gibson and Drake still held on to, as he said, fourth-year hang-ups and crushes? That's why she stayed her hand and didn't torch the place just yet; that is why she didn't immediately ignite the rockets and watch hot, gray steam vent as they shot forward and sent the concrete and steel shooting about in all directions. She wanted answers, and only because she wanted understanding. Once she had the understanding, she rationalized, she might then accept the situation and kill the bastard and the bitch for even thinking about what they had done to start this whole mess.

Jaclyn exhaled hard.

If I can't do it now, her thoughts continued, *then I have to do it later. But there is the chance I have to do it when I'm inside the place. That could mean—*

"HUD, will I be able to remote start the missiles from inside the building?" she queried. The HUD beeped as it made its calculations. Nothing came through the Bluetooth from the other end, and Jaclyn didn't know if Tom and Tasha had heard her correctly. Certainly they would have stopped her if they knew what she had planned.

Affirmative, the HUD replied across the lenses. *Your iPad should be able to do it, but the Bluetooth is wired to Lucy, and Lucy can command the weaponry.*

Jaclyn's lips became a line as she nodded. She took the bottom one between her teeth for half a heartbeat.

"Good. Scouser, Sex Kitten, I'm moving in."

"Roger that, Snapshot," Tasha said. "She's going in, boys."

Jaclyn heard the tremors of engines turning over as she exited the Cruze. She didn't set its lock. She flipped the safeties to her Walthers—un-suppressed this time; she wanted anyone listening to know that there was a shootout in progress, in their neighborhood, if she needed to fire off a few shots—off as she stalked in, her heels clicking off the asphalt. The purpose and strength behind her steps made the ground tremble and quake as her presence sent the shadows scurrying away to more hospitable locales.

Opening a slightly recessed door roughly the same color as the concrete, she slipped into the building, one Walther drawn. Darkness surrounded her, and her footsteps immediately bounced back at her in a half-hearted attempt to disorient her. It was a concrete corridor, and she had the feeling it would lead her right to her targets. Every breath felt strangled and labored, clenching at her throat with unseen fingers, and it only fueled the ache which kept growing, kept spreading, until it made her gasp. Every staccato breath melded with her footsteps and the shifting of the jumpsuit, her bodily functions giving her the feeling of a one-woman band. Even so, it was that desire to breathe freely again, and the desire to eliminate Drake and Perkins, which kept her feet from faltering underneath her.

She moved further into the building.

It was when she came to the center of the plant some five minutes later she finally found Drake, standing with the woman once known to her as Kim Gibson. They stood side by side on the floor of the large plant, motionless, as if waiting for her. There was a touch of steam lingering about, as well as vats of all shapes and sizes lining the walls. Jaclyn figured, her nimble mind working away, this was the place where they stored whatever toxic chemical Seattle Police had spied with the drones in recent weeks. Walking forward, Jaclyn felt the air grow warmer, as if they stood in a heat vent that rivaled the pits of Hell itself.

"Engaging," she whispered. She didn't hear a response. She drew closer.

"That's far enough, Jaclyn," Drake said just before he applied a rather smooth—yet rather slimy, in Jaclyn's estimation—grin. "There's no need for a gun. We're all friends here."

She paused immediately, but didn't holster her weapon. Jaclyn had it up but not aimed, and she let her eyes, hidden by her dark Foster Grants, dart between the two.

"You want to turn yourself in, I understand," she said, her left hand on her hip.

"No," Gibson said, her smirk clear as day. "We want you to die."

Jaclyn felt her rage burning in the pit of her stomach, but she didn't allow it to race to the surface. She needed to remain in control right now, and matching scathing remarks with one such as Kim Gibson really wasn't called for. She shifted her weight, moving her hip to the left a few inches.

"I'm sure I will at some point in the future, Kim," Jaclyn replied, "but it is sure not going to be today."

Gibson's nostrils flared as if she stared through flames.

"You will die today, bitch." Jaclyn saw her level a claw-tipped finger her way; it didn't bob or move, as if it were made of hard iron. "And I'm going to laugh while standing over your corpse."

"Seriously, I have to ask," Jaclyn said, shifting her weight again, "when was the last time we saw other? Fifteen years ago? Sixteen? I've lost count of all the years I've been away, fighting terrorism and keeping this country—and to a lesser extent, you—safe, and yet you're still clinging to whatever hatred you had of me back in middle school? Back in freshman year?" She spat a sigh that resembled a deflating bicycle tire. "Haven't you matured even a little bit?"

"Oh, I have," the woman replied, "believe me, I have. But whenever your name pops up, I can't help but slide back into the angry me, the me who wanted to make sure you were ground under my heel every morning back at Woodbrook." Jaclyn noticed the woman kept sneering at her, as if she had plastered the look to her face before the arch-nemesis from her youth even entered the room. Her eyes glittered with lingering fanaticism, the pupils turning darker with each passing word of anger that slipped through her teeth. "And I can't wait to do it again." She suddenly lurched forward, as if ready to steamroll her.

Jaclyn snapped the Walther back into place, the barrel pointed straight at Gibson's forehead. The woman across from her stiffened and halted.

The counterterrorism agent grinned wide as she noticed the blood rush out of Gibson's face, leaving behind a pasty shell in its place.

"Come at me, bitch." Jaclyn pursed her lips into a smile as she inhaled, then relaxed her mouth as she exhaled. "See what happens."

Gibson looked to Drake. Jaclyn's eyes stayed on the woman, all while her chest heaved with her developing anger.

"Jaclyn, put down the weapon and we'll talk," Drake said.

Jaclyn answered with a simple draw of her second Walther. She pointed it right at his heart, and she felt her own heart swell as she watched his Adam's apple bob twice.

"We'll talk like this," she countered.

"Statements made under duress like this are inadmissible in a court of law, and you know that."

"Whoever said you'll make it to a court of law? The people you used to set up your scam are dead. There's no one to testify against you. It's your word against mine, and who do you think the federal prosecutor will believe?"

"Not all of them," Gibson snarled.

Jaclyn blinked, but she recovered quickly.

"We'll round them up in due course, don't you worry your pretty little head about that. But I think I will save the taxpayers the cost of a trial and just kill you after you confess every little one of your crimes to me. How about it? Ready-made judge, jury, and executioner, right here. And in a way, Kim, you're the one who created me." She chuckled through a closed mouth, making it sound as if the chuckle came from her feet. "How does that knowledge sit?"

"You'd never get away with it, Jaclyn," Drake said.

Jaclyn chuckled harder this time.

"You obviously have no clue of the cliques I run with now," she countered. "I've come a long way from Woodbrook Middle School; a lot further than you two have come."

"Yes, yes," Gibson said as she rolled her eyes. "You're friends with the good ol' President of the United States. Pfft. Big fucking deal. You're friends with a piece of shit liberal, that's so cute and cliché. Gag me."

Jaclyn watched as Drake nodded along.

Well, she thought, *that confirms that little nugget. Tasha will be so glad to hear that my hypothesis was correct.*

"With lead? It would be my pleasure, Kim," she said. "So, while we're standing here, I want to get a few things straight before I impose your sentence. My first question is why? Why did you kill Alex?" There was no emotion behind the question; she kept her anger at bay. She wanted the truth, and with a gun pointed at them, with no wind or rainstorm to distract them, the truth would come. Jaclyn was sure of it.

"I think I've already told you why," Drake said. "I wanted to kill you for leaving me all those years ago, and this was the first time since then that you were within killing distance. The bitch that stole you from me—"

Jaclyn automatically lowered the Walther and fired without further thought, the concussive blast making the other two parties leap out of their socks. The bullet, Jaclyn noted through the HUD, skipped off the concrete between Drake's legs with a clink.

Drake gasped as he looked at Jaclyn with fear flooding his face.

"Care to rephrase that?" she said. "Consider that a warning shot, Darren. Next time, I won't be so careless with my aim."

"The woman that stole you from me got what she deserved, even though she was simply in the wrong place at the wrong time," Drake corrected, his tone stern. "I am not sorry that she died, Jaclyn. She hurt me more than you could ever know."

"So you killed her because of a crush that you never let go of? You need help. Serious help."

He stepped forward, his eyes wide. Jaclyn noticed Gibson's mouth opened, as if in shock at what he was doing.

"Yes. I do. Help me. If you ever had an ounce of love for me once, and you kissed me on the cheek when you left, help me."

"The kiss I gave you was thanking you for being kind to me and accepting of my handicap," Jaclyn said. "You were kind to me when bitches like this," she gestured toward Gibson, "did their level best to make my life here a living hell every single fucking day. It wasn't an engraved invitation to try to separate me from my panties. And all the letters you've written me since I came home from London went right into the circular file, if you catch my drift. Quite a few of them were unopened."

That last admittance, Jaclyn saw, had two different reactions shooting back at her, and to her, it was a reaction of triumph—a personal triumph at splitting these two up and getting them to turn on each other; it had already worked once, when she managed to have Kerri Davis turn on Senator Jennifer Farrell and Davis's own ex-husband, Robert Letts.

This was nearly an exact carbon copy of that event in Kingman, Arizona.

Drake's face had automatically fallen, as if on command: her words, words which shattered his heart and flogged his dreams into submission, had defeated him and sent him spiraling toward a depression Jaclyn knew quite a bit about. She recalled what had occurred in her mind after she had refused Forrister's order to come home, the feeling of loneliness that enveloped her until Tom finally tracked her down in that pizza shop near Highbury in North London.

Meanwhile, Gibson's face turned from a look of disbelief to one of feeling a costly betrayal. Jaclyn's heart did not go out to her, the conniving snake that she was.

"You what?" Gibson said. "You wrote to her?! You wrote to the blind bitch?"

"I'm in the room, you know," Jaclyn said, feigning shock. She kept her guns pointed on her targets, regardless of the levity. "And I'm partially blind. Sheesh, get it right."

Gibson went on with her raving lunacy as if she didn't hear.

"You've been inside of me for how long, and you've been writing to her on the fucking side? Shit, now I don't feel bad for taking your money every fucking chance I got!"

Jaclyn stared at the two, noticing that Drake appeared ready to weep at the knowledge he had no chance any longer. Yet as she looked back to Gibson a few moments later, she immediately noticed the woman was in the process of having a rather large epiphany—a necessary epiphany—that would help push her mission over the top, and allow her to pull the trigger on both of them.

"So about that," Jaclyn said after the silence had lingered for a few extra minutes. Gibson stared hard at Drake before finally turning her attentions to the counterterrorism agent. She had taken a few breaths once Jaclyn interrupted "What is that money for? There is tons of it passing back and forth. Well, mainly forth. I guess the back part is what she gives you."

"Shut up!" Gibson snarled.

Well, Jaclyn thought, *there goes that epiphany, right out the ol' window.*

A rush of adrenaline fueling her footsteps, Jaclyn powered forward and shoved the barrel of her right side Walther right up against Gibson's nose, the steel smashing against the bone. Gibson stiffened again. She kept the other one right on Drake, but out of the corner of her HUD, he didn't look like he wanted to make a move against her.

"No, you shut up. Right this second. I will fucking take you out of the picture so fast that I know that they'll erase your pug face from the yearbook." The two women locked eyes, Gibson trying to search for Jaclyn's through the heavily-tinted lenses; Jaclyn wondered if she saw the telemetry read-outs, her face was so close. "Now, tell me about the money."

Still staring, Gibson remained defiantly quiet until Jaclyn pressed the barrel harder.

"We're here, Snapshot," Jaclyn heard Tom's voice through the headset. "Shall we knock?"

"Yeah, why not?" she answered before turning her tone a little darker. "Tell me about the money, Kim."

Gibson's lip curled into a remarkable evil grin. Then she let loose a torrent of information, confirming everything Jaclyn already knew.

"Drake's company, while legitimate, passed money to me in order to fund a rather complex project."

"Kim, stop—"

"Oh, fuck off." She turned to Jaclyn. "It was his idea."

"No, it wasn't!"

"He wanted to sell as many of his cheap-ass computers as he could. Then he funneled the money to me so we could destroy Seattle inch by inch, block by block, mile by mile. You see something, Jaclyn: you may hang with the liberals, and this is a very progressive state. Darren and I prefer to hang with conservatives, of course, and we're tired of the total green-ness of Seattle. Such a bore, if I'm being completely honest with you. Sure, my company provides solar energy to thousands. That's great, and I've made millions of dollars in exchange. But what if, what if, Seattle turned hotter than the surface of the sun itself?"

Jaclyn blinked.

Where is she going with this? she thought.

"How would you do—oh," she said, the realization suddenly dawning. "So—let's talk about the chemicals."

Gibson blanched.

"How do you know about those?"

Jaclyn showed two rows of white teeth. Nearby, Drake took several steps backward.

"I usually don't divulge information to criminals like this, but since you're going to be dead soon anyway, I don't see why not. Seattle Police used drones to fly by your facility once. They saw the chemicals and didn't know why a supposedly green company like yours would need anything chemical."

"Kim, please, don't—"

"We're dead anyway, Darren. She just told you that. It doesn't matter any longer," Gibson said. Her tone had sobered so much that she looked slightly unsteady on her own feet. "We have a controlling interest in several insurance companies. Mostly home owner's insurance."

"I do not like where this is going," Jaclyn said.

"No, I don't think you would, Miss Goody Two Shoes. We've shipped the chemicals to Vancouver. There's an airstrip there, and we've hired—well, hired is such a loose term; let's just say we have some pilots who we had planned to kill after it's all said and done. They are going to spray Seattle with them. And then, we were supposed to get on a boat, head out to the Sound, then wait for some dumbass to simply light a cigarette." Gibson showed teeth and let her fingers spring away from her balled-up fists. "Kaboom."

Jaclyn choked on her breath as she realized exactly what Gibson meant.

"Wow," she whispered. "You are incredibly delusional."

"No, I am pragmatic and thinking three steps ahead of everyone else. The city goes up in flames. There will be deaths, yes. But there will be some who live, and those people will try to claim what is rightfully theirs. Alas, Darren and I will declare that we are unable to pay, and we leave the country. Right, Darren?" Jaclyn watched as Gibson turned toward him, then watched as she blinked in disbelief. "Darren?!"

Jaclyn kept her Walther primed on Gibson as she turned her head toward where she had thought Drake stood—but he had left rather silently. The door off to the side, though, clanged shut. She gasped as she realized her error. She touched the Bluetooth device in her ear canal.

"Shit! Scouser, Sex Kitten, move in," Jaclyn ordered as soon as she recovered. "Everyone, move in. We're short one, and it wasn't by a bullet."

"As ordered," Tom answered in her ear.

The sounds of bullets spraying against the metal outside made the interior sound like a hailstorm. Soon, the sound of venting steam zipped quickly, just before it exploded against the building's façade. A yell from nearby preceded Jaclyn raising her gauntleted arm to guard her face from any shrapnel drawing close to puncture her skin. Mere seconds later, hot white light filtered in through the growing smoke cloud. Lowering her arm, Jaclyn stashed the now-unneeded Walther just as Gibson seethed and screamed—but not for Drake running out on her.

"I said no cops, bitch," Gibson said from the floor, the blast knocking her askew and off her feet. "I wanted no fucking cops!"

"And I didn't bring any," Jaclyn countered. "I followed your request. No cops. I brought something even better." She grinned as she laid out her riposte with a stunning bit of flair. "The late General Edward Johnson's Fighting 50th Infantry Division. Fort Lewis. Familiar with it at all?"

Gibson, defeated, scrunched her face up as disbelief registered in her shimmering eyes. She wept hard, just as Tom and Tasha—followed by several members of the United States Army—swarmed in. The soldiers surrounded Jaclyn's old classmate.

"Drake got away," Jaclyn told them. "We need to go now. You, keep an eye on her and take her into custody."

"Yes, Commander," the soldier said.

Without another word, Jaclyn, Tom, and Tasha trotted off toward the door that Drake had seemingly escaped through.

“You’re never going to get away with this, Johnson!” Gibson yelled as the soldiers heaved her to her feet. Even though she would lose precious seconds, Jaclyn made her companions halt right away, then turned back to face the woman that had once tormented her through her formative years, a woman she had once thought out of her life for good. “I have powerful lawyers. They won’t stand for this. I will make sure you rue the day you ever met me, you blind Army bitch!”

Jaclyn frowned if only for half a second, but it was half a second longer than necessary. She leveled her Walther at the bitch again.

“I already do. Stand aside, private,” she ordered.

The soldier, she saw, did not disobey, raising his rifle to make sure she stayed put.

“No!” Gibson shouted, her eyes widening. She didn’t move; instead, she stood rooted to the spot.

Without another second’s hesitation or wondering if Gibson would flee, Jaclyn immediately pulled the trigger. The shot cracked the air, sending Gibson spinning backward half a second later, taking her clean off her feet. She collided against the concrete floor with the force of a rag doll.

Immediately letting go of a long-held sigh, Jaclyn didn’t need to see if Gibson was dead. She had bigger fish to fry, so to speak, and no more time to lose.

“Let’s go,” she said, turning and heading toward the door. Jaclyn smacked it aside. Tom and Tasha followed, hot on her heels.

They found themselves in the same hallway Jaclyn had used upon entering the facility, except there were exposed pipes running the length of the curving wall on this side of the building. Bare light bulbs provided a pale glow, making the corridor look like the final approach for a death row inmate rather than the service passageway for a major utility provider in a metropolitan area.

“If you were running scared,” Tasha said, “and your worst nightmare was coming to get you, what would you do?”

Jaclyn nodded, knowing what her ward meant.

“I’d run like my ass was on fire. Good job, kiddo. HUD, give me a schematic of this floor, and heat signatures on, please.”

The Foster Grants beeped in response. Red lines formed as the lenses painted the picture right before her eyes. The corridor was long and curved a little toward its right, but the heat sensors told her the story: with the exception of the mass of people inside the plant’s main room, there were no other signatures hot enough to tell if there was another person on that floor.

“He’s definitely not in the building. He’s not going to go up; he’d only trap himself there. There’s no downstairs, either.”

“So he’s out the door,” Tom said.

Jaclyn tapped the side of her nose.

“Lead the way, Snapshot,” Tasha added.

Jaclyn, Tom, and Tasha raced down the hall. Jaclyn felt the sweat coating her spine while her skull throbbed under the pain of adrenaline coursing through her blood vessels, but she didn’t even acknowledge it as she shouldered the door aside. She used enough force to make the door carom off the building’s face, so much so that the crack reverberated out across the water.

Cool air off the Puget met their faces as Jaclyn and Company stared across the utter blackness, the water slurping against the docks. They were on the north side of the plant, whose western side was practically flush with the Duwamish Waterway running from northwest to southeast, and about as tight to the building just to the north of it. A chain link fence ran along the east side—and there were soldiers stationed on the southern side, near Jaclyn’s and presumably Tasha’s Cruzes. There wasn’t much room for anyone to get around to the north side from the outside; the curve there was treacherous, if one didn’t want to get wet. A distant bell tolled on the water, rolling across the expanse.

Jaclyn fixed her HUD that way. It was the only possible escape route, she saw. And since Drake couldn’t walk on water, that meant—

Refusing to spit her frustration, she kept her jaw clamped as she let the device work. There were boats out there, yes, but they were too far out to see them with the naked eye. None were motorboats that she could tell, just simple light pleasure crafts taking advantage of a Sunday night with no one else on the water—save a terrorist trying to make a getaway into the rigid darkness.

"Anything?" Tom asked.

A frown creasing her mouth, Jaclyn shook her head.

"He didn't have that much time to get away," she mused, her thoughts rolling like fog. "He would have had to fire up his engine to break away and kill it no more than ten seconds before we barged outside. Firing the engine would have alerted the soldiers, but he only heard them assaulting the building well after he raced away. He could have used the shots to camouflage his escape." She knew she spoke loudly; she hoped her voice carried a little further than just the three of them. "Darren! I know you're out there! Come about and give yourself up right this second, or take your chances with the Coast Guard!"

Then, unexpectedly, a voice came calling back after a five count.

"Not a chance, Jaclyn! I'll take my chances with the faux Navy, thank you very much. Thanks for the swell evening, and thanks for getting her off my hands."

Jaclyn's jaw dropped as Drake's raised voice, albeit a little on the sarcastic side, met her ears. She felt a shiver overtake her, but she realized that Drake was still relatively close to the plant. He couldn't have been more than a football field's length away, and barely at the mouth of the Duwamish, for that matter.

Voices carry over water, and he's still within range, Jaclyn thought, her chest swelling as the idea sprang to her mind. Under her HUD, her eyes widened.

"You've got a plan," Tom said.

"Yeah. The plan is turn my classmate into a roast chicken." She touched her ear canal, the Bluetooth earpiece shifting a bit under her touch. "Lucy, fire up the engines and get as close to the water as you can, with plenty of S-T-A clearance. Ass out toward the water."

"As ordered. This car," Lucy called back through the Bluetooth, "is a big fine woman. I will gladly back her ass up."

Jaclyn immediately rolled her eyes as the sentient GPS unit finished.

A few seconds later, Jaclyn heard the engine to her Cruze turning over, followed by the squealing tires applying a bit of fresh rubber to the asphalt, then the screeching skid as the car swung around into position like she had ordered. The churning of servos and gears told Jaclyn the rack was on its way up. A cha-clink locked it in place.

"Target toward the mouth of the waterway," Jaclyn ordered.

"Target acquired. Running through registry."

Jaclyn's sternum groaned under the constant strain of her racing heart, and right about now, all she wanted was for the operation to end so her heart rate could return to something resembling a normal speed. She whispered, "Come on, quicker," several times as Lucy went through the ship's registry database, until she chimed in with the official word less than a minute later.

"Ship's registry provides a match. *Half-Blind Angel*," Lucy said, "owned by—"

"I know who owns it," Jaclyn snapped. She took a deep breath and let it out, grimacing a little as she regained her composure and letting the impatience roll off her back; it was almost over, her personal nightmare. "I'm sorry, Lucy. You may fire at will."

"Apology accepted, Snapshot. Box One, releasing."

The thrum of the surface-to-air missile came to life as it vented steam, then shooting away in a cloud of displaced air; Jaclyn's hair whipped about as it rocketed past the trio with a heavy whine and a shiver-inducing breeze. They stood in silence as orange flames and dirty gray smoke trailed and whittled away until it connected violently with the target seconds later. The vicious explosion turned the boat into a floating fireball, the areas off to the shore reflecting the brightness of the conflagration now adrift only a few meters into Puget Sound.

Watching the explosion, Jaclyn's heart swelled. She sighed and tightened her eyes, her shoulders and form drooping as the sounds of the roaring flames drowned out her tears. Several pieces of the vessel tumbled into the water with a light splash while Tom reached around to her right shoulder and pulled her close. She instinctively sought out his waist, but she didn't pull her HUD away from the burning carcass of Drake's boat. The gravity of the moment threatened to overwhelm them as they reflected on the last few weeks in silence.

"Gee," Tasha said after a few minutes, breaking the quiet, "the Coast Guard is really going to be pissed at us, aren't they? We're turning the Sound into a junk yard. First the police chopper, now Drake's boat."

"It's a morgue, too," Jaclyn said, her tone sobering. She pulled out of her husband's embrace, yet still held onto his hand. "Somewhere, the body of Alex's true killer—someone who I once called my friend so long ago—is in the process of burning and hopefully sinking to the bottom of the Sound." A heavy sigh rattled her teeth and made her gums quiver. "Truthfully, and I mean this from the bottom of my heart, I hope they never bring his body back up."

They continued to watch the raging inferno from the docks, the flames dancing across the stern.

Chapter 23
Arlington National Cemetery
Arlington, Virginia
Monday, July 7
10:22 a.m. PT/1:22 p.m. ET

They let her have a few moments alone at the gravesite before beginning their long cross country trip.

The president's cortege had filed into the cemetery only a few minutes before. Jaclyn tried not to look out at the lines of quiet, respectful people standing aside in awe as they passed, knowing some would be frustrated as their own plans took a back seat to the president's. She took a deep breath of cool, recycled air as they drew closer.

Another crisis was over, another terrorist dead. The trio of counterterrorism agents, with Canadian authorities present, raided the hanger in Vancouver and prevented the planes laden with the toxic, flammable chemicals from taking off. Hazmat teams carefully removed the canisters, bringing the ordeal to a fitting conclusion.

And now, a week later, Jaclyn needed to honor its beginning.

The motorcade rolled to a stop with historic Arlington House in front of them. The Secret Service jumped out first and opened the squeaky side door of Cadillac One, letting in a wash of hot, early July air. With flowers in hand, Jaclyn, along with Tom, Tasha, the president, the first lady, Melanie Ruoff, and little Maryah all stepped out. Another limousine had pulled up behind it, the Secret Service agents there letting the vice president and her husband out. Together, everyone else hung back as Jaclyn, wearing a tea-length black dress, walked some twenty yards to the final resting place of her mentor, Alexandra Dupuis.

Accorded a space in Arlington due to her unused and rarely-brought up military rank, Alex's family had buried her near the graves of both Nathaniel Dyer and Sarah Kendall in the days after she had died, some forty-eight hours before Jaclyn had returned to Seattle in order to seek Drake. She had gone to the funeral, albeit in the back so as not to disturb

Tommy, and she had stayed a good distance away as they laid her to rest. Now, several weeks later and five days after Jaclyn, Tom, and Tasha had returned to the capital following the denouement on the Puget, Jaclyn found the time right to finally pay her respects to the woman who acted as her mother in the days, months, and years after terrorists took her own mother away.

The grave was still rather fresh, she noted, with a few plugs of returning grass springing up where the earth had been turned. In time, the grass would fully return: there was a bit of seed there, too. Hitching her dress up by the hem, Jaclyn stepped out of her heels and went to her knees some five feet from the base of the plain white headstone. The warmth of the grounds seeped into her joints.

She ignored it. She ignored it all. She shut out the rest of the world, the galaxy, the universe, as she turned her gaze to the stone which now held Alex's name for the rest of eternity. Jaclyn breathed easily as she stared, until she felt the grief welling in her chest. She bowed her head and bit her lip, taking a rather deep breath as warm, humid air filled her lungs.

"He's dead, Alex," Jaclyn whispered. "They're all dead. All the ones that hurt you and put you here long before your time, they're all dead. Some tried to run, but I caught up with them for you."

Another slightly labored breath came as her tone changed. A tear ran down her cheek from underneath her HUD.

"You can rest easy now. Your part of the fight against terror is over. I'm going to continue your fight, because that's what I know you'd expect from me." She inhaled and let the breath go just as quickly as it had entered. "I don't know if I said it much, but thank you. Thank you for being there for me all those years ago after you came and got me when my head swam with the thoughts of my loss. Thank you for being there, for kicking my ass when I needed it. Thank you for stepping in even though you didn't have to. I'm so thankful that you did what you did, and so thankful for turning me into the woman that I am today.

"I promise you that I'll keep up the fight. I'll keep to the path you put me on." She leaned a little closer to the stone, as if what she had to say next was between them and them alone. "I'll keep your boys safe. I love you, Alex. I'll keep your memory close to my heart."

Jaclyn set the flowers down at the base of the headstone and bowed her head one last time.

"Good bye, dear friend," she whispered.

She stood and straightened her dress, not caring about the imbedded grass marks on her knees. She stepped back into her shoes and walked around the gravestone, heading back to where the entourage stood.

Tasha met her and hugged her, followed by an equally long hug from her husband; they held onto each other for several minutes, Jaclyn's shoulders bobbing as she soaked his dress shirt. Melanie and Veronica Forrister followed—even little Maryah had her arms outstretched, ready for a hug. Jaclyn, finally smiling, wiped the trails of tears away and scooped the little girl up into her arms. She hugged her tight as she walked to where the president stood near Cadillac One.

"Are you all right, Snapshot?" Forrister asked.

Jaclyn nodded.

"I am, sir. Thank you for the detour."

Forrister's smile was genuine.

"We were on the way," he said, shrugging off her thanks.

"And speaking of that," Jaclyn said, "did someone contact my aunt and uncle and let them know about—"

"I took the liberty of calling myself," Melanie interrupted. "I didn't think this was something I could let an Advance handle."

"And your uncle and I had a little chat afterward," Forrister added. "He's a good man. Just like your father was."

Jaclyn's grin spread easily.

"I know. I can't wait to see them again." She turned her head back to Alex's headstone and let the smile drift a little further. "She did the right thing, you know. As much as I love my aunt and uncle, she did the right thing. Things would be different." She set Maryah down after giving the little girl a kiss on the cheek, then grabbed Tom's hand. "And honestly, I wouldn't have it any other way than the way it is now."

Forrister's grin matched hers. "Take all the time you need. Our flight leaves when I say it leaves."

"Thanks, sir."

He gave her a peck on the cheek, before he moved toward the back door of Cadillac One. Veronica and Maryah followed, leaving Jaclyn, Tom, and Tasha alone.

"I love you, Scouser," she said, kissing him tenderly. "Please, for all the love in the world you hold for me, make sure I keep my promises."

Tom blinked, and Jaclyn saw that he had no idea what she meant.

"Just promise me that you'll make sure I keep them."

Tom smiled and nodded.

"You bet your arse I will."

Then, without another word but with a glance back at Alex's stone, they returned to the president's limo, ready to head to Andrews.

***

Home of the Reverend James McAllister
Huntsville, Alabama
Monday, July 7
11:15 a.m. PT/2:15 p.m. ET

Stepping through the threshold, James McAllister welcomed him with open arms.

"I'm so glad you were able to escape, Darren," he said. "Your cousin kept me aware of everything that was going on."

Darren Drake smiled at his host.

"She does have a habit of loose lips, but I am grateful that she told you. I am, of course, one of your best donors."

McAllister bowed his head for only a few moments before he lifted it.

"May I offer you some sweet tea? Best in the South."

"I am rather parched from my journey, yes, thank you."

"I'm sure it's a journey rife with a tale to tell," McAllister said as he led Drake toward the kitchen. He grabbed two chilled pint glasses from the freezer, a light frost coating the surface. He set them down on the counter—Drake sidled up—and grabbed the pitcher from within the refrigerator. He poured a hefty amount into each glass. "To our Lord Jesus Christ," he said as he set the pitcher down and lifted his glass. Drake did the same.

"To our Lord Jesus Christ," He drank deeply, the distinct flavors of Lipton's finest mingling with a strong hint of Jack Daniels dancing against his tonsils as he swallowed.

"Tell me, Darren. The escape. Did it go the way you planned?"

Drake grinned over the brim of the glass.

"Almost. Kim is dead. She wouldn't have come along anyway after—" His thoughts drifted away, unable to say the words he wanted to so desperately forget.

"It is okay, my son," McAllister said. "Tell me."

Drake cleared his throat and took another deep sip of the spiked sweet tea.

"Having a submersible on board your pleasure craft is always a welcome thing. I pushed the boat away from the dock and hopped in; the Army fired off shots, so I rushed to the front and gunned the engine, then turned it off as soon as I had momentum. Then, I ducked underneath and entered my submersible. I was out of the boat proper when Jaclyn shot it. The boat exploded."

McAllister frowned.

"And yet you made it to safety."

Drake nodded.

"I brought the submersible back toward the plant, passing it," he said. "The Duwamish goes toward the southeast, of course, going against the current from the Puget, as you know. It was a bit of a fight to keep it steady and not send it back into the Sound. I docked at the end of the Duwamish and waited. I waited for everything to blow over, even if it took a few days. That area is barren, so I had no worry of someone seeing the submersible if the sun struck the water just right. Then I got out. I had plenty of supplies inside to last me until yesterday. I had some cash on me; I bought a Starbucks coffee and a sandwich, then bought a ticket to Huntsville under an assumed identity. TSA didn't even stop me, bless them. And now, I'm here."

McAllister stood and looked the man right in the eye.

"Are you ready to do God's work?"

Drake nodded again.

"Yes."

McAllister felt his cheek twitch.

"Good. Are you ready to absolve yourself of all materialistic things and give your soul to Christ the Almighty?"

Drake gave a hard swallow, then nodded.

"Good. Confess your sins before God, and everything will be forgiven. You will become His right hand, Darren. You will be able to right the wrongs against you, all in Jesus's holy name."

"Will he," Drake said, stammering his words, "will he forgive me again when I eventually kill Jaclyn Johnson?"

The preacher's smile was oily.

"He always forgives. People were created to sin, even those who have been forgiven. He wants her death to be so, for she is the tool of a dirty, overreaching Liberal government," he said, spreading his hands apart as if the answer was crystal clear. "You will not only kill her on Jesus's orders, but there may also be some other undesirables that need eliminating. But we must only wait until it is His time to act. Everything is in His time, Darren. You know this, correct?"

Drake nodded and grinned.

"I know that. I will wait for Him to bless me, and then, when the time is right, I will do as I originally intended." He sniffed as his grin touched his ears. "In Jesus's holy name, I will kill Jaclyn Johnson in punishment for her sins."

Satisfied with Drake's reply, McAllister embraced him once again. He was now confident that God's will would get carried out.

TO BE CONTINUED

Like what you've read? Sean Sweeney has something for every member of the family: check out more books and stories!

For kids:

Furball And Feathers: The Cat Food Caper!
Furball And Feathers: The Birdseed Bugaboo!
Furball And Feathers: The Case of the High-Wire Horse!
My Sister Is An Alien…(I Think)

For young adults:

Zombie Showdown

For adults:

The Jaclyn Johnson, code name Snapshot series
Model Agent: A Thriller
Rogue Agent: A Thriller
Double Agent: A Thriller
Promises Given, Promises Kept: A Jaclyn Johnson novella
Federal Agent: A Thriller
Literary Agent: A Thriller
Jail Bird Jenny: A Jaclyn Johnson short story
Travel Agent: A Thriller
Chemical Agent: A Thriller
Currently untitled eighth Jaclyn Johnson Thriller (coming early 2017)

Redeemed
Scollay Love (under the name D.L. Boyd)
Royal Switch: A Major League Thriller
An Invitation to Drink… and to Die
The Lone Bostonian
The Long Crimson Line

The Alex Bourque Small Town PI series

Cold Altar
Voir Dire
Beach Blanket Bloodshed (Coming Summer 2016)

The Obloeron Saga
The Rise Of The Dark Falcon
The Shadow Looms
Krampel's Revenge
The Quest For The Chalice
The Return To Lowbridge
The Fall of Myrindar

Short stories
Belief Debt: Paid In Full (Part of Christopher Nadeau's Not in the Brochure anthology)
C is for Coulrophobia (Part of the Phobophobia anthology)
Red Christmas (Part of the Bump in the Night 2011 anthology)
Refugees: A short story of survival

Writing As John Fitch V

One Hero, A Savior
Turning Back The Clock
A Galaxy At War
The Mastermind: A novella

Short stories
Sidetracked
Amber Twilight
Vuvuzombie

About the Author

Sean Sweeney's love of reading began in 1988, when he was handed J.R.R. Tolkien's classic The Hobbit. His passion for writing began in 1993, as a sophomore in high school, when he began writing sports for his local newspaper. Born and raised in North Central Massachusetts, Sweeney has written for several newspapers. When he is not writing, he enjoys playing golf, reading, watching movies, enjoying Boston sports teams, Arsenal F.C., and the Gold Coast F.C. He and his wife, Jennifer, have two horses—Alex and Jesse—as well as five cats: Ziggy Puff, Diva, Spooky, Squeaky, and Roxie. They live in Bolton, Massachusetts.

Visit Sean online:
www.seansweeneyauthor.com

Join Sean's mailing list and get updates on his work straight to your email!
eepurl.com/NR259

Email Sean!
seansweeneyauthor@yahoo.com

Fan of Sean's work? Find him on Facebook
https://www.facebook.com/seansweeneyauthor

Made in the USA
Charleston, SC
13 July 2016